The Forgotten Night

A Lexie Logan Thriller - Book One

J. T. Bishop

Eudoran Press

Eudoran Press LLC

6009 W. Parker Rd. Su. 149, #205

Dallas, TX 75093

www.jtbishopauthor.com

Book Cover by J. T. Bishop

Book editing by P. Creeden, C. Marquis, C. Maguire and G. Enstam.

The Forgotten Night/2026 – 1st edition

ISBNs: 978-1-971350-02-8, 978-1-971350-03-5

To all the intrepid reporters out there, whether you're a journalist or not, here's to your search for the truth.

May that always be your guiding light.

Other Books by J. T. Bishop

The Red-Line Trilogy

Red-Line: The Shift

Red-Line: Mirrors

Red-Line: Trust Destiny

The Red-Line Trilogy Boxed Set

Red-Line: The Fletcher Family Saga

Curse Breaker

High Child

Spark

Forged Lines

The Fletcher Family Boxed Set

The Family or Foe Saga with Detectives Daniels and Remalla

First Cut

Second Slice

Third Blow

Fourth Strike

The Family or Foe Saga Boxed Set

Detectives Daniels and Remalla standalones/novellas

The Girl and the Gunshot (subscribers only)

A Hamburger Christmas

The Magic of Murder (subscribers only)

Murder Unveiled—a prequel to Haunted River

Detectives Daniels and Remalla

Haunted River

Of Breath and Blood

Of Body and Bone

Of Mind and Madness

Of Power and Pain

Of Love and Loss

Dominion

Illusions

Vendetta

Black Bird

The Redstone Chronicles

Lost Souls

Lost Dreams

Lost Chances

Lost Hope

Lost Lives

Lost Time

Lost Love

Lexie Logan

The Forgotten Night

The Silent Sister

Chapter One

"What do you mean you can't tell me anything? That is absurd. What kind of hospital is this?"

Lexie registered the words but barely made sense of them.

"And what kind of doctor are you? Look at you. You can't be over forty."

Lexie recognized her mother's voice.

"Mrs. Logan, I understand your concerns, but until she wakes up, I can't tell you much more."

The male voice wasn't recognizable.

Her mother spoke. "But you've done all those tests."

"I've already told you, Mrs. Logan. The tests don't tell us everything. We need your daughter to tell us the rest."

Lexie clenched her eyes. Were her mother and the man talking about her? Where was she?

"Doctor McCabe." Her mother's voice took on the impatient tone Lexie recognized well. "Please don't take this the wrong way, but I think I'd like someone with more experience. I want another opinion."

Doctor? Stirring, Lexie fought to get her brain to engage. She wanted to speak, but her mouth wouldn't comply.

The man's voice sounded equally impatient. "That is your right, Mrs. Logan, but another doctor will only tell you the same thing. Your daughter will come around. Just give her some time. Considering her state when she was brought in, she's lucky to be alive."

Hearing that, Lexie fought harder. Becoming more aware, she determined she was lying in bed. The soft sounds of beeping and the feel of the sheets under her fingers made her fear bloom. Was she in a hospital? She tried to open her eyes.

"I'm aware of how lucky she is, doctor. The staff around here never cease to remind me."

"Your daughter needs time to regain consciousness. She had a substantial amount of alcohol and drugs in her system."

Lexie couldn't keep up. *Alcohol? Drugs?*

Her mother's impatient tone softened. "I understand."

Inside her head, Lexie struggled to respond. *I'm awake. I'm right here.* She heard soft footsteps and felt a presence near her. Someone touched her forehead.

"Just try to be patient, Mrs. Logan."

Her mother scoffed. "Patience is *not* my strong suit, Dr. McCabe."

Warm breath brushed her cheek, and her mother whispered in her ear. "You listen to me, Lexie Rose Logan. You need to wake up. Right now. I've got an inane doctor telling me you need more time, and I'm missing my trip to the Appalachian Trail. Gary isn't thrilled, but he can wait. I told him how tough you are and that you will be up in no time. So don't make me a liar."

Fingers stroked Lexie's cheek.

"So, if you can hear me, sweetheart, open your eyes. Right now."

Lexie tried.

Her mother sucked in a breath. "Her eyelids fluttered."

Sounding closer, the doctor spoke. "Keep talking to her."

Her mother raised her voice. "Can you hear me, honey? Open your eyes."

Her mother took Lexie's hand, and Lexie gripped her fingers.

"She squeezed my hand," said her mother, clutching her fingers around Lexie's. "You can hear me, can't you?"

Lexie tried again to open her eyes, but they felt cemented shut. A hand jostled her shoulder.

"C'mon, Lexie. You can do it." The hand jostled her some more. "Open your eyes."

"Mrs. Logan. Don't rush it."

Her mother's voice turned harsh. "Don't tell me how to talk to my daughter. I'm the only one around here who seems interested in rousing her." Her voice relaxed. "Lexie, honey, open your eyes."

Lexie tried again. It felt like she was blinking, but her eyes didn't actually open.

Her mother's voice got louder in her ear. "Lexie Rose. Open your eyes, or I will contact your brother, sister, and your father and tell them you're in the hospital, fighting for your life from a drug overdose."

Lexie clutched her mother's fingers.

"Ouch," said her mother.

Lexie forced her eyes open. The light blinded her, and she shut them again.

"I knew it." Her mother's tone turned impatient again. "See, doctor. I told you."

He sighed, and Lexie opened her eyes again. Everything was blurry, and she blinked several times. She adjusted to the light, and her vision slowly cleared.

"Honey. Can you see me?"

Her mother's face sharpened into focus, and Lexie tried to speak. "Mom?" it came out more as a croak.

Her mother reached for something, and Lexie saw a cup with a straw. "Here. Take a sip." She helped Lexie raise her head.

Lexie sucked on the straw. Blessedly cool water hit her tongue, and she swallowed.

The doctor leaned over the bed. "Take small sips."

Lexie swallowed some more and lay back. "That's better," she whispered. Her voice sounded stronger.

Her mother returned the cup to the table. "How do you feel?"

Lexie had no idea how to answer. "Where am I?" It seemed like the better response.

"You're in the hospital, dear." Her mother looked behind her. "This is Dr. McCabe. He's been supposedly treating you."

Lexie didn't miss the slight tightening of the doctor's shoulders before he slipped back into professional mode. "Hello, Miss Logan." He stepped closer and held up three fingers. "How many fingers am I holding up?"

Her mother grumbled. "You're kidding? That's what you want to ask her?"

"Three," said Lexie.

"Good." He eyed her mother. "If you don't mind, Mrs. Logan. I'd like to examine your daughter. Would you please wait outside?"

Her mother's mouth fell open. "I will not."

Her focus improving, Lexie could almost read the doctor's mind. His fuse was growing shorter by the second. It was a common trait among most who spent time with Leona Logan. "It's okay, Mom."

Her mother stared at her, and then at the doctor. "Fine." She straightened and smoothed her pink silk shirt. Even in a hospital, her mother still dressed to impress. "I'll be right outside."

"It won't take long." The doctor gestured toward the door.

Her mother scowled. "Nothing happens fast at this hospital. It's unbelievable the amount of time wasted around here. Someone should talk to your supervisor."

"I'd be happy to give you the hospital administrator's name." He stared without a hint of empathy.

Her mother huffed, found her purse, and walked out of the room.

Lexie blinked again and focused on the doctor. Her mother had been correct. Lexie put him at around forty. He had short, brown, manicured hair, a firm jaw, and thick eyebrows. He wore glasses that emphasized his brown eyes and wore the typical long white doctor's coat with Dr. William McCabe embroidered on the pocket. He asked her several questions that she answered, studied the machines in her room, and made notes on a tablet he held in his hand.

While he focused on the tablet, Lexie, feeling more alert, raised the bed and sipped water from the cup he'd handed her.

He lowered the tablet. "Good news. I think you're going to make a full recovery." He slid the tablet into his pocket. "Any questions?"

Now that she'd had a few minutes to assimilate where she was and felt stronger, she had plenty. "What happened to me? Why am I here?"

He crossed his arms. "You were brought into the ER early yesterday morning unconscious. Your blood alcohol level was twice the legal limit, and your blood tox came back positive for cocaine and fentanyl. You're lucky someone found you when they did, or you wouldn't be here right now."

Lexie's head swam. She couldn't understand any of that. "There's a mistake. I don't drink. And I don't do drugs." He studied her, and her cheeks reddened at his appraisal. "I'm telling you the truth."

"Miss Logan. What happened to you is not for me to judge, and it's none of my business who you associate with, but as your doctor, I would be remiss not to suggest addiction counseling." He glanced toward the door. "I'm sure your mother would agree."

Lexie's face burned. The slight headache that had been threatening intensified. She wondered what her mother had told Dr. McCabe. She thought back to her last few days, but they were a blank.

"What do you remember?" he asked.

Lexie rubbed her forehead and closed her eyes. The last thing she recalled was sitting and eating dinner at her place. She opened her eyes. "Nothing about taking any drugs or drinking."

"That's not unusual for an overdose. Your memories will come back with time. I suggest lots of water and rest. Healthy food, and..." he eyed her solemnly, "no more substance abuse."

Lexie shook her head and regretted the action. Her head hurt, and her stomach flipped. "Doctor. I don't know what happened. I haven't had a drink...in a long time. I have no reason to do this."

He tipped his head toward her. "Have you been stressed lately? Under a lot of pressure? What do you do for a living?"

"I'm an investigative journalist." She thought back on her previous few months. It had been a whirlwind of activity. After breaking the Damien Rook case and exposing his secret society and their multitude of crimes, she'd been on a nonstop press junket. Her reporting had gone national, and she'd been in demand with several news organizations. She'd even started her own podcast to expose all she knew about Rook and his members' extensive and nefarious activities. Her mother, who worried about her attracting the wrong attention from those who'd been exposed, had warned against it, but to Lexie, it seemed like the next logical step in her career.

"Your mother implied you'd been under considerable strain recently."

Lexie rolled her eyes. "She worries too much."

McCabe slid his hands into the pockets of his coat. "She does have her opinions."

"She's a former advice columnist. It comes with the territory."

He knitted his brow. "She's not Leona Logan, is she? From *Ask Leona*?"

"The one and the same."

"Now I understand the alcohol and drugs."

Lexie frowned at him.

He frowned back. “Sorry. That was unprofessional.”

“Doctor, I didn’t take drugs or drink.”

“Your toxicology report says otherwise.”

Hating that he didn’t believe her and knowing his reaction would be exactly what she could expect from everyone else, Lexie’s emotions stirred. “I’m telling the truth.”

“If that’s true, then how did this happen? Were you forced to do this? And how so? Do you have any recollection of an assault? Or do you know someone who would want to hurt you?”

A tear threatened to spill over her lashes, and Lexie wiped it away. Her mother’s warnings echoed in her mind. Had someone from Rook’s society decided to pay her back for revealing their crimes? She had to consider it. “Maybe. I’ve made some enemies.”

“Then I suggest you talk to the police. If something happened to you, they would need to take it from here.” He stepped away from the bed. “I’d like to keep you another night for observation. Assuming there are no complications, I’ll approve your discharge tomorrow.”

She toyed with the edge of the sheet, still trying to recall what had happened to her. “Thanks, Doctor.”

“You’re welcome.” He reached for the door handle. “And my advice? Reduce your stress and keep a reasonable distance from your mother.”

“Easier said than done.”

“I’ll be back tomorrow. Get some rest.” He pulled the door open just as her mother pushed it from the other side.

Lexie moaned but tensed when she saw two people walk in behind her mom.

“Are you done?” asked Leona with a withering stare at Dr. McCabe.

“We are. She’s all yours, but don’t overdo it.” The doctor walked around her and left the room.

Leona walked past him with a glare, and the two people—one a younger woman around Lexie’s age and an older man who looked to be in his sixties—entered the room. They wore slacks, collared shirts, and jackets, and looked serious.

"Lexie," said her mother. "These are detectives from the SDPD. They want to talk to you."

The man and the woman flashed their badges. The woman spoke first. "I'm Detective Samantha Carlson, and this is my partner, Detective Phil Justini. You're Lexie Logan?" Carlson was an attractive woman with dark brown shoulder-length hair and a slim but sturdy physique.

"Yes." Lexie wondered what was happening. Was she in trouble?

Justini stepped closer. He had salt and pepper hair and a mustache, and the intense gaze of a man who'd seen a lot of awful things and wished he could forget them. "We'd like to ask you about two nights ago."

Her mother walked up to the side of the bed. "You don't have to say a word, Lex." She pulled out her cell phone. "I'm calling Gary."

"Appalachian guy?" asked Lexie.

"Yes." She held the phone to her ear. "He's an attorney, and a prominent one." She shot laser beams with her eyes at Carlson and Justini.

"That's your right, ma'am," said Carlson. "But we just have a few questions for your daughter."

"Questions now. An arrest later." She cursed at the phone. "Damn it, Gary. Pick up."

"It's okay, Mom. I'll talk to them. Just give us a second."

Her mother scowled. "I am not going anywhere."

Lexie rubbed her forehead again. Her headache was growing by the second. "What are your questions?"

"We understand you were brought in early yesterday after an overdose," Justini tucked his badge into his jacket pocket. "Is that correct?"

Lexie debated how to answer. "I suppose that's the way it looks."

"What does that mean?" asked Carlson.

"It means I almost died from an overdose of alcohol and drugs, but I didn't take them. Not willingly." Lexie anticipated their response and wasn't disappointed.

Justini half smiled. "So who took them? Your alter ego?" He paused. "You have a mental disorder?"

"Certainly not," added Leona. "Don't be vulgar, Detective."

Justini shrugged.

The urge to cry returned, but Lexie forced back her tears. "I have no memory of what happened to me. The last thing I recall was eating dinner at home. After that...it's a blank."

Justini's smile grew. "It must have been one hell of a party."

Lexie clenched her jaw.

Detective Carlson stepped closer. "Do you have any knowledge of how you ended up in an alley outside an abandoned warehouse?"

Lexie stiffened. "Alley? What alley? I assumed I was found at my duplex." She looked at her mother.

Her mother lowered her phone. "No dear. Someone found you and called an ambulance. You should stop talking now." Leona put the phone back to her ear. "I'm trying Gary again."

Lexie spoke to the detectives. "Who found me?"

"A maintenance worker, who just happened to walk outside to smoke. He wasn't supposed to be there, but you're lucky he was." Carlson pulled a notebook from her pocket. "Does the name Dr. Mira Patel ring a bell?"

Lexie opened her mouth to say "no" when an image flashed in her brain. She'd been working late. Her phone had rung, and she'd answered.

"Miss Logan?" asked Carlson.

Lexie held her stomach, which was churning. "She called me."

Leona lowered her phone again.

"Dr. Patel called you?" asked Justini. "When?"

Lexie clenched her eyes shut as the images flashed again. "It was late. She asked if I was Lexie Logan, the journalist. I said yes. She said she wanted to meet but wouldn't say why. Only that it was important and it had to be right then. She gave me an address."

"You typically meet strangers in strange places at night?" asked Justini, looking dubious.

Lexie fought to recall everything Dr. Patel had told her. "She asked what kind of phone I used, and I told her."

Carlson and Justini glanced at each other. "Why would she ask that?" asked Justini.

"I don't know." Lexie rubbed her temple. "She implied that she had information about her employer."

Carlson found a pencil and scribbled in her notepad. "Did she give any details?"

Lexie shook her head. "No."

"How'd you get there?" asked Justini. "We didn't find your car."

Lexie thought back. After talking to Patel, she'd hung up, grabbed her purse, and headed out the door. "I took a rideshare. My neighbor, Lynn, borrowed my car to go on a date. Her car's in the shop."

Carlson took more notes.

Lexie sat up. "This must have something to do with what happened to me. Have you talked to Dr. Patel?" Lexie had to wonder if Mira Patel had some connection to Rook's fallen black bird society. "I'm a journalist. I broke a big story recently that exposed a lot of people and their crimes. This must be some sort of payback." Feeling like some pieces were falling into place, she hoped the detectives would have more reason to believe her. "She must have lured me out to give someone access to me."

Carlson and Justini glanced at each other again.

"My daughter wouldn't lie." Leona faced the detectives as if she were their superior. "This Dr. Patel must know what happened. My daughter's reporting took down powerful people. Someone tried to kill her. I demand that you figure out who. This doctor needs to be questioned immediately."

Carlson didn't act the least bit fazed by Leona. She eyed Lexie. "Miss Logan, Dr. Patel was murdered. Her body was found in the warehouse next to the alley where you were located." She paused. "And we'd like to know why."

Justini crossed his arms. "Care to explain, Miss Logan?"

Leona's composure slipped. "Don't say one word, Lexie."

Lexie did the opposite. Realizing the implications, she couldn't help but curse.

Chapter Two

Lexie walked up the steps to her duplex and pulled out her keys. She turned and waved at her mom, who'd driven her home after being released from the hospital. Her mom had wanted to walk her in and help get her settled, but Lexie had insisted she was fine. While that was true, the main reason was that Lexie needed space. She'd spent the last day lying in bed with her mother beside her. By the time she was discharged, the nurses were as eager to be rid of Leona as Lexie was.

Happy to be home, she slid the key into the lock as her mother drove away, and Lynn, her neighbor, opened her front door. Her long blonde hair ran down her back, and she wore yoga pants and an oversized T-shirt that read *Save the Elephants*.

"There you are, Lex." Lynn held a leash, and her dog Foster, a small mutt with wiry hair, ran out onto the steps and jumped up on Lexie's leg.

"Hey, Lynn." She petted the dog's head. "Hey, Foster."

"Did you go out of town again?"

Lexie shook her head. "I, uh, no." She hadn't considered how to answer people's questions about her absence. "I was with Mom for a couple of days."

"Everything okay?" She knitted her brow. "You look tired."

Lexie opened her door. "I am tired." She dreaded seeing Lynn's look of doubt if she heard about the overdose, so Lexie kept it to herself. "I just need some rest. I'll be fine."

"Doris was here yesterday, looking for rent."

Lexie sighed. "I forgot. I'll stop by later and pay it. Thanks, Lynn."

"And I put your car keys on your entry table, along with your mail. I used the key you gave me. Is that okay?"

"Sure. That's fine."

"Thanks for letting me borrow the car. I appreciate it."

"No problem. I hope your evening went well." Lynn had a history of dating disastrous men. The last man she'd gone out with had been arrested for unpaid parking tickets while they'd been out at dinner, and the one before that, who Lynn believed was an accountant making six figures, turned out to live in his mother's basement and was six figures in debt.

Lynn's face fell. "It did if you like men who smell like cigarettes and drink a lot of beer. He could have been Doris' brother."

Lexie thought of her landlady, who smoked like a chimney and drank beer like water. "That good, huh? Sorry about that."

Lynn smiled. "That's okay. I've got my eye on a cutie I met at the dog park yesterday. Foster and I are going there now. You want to join us?"

Lexie shook her head. "Not today. You guys have fun. Hope you bump into Mr. Cutie."

"Me too." She tugged on the leash. "C'mon, Foster. Let's go."

Lexie paused on the step. "Hey, Lynn?"

Lynn turned back. "Yeah?"

Lexie hesitated but asked her question anyway. "The night you went out on the date, when you came back, did you see anything weird?"

"Weird?" Lynn wrinkled her nose. "How so?"

Lexie wasn't sure what to say. "I don't know. Anybody walking around that shouldn't be? Anything out of place?"

Lynn paused. "No. Should I have?"

"No. I was just wondering." She waved her hand. "Ignore me. I need sleep."

Lynn watched her for a second. "Are you sure you're okay?"

Lexie nodded. "Have fun on your walk." She pushed her door open and stepped inside. Her place looked exactly as she'd left it. Boxes, some open and others still taped shut, were pushed against the walls of her small living area. Her meager breakfast table, next to her tiny kitchen, sported her closed laptop and various notebooks. She dropped her purse and house keys next to the mail on the entry table.

Apparently, when she'd been found in the alley, her purse and everything inside it had still been with her and untouched. Carlson and Justini had asked to go through it, but her mother, who'd eventually contacted Gary, had refused. Lexie did give them the number Dr. Mira Patel had called her from but did not provide access to her phone; not because she had something to hide regarding Dr. Patel, but because, as a journalist, she had to protect her sources.

She'd told the detectives as much as she could recall from that night, but Gary had advised her to say little else. She didn't enjoy hiding anything, especially about her past, because she knew it looked bad. But she understood her mother and Gary were only protecting her, and since Lexie couldn't remember much, it was the smart thing to do.

After closing the door behind her, she went into the bathroom to wash her face and brush her teeth. After drying her skin, she stared at herself and noted the circles beneath her eyes, her sunken cheeks, and her limp brown hair. She gathered her hair into a ponytail, twisted it around her fingers, and clipped it up to get it off her shoulders.

Needing a few minutes before she got into the shower, she went into the kitchen to get something to drink. Another open box she had yet to unpack sat in the corner. She filled a glass with water and ice and, leaning against the counter, took a second to breathe. It was her first chance to be away from her mom and think since this ordeal began, and she relished it.

Her mind wandered, and she thought about the last few months. Not long after breaking the Damien Rook case, she'd moved out of her apartment because her neighbor and friend, Lonny, had died there, and she couldn't stomach staying. After that, her apartment manager kindly let her out of her lease, and Lexie moved into this duplex. So much had happened since, though, that Lexie still hadn't unpacked all her boxes.

Lexie stretched her neck and thought again about Dr. Mira Patel. Who was she, and why had she called? Lexie tried again to remember more, but it remained a blank. Eyeing the notebooks on her table, she pushed off the counter and sat at her dining table. She set her water glass down and opened her yellow notebook. She flipped to the last page and stopped. In pencil, she had written Dr. Patel's name and an address.

She pulled out her phone and typed in the address. A map pulled up, and she studied it. The location wasn't close by but over on the east end of town, and it pinpointed a warehouse, which was near the headquarters of the tech company Omnivista. Behind it was an alley, and Lexie wondered if that's where she'd been found.

Setting her phone down, she rested her elbow on the table and her jaw in her palm. What had happened that night? Had she made it to the warehouse? Had she gone inside? Had she met Dr. Patel? She closed her eyes but failed to recall anything.

Her next thought was about Dr. Patel's murder. All Carlson and Justini would tell her was that the doctor had been shot and that her time of death was around the time Lexie had been found. While that was alarming, it certainly didn't prove Lexie was involved. After the detectives had left, Lexie questioned every doctor or nurse who'd been in her room, wanting to know about when she'd been brought into the ER. Had she said anything? Had there been blood on her? Had there been any sign she'd been knocked out first before taking the drugs or alcohol? Her mother had told the nurses to toss the clothes Lexie had been wearing since they'd been cut off in the ER, so they were no longer a source of information. No one she spoke with could offer anything helpful, though, and she'd left the hospital with more questions than answers.

Sighing, she glanced at her phone and considered calling Daniels and Remalla, the two detectives she'd worked closely with on the Rook case. They'd risked their lives to infiltrate Rook's society, which ultimately had led to his demise. Despite their relationship starting on shaky ground, over time, they'd formed a bond of mutual trust and respect.

She considered asking them to find out more about Carlson and Justini, and Mira Patel, even though it wasn't their case. But if she asked, they'd want to know why, and that would mean divulging her overdose and memory loss, plus a few other things they didn't know. The thought of them believing she was hiding from the truth almost made her ill, so she held off. She had other avenues she could pursue before she had to use that card. Besides, she didn't want to cause any friction with Carlson and Justini if they learned she'd involved two other detectives.

She opened her laptop, typed Mira Patel's name and started doing research. It didn't take long to find an article about her murder. It revealed little, but it mentioned where Dr. Patel worked–Omnivista.

Lexie opened another browser window and searched for information on Omnivista. The giant from Silicon Valley was known for its global, innovative social media platforms and cutting-edge AI technology. The company prided itself on its "connect the world" mission and its commitment to user privacy. CEO Nolan Sorrento had been directing the company to record growth for the last eight years. Lexie pulled up a picture of him. Sorrento looked to be in his mid-fifties, with short, perfectly cut wavy black hair with hints of gray, and a trim but muscular physique. Wearing tailored slacks and a shirt but no tie or jacket, he appeared every bit the country-club type who golfed during the week while doing million-dollar deals.

Lexie opened her yellow notebook and took notes. If Dr. Patel had been legit and had dirt on Omnivista, and she'd planned to tell Lexie about it, Lexie needed all the information she could get on the company.

Setting her pen down, she still had to consider whether any of this had to do with taking down Rook's society. After going through his office, the police had found a trove of evidence incriminating numerous people in powerful positions, but there was no way to know if they'd caught everyone. From what Lexie knew, neither Patel's nor Sorrento's names were on the list of members, but that didn't mean they weren't connected. Lexie would have to do some digging to find out more, but she'd need help. An investigation like this required more hands. She had to consider that someone out there considered her a threat, or at least wanted payback, so she couldn't afford to do this alone.

She picked up her phone, hit a button, and listened to it ring until a male voice picked up.

"Hey, kiddo. I was just getting ready to call you. What's this business about you being in the hospital? Are you okay?"

Lexie slumped. Her mother had struck again. "Hey, Frank. You talked to Mom?"

"I just got off the phone with her. She's worried sick about you."

"She still heading off to the Appalachian Trail with Gary?"

"They leave tomorrow."

"I figured."

"That's how your mom copes. She extreme travels. At least this time, she's not climbing Everest. Not yet, anyway."

Lexie dropped her head into her hand. "Yeah. I know." She fell back in her seat. "How much did she tell you?"

"Enough."

Lexie closed her eyes. "I'm not drinking or doing drugs."

"I never said you were."

"But you're thinking it."

He paused. "Hell, kid. I know what you've been through. I wouldn't blame you if you fell off the wagon. But even at its worst, you never touched drugs."

"I didn't fall off the wagon."

"There's no shame in it, Lex."

Her chest tightened. Even Frank didn't believe her. "I'm telling you the truth. I didn't do this. I don't know how I ended up in that alley. All I know is I got a phone call, and I went to see someone, and the next thing I know, I'm waking up in a hospital." She gripped her temples. "Someone targeted me, Frank. I was set up." Her voice caught at the end of the sentence.

Frank stayed quiet for a second. "You home?"

Lexie collected herself. "I am."

"By yourself?"

"Yes."

"I don't like that."

Lexie clenched her eyes shut. "I'm not drinking, Frank."

"That's not what I meant." He paused. "Listen. Grab a few things and come stay the night here. We'll talk. I'd come there, but Elaine's gone for the weekend, and I've got the dogs. I'll send a car. Be ready in thirty minutes."

She sniffed. "Frank, I—"

"No arguments. Just do what I say. Your father told me to keep an eye on you, and that's what I'm going to do."

Lexie took a deep breath. Her father was the last thing she wanted to discuss. "Okay. I'll grab a few things. Make it an hour, though. I need to take a shower first."

"Okay. I'll see you soon. And don't worry. We'll figure this out."

A small measure of hope bloomed. “Thanks, Frank.”

“Love ya, kid.”

“Love you too.” She hung up and put her phone down. Still emotional, she wiped at her eyes, sniffed and brushed a strand of hair that had come loose away from her face. She had to pull herself together, or she’d never figure this out. Shaking out her hands, she stood and thought about what to bring to Frank’s for the night. For a long second, she thought about bypassing him and getting a drink at a local bar, and immediately chastised herself. She’d made that mistake once before and swore she’d never make it again, no matter what she was dealing with. She considered calling her sponsor, Mickey, but dreaded telling him the news. Would he believe her? Probably not.

Gathering herself, she closed her laptop and slid it into one of her large purses, adding her yellow folder and some pens. She stood, grabbed her water glass, and took it into the kitchen. Scratching at the shirt her mother had brought for her to wear home, she walked out of the kitchen to start the shower when she heard a muffled buzzing. She stopped, listened and heard it again. It sounded like a phone ringing, only it wasn’t hers. Following the sound, she neared the entry table where the buzzing grew louder. Frowning, she dug through the mail and picked up a brown manila envelope, which buzzed again in her hand.

“What in the—?”

The envelope had her name written on the front in black marker but nothing else, so someone had slipped it into her mailbox. She opened the envelope and pulled out a small black cellphone. Staring at it, it buzzed once more. The display read “unknown,” and wondering what was going on, she answered. “Hello?”

A muffled voice answered. “Lexie Logan? The journalist?”

Her heart raced when she recalled Dr. Patel asking her the same question. “Who is this?”

"A friend." The voice sounded odd, as if the speaker was talking through a filter.

Lexie gripped the phone. "You got a name, friend?"

"You can call me Zephyr."

Lexie almost hung up. Was this some sort of joke? "You sent me this phone?"

"I did."

"Why?"

"Because you need help."

Lexie paused. "What kind of help?"

"I know what happened to you."

She froze. "Who is this?"

"I knew Dr. Patel."

She widened her eyes and got angry. "Listen. I don't know what kind of game you're playing, but this isn't funny. Dr. Patel was murdered."

"She was murdered because she was going to tell you everything."

Lexie stilled. "Like what?"

"That answer takes time. More than I have right now. But I know things. Things that could get me killed, like Dr. Patel. And if you choose to talk to me, they could get you killed too. They've already tried to discredit you. They won't stop there."

Lexie tried to grasp what Zephyr was telling her. "How do I know I can trust you?"

"You'll figure that out soon enough. You don't want to talk to me? Throw this phone into the river. But if you want to know the truth, keep this a secret and tell no one, and I'll be in touch. You tell anyone about me, and I'm gone."

Lexie sputtered. "Wait a minute. How do I—?" It was pointless though, because Zephyr had hung up.

Chapter Three

Sitting at the kitchen table, Lexie watched Frank work in the kitchen. "You didn't have to go to this trouble. I would have been fine with sandwiches."

Frank sprinkled basil on top of the red snapper. "Sandwiches are for kids. You need something decent to eat." He set the spice bottle down, picked up the pan, and slid the fish into the oven. "Besides, you know cooking is my way to relax." He set the timer and started making a salad.

Lexie sipped on the glass of sparkling water with a slice of lemon he'd given her. "I wish that worked for me."

He added lettuce to a bowl. "It might if you actually cooked."

Barney, Frank's golden retriever, sat beside Lexie's chair. Lexie petted his head. "It's not my strong suit. Cooking only makes me anxious."

"That's because you're always in a hurry." He cut a tomato. "You need to stop and smell the roses more often."

Lexie almost chuckled. "Have you forgotten who my parents are? Smelling the roses was never on their list of priorities."

"Your dad's rethinking that. He's got nothing but time now."

Lexie didn't respond.

Frank glanced over at her. "I saw him last week."

The familiar constriction in her stomach whenever the conversation shifted to her father flared. She played with the stem of her glass. "How is he?"

He arched his eyebrow at her. "Nice of you to ask."

The constriction tightened. "Don't start with me, Frank. I've got enough on my plate right now."

He stared for a second and added the tomatoes to the bowl. "It's just that you rarely mention him."

Lexie wanted to change the subject. "You need help with anything?"

He shook his head. "No." He picked up an avocado. "Did you know he's up for parole in a couple of months?" He pierced the avocado with his knife.

Lexie sat up with a start. "What? Already?"

"It's been eight years."

Lexie tried to comprehend how quickly those years had gone by.

"I'm sure he'd appreciate it if you came to the hearing."

Lexie's stomach flipped. "No way. He made it very clear how he felt about my coming around. That's not going to change just because he's up for parole."

Frank stopped cutting the avocado and turned toward her. "He's your father, Lex."

"He's also in prison for embezzlement. And he's an alcoholic who cheated on Mom for years. And he lied to me."

Frank set his knife on the cutting board. "How did he lie to you?"

Lexie shrank back into her chair. She hated thinking about those days. "He told me I wasn't like him when I'm exactly like him. I drank as much as he did, and when things got bad for me, he'd tell me to toughen up and have another drink. He lied to Mom about his affair, and he lied to all of us when he told us he never embezzled anything when he clearly did."

Frank's shoulders fell. "Lex—"

"And that's not even the worst of it." Now that she was talking about it, she found it hard to shut up. "He knew I worshipped him. Despite everything, I always justified everything he did. I supported him until the end, even when they found him guilty. And after all that, what did he do? He told me he didn't want to see me. That it was better for him to make a clean break from everyone." She patted her hand against her chest. "When I was the only one still sticking beside him. Natalie was in Arizona, and Jonah, wherever he was, barely spoke to Mom or Dad, and Mom wanted nothing to do with Dad since the divorce. So what Dad was really saying is he wanted nothing to do with me."

Frank softened his gaze. "Your father was not in a good place, Lex..."

Her anger bubbled up. "You think I was?" She banged her palm against the tabletop. "I was in recovery. He knew I was trying to get my act together back then. I was coming out of an abusive relationship, trying my damnedest to be there for him and for Mom, and he had the nerve to tell me he didn't want my help anymore. That all I did was remind him of all he'd lost, and it was too painful." Tears made her vision blur, and she swiped at her eyes. "So, no. I will not be at his hearing. He made his wishes very clear, and I won't be made to feel guilty because I'm honoring them."

Frank paused, then sighed. "Then I won't pressure you."

Lexie stood. "Maybe I should go." She sniffled and wiped a tear that slid down her cheek. "I've had a hellish two days. I don't need any more."

Frank walked over to her. He put his hands on her shoulders. "I'm sorry. I shouldn't have brought it up. It's just that you never talk about him."

She sniffed again. "Now you know why."

He guided her back into the chair. "Leona won't discuss him either."

"Dad made that bed."

Frank sat beside her. "Listen, kiddo. I've known your dad for twenty-five years. Believe me. I'm aware of his faults. He'll never win Father or Husband of the Year, but I know he loves you. Natalie and Jonah, too. But he's always had a soft spot for you."

Lexie picked up a napkin from the table and dabbed her eyes with it. “Probably because I’m the only one who’d drink with him.”

He smiled. “He was proud of you when you stopped drinking, but it was hard on him because he couldn’t do the same.”

“He could have. He just didn’t want to.”

“He was in the middle of a trial. It’s a lousy time to go on the wagon. And your father, no matter how hard he tries to convince people otherwise, is not a strong man.”

Lexie recalled those tough days. “I always thought he was.”

“Most kids do, especially ones who idolize their fathers. But it’s a hard day when you realize your parents aren’t heroes. They’re trying to figure things out just like everyone else. And your dad, when he saw that realization hit you, well, it just about broke him.”

Lexie looked away.

“And I’m sorry I wasn’t there for you. I could see the strain you were under, but I was so focused on being your father’s attorney and trying to defend him that you fell through the cracks.” He sighed. “And after the guilty verdict, it was all about appealing. And when that fell through, I was so fed up, I left the legal profession.”

Composing herself, Lexie closed and opened her eyes. “That trial did so much damage. To all of us.”

He paused. “It wasn’t all bad. Look at you. You’ve become a first-rate journalist. You broke a huge national story, and your career is thriving. Your mom has discovered a whole new side of herself she never would have found otherwise. She’s dating, traveling, hiking, and climbing. You think she would have done any of that with Tobias still in the picture?” He pointed at himself. “And I started my investigation firm, which allowed me to help you when you needed it.” He squeezed her arm. “I’d say we’re all doing okay, kid.”

“I think Natalie and Jonah would say otherwise.”

"Your brother and sister have their own issues to address, and they have nothing to do with you."

Lexie scoffed. "Natalie married my ex behind my back and had his kid, and Jonah, the brilliant one," she used her fingers as quotes, "rarely speaks to any of us. His last argument with Dad was about how Dad always favored me and Nat over him, which is ridiculous. No matter what Dad did, Jonah was never happy."

Frank rested his elbow on the back of his chair. "I wouldn't worry about Jonah. I've learned over the years that those with high IQs get shortchanged in the common sense department. He's held a chip on his shoulder ever since his biological father disappeared, and when Leona remarried, Tobias never measured up. One of these days, Jonah will figure it out. And I think your sister is rethinking her choices right now."

Lexie studied her fingers and thought of her ex. "Walker was a good guy, at least when I was dating him. Hell. I thought I would marry him."

"And if you had..."

Looking back, Lexie felt certain it would have been a disaster. At the time, though, she'd been in love. She and Walker had both been studying journalism in school, and she'd fallen head over heels. They'd planned to marry after graduating, but when that time had come, her drinking had picked up, and her focus had been on proving herself at her first big job at a major paper. She'd believed their relationship was fine, but a year later, Walker had told her he'd met someone else and was leaving. She was devastated when he moved out and left town. Her drinking got worse, and she ended up losing her job when she'd missed too many deadlines. Things only declined when her sister, Natalie, who'd been attending ASU, showed up at Mom's door, married and six months pregnant.

Lexie had been happy for her sister until Natalie had informed them she'd married Walker and was carrying his child. Drinking heavily by then and heartbroken, Lexie had broken off all ties with her sister, who'd returned to Arizona.

Soon after her sister left, Lexie started dating Judd, who was an editor at another big paper where she'd found work. It was a rocky relationship from the start because Judd drank too. They argued a lot, and after one bad altercation, he hit Lexie.

After his many apologies, she justified it by telling herself he'd never do it again, until he did. Again and again. Her mother had begged her to get out of the relationship, and her father had encouraged her to leave, but his revealed affair and arrest had changed things. Lexie's private life had taken a back seat to his own issues.

Her father's troubles had only exacerbated the problems between her and Judd until they'd culminated in an ugly argument. Lexie had ended up with two black eyes, a bloody nose, and a swollen, split lip when the cops arrived.

Prior to that, Lexie had always made excuses for Judd and never pressed charges. But that night, an officer had pulled her aside and talked to her. Lexie could remember him clearly. His name was Connor Diamond. He'd found her some ice, sat with her on the curb, and talked to her. Before then, she had always been an object of pity, but Officer Diamond told her she didn't deserve the treatment she had endured. That no matter what she'd done in the past, or how much Judd apologized or said he loved her, nothing would change until Lexie did.

Lexie had listened but still felt like she knew better until Diamond told her he'd lost his sister to domestic abuse, and it was why he'd gone into law enforcement–to prevent other brilliant, amazing, and beautiful women from dying.

That had struck Lexie in a way nothing else had. In her world, her older brother Jonah had been the brilliant son, and Natalie had been the beautiful younger daughter. Lexie had always seen herself as the people pleaser, always trying to prove herself. Had she been making herself small because she felt that way? And if she stayed with Judd, would he eventually kill her?

In that moment, she'd witnessed Judd arguing with Diamond's partner about how he'd only been defending himself. Something inside her had shifted, and when Diamond had asked her if she wanted to press charges, she'd said yes.

They'd handcuffed Judd, who'd lunged at her and called her awful names until Diamond walked up and said something to him. Judd had paled, gone quiet, and Diamond had shoved him into the back of the patrol car.

Before Lexie had gone off in the ambulance, Diamond had assured her that Judd would never harm her again, provided that's what she wanted. On the way to the hospital, she'd decided that's exactly what would happen. Judd ended up taking a plea and doing nine months in jail, and Lexie went into rehab. She'd stayed sober throughout her father's abysmal trial, and even after Judd got out and came to see her, expecting to reconnect. The nine-millimeter her mother had bought Lexie, and she'd taken shooting classes with, had been enough to convince him she'd moved on and he should too.

She hadn't seen him since, nor had she seen Officer Diamond after the night of the fight, but every once in a while, she thought of him. If she ever saw him again, she planned to thank him. He'd been the only one to get through to her, and he deserved to know that.

Frank nudged her. "Hey. You there?"

She pulled back from the memories. "Sorry. I was just thinking. You're right. Walker and I would have been a disaster if we'd stayed together."

"You wouldn't be the Lexie you are today. And that would be a shame."

Her present problems surfaced. “You sure about that? I almost died from an overdose I have no memory of, and the woman I was supposed to meet is dead. I’d say that’s a serious issue.”

Frank stood and went into the kitchen. “Let’s talk about that.” He resumed cutting the avocado. “Tell me what you know.”

Lexie settled back in her seat and told Frank about her talk with Detectives Carlson and Justini, and what Lexie had learned about Dr. Patel and Omnivista from the internet. She didn’t mention the call from Zephyr. As a journalist, so-called informants sometimes contacted her, but most never panned out. Although Zephyr had sent her a burner phone, until she heard from him again, she couldn’t rely on him.

Frank mixed the salad in the bowl. “What does your mother think of all this?”

Lexie leaned over the table and rested her chin in her palm. “I’m not sure. On the way back from the hospital, all she could talk about was how handsome Dr. McCabe was and how maybe I should get to know him better.”

Frank laughed out loud. “Leave it to Leona to play matchmaker.”

“She drove the man nuts while I was there, but you’d have thought he’d cured cancer by the way she talked about him on the way home.”

Frank poured olive oil into a measuring cup. “God help the man you choose to invite into your life.”

“If that ever happens, he’ll deserve sainthood.” She sat back with a sigh. “After talking about St. McCabe, Mom just told me not to talk to the cops and to call Gary’s partner at their firm if they want to question me again before she and Gary get back.” She paused. “I’m still not sure if she believes me about the overdose.”

Frank added vinegar to the olive oil. “Regardless, she’ll defend you to the death.”

Lexie watched Frank add some mustard and spices to the olive oil and stir the contents. “Do you believe me?”

He picked up the measuring cup and turned toward her. "Of course I do. But if Dr. Mira Patel got killed for her attempt to whistle-blow, then you've got a target on your back."

"Omnivista is a monster company. Investigating them won't be easy."

"No, it won't. But how can you be sure this doesn't have something to do with the black bird group you exposed?"

Zephyr's call suggested her assault had everything to do with Dr. Patel and her employer, but could she trust this Zephyr? Was he leading her in the wrong direction to protect someone? "None of the names connected to Omnivista have any connection to the members of that society."

He poured the dressing onto the salad in the bowl. "That you know of. You told me there was loads of evidence to go through in the Rook investigation and it would take months to unravel. Maybe there are more names that have yet to surface. Your podcast has attracted interest, and before you expose anyone else, maybe someone's trying to discredit you. Or some member you've exposed is pissed." He mixed the salad. "Any way you can find out? What about those two detectives you worked with? Can they help?"

Lexie thought of Daniels and Remalla. "Probably. But I don't relish revealing my supposed overdose."

"They don't have to know." He set the salad bowl to the side. "Use those journalistic skills of yours to get to the truth without exposing your own."

She considered her history with the detectives. She'd never told them about her alcoholism, but if they'd checked her background, they'd have found two DUIs, an arrest for public intoxication, and a brief stint in court-ordered rehab, but those were over a decade old, and they'd never asked her about it. If the overdose came up, would they suspect she was an addict? If they asked about it, she'd have to explain a few things she'd planned to keep to herself. Could she do that? Could she risk losing their respect? Despite the risks, she knew she couldn't avoid them. "It wouldn't be the first time, would it?"

He grabbed some oven mitts. "Besides, if you eventually need their help, better to include them now and not later." He opened the oven and pulled out two foil-wrapped potatoes. "We eat in twelve minutes. That's plenty of time to make a phone call."

Realizing he was right, she stood and reached for her phone. "I haven't talked to them in a while, anyway. It's about time for me to get an update. Be right back." She walked to the back door, stepped outside, and called. Nervous, she listened to the phone ring.

Remalla picked up. "Well, well, well. Look who's calling. You finally taking a break between interviews and podcasts?"

She smiled. "Just a short one. How are you and Daniels?"

"We're finally catching our breath after all the news coverage. You caught us at a good time. We're in line at the taco truck. I'll put you on speaker."

Lexie heard a click and heard Daniels' voice. "Hey, Lex. Any chance you can stop by with some bug spray?"

Remalla responded. "Would you stop complaining?"

"Your Taco del Fuego should be called Taco de Fly. I'm amazed you're not dead from some bug-borne disease."

"What do you want to eat?" asked Rem. "I'm buying."

"You always say that when you know all I want is water."

"One water coming up."

Lexie heard Daniels groan. "Take me out of my misery, Lex."

Lexie was happy she'd called. She'd missed these two more than she'd realized. "He's all yours, Daniels."

"I figured. What's up? This a social call or business?"

"Both, I guess. I hate to admit it, but I've missed you guys."

"Aww, Lexie misses us," said Rem. "We miss you too, especially your sarcasm. Nobody can drive us crazier."

"I take pride in that," she said.

"We know," said Daniels. "What's the business part?"

Lexie took a deep breath. "I'm curious about a couple of names. Dr. Mira Patel and Nolan Sorrento. They're both connected to the global tech company Omnivista. I'm sure you're familiar with it."

"It's only slightly smaller than Amazon or Facebook. What's your interest?" asked Rem.

"I'm wondering if those names ever showed up in the black bird member file. You guys hear whether more names were discovered?"

"Mel and Garcia are handling that side of the investigation," said Daniels. "Lozano has Rem and me prepping to testify against the ones we know of."

"Why the interest?" asked Rem. "Something come up with this Patel and Sorrento?"

Lexie hesitated. "Maybe. A potential whistleblower contacted me about Omnivista, and I'm wondering if it has to do with my connection to Rook and his society, or if it's unrelated."

"The press coverage may have led this person to you," said Daniels, "but why connect those two to Rook? Did something happen?"

Lexie stilled. She'd expected these two would want details but hoped she could maneuver around them. "Maybe. I just need to know what I'm dealing with."

There was a pause, and she cursed herself for calling.

"What's going on, Lex?" asked Rem. "Do we need to get out of the taco line?"

"Please say yes," added Daniels.

Lexie swallowed and gave in. "I got a call from Dr. Mira Patel. She said she had information about her employer, Omnivista. I went to meet her and ended up in the ER. I was told I'd overdosed on alcohol and drugs, but I have no memory of it." She gripped the phone and waited for the pity and doubt. She expected they'd think the worst, as most seemed to do.

Remalla responded. "I hope you told them that's bullshit."

"Who did this to you, Lex?" asked Daniels. "Are you okay?"

Her emotions bubbled up again as relief fluttered through her. "Thanks, guys."

"For what?" asked Daniels. "We haven't done anything yet."

"You're thinking this has something to do with the black birds?" asked Rem.

She blew out a long breath. "It might if someone's pissed at me. Or maybe this is really an Omnivista thing. I'm not sure yet."

"What about this Dr. Patel?" asked Daniels. "Any insight from her?"

She paced next to Frank's outdoor table. "She's dead. Someone shot her. I was lying in the alley outside the building where she was found."

It was quiet for a second.

Daniels spoke first. "I owe you, Lex. We're officially out of the taco line."

"You want us to do some digging?" asked Rem. "Find out what's going on?"

"I didn't call to get you two involved. Two detectives have already spoken to me. Carlson and Justini from another division. They haven't arrested me, so I'm guessing that's a good sign. But I don't want them mad because I contacted the two of you."

"Don't worry about that," said Rem. "Daniels' specialty is getting nosy about other investigations not assigned to us."

"That's only because you're lousy at it," replied Daniels. "We'll see what we can find out, Lex."

"And we'll talk to Mel and Garcia," added Rem. "See if Patel and Sorrento are on the black bird list. Where are you?"

"I'm out of the hospital and staying at a friend's house. But I'm plenty unnerved by what happened. The sooner I know what I'm up against, the better."

"We'll call as soon as we know something," said Daniels. "And be careful. No more going off to meet strange people. You get another call like that, contact us."

"I will. And you two be careful too. If some society member is pissed off, I'm not the only one they'll be mad at."

"Don't worry about Rem," said Daniels. "The tacos will finish him off before anyone with a grudge does."

"At least I'll die happy," said Rem. "Take care, Lex. We'll call soon."

"Thanks, guys. I appreciate it." They said their goodbyes, and she hung up. She stared out at Frank's pool and wondered if she should have told them more, but decided that was a conversation for later. She went back inside just as the timer went off. Frank turned to get the fish. "How'd it go?"

She put her phone down. "I told them about the overdose. They're too perceptive, and I don't want to lie to them."

Frank set the pan on the counter and added the fish to a plate along with a steaming baked potato. He set the plate in front of her, grabbed some napkins and silverware, and brought them to the table. "You trust them?"

"They're two of the few I do."

"Good. Then I hope they can help." He put the bowl of salad and a butter dish on the table. "Now, dig in."

He sat, and Lexie grabbed her knife and cut into the potato. "This looks great. Thank you."

"You're welcome." He placed his napkin on his lap.

She split her potato in half. "But they're not the only ones I'll need help from. I need your help too. If this involves Omnivista, your investigative skills will come in handy."

He reached for the salad. "I can't help you there, Lex. I sold the agency last week."

She stopped slathering butter on her potato. "What are you talking about? When did this happen?"

He chuckled. "Kiddo, this is nothing new. I told you I planned to make some changes, but you were so caught up in the black bird investigation and its aftermath that you missed the part where I was retiring. Elaine and I plan to use the RV, take a page from Leona, and start traveling."

Lexie dropped her jaw in shock. "I can't believe this. You're retiring?"

He scooped out some salad and handed her the bowl. "Correction. I've retired. The papers are signed, and it's official." Frank's other dog, a senior boxer named Sally, trotted through the dog door and sat next to Frank's chair. Frank handed her a piece of lettuce, and she snapped it up with her tongue.

Lexie set the salad bowl beside her plate. "But...but..." She shook her head. "Sorry, but this came out of left field."

"Not really, but that's okay. You've had other things on your mind."

Lexie held her fork and took a few seconds to adjust to Frank's news. "Don't get me wrong. I'm happy for you, but I'm bummed that I'll have to find another investigator." She sighed. "Darn it."

"No, you won't. I left you in good hands." He cut into his potato. "I sold the agency to a former detective. He's smart and knows his stuff. He's taking over my clients, and I told him he's expected to help you. That was part of the deal."

Lexie sputtered. "You did what? But how do you know if I'll even like him?"

"You will because I like him. He's a good guy, Lex, so give him a chance before you make any assumptions."

Uncertain, she placed her napkin on her lap. "He'd better be as good as you, but that's a high bar to reach." She scooped up some salad with the tongs. "Who is he?"

Frank scooped some butter out of the tub with his knife. “His name’s Connor Diamond, and I promise, you’re gonna love him.”

Chapter Four

CARRYING A FOOD BAG, Carlson knocked on Captain Octavia Dolan's door. Her captain waved her in, and Carlson entered her office. Justini, carrying two bottles of juice-one apple and one orange-followed her inside.

An African-American woman, Dolan had short gray hair cut in a pixie style, which emphasized her wide dark eyes and prominent cheekbones. She wore no makeup other than dark red lipstick, and large silver hoops dangled from her earlobes. Her bright red, long fingernails flashed in the light from the window beside her desk, and she shoved a pile of folders closer to another pile of similar height. For as long as Carlson had known Dolan, she'd had a cluttered desk. Dolan insisted she worked better that way. Organization distracted her.

"You get me the tuna on rye?" asked Dolan.

Carlson set the bag on the edge of Dolan's desk. "Right here, Cap." She pulled out a wrapped sandwich and handed it to Dolan.

Justini handed Carlson the apple juice, and Carlson gave him his chicken salad sandwich and chips.

Carlson grabbed her turkey and swiss on a baguette and sat across from Dolan's desk to eat. She cracked her juice open and set it on the floor beside her chair.

Dolan took a gulp of her large coffee, unwrapped her sandwich, and pulled a napkin from her desk. "So, what's new with the Patel case?" She took a bite of her food.

Carlson opened her wrapper, set it on her lap, and picked up her sandwich. "We've been to Patel's apartment and talked to her employer and coworkers. Right now, there's no smoking gun." She bit into her sandwich.

Justini chewed and swallowed his bite. "Not yet, anyway, but I'm not convinced our reporter, Lexie Logan, doesn't have something to do with this."

Dolan wiped mayonnaise off one of her red nails with her napkin. "You find something to connect her to this other than the phone call from Patel and where Logan was found?"

"No." Carlson chewed and swallowed. "There are no fingerprints at Patel's home other than her own and her housekeeper's. No unexpected fibers, either. Her car's clean too."

Justini drank some orange juice and set the bottle on the edge of Dolan's desk. "Nothing at the crime scene either, other than Patel's prints. But the morning crew came in and found Patel, so prints could have been compromised."

Carlson pulled out a slice of onion from her sandwich and set it aside. "So far, nothing suggests Logan was there."

"But that doesn't exclude Logan. She could have worn gloves." Justini reached over and grabbed the discarded onion. "I'll eat that." He dropped it into his mouth and chewed.

Carlson made a face at her partner. "Do me a favor and pop a breath mint when you're done."

Justini smiled. "No promises."

Dolan opened her top drawer and pulled out a stick of gum. "Here, Phil. Do us all a favor."

Justini caught the gum. "Jeez, Cap. I thought I put up with enough crap from Sam. You saying my breath is bad?"

Dolan shut her drawer. "I'm tempted to open my window."

Justini breathed into his hand and sniffed.

Carlson pulled another slice of onion out of her sandwich and set it on her wrapper.

Justini left it alone and set the stick of gum next to his juice. "We need a warrant to search her place."

"We don't have probable cause," added Carlson.

"The phone call isn't enough," said Dolan. "We need to place Logan at the crime scene, not outside of it. Or show she has a connection to Patel beyond the phone call."

Carlson wiped a crumb off her pants. "Based on what we know, Logan is telling the truth."

"I'm not convinced of that," said Justini. "We may not have found a smoking gun, but Logan's not clean. We found two old DUI charges against her, plus a public intoxication charge, so she's got issues with alcohol."

"All of those charges are from years ago, and they don't make her a murderer today," added Carlson.

Justini spoke through a mouthful of food. "But I think it should make you question her story about not drinking or doing drugs."

"She told us she's sober. You don't believe her?"

"She didn't say how long she's been sober. She almost overdosed outside the warehouse where Patel was killed. That doesn't make you suspicious?"

Dolan swallowed another bite of her sandwich. "You two seem to have different opinions about this case."

"We do." Carlson picked up her juice bottle. "Phil and I are pursuing both angles. I'm investigating whether Logan is telling the truth. He's digging into whether she's lying. So far, I'm winning." She drank some juice. "I've decided I want a tasty fish dinner with a beautiful view of the beach, and a glass of Chardonnay."

Justini smirked. "You haven't won anything yet."

Dolan sat forward. “It’s not looking good, Phil. You’ve got no murder weapon, no witnesses, and no connection between Logan and Patel other than that call. And those old charges are circumstantial.” She took another bite of her sandwich.

“It’s only been a couple of days.” He drank some orange juice and set the bottle down. “But Logan wasn’t there by accident.”

“No, she wasn’t,” said Carlson, “which gives her story credence. She is a reporter. She recently broke a big story, so it makes sense Patel would call her if she had damaging information to share about her employer.”

Justini set his food down and opened his bag of chips. “The phone number Logan says is the number Patel called her from led nowhere.”

“If you were a whistleblower in a company as big as Omnivista, would you call from your own phone?” asked Carlson. “We pulled Patel’s phone records, and there’re no calls or texts between Logan and Patel. Patel obviously had a burner.”

“Which we never located, along with her personal cell.” Justini ate a chip.

Carlson lowered her sandwich. “What do you think happened in that warehouse? You think Logan somehow shot Patel, exited the scene with Patel’s phone or phones and the murder weapon, hid them, and loaded up on tequila and cocaine right outside in the alley?”

“She’s got a point, Phil.” Dolan wiped her lips with her napkin. “What’s your theory?”

“And what’s Logan’s motive?” asked Carlson. “Why kill Patel?”

Justini shrugged. “Listen. I got no beef with the reporter, but I’m not ready to let her off the hook. She claims Patel called with dirt on Omnivista, but what if that’s not true? What if Patel called with dirt on Logan?”

Questioning Justini’s line of thought, Carlson frowned. “What are you talking about? What dirt?”

Justini picked up his sandwich. “She’s a big-time reporter, right? Who just broke the Damien Rook story? That went national? It wouldn’t look too good if Patel had evidence that Logan is an addict.” He took another bite, chewed, and popped another chip into his mouth.

Carlson tried to give her partner the benefit of the doubt. “Patel threatens Logan, Logan meets her in the warehouse, and what? Is Logan going to give Patel cash to shut her up? How does Patel know anything about Logan, and why would she care?”

Dolan swallowed another bite. “And you still have the problem of how she got out of the warehouse without leaving evidence behind. And why would she get wasted out in the alley?”

Justini drank some more water. “She could do it if she weren’t alone.”

“Now you’ve got an accomplice?” Carlson munched on a mouthful of turkey and swiss. “We have no evidence of that.”

“Because we haven’t been looking for it.” Justini grabbed a napkin from the lunch bag. “Think about it. Patel calls Logan and threatens her. Logan agrees to pay whatever Patel’s asking for and to meet at the warehouse, only she doesn’t go alone. Someone goes with her. The accomplice shoots Patel and grabs her phone or phones and any evidence she brought to bribe Logan, then takes off. Logan, who I’m going to assume was drunk and high when she arrived at the warehouse, decides in a moment of celebration to have another snort, only maybe what she got was laced with more than she expected. She wanders down the alley and collapses.”

Carlson tried to imagine her partner’s scenario. “Then where are these drugs? And the gloves she supposedly wore?”

“The accomplice was with her, saw Logan was in trouble, grabbed everything, and took off. He or she either still has it all or tossed it in the trash away from the scene.”

Dolan shook her head. “That’s thin. And you’ve got no evidence.”

"Not yet, but I'm working on it. If I can find a relationship between Patel and Logan, then you'll have to admit I may have something."

"I'm already smelling that fish dinner." Carlson smiled and took another bite of her sandwich.

"Since you're so confident, tell me what you've got to support Logan?" asked Dolan.

Carlson picked out a piece of turkey from her sandwich and ate it. "That's easy. Logan's explanation makes sense. As a reporter who's in the headlines, it's logical Patel would contact her if she wanted to report on her employer. And if that's true, and her employer found out, that makes Patel a target. Someone finds out she's about to blow the whistle, and they kill her in the warehouse. Logan arrives to talk, but she's incapacitated, given drugs and alcohol, and left in the alley, likely to die. But if she doesn't, at least she's discredited. And the DUIs on her record don't help. The killer takes whatever incriminating evidence Patel had against Omnivista and gets away, and Logan looks complicit."

Dolan drank some coffee. "How'd it go when you talked to Patel's boss?"

Carlson recalled her and Justini's visit to Omnivista that morning. They'd introduced themselves to a receptionist who'd asked them to wait in the lobby, and minutes later, they'd met Dr. Eliza Thorne, who had been Dr. Patel's immediate supervisor. With her glossy black hair pulled back in a perfect bun, and wearing an immaculate narrow-cut white suit with a thin black leather belt and black pumps, Thorne had shown them to her office, which was as white as her suit, and as polished as her hair.

Thorne had said all the obligatory words–that Mira Patel was an outstanding researcher with a tremendous work ethic and unquestionable commitment to Omnivista and its projects. She'd worked there for ten years without a blemish on her annual performance reviews. She'd been awarded a raise every year and promoted accordingly. Thorne and Mira's coworkers, including their CEO Nolan Sorrento, were all shocked and appalled by what had happened to Mira, and hoped the police could find who did this to her as soon as possible.

Despite all of that, because of privacy concerns and to protect proprietary information, they couldn't provide Mira's computer or any information regarding her work without a court order.

Before leaving, Nolan Sorrento, Omnivista's enigmatic CEO, had stopped by Thorne's office to convey his dismay about what had happened, and had offered to help with the investigation, provided it didn't curtail any of Omnivista's current projects or risk its stellar reputation.

Carlson and Justini had left knowing little more about Mira Patel than when they'd arrived.

"We got the usual runaround," said Carlson. "Patel was the best employee ever, and they're all shocked by what happened to her."

Justini grunted. "We want anything from them worth more than this sandwich, a judge is going to have to sign off on it."

"Not surprising," added Dolan. "And with Omnivista's clout, we'll need a signed confession before we go before a judge."

Carlson wrapped up the rest of her sandwich to eat later. "The entire visit left a nasty taste in my mouth. It wouldn't surprise me at all if those people had something to hide. They're so big, they think they're invincible." She set her sandwich on the edge of Dolan's desk. "Which is why I'm siding with Logan on this one. Patel knew something, and someone shut her up."

"You may be right," said Justini, "but just because they're big doesn't make them bad. I'm not giving up on my theory."

Dolan ate a bite of tuna that had fallen out of her sandwich. "Why are you so confident Logan is lying?"

"I've been doing this job too long," said Justini, "and this whole whistleblower thing is too easy. Logan's got secrets. Did you know her father's doing time for embezzlement? He's been in prison for eight years. He's got a parole hearing coming up."

Dolan sat up and pushed her sandwich to the side. "That's interesting."

Carlson thought about it. "You think Patel was threatening Logan by somehow using her father against her?"

"Maybe, but that's not what I'm curious about." Justini's phone rang, and he pulled it out of his pocket.

"What are you curious about?" asked Dolan.

"One sec." He set his sandwich down on the wrapper. "This may answer that question." Wiping his fingers on his jacket, he stood, walked to the window, and answered. "Justini speaking."

Carlson waited with Dolan as Justini offered basic one-word responses, making it impossible to decipher who he was talking to or what it was about.

When the conversation ended, he turned, smiled and hung up.

"Well?" asked Carlson, not liking the grin on Justini's face.

Justini sat again and picked up his sandwich. "Tobias Logan embezzled over half a mil from his employer and clients. He got fifteen years and a hundred and fifty thousand dollar fine."

"He's lucky he didn't get more of both," said Dolan.

"What's the point?" asked Carlson. "How does this help us?"

Justini sat back. "The sentence doesn't matter. It's just good to know. What matters is who he stole from." He picked up his sandwich and took another bite.

Carlson raised an eyebrow. "Stop being so annoying. What are you not telling us?"

Justini took his time chewing and finally swallowed. "That one of those clients was Dr. Oleg Najinsky."

Dolan knitted her brow. "Who?"

Justini's smile widened. "Dr. Mira Patel's ex-husband. They divorced not long after they lost their money to Tobias Logan."

Dolan sat back and crossed her arms. "Well, well, well."

Carlson cursed.

Justini chuckled. "I'm thinking a steak dinner in an oak-paneled room with fancy plates and an expensive cabernet sounds really nice."

Carlson shot the finger at him.

Chapter Five

Lexie pulled into a parking space in front of the blue door with two small windows on either side of it. The sign *Storm Investigations*, which used to hang above it, was gone, and in its place was a temporary sign printed in bold font on a piece of paper. It read *Diamond Investigations*, and beneath it in a smaller font, *New Clients Welcome*.

Lexie turned off the ignition and stared at the sign. She still found it hard to believe that Frank had sold his agency to the man who'd changed her life. At first, she believed it had to be another Connor Diamond, but based on Frank's description of Connor and his background with law enforcement, Lexie realized it had to be the same person.

Still staring, she opened her car door, grabbed her purse, and got out. Her heart thumped at the thought of seeing him again. Would he remember her? She'd always wondered what it would be like if she were to bump into him, but she'd never imagined it would be like this.

Sliding her purse over her shoulder, she closed her car door and stepped up onto the sidewalk. Frank had suggested she stop by and introduce herself because he'd told Connor to expect her. She hadn't mentioned her history with Connor and wondered if Connor would recall her name. Was he expecting her?

Approaching the door, she took a deep breath, smoothed her shirt and hair, and then opened the door. She entered the familiar front office with a worn brown carpet and beige walls. The same unused desk with a few magazines, business cards, and a phone on it remained against the wall, although Frank had never used a receptionist. When the phone rang, Frank would pick it up in his office, which was behind another door just past the front desk.

The wall to her right had one narrow couch pushed against it, and two dinged wooden chairs sat at a right angle to the couch. If it hadn't been for the sign on the door, no one would know anything had changed. Everything looked the same.

Preparing herself, she moved up to the door that led to the main office. She didn't hear anything and wondered if anyone was even here. She knocked softly.

"Come on in," said a muffled male voice.

Nervous, she turned the knob, pushed the door open, and poked her head inside. A man sat behind the desk, but his head was down as he wrote something.

"Be right with you." He kept writing.

She stepped inside and closed the door.

"Have a seat." He looked up.

Lexie instantly remembered his eyes. The night he'd helped her with Judd, those same hazel eyes with the dark brows had bored through her, and she inhaled at the memory. "Hello." It was the only word her mouth would form.

He stopped writing. For a moment, his eyes widened, and he studied her. He put his pen down and stood. "Hello."

He wore a navy button-down shirt and brown slacks. His light brown, wavy hair was longer than she recalled, but it was brushed back in the latest style. His stubbled jaw gave him a rugged look. His broad shoulders led to a narrow waist, and he was taller than she remembered. More handsome too. For a moment, she was tongue-tied. "Sorry. I hope this is a good time." She didn't know what else to say. For some silly reason, she felt like an inept high school girl talking to the quarterback of the school's football team.

His gaze softened. “No. Sorry about that. I was expecting someone else.” He gestured at the two upholstered chairs in front of his desk. “Have a seat.”

Lexie walked up, put her purse down, and sat. “You’re the new owner?”

“I am.” He offered his hand. “Connor Diamond.”

She paused and reached up. “I’m Lexie—”

“...Logan.” He took her hand and clutched it.

Heat traveled up her arm. “You remember me?”

He smiled, revealing his white teeth. “I do. You remember me?”

She nodded. “Vividly.” Feeling his fingers against hers, she felt sure she was blushing and let go of his hand.

He sat. “You’re Frank Storm’s niece?”

She tried to relax. “Not biologically, but I might as well be. He’s my father’s best friend. I’ve known him since I was six.”

“He’s a good man.”

“One of the best.”

Connor set the paper he’d been writing on aside. “When he told me your name, I wondered if it was the same Lexie Logan.”

“I wondered the same about you. Small world.”

“Indeed, it is.”

His gaze made her fidget.

“You okay?”

She told herself to stop acting so silly. “I’m fine. I just always imagined this moment and how I would handle it.”

He frowned. “You mean meeting Frank’s replacement?” His frown deepened. “Let me guess. Was this all a surprise? Did you even know Frank was selling his agency?”

She shook her head. “I didn’t know, but not because of Frank. I’ve been preoccupied lately, and I missed the signs, but that’s not what I meant.”

"What did you mean?"

Now that the moment was here, she found it hard to explain. "That night...when we met."

He tensed. "That was a long time ago."

"It was." She bit her lower lip as the memories flashed through her mind. "It was a difficult period in my life."

"Listen, you don't have to explain anything to me. I've seen a lot of people at their worst."

She thought back. "I don't recognize that person anymore."

"It seems like you're doing well now."

She nodded. "I am."

"And the boyfriend?" He arched his eyebrow.

"History. For a long time now."

His shoulders relaxed. "I'm glad to hear it."

"That's what I'm trying so poorly to tell you. That night. What you said to me. It got through and changed everything. And I wanted to thank you."

He raised his hand. "You don't have to thank me at all. That was my job."

She blew out a nervous breath. "Well, I just wanted you to know that you made a difference."

He held her gaze and smiled softly. "I appreciate that. And thank you."

"You're welcome." She cleared her throat and asked another hard question. "What you said that night about your sister. Is it true? Was she a victim of domestic abuse?"

He set his jaw. "Emily was four years older than me. Her boyfriend stabbed her when she tried to break up with him." He paused. "It's what made me want to become a cop."

Lexie's throat tightened. "I'm sorry to hear that, but if it's any consolation, her death saved me, and I suspect countless others too."

He fiddled with the paper on his desk and set it aside. "I try to remind myself of that every time I think of her."

"Were you close?"

"We were, yes."

They were quiet for a few seconds until he broke the silence. "So, did you find a stand-up guy who treats you right?"

The question made her fidget again. "No. Not yet, at least. After Judd, I spent time on myself. I got sober and tried to get my life together. I focused on my career instead of men."

"I heard about your work. Frank couldn't stop talking about what an accomplished journalist you are. You broke the Damien Rook case?"

Her cheeks warmed again. "Not on my own. I had a lot of help."

"Still. That's impressive."

"What about you? What made you leave law enforcement to become an investigator?"

Looking more at ease, he leaned back in his leather chair. "Not long after I helped you, I got bumped up to detective. But the job takes a toll. I ended up divorced and sharing custody of my daughter." He reached behind him and picked up a small, framed picture on the shelf behind him. "This is Brooke." He handed her the picture. "She's seven."

Lexie took the picture and smiled at the pretty brown-haired girl with pigtails. She was sitting on a swing hanging from a branch of a large tree. "She's adorable." She handed the picture back to him. "You're obviously a proud father."

"I am." He put the picture back on the shelf. "After the divorce, spending time with her got harder. I knew I had to make a tough decision."

"Family or the job?" She recalled her father and mother, and how much time they'd devoted to their careers. "It's a difficult choice."

"Very. I wasn't sure what to do until I learned through a colleague about Frank's agency being up for sale. The minute I heard it, I knew it was the right move."

"Frank's got a reputation, doesn't he?"

"A stellar one. A former cop who moves up through the ranks, goes to law school and becomes an attorney, and then reinvents himself again to become an investigator. I was impressed."

"That's Frank Storm for you. When it's time for a change, he doesn't hesitate."

"He inspired me."

"Let's see how he handles retirement."

Connor chuckled. "I was wondering the same." He swiveled in his chair. "Frank told me he worked with you on your various investigations."

"He did. Not all the time, but his connections and suggestions came in handy."

"He told me that one of his requirements is that I continue to help you out."

"I hope that's not a problem. I'd pay you, of course."

"It is a problem. I'm not allowed to charge you. It's in the contract."

She scoffed. "Well, that's just silly. You can't work for free."

"Don't worry. I'll be charging the other clients Frank passed on to me. You're the only one who gets the deal."

Lexie wasn't sure how she felt about that. "That's nice of you, but I'm happy to pay."

He shrugged. "I can charge you, but any payment will be given to the local women's shelter. They need it more than I do."

She poked at the fabric of her chair. "I can live with that."

"Good." He sat up and rested his elbows on his desk. "Now that we've got that out of the way, are you here to say hello, or is this about business?"

"Both, actually."

"Now I'm intrigued. What case are you working on now? Another big story?"

"You could say that."

He pursed his lips. "Don't keep me in suspense."

Lexie nibbled her lip again. The familiar dread of having to tell someone about her overdose flared once more. And telling Connor seemed even harder. Would he believe her? Or would he assume she'd slipped back into bad habits? The thought of that made her want to leave and find another investigator.

"Miss Logan?"

She rolled her eyes. "Oh, God. Don't call me that. I think we can use first names at this point."

He smiled. "Okay, Lexie. What's up?"

She crossed and uncrossed her legs and wiggled in her seat. His gaze bored into hers again, as it had the night they'd met.

"Is it that terrible?" he asked.

She clenched her fingers together. "I seem to be attracting trouble of late."

"How bad can it be?"

She steeled herself and blurted everything out. She told him about Mira Patel's phone call, the overdose and waking up in the hospital, the talks with the doctor and the detectives, plus her mother and Gary, what she'd learned from her research, and her history with the black bird investigation. The only thing she didn't mention was Zephyr.

He listened and didn't interrupt. When she finished, she swallowed and waited.

He sat back again and swiveled in his seat with a serious look.

Anxious, she had to fill the silence. "I realize I laid a lot on you, and I have no idea where this might lead. I could have met with Dr. Patel, but there's no way I killed her. But these detectives, Carlson and Justini,

I don't think they believe that. And if Patel really is a whistleblower, then that means digging into Omnivista, which is no small task. Or even digging into a possible black bird member who has it out for me. I mean, the implications of this are enormous." Grasping that she was rambling, she tried to relax. "Sorry. I'll shut up now. Except to say that I did not go on a bender out of the blue. I'm sober and plan to stay that way. Maybe I'll remember something about that night, but maybe I won't. And I understand if you'd rather leave this can of worms alone. Contract or no contract."

He stared at her silently.

His silence made her more nervous. "Please say something."

He finally sat up. "It seems to me that the local women's shelter is going to do just fine this year."

Sighing with relief, she smiled.

He reached for his phone. "Let me make a phone call to rearrange something, and then you and I are going to talk."

Chapter Six

ELIZA THORNE WALKED DOWN the sunlight-brightened hall, her high heels clicking on the white polished tile. Approaching Nolan Sorrento's office, which occupied one corner of the top floor of the Omnivista building, she smoothed her polished hair, which was pulled into its usual tight bun without a single errant hair, and buttoned the jacket of her slim red pantsuit. Holding a folder, she approached Nila's desk.

Nila was Nolan's long-standing receptionist, who watched over him like a hawk. Eliza suspected she was around sixty, but a couple of facelifts put her closer to fifty, but only because Nila had let her gray hair grow out during the pandemic. She kept it cut short, and her manicured nails clicked on the computer keyboard as Eliza approached.

"I need to see him."

Eliza and Nila had never been friends. Nila had never been secretive about her dislike of Eliza's close relationship with Nolan.

Nila didn't look up. "He's busy." She kept typing. "He's getting ready to go to the fundraiser tonight. I'll tell him you stopped by."

Eliza tightened her grip on the folder. "I'll tell him myself." She walked past Nila's desk to Nolan's door.

Nila swiveled in her chair. "Wait a minute."

Eliza knocked. "I'm coming in." She opened the door.

"I told you. He's busy." Nila followed her.

Eliza didn't see Nolan at first. His large desk was unoccupied, and no one was at the conference table or in the sitting area with a view of the downtown skyline. "Nolan?"

Nolan emerged from his private bathroom. He had slicked back his salt and pepper hair from his face, and he wore black slacks and an unbuttoned white shirt.

"I apologize, Mr. Sorrento," said Nila with a glare at Eliza. "I told her you were busy."

Eliza held up the folder. "I have the information you've been waiting for."

His blue-eyed gaze fell on the folder. "It's okay, Nila. Call Ramona and tell her I'll be a few minutes late picking her up."

Nila shot another glare at Eliza, who smiled at her. "Very well, sir." She turned, left the office, and closed the door behind her.

"Sorry to interrupt." Eliza eyed his exposed chest. For a man in his mid-fifties, he maintained an attractive, muscular physique.

"I've got his damn charity thing I'm committed to." He buttoned his shirt. "Bring the folder over here." He walked to the sitting area with the view and sat on the leather couch. He held his hand out.

Eliza put the folder in his palm and sat beside him.

He glanced at her and opened the folder. "Tell me what I'm looking at here." He pulled out some papers. "And summarize. Time is short."

Eliza eyed the pictures in the folder. "The woman is Detective Samantha Carlson, and the man is her partner, Detective Phil Justini. They're assigned to Patel's murder investigation. They are stand-up detectives. Carlson has been a detective for a year and was partnered with Justini. She lives alone and is single; is a workaholic; and she has a father and stepmother in San Francisco. Her mother died when Carlson was ten. Justini has been married for twenty-six years, has two kids in college, and a mortgage payment. He's by the book and has several commendations."

Nolan rubbed his jaw. "That's too bad." He flipped to the next page. "This is our fly in the ointment?"

"Yes, that's Lexie Logan. Independent journalist."

"She's the one who took down Damien?"

Eliza nodded. "She's the one who broke the story. She worked with two other detectives who infiltrated Rook's group. Lexie helped them and got the scoop."

He took a breath. "Rook was stupid. He should have known better."

Eliza recalled meeting Damien Rook in this office a few years back. He and Nolan had occasionally seen each other on the social scene and had had dinner once or twice. "He made poor choices."

"Yes, he did." He studied Lexie's picture. "Tell me about her."

Eliza leaned against the couch cushion. "Her mother is Leona Logan, former advice columnist. Her father is Tobias Logan. Former investment manager who is doing time for embezzlement. He's been in prison for eight years and is up for parole soon. Her sister is Natalie and her brother is Jonah, but Logan is estranged from both. Her father, too."

He set the picture down and finished buttoning his shirt. "Typical happy family."

"Logan is also an alcoholic. Same as her father. She got sober after a bad altercation with a boyfriend eight years ago. From what we know, she hasn't touched a drop since, at least until the other night."

"What's the boyfriend's name?"

"Judd Ballard."

He finished buttoning his shirt and stood. "Keep talking. I need to get a tie."

Eliza reached for the folder. "Since leaving the hospital, Logan's been in touch with Frank Storm, a close family friend. He's a former attorney who defended Tobias in his trial. Afterward, Storm left the legal profession and became a private investigator who helped Logan when needed."

Nolan opened a narrow door in a freestanding mahogany bureau that took up the far wall of his office. Behind the door was an assortment of ties. "You think she'll keep digging?"

"She will. She knows she didn't overdose, and she has no memory of that night. But Storm's retired, so he won't be helping her."

Nolan pulled out a black tie with red stripes. "Who will?"

"Yesterday, Logan met with Storm's replacement. A former detective named Connor Diamond."

"Any information about him?"

"He's divorced with a seven-year-old daughter named Brooke. His sister is deceased, and his parents live in Florida. We can dig deeper if needed."

Nolan slipped the tie around his neck. "Do it."

Eliza closed the folder. "Logan recalls Patel's phone call, and as far as we know, nothing else."

Looking in the mirror on the door's side, Nolan knotted his tie. "Then why are we concerned? She has nothing, and the police suspect her of the crime."

"We're working on what Carlson and Justini know. My source tells me that Logan also suspects that someone from Rook's group could be behind the assault on her."

Nolan paused while straightening his tie. He glanced at Eliza in the mirror. "Really?"

"But the police are also looking at Logan possibly killing Patel because Patel was framing her."

"Framing her for what?" Nolan adjusted the tie's knot in the mirror.

"Exposing her as an addict."

"For what purpose?"

"Patel's ex is one of Tobias Logan's former clients. They lost close to seventy-five thousand dollars in the scam."

Nolan smoothed his collar over the tie. "Do the cops know that?"

"They do. That information gives Patel a motive to expose Logan and blackmail her, which gives Logan a motive to silence Patel."

Nolan closed the door. "So Logan shouldn't be much of a threat."

Thorne paused. "Not necessarily. We may have a problem."

He faced her. "I thought we had eliminated our problem. You said it was handled."

"Patel was taken care of, but what she took is not accounted for."

He returned to the couch but didn't sit. "You said it was confiscated."

Eliza didn't relish telling Nolan this part. "It was, but when the drive was opened, it was blank." They spoke openly since Nolan was hyperaware of security. The cleaning crew, who cleaned his workspace and bathroom every weekend, had been carefully vetted, and security swept his office for listening devices every Monday morning. And it was well known that, except for Nila, who Nolan trusted implicitly, no one was ever allowed in Nolan's office alone.

Nolan's features clouded. "It was a decoy?"

"We believe so. The USB she took is still out there. Patel must have hidden it."

Nolan's cheeks turned red, and he cursed.

"She probably planned to tell Logan the location," she said, "but was compromised first."

Nolan glowered. "Why bring a damn decoy in the first place?"

"She may have suspected she was being followed or was in danger."

"Son-of-a-bitch." Nolan yanked at the tie he'd just perfectly knotted. "I don't have to tell you what's at stake if that drive falls into the wrong hands?"

Eliza straightened. "No, you don't."

Nolan stood over her. "Does Lynx have any knowledge of this?"

"Not yet, no."

He aimed his finger at her. "You keep this quiet, you hear me? If Lynx finds out, we'll all be at risk. You think my temper's bad? It's nothing compared to his, and he doesn't suffer fools." He paused. "You think he's named on the USB?"

Eliza braced. "It's possible. We can't be a hundred percent sure how much information left the building. Patel had high-level access."

Nolan yelled a nasty epithet and kicked the couch. He took a second to collect himself, and after a breath, he tightened his tie again. "I don't have to tell you what needs to be done, do I?"

"No. We've got surveillance on Logan. If she moves, we'll know it. And we're amping up our online surveillance. It's taking time to shift resources, but once everything's in place, we'll be able to monitor her better."

"Good. And keep that source of yours close. I want to know what's going on with the detectives, and that Diamond fellow."

"Will do." She stood. "I'll keep you updated." She picked up the folder and tucked it under her arm.

"And shred that."

"I will. Is there anything else?"

He straightened his tie. "Just find that damn drive."

"I will." She turned to leave.

"And Thorne?"

She turned back.

"If anyone gets too close, I don't care who it is. Journalists, detectives, investigators, family, friends—nothing stands in the way. You understand?"

Eliza tipped her head forward. "Completely."

"Good. Now get out of here."

Considering her next steps, she turned and left the office.

Chapter Seven

LEXIE UNLOCKED HER DOOR and kicked it open. With her large purse slung over her shoulder, she carried three grocery bags into her duplex and kicked the door shut behind her.

She carried the bags into the kitchen and set them on the counter. Since returning from the hospital, she'd been living on cereal and oat milk, stale bread with peanut butter and jelly, and frozen meals. As she unloaded her groceries and put them away, she thought again about her meeting with Connor Diamond the previous day and what they'd accomplished.

Connor planned to dive into Omnivista and its CEO, Nolan Sorrento, and Lexie would learn more about Mira Patel. She'd also work on the black bird angle in case someone from Rook's society had something to do with Lexie's assault. Zephyr's phone call suggested that Omnivista was the culprit, but since she hadn't heard from Zephyr again, she could no longer be sure what to believe.

She put the milk and eggs in the refrigerator and debated calling Connor. They'd planned to meet up again in a couple of days to review their findings, but she'd been thinking about him frequently since leaving his office.

After their meeting, she'd been strangely elated, as if she'd seen a long-lost friend after years of separation. But she had no reason to think of Connor like that. She barely knew the man. She was happy he'd agreed to help her; she wasn't sure what she would have done if he'd refused. But it was more than that. She enjoyed his company and genuinely liked him. That was rare for her. She found most people annoying and didn't make friends easily. But being with Connor felt like wearing her favorite pair of jeans. She was comfortable and at ease with him.

Wondering if that was good or bad because the last thing she needed was to fall for her investigator, she heard a familiar buzz. She set a bag of potato chips down and ran for her purse. She opened it, dug into the side pocket and pulled out the burner phone Zephyr had used to call her.

Nervous, she hit the button and put the phone to her ear. "Yes?"

The same filtered voice spoke. "Can you talk?"

She pulled out a dining chair and sat. "I can." Despite the filter, she felt certain it was a man. "I was wondering if you'd call back."

"I call when I can. What have you learned since we last spoke?"

She hesitated. "How do I know I'm not talking to someone from Omnivista, or a cop?"

"Because the cops can question you face to face, and this conversation wouldn't hold up in court, and you are talking to someone from Omnivista. But I haven't worked there for years. That's where I met Mira."

"Then how about we start with what *you* know about her? So far, all I know is what I've learned on the internet, and it isn't much."

"Mira was a brilliant researcher and a technological wizard. We became immediate friends when we were assigned to work on the same project at Omnivista."

"What project is that?"

"The very project that ultimately led to my firing and her death. Project Prometheus."

Lexie grabbed a nearby notebook, opened it, and flipped to the first clean page. "Tell me about it." She found a pen and scribbled *Project Prometheus* on the paper.

"You're familiar with Omnivista's smart devices? That users call Prometheus? It's used in Omnivista's cell phones, too."

Lexie thought of the device in her mother's home, which her mom used mostly to get the weather or set a timer. "I am."

"Mira and I were the researchers at the forefront of that technology. At first, it was a promising assignment. Artificial intelligence was in its infancy, and we were creating the interface that would ultimately connect that intelligence to the user. It was exciting to work on. Mira and I were developing the building blocks that ultimately would change the world."

Lexie took notes. "What went wrong?"

"That technology developed and expanded at a rapid rate. While it has enormous potential and benefits, its power in the wrong hands makes it extremely dangerous. Omnivista was growing exponentially, and when Sorrento took over, he wanted to beat its competitors in the AI era. Mira and I were tasked with making it better, faster, and more efficient. We were told to cut corners if necessary."

"What corners?"

"Omnivista is known for its smart devices and phones, but also for its global social media platforms. Its presence is in almost every living room around the world. Like all major companies, they are committed to user privacy. It's the cornerstone of their mission statement. The amount of data they have access to is massive, and with the advent of AI, that amount of data is now colossal. Mira and I added user protections to the AI interface. Only certain data could be stored. But after a certain point, we were told to modify that."

Lexie sat up. "Modify it how?"

"Nothing was to be purged. They wanted everything. When we realized the implications, we complained and brought our concerns to our supervisor. We were ignored and told either to continue and we'd be rewarded for our efforts, or we could quit."

"They were bribing you to shut up?"

"Yes. They tried to convince us that the data would not be used without the user's consent. We believed them for a while until it became obvious that it was a lie."

"What kind of data are we talking about?"

"Everything. From your internet searches, what you read, watch, or download online, your personal photos, text messages, and the private conversations heard in your home and on your phone through any Omnivista devices or apps. It's the kind of data that, once collected and analyzed, can manipulate a user's behavior and beliefs. In the wrong hands, it could sway elections, target enemies, blackmail individuals and organizations, and steal proprietary information. As this technology developed and improved, and the amount of information multiplied, Mira discovered Omnivista was doing exactly what we feared–selling this user data to third parties, including governments and political organizations, foreign and domestic. And Mira told me that since I left, Prometheus has evolved, and with the proper resource allocation, it's better at targeting certain individuals and groups."

"Is that unusual?"

"Prometheus was built to work with large swaths of data. It's what it does best. Focusing in on smaller targets requires more finesse, time, and human resources. And it's not always accurate, so the data is double-checked. That can detract from the larger focus of disseminating massive amounts of data. But Prometheus is getting better, so that will change."

Lexie tightened her grip on her pen. “You’re telling me Omnivista has been spying on its millions of users and selling their private information to the highest bidder?”

“Yes. When Eliza Thorne was assigned to Project Prometheus, Mira and I brought our concerns to her, but she continued to tell us our fears were unfounded. Ultimately, we were removed from the project and reassigned, but I made the mistake of telling an outside party about my reservations. Thorne found out. I was threatened and eventually fired.”

“And Mira?”

“She stayed on.”

“Why?”

“Mainly because she was scared. She saw what had happened to me. And she was going through some personal problems. Problems that connect back to you.”

Lexie stopped writing. “Me?”

“More specifically, your father. Which is why it’s important that after we hang up, you hide this phone somewhere other than in your home or car.”

Lexie narrowed her eyes. “What are you talking about?”

“Back then, Mira and her husband, Oleg, had invested a significant amount of money with your father’s investment firm. According to the police, your father embezzled it. Because of that loss, Mira chose not to quit.”

Lexie couldn’t believe what she was hearing. “Mira and her husband were my father’s clients? How is that possible?”

“The how is no longer important. What matters is that once the police discover this connection, that gives them probable cause to get a search warrant.”

Lexie sucked in a sharp breath. “A search warrant? Here?”

"Put this phone somewhere they don't have access to. The warrant will extend to your home and car, so put the phone somewhere else. And anything else you don't want found."

"I have nothing to hide."

"Then that makes it easier. But don't dawdle. Do it now. If they find this phone, it makes you look more suspicious, and I'll disappear."

"But where am I supposed to hide it?"

"You're smart. You'll figure that out. If you're successful, I'll be in touch, because there's more to tell."

"Wait a minute—" She heard a click, and the line went dead. Staring at the phone in shock, she tried to grasp what Zephyr had told her. Mira and her husband had been her father's clients? He'd taken their money, which had forced Mira to stay at Omnivista? Then she'd stolen Omnivista's secrets? And contacted the daughter of the man who'd taken her life savings? The whole thing sounded crazy.

But she realized Zephyr was right. If Carlson and Justini made the connection between her and Mira, they'd get a search warrant. And it wouldn't take them long.

She stood, her mind racing with where to hide the phone. Could she bury it outside? Imagining an officer finding the disturbed grass, she discarded that idea. The next logical thought was her mother's house. She could easily put it there. Moving fast, she grabbed her purse and keys and hesitated. Eyeing her notebook, where she'd written her notes on Project Prometheus, she ran back and grabbed it too.

As she opened the door, something nudged her to move faster. As a journalist, she'd learned to trust her intuition. Lynn's key dangled from the chain. Lexie recalled her neighbor, who normally worked remotely, telling her that this was her week to work on site. Moving fast, Lexie grabbed Lynn's house key, unlocked Lynn's door, and stepped inside. Foster barked and ran up to greet her. She patted the dog's head, opened a drawer on the front table that was along the wall, and dropped the burner phone and notebook into it.

Foster watched her, and she put her finger to her lips. “No telling, okay, Foster?”

The dog tilted its head. Lexie left Lynn’s and closed and locked the door behind her. Just as she stepped back into her place, two police cars rounded the corner, drove up, and stopped in front of her duplex. Behind them, another car arrived and parked. Carlson, Justini, and four officers emerged from their vehicles and strode toward Lexie’s door.

Chapter Eight

Lexie stood on the sidewalk while the police went through her duplex and her car. She'd called Frank, who'd told her he'd come over and to sit tight, and not to speak to the police. Her mother would have wanted her to call Gary's law partner since he was a practicing defense attorney, but Lexie didn't see the point. Frank was just as good and way cheaper.

As an officer dusted her car for prints, Detective Carlson emerged from Lexie's duplex and joined her on the sidewalk.

Lexie debated not speaking, but that was rare for her. "Did you find the bloody knife in the library next to the blood-spattered shoes?"

Carlson glanced over at her. "I'm sure your attorney advised you not to speak with me."

Lexie shrugged. "I figured it couldn't hurt for *you* to talk to *me*."

Carlson watched as an officer carried a box of items out of the duplex.

Lexie sighed. "I guess that's one way to unpack my stuff." She looked closer and saw her laptop in the box. "You're taking my laptop?"

Carlson nodded. "And your phone."

Lexie dropped her jaw. "How am I supposed to work?"

"Borrow someone else's."

Anger bubbled up. "That phone contains the names of protected sources. I'm a journalist. My career depends on maintaining confidentiality."

Carlson stepped back and leaned against one of the patrol cars. "We're not interested in your sources. Just Mira Patel. As long as we can't connect anyone in your phone to this crime, the names won't be divulged."

"Does that promise extend to your partner, too? Something tells me he doesn't care about my career."

Carlson studied her. "Phil's a good detective, but I'll talk to him. And if I can get your phone back to you sooner rather than later, I will. Can't promise about your laptop though."

Lexie thought of the burner cell and her notebook and was thankful she'd hidden them. "I'd appreciate that."

"And speaking of guns, we found a nine-millimeter in your closet."

Lexie smirked. "Good for you. I haven't touched that thing in a while." She recalled a few perilous moments during the Rook investigation. "Except for a couple of times during the Rook case. But it's not your murder weapon."

"Guess we'll find out soon enough." She slid her hands into her pockets. "Where are the clothes you were wearing when they took you to the hospital?"

"In some trash bin. They cut them off me. Did you expect me to keep them?"

"That's too bad."

"Why?" She slumped when she realized why Carlson wanted them. "You wanted to check them for blood?"

"And gunshot residue. A negative test would help your story."

"It's not a story."

"How do you know? You can't remember anything."

"I feel pretty certain that if I'd killed someone, I'd recall it."

"Maybe, but maybe not."

Lexie realized she was talking when she shouldn't have been, but didn't care. Detective Carlson struck her as a levelheaded detective who wanted the truth as much as she did. "You know about my dad?"

"Of course we do."

"You know Mira and her husband were his clients?"

"Apparently, you do too."

Lexie looked back toward her home as another technician emerged with a box. "It recently came to my attention."

"Who told you?"

"A friend."

"This friend have a name?"

Lexie could imagine what Carlson would think if Lexie mentioned Zephyr. "Not one I plan to share."

"The more you cooperate, the sooner we can clear your name."

"And if someone's framing me, the sooner you can arrest me."

Carlson crossed one foot in front of the other. "This connection between Patel and your father gives her a motive to contact you. We know about your past DUIs and arrest for public intoxication. If Patel did too, she could have threatened to go public with your addiction issues. Your overdose in the alley supports that."

Lexie's heart pounded. "And you think I killed her before she could retaliate?"

"It's a theory."

"It's a stupid one."

Carlson lifted an eyebrow at Lexie.

Lexie faced her. "First of all, Detective, I've never taken drugs. And why would Mira Patel care about my alcoholism years after my father went to prison for his crimes?" She flapped her hands. "She could have come after me, or any member of my family at any time. And what would she hope to get from me?"

"Money, I'd guess."

Lexie scoffed. "Something tells me Dr. Patel makes a handsome salary at Omnivista. And I'm a freelance journalist. I'm not exactly rolling in dough."

"Your recent news exposure and your popular podcast may have made her think otherwise."

Lexie crossed her arms. "You strike me as being smarter than that, Detective Carlson." She paused. "Can we think logically now? Mira Patel worked at a global tech company. I remember her phone call. She said she knew things about them she wanted to share. My recent exposure put me on her radar."

"Why would she call the daughter of the man who took her and her husband's money?"

"Maybe she didn't know that I am his daughter."

"You've got his last name. And you were at his trial every day."

Lexie tensed. "You've done your homework."

"That's my job."

"It's my job, too." She stepped closer. "Doesn't it make more sense that someone from Omnivista knew Patel was about to expose something incriminating? And they eliminated her and assaulted me?"

Carlson pushed off the patrol car. "Believe me, Miss Logan..."

"Call me Lexie."

Carlson paused. "That's why we're here. To eliminate you as a suspect. If we do that, then I'm happy to pursue your theory."

"But while you're focusing on me, Omnivista is obliterating any evidence connecting them, and maybe considering new ways to connect me to the crime."

"If they have anything to do with this, we'll find out."

"Will you? We're talking about a billion-dollar corporation here. Power and money like that can corrupt."

Carlson stiffened. "Are you suggesting that either I or my partner is on the take?"

"Doesn't feel very good, does it? To be falsely accused of something?"

Carlson held a look with Lexie. "What about your theory that this has some connection to your investigation of Damien Rook and his organization?"

Lexie again thought of Zephyr and wished she could tell Carlson about him. "The more I consider that, the less likely I think it is. Why use Dr. Patel to get to me? They could have attacked me anywhere at any time."

"From what I understand, this secret society had a long reach. Maybe Patel was involved?"

"Until either of us has proof of that, we have to assume she had no connection to Rook's black bird group."

The crease between Carlson's brows deepened. "Excuse me. Us? We?"

"What do you expect me to do? Sit on the sidelines while Omnivista smears my name and you and your partner attempt to clear it?" She waved her hand at her duplex. "While you search my home and car? And take my laptop and phone? The only person under investigation here is me."

Carlson's tone turned more serious. "I would advise you to stay out of this, Miss Logan, until we can determine your innocence or guilt."

A press van pulled up on the other side of the street. Seeing it, Lexie's heart skipped. "Don't tell me. Did you call them?"

Carlson glanced at the van. "No. But you have to assume that this would hit the news."

Lexie didn't know what to believe, but it was obvious the smear campaign against her was in full swing. "I assume nothing in this business. How much you want to bet they're going to ask me if I'm an alcoholic?"

Carlson straightened. "If you're suggesting that I had anything to do with this—"

"Get your head out of your ass, Carlson. I'm being set up." Another car pulled up, and Lexie recognized Frank's SUV. He parked and got out. Relief fluttered through her. "I didn't do this. Patel had information on her employer, and she was silenced, and whoever killed her is terrified Patel told me something." She narrowed her eyes. "And I think you know that."

Carlson's gaze settled on the press van as the door opened, and a woman in a gray suit and wavy long hair slid out of the front seat. A man with a video camera came around the other side of the van and joined the woman. "I would advise you to take a lie detector test, Miss Logan. That would help sort all of this out."

Lexie almost laughed. "Are you going to vet who's administering the test?" She recalled Zephyr's warning. "Sorry, but right now, I don't trust you or anyone else."

The crease between Carlson's brows deepened. "I have full confidence that the test will be accurate and reliable. You should too."

Frank ran up and took Lexie's arm. "This conversation is over."

Lexie resisted Frank and spoke to Carlson. "Open your eyes, Detective. You're being played almost as badly as I am."

Carlson didn't respond, and Lexie turned and walked away with Frank.

The reporter caught up with Lexie and shoved the microphone in her face. "Is it true that you're suspected in the murder of a prominent researcher at Omnivista, Miss Logan?"

Frank waved his hand at the camera. "We have no comment."

The reporter persisted. "Is it true you're an alcoholic, Miss Logan? Were you drinking during the Damien Rook investigation? How did that affect the reliability of your reporting?"

Lexie shot a look back at Carlson, who stood on the corner and watched with an unreadable expression. "No comment." She jogged to Frank's car, and he opened the passenger door. She got in, and Frank shut the door before the reporter could ask another question. Frank ran around the front of the car and jumped into the driver's seat. He shut the door and faced Lexie, who put her hand up to block the cameraman's view. "What the hell are you doing?" he asked her.

Lexie slumped against the seat and turned away from the window. "Watching my life fall apart." Her vision blurred as her eyes swirled with tears.

. . . .

Carlson remained on the sidewalk and observed the reporter knock and shout questions through the glass as the cameraman filmed. Something inside her twisted, and she was tempted to yell at the reporter to get lost when Justini came up beside her.

"How'd it go?" he asked. "You get anything out of her?"

Carlson shook her head. "Nothing we don't already know."

"Too bad. It was worth a try." Justini looked toward the reporter. "Looks like the sharks have arrived and are circling." He chuckled. "I wonder how it feels for a reporter to become the main dish. The tables have turned, haven't they?" He chuckled again.

Carlson shot a look at her partner. "Did you have something to do with that?" She gestured toward the reporter.

Justini raised the corner of his mouth. "I may have put a bug in somebody's ear."

Carlson's body warmed with anger. "Why?"

"It's called pressure. Logan's used to being on one side of the camera. Maybe she needs to know what it's like on the other."

"We don't know she did this."

"And we don't know she didn't."

"Isn't it innocent until proven guilty?"

He scrunched his face at her. “You’ll learn eventually that you do what’s necessary to get to the truth.”

“How is this getting to the truth?” She jabbed her hand toward the badgering reporter and cameraman. “Logan believes this is a smear campaign, and I was telling her it isn’t. But now you’re telling me you did this? On purpose?”

“It’s not like it won’t come out, anyway. It was just a matter of time.”

“That is not the point.”

Justini raised his voice. “That is exactly the point. You think if we make this easier for her, she’ll tell us the truth?”

Carlson gaped at him. “You act like she’s guilty, and you’re trying to prove it, instead of the other way around.”

“I’m doing my job. Just like you should do yours.” He lowered his voice when an officer leaving the duplex glanced over at them. “And if you’ve got a problem with that, you can take it to Dolan.” He brought his face closer to hers. “Otherwise, welcome to police work, Detective.”

Stunned, Carlson dropped her jaw as he walked away.

Chapter Nine

Detective Aaron Remalla sat at his desk and typed. "Was Rhubarb's assailant wearing blue jeans and a pink T-shirt?"

Daniels looked up from his keyboard. "No. He wore blue pants and a red T-shirt. And it's Rhubarn. Not Rhubarb."

Rem grunted and hit the backspace button several times.

"You know, if you'd take notes, you'd know all this information."

Rem started typing again. "I rely on my superior memory."

Daniels resumed his typing. "I can see how superior it is."

"Besides, you take all the notes. Why do it twice?"

"Because I'm not always around, and it doesn't hurt to have a backup."

"We've survived this long, haven't we?"

"There's always room for improvement."

"If it ain't broke, don't fix it."

Daniels sighed. "You're the one whose superior memory is on the fritz."

"And you helped me out." He smiled at his partner. "See? It all works perfectly."

Daniels rolled his eyes and resumed typing. "I don't know why I bother."

The squad doors opened, and their captain, Frank Lozano, walked in. He wore his usual suit with a loosened tie, and he ran his hand over his short salt and pepper hair. He carried a folder and had a newspaper tucked under his arm.

"Hey, Cap," said Rem.

"Captain," said Daniels.

"Morning, you two." Lozano stopped by their desks. "How's it going with the Rhubarn case?"

"Typing up the report as we speak, Cap." Rem swiveled in his chair to face Lozano. "It'll be in your inbox within the hour."

"As long as he has my notes," mumbled Daniels, picking up his water bottle. He took a drink.

"What?" asked Lozano.

Daniels lowered the bottle. "Um, just saying it's good I have my notes. Accuracy is key."

"You bet it is." Lozano eyed Rem. "And so is punctuation. You got that?"

"I'll dot every 'i' and cross every 't.'"

Lozano huffed. "Periods would be nice, too."

Rem smiled. "You got it, Cap. I'm in a good mood today."

Lozano grunted. "We'll see how long that lasts." He pulled the paper out from under his arm. "Have you two seen this?" He dropped the paper on Daniels' desk.

Daniels picked it up and studied it. "Studies show extra weight tied to hair loss?"

Rem eyed Lozano's round belly. "I wouldn't worry, Cap. You've got plenty of hair."

Lozano glowered at Rem and grabbed the paper from Daniels. "Not that." He turned the paper over. "This."

Daniels took it again and read it. "Reporter suspected of alcoholism and…" He sat up. "…murder?" He frowned, read some more, and looked up at Rem with wide eyes. "This is about Lexie."

Not expecting that, Rem sat up. "What?" He stood and walked over to Daniels' desk.

"Lexie Logan is in some trouble," said Lozano. "Did you two know about this?"

Rem leaned over Daniels' shoulder to read the article.

"She called us a couple of days ago," said Daniels, still studying the article. He looked up. "She told us she'd woken up in a hospital after an overdose with no memory of what happened to her. She was worried someone from Rook's group was responsible."

Rem finished skimming the article. "Whoever wrote this is a complete hack. No doubt it's online as clickbait."

"Damaging clickbait," added Daniels. "It'll only attract more attention Lexie doesn't need."

"Is it true about the murdered woman?" asked Lozano. "Was Lexie found nearby?"

"She was," said Daniels. "The woman was a whistleblower who was targeted after she tried to contact Lexie, or that's the theory."

Lozano slid the folder under his arm. "Well, Lexie better hope she's exonerated, or this is going to blow up fast. It'll cast doubt on her reporting of the Rook investigation too, which doesn't help us any."

Rem straightened. "What do you mean? Our investigation is rock-solid."

"It may be, but the court of public opinion matters, Remalla. We don't need to give any defense attorneys help with their cases." He pointed at the paper. "Is it true about her alcoholism?"

Daniels dropped the paper on his desk. "I don't know anything about her issues with alcohol, but she was sober when we worked with her. No issues at all."

Rem recalled an instance during the Rook investigation where Lexie had shown up drunk at Daniels' place, but he kept it to himself. "Whatever history she may have with alcohol is just that. In the past." He hoped that was true.

"And everything she reported was accurate," added Daniels.

Lozano tugged at his tie. "I'm not saying it wasn't. I know she's a talented reporter. But based on her involvement in the investigation, she may have to testify. Let's just hope that after this, it's for the right side."

Rem hoped it wouldn't get that far. "It seems Lexie's fears are legit. Someone's trying to discredit her."

Lozano pulled his tie off. "What did she ask you two to do?"

"Look for some names in the Rook files." Daniels rubbed his neck. "We asked Garcia and Mel, but haven't heard back."

"She also asked us to see what we could learn about the murdered woman," said Rem. "We tried to contact the detectives in charge, but no one returned our calls." He eyed his partner. "Maybe we need to get more involved."

Lozano stuck out his hand. "You two have enough to do. I don't need you butting your noses into another officer's case." He grabbed his folder and gestured at the paper. "According to that article, they searched Lexie's home, which means they've got probable cause."

"That's easy to get if someone's being framed." Rem walked back to his desk and sat in his chair. "Lexie's not a murderer, Cap."

"I'm not the one you have to convince." After a pause, his gaze traveled between the two of them. "Just be careful how you go about it. Check with Mel and Garcia about those names and figure out what kind of case there is against Logan. We need to know what we're dealing with here." He jabbed the folder at them. "But keep your distance, you got it? I don't need any pissed-off phone calls from another captain from another division."

"You got it, Cap," said Daniels. "We'll be as cool as Rem after a dip in the plunge pool."

Rem shivered. "I am never doing that again. That was horrible. I almost lost a toe to frostbite."

Lozano shot a look at Rem. "How about considering losing some of that hair instead, Remalla? It's getting too long."

Rem ran his fingers down his almost shoulder-length locks. "I'll make an appointment."

"That's what you said the last time I brought it up."

Rem picked up his pen and wrote a note on his calendar. "It's on my to-do list, Cap."

"Since when do you have a to-do list?" asked Daniels.

Rem smirked. "Since right now."

Lozano smirked back. "Just take care of it. I don't need you on the stand looking like a homeless detective." He grumbled and picked up the newspaper. "Keep me posted on Logan." He headed toward his office.

"Will do, Cap," said Daniels.

Ensuring Lozano was out of earshot, Rem eyed Daniels. "Hey. Did you forget when Lexie spoke to Miguel for us? To get information? She got drunk and came to your place afterward."

Daniels furrowed his brow. "Hell. That's right. I forgot about that." He leaned over his desk. "And do you recall when we pulled her file and found the DUIs?"

"Plus the public intoxication, but that all happened a long time ago."

"And we only saw her drunk that one time. If she'd been drinking more, there's no way we could have missed it."

"I agree, but if alcohol is an issue, and she's insisting she's been sober, we know she went off the wagon."

Daniels stared off before looking back up at Rem. "Are you questioning her reporting or her work on Rook's case?"

"Hell, no. She got important info the night she talked to Miguel. It led us to the initial list of black bird members. If she weren't a journalist, she'd make a great cop."

Daniels paused. "As far as I am concerned, one recent mistake doesn't mean she isn't sober now. And we know she's not a murderer."

Rem set his calendar aside. "Then let's do what we need to do. And keep Lexie's little slip to ourselves."

"Unless there's a reason to reveal it."

Rem nodded. "I'm good with that."

"Me too."

"Then where do you want to start?" Rem sipped from his thermos of coffee. "You want to talk to Mel and Garcia, or the detectives on Lexie's case?"

Daniels tossed one of his pens into the cupholder on his desk. "Is that a trick question?"

Rem picked up his phone to call Garcia. "Just double-checking."

···········

Lexie cracked her eyelids open, and seeing the bright sun illuminating the borders of the curtains, she shut her eyes again and pulled the covers over her head. She'd been in bed for the last twenty-four hours, ever since Frank had dropped her off at her mom's house. Not long after the search of her duplex had ended, she and Frank had gone back inside. Lexie had been dismayed to see all her boxes open and her belongings strewn all over her floor. They'd rummaged through the items in her cabinets and drawers, and fingerprint dust coated everything. Her emotions already jumbled after dealing with the reporter, her heart hurt at the mess the officers had left behind, and she could barely hold it together when another press van pulled up outside.

Frank had immediately taken over. He'd told her to grab whatever she needed for a few nights away. She'd argued about going back to his place, but he'd told her he would take her to her mom's, who wasn't due back for a couple of days. She lived in a gated community, where the press couldn't get to the house, and Lexie could have some peace. Once she had regrouped, she could decide what to do next.

Lexie hadn't argued. Moving through the mess of her home, she'd grabbed her stuff and, under the guise of checking on Foster, she'd gone next door to get her notebook and burner phone, which she hid in one of her big purses. She left with Frank, who'd successfully navigated her past the second reporter and cameraman, and he'd dropped her off at Leona's. He'd offered to come in, but she'd told him no. She needed to be alone to think. Clearly worried about her, he told her he would check in the next day and had left.

Lexie had gone inside, went to one of the upstairs bedrooms she typically used when she stayed over, dumped her stuff on the floor, stripped down to her underwear, and crawled into bed. She'd been there ever since.

Since becoming sober, her bouts with depression had been rare and short-lived, but after the recent events, it enveloped her. Knowing what would be written online and in the papers, she'd cried into her pillow for most of the night. All the hard work she'd done to build her reputation after dumping Judd, surviving her father's trial, and getting sober was gone. She knew people would think the worst. They'd say she was a lousy drunk; that her reporting couldn't be trusted, and no one would believe her again.

She could imagine her phone was blowing up and was glad she didn't have it. Those she'd promised confidentiality to would be scared they'd lost it. The media organizations she'd worked with and the press she'd done interviews with must all be questioning her reliability and pulling any articles she'd sold them. She could imagine the reactions on social media and her podcast and wondered if she'd ever do another. Everything she'd worked so hard for had vanished overnight, and it ate at her soul.

Feeling sorry for herself, she craved a drink. Her mother kept her alcohol in a cabinet in the bar next to the living room. When Lexie initially got sober, her mother had tossed all her alcohol down the sink. But Lexie had told her that wasn't necessary. She could be around liquor without having to drink it. Learning to live with its presence was part of sobriety.

The temptation to go downstairs and pour herself a shot depressed her more, and even though she hadn't eaten, she'd stayed in bed, refusing to move.

On the way to her mom's, Frank had stopped at an electronics store and bought Lexie a phone. It was still in its packaging, though. The only usable phone she had other than her mother's landline, which received mostly spam calls, was the burner Zephyr had provided. Lexie wondered if he'd care whether she started using it as her cell. Despite her emotional state, she chuckled. She figured he wouldn't be pleased.

Her stomach rumbling, she thought of Connor Diamond. She could imagine what he would think of her now. She'd told him she'd turned her life around after what he'd done for her, but now he'd likely think she'd lied to him. Lexie wouldn't blame him if he chose not to work with her anymore.

Having no idea what time it was, she peeked out from under the covers and eyed the antique clock by the side of the bed. Her mother was an antique nut. She loved antique shops and never passed a garage sale without wanting to stop and look for hidden treasures. The clock ticked softly, and Lexie sat up abruptly when she saw it was three o'clock in the afternoon. She was supposed to have met with Connor at his office at one o'clock, and, stuck in her misery, she'd forgotten.

Cursing, she pushed the covers back and moved to the edge of the bed, but paused before getting up. Was there any point in contacting Connor? Maybe it was better this way. She'd let him off the hook and give him a simple reason to back away from her and this investigation. The way it looked, she'd be in jail soon, anyway.

Dropping her head into her hands, she thought of her father. Had this been how he'd felt during his trial? Knowing he'd lost everything that mattered to him? Her heart ached at the thought.

The bar beckoned downstairs, and she considered again whether to get a drink. It would take all these bad thoughts away, and she might even sleep. She could deal with the repercussions later. She reluctantly recalled letting her guard down six months earlier, when she'd gone through a rough period during the Rook investigation. She'd met a man at a bar to get information from him and ended up getting drunk with him. It had worked, though, and she'd learned crucial information for the case. But the next morning had been a wake-up call, and despondent over her screw-up, she'd called Mickey, who'd talked her through it and taken her to a meeting. She'd been back on the wagon ever since. The only people who knew about it were Daniels and Remalla, and now she had to guess they were questioning her integrity too, and that made her more miserable.

Lost in her thoughts, she sat up when she heard footsteps outside her door and jumped when it opened.

Her mother stepped inside. "There you are." She wore navy slacks and a red sweater with a flower-patterned scarf tied around her neck.

Shocked by the interruption, Lexie grabbed at the sheet and pulled it over herself. "Mother. What are you doing here? You're not supposed to be home until tomorrow."

Her gaze traveled over Lexie, and she grimaced. "You need a shower."

Lexie could imagine how she looked. "Mom, please." She dropped her head back into her palm. "What are you doing here?"

"It's my house. I live here."

Lexie groaned.

"And I heard what happened, so I came home early."

"You didn't have to do that."

"It wasn't the only reason, but I talked to Frank. I don't know why you called him. I told you to contact Jeremy, Gary's partner."

"Frank is just as capable. He's a former defense attorney, Mom."

"Exactly. Former. Not current. And not a good one, if we're honest."

"Just because he lost Dad's case doesn't make him a bad attorney."

"It's not exactly a rave review either."

Lexie didn't have the strength to argue that her father's case was basically open and shut and that Frank had encouraged him to take a plea, but her dad had refused. Feeling the onset of a headache, Lexie gripped her temples. "How was the Appalachian Trail?"

"As trails go, not bad." She walked closer and sat on the edge of the bed. "When's the last time you ate something?"

"I don't remember."

Leona stood. "Then get up and hop in the shower. I'll order us some food."

"I'm not hungry."

"Lexie Rose Logan. I didn't raise you to hide in this house and mope."

Lexie faced her mother. "I just need some time to think."

"Think about what?"

Lexie scoffed. "My career, or what's left of it. And maybe going to jail for murder?"

Her mother put her hand on her hip. "The last time you felt this sorry for yourself, you were plastered on the downstairs sofa." She looked around the room. "Have you been drinking?"

The question made Lexie gasp. "No."

"But you've thought about it, haven't you?"

Clenching her jaw, Lexie turned away. “No…well, maybe.” Tears welled up in her eyes. “Is that how you think of me? Like you thought of Dad?”

“Certainly not. Your father never had the strength to get sober until he had no choice.”

“But you still think I’m weak.” She looked back at her mom again. “Be honest. Do you believe me when I tell you I did not overdose in that alley, and that I had nothing to do with Dr. Patel’s death?”

Her mother’s face tightened. “How can you ask that?”

“Because I see it in your eyes. Your doubt. I see it in other people’s eyes too.”

Her mother paused, and she sat again beside Lexie. “You are so much like your father.”

Lexie held her churning stomach. “Who you hate.”

Leona sighed. “Hate is a strong word, but just because you’re like him doesn’t mean anything. He had the same penchant for thinking the worst when things got tough. He’d turn to alcohol to deal with it. Tobias was smart, funny, and handsome, but he couldn’t see that at all. If things were going his way, he’d celebrate. If they weren’t, he’d blame himself, get depressed and disappear.”

Lexie swiped a tear away from her cheek. “Guess I’m doomed, huh? I’m going to end up just like him. In jail, with no one but myself to blame for this mess.”

“Oh, for heaven’s sake. Put the violins away, my dear. They’re hurting my ears.”

Lexie sniffed. “What am I going to do?”

“You’re not just your father’s daughter. You’re my daughter too. You’re going to get up, get showered, eat something, and then figure out your next step. You didn’t overdose, and you didn’t murder anyone. Now you have to prove it. And you can’t do that by lying in bed.” She stood, went to the curtains, and flung them open.

Lexie squinted.

"Now get moving." Leona walked to the door. "We'll talk more when you're clean." She left and shut the door behind her.

For the first time since seeing the police cars pull up to her home, Lexie felt a little hope. Rousing herself, she tossed the sheet aside and went into the bathroom.

After a quick shower, and feeling more like herself, she'd gathered her things, repacked them, and carried them downstairs. Her mother sat in the kitchen, texting on her phone, and Lexie set her bag and purse at the end of the sofa near the side table. She immediately saw the small, oval Prometheus smart device sitting beside the lamp and thought of what Zephyr had told her.

She stared at it. "Prometheus?"

The device lit up.

"Are you listening to me?"

A soothing male voice responded. "Yes. I can hear you. How can I help you today?"

"Prometheus, do you record conversations?"

The light brightened. "I can record your conversation. Would you like me to do that now?"

"Do you do that without my permission?"

Her mother looked over.

"No," Prometheus answered. "I do not record conversations without your consent."

"Have you ever been asked to record conversations without consent?"

The light swirled. "Sorry. I don't understand."

"Somehow, I think you do."

Her mother walked into the room. "What are you doing?"

Lexie followed the cord from the device to an outlet and unplugged it. The light on Prometheus went out. "Do me a favor, Mom. Don't use this right now."

"Why not?"

Lexie tucked the cord under the couch. "Just humor me."

"But how will I set a timer, or get the weather?"

"You can use your phone for both."

Her mom hesitated. "Is this some weird conspiracy theory?"

"Maybe. I don't know. But just go with it for now."

Her mother shook her head. "Fine." She eyed Lexie's bag. "I didn't say you had to leave."

Lexie walked into the kitchen. "I know. But you're right. I can't hide here. I need to go home and clean the mess the police left me and figure out what to do next."

"I ordered us some sandwiches. At least wait and get some food before you head back."

Lexie ran her fingers through her damp hair. "Okay." She looked around the kitchen. "You mind if I borrow your laptop? Mine's been confiscated."

Her mom texted something and looked up. "That's why you should have called Jeremy. He could have prevented that."

"They had a warrant, Mom." Lexie didn't feel like arguing. "They took my phone too, so for now," she held up the phone she'd removed from its package and activated, "I'm using this." She sighed. "And don't tell me Jeremy could have prevented that either, because he couldn't have."

"He would have done a lot better than Frank."

"Mom, please..."

Her mother stood. "Stay put. I'll be right back." She gestured toward the counter. "I made some coffee. Help yourself."

Lexie eyed the full coffee pot. "Thanks. I will."

Her mother left the kitchen, and she poured herself a cup of coffee and added some sugar.

Her mother returned, holding a laptop bag. "Here. The charger's there too."

Lexie took the bag. "You sure you don't need it?"

"I don't use it often. Besides, I can work on the desktop. And the less time I spend on the computer, the better."

"I appreciate it. Thank you."

Leona pointed. "You just prove your innocence. That's all I care about."

Lexie stirred her coffee. "I will."

"Good. That's the positive attitude I expect from you."

Holding her coffee mug, Lexie set the laptop bag down next to her other things and returned to the kitchen. "So, tell me what's on your mind." She sat at the kitchen table.

Leona found her own mug and added coffee to it. "Besides the obvious?"

"You never make coffee unless you want to talk. You did it with Dad all the time. And I heard you mention upstairs that there was another reason you came home early."

Leona's phone dinged. She read the text, frowned, and responded.

"Mom?" asked Lexie. "What is it?"

After texting, Leona sat at the table with her coffee. "I need to talk to you about something."

"Other than the pothole that is currently my life?"

Leona set her phone on the table. "Yes."

Seeing her mother's expression, Lexie gripped her mug. "Please don't tell me that pothole is about to get deeper."

"Certainly not. In fact, I think this could be good."

That made Lexie worry more. "Oh, God. I'm afraid to ask."

The doorbell rang, and her mom stood. “That’s the food. I’ll get it, and then we’ll talk.”

Lexie set her mug down and wondered what her mother wanted to discuss.

The front door opened, and her mother spoke. “Oh, hello. Who are you?”

A male voice responded. “I’m Connor Diamond. I was looking for Lexie Logan.”

Not expecting to hear that, Lexie stood and raced over to the door. “Connor?”

He stood at the threshold. “Hi. Sorry to interrupt.” He spoke to Leona. “You must be Leona Logan?”

Her mother stared with wide eyes and smiled. “Yes. I am.” She shot a look at Lexie.

“Come in, Connor.” Lexie ignored her mother’s look. “How’d you get past the gate?”

Connor stepped inside. “I told him I was here to see you. Security just let me in.”

Leona shut the door and grumbled. “They must have thought you were delivering the food.” She looked him over. “Not that you look like a delivery person. Far from it.” She stepped closer, and her eyes sparkled with curiosity. “How do you know my daughter?”

Lexie knew that look. “Connor bought Frank’s agency. He’s helping me out of the pothole.”

“When you didn’t show up for our meeting,” said Connor, “I called Frank. He told me what happened. He gave me this address and suggested I come here and check on you. I think he’s worried.” He glanced at Leona, who was staring up at him with a smile. “I hope I’m not intruding.”

Lexie shot a hard stare at her mom, who was ogling Connor. "Mom came home early." Lexie almost poked her mom in the arm to snap her out of it.

"Connor," said Leona, "why don't you go into the kitchen and help yourself to some coffee?"

Connor glanced at Lexie.

"There are mugs in the cabinet above the machine," said Lexie. She could imagine how he felt under her mother's scrutiny. "I'll be right there."

"I could use a cup. Thanks." With another look at Leona, he walked into the kitchen.

Leona immediately grabbed Lexie's arm and pulled her away from the kitchen. She whispered. "Since when have you been working with Robert Redford?"

Lexie rolled her eyes. "I just met him, Mom."

"Is he married?"

Lexie stifled a groan. "He's divorced with a seven-year-old daughter."

"Nothing wrong with that." She leaned in to look into the kitchen. "What's his background? Is he qualified to help you?"

"He's a former detective, so yes. He's qualified."

"He's damn sure better than Frank, and way better looking."

"Mom, please. Stop playing matchmaker."

"Just promise me you won't screw this up."

Lexie widened her eyes. "Screw what up?"

"The obvious attraction between the two of you."

Lexie couldn't believe her ears. "I barely know the man."

"That will change."

"Mother, will you please..."

"I think he's more handsome than Dr. McCabe, don't you?" She looked back at Lexie. "Have you scheduled a follow-up appointment with him, by the way?"

"I am officially done here." Lexie turned to walk away, but her mother grabbed her arm and whispered again.

"Just try to be less abrasive."

Lexie couldn't believe what she was hearing. "Less what?"

Connor's voice interrupted. "If I interrupted something—"

Lexie and her mom swiveled to face him. "No," they both said at the same time.

Her mom stepped toward him. "I'm just happy to finally meet one of Lexie's friends. You think you can help her out of this mess?"

Connor, who was holding a coffee mug, nodded. "I'd certainly like to try."

"I'm sorry about missing our meeting and not calling," said Lexie. "I was...um...not myself. I should have gotten in touch."

"I tried calling, but it only went to voicemail."

Lexie held her head. "That's because the cops have my phone." Feeling her damp hair, she tossed it with her fingers.

"That's what Frank said." He lifted his coffee. "I'm just glad you're okay."

Leona took his arm. "Why don't you two have your meeting here? We've got sandwiches coming."

Lexie stepped closer. "That's okay, Mom."

"No, really..." Her mom's phone dinged again, and she glanced at it, just as the doorbell rang.

"I'll get it." Lexie headed toward the door.

Her mom lowered her phone. "Wait." Her face fell as she walked toward Lexie. "I can answer it."

"It's just the food, Mom." She opened the door and stopped cold. Standing on the porch was her sister, Natalie. Lexie froze.

Natalie stared at her and put her hand on the shoulder of the boy standing beside her. Lexie recognized her nephew, Chase.

Neither sister moved until Natalie spoke first. “Hey, Lex.”

Chapter Ten

SEEING HER SISTER, A thousand responses came to mind, but Lexie held her tongue. Her nephew didn't need to hear any of them.

Her mother walked up. "Natalie. Chase." She leaned over and ruffled Chase's hair. "It's so good to see you. Come in."

Chase smiled. "Hi, Nana."

Lexie stepped back, and Natalie and Chase walked in, and Leona hugged them both. She eyed Lexie with a wary gaze.

Natalie did too. "Thanks, Mom."

Lexie still didn't say a word.

Her mother closed the door. "The food should be here any minute. You two hungry?"

That sentence pulled Lexie out of her shock. Mom had ordered food for all of them. Now all the texting made sense. Her mother had known Natalie was on her way. Was that the real reason Mom had come home early?

Before she could say something awful, Lexie ignored her mom and sister and spoke to Connor, who stood still in the room like one of Leona's antique grandfather clocks, of which she had several. "Connor, would you mind driving me home?"

Her mother swiveled toward her. "Lexie, please. Stay and eat something." She glanced at Connor. "You too."

Natalie patted Chase on the shoulder. "Honey, why don't you go with Nana into the kitchen? I bet she has some hot chocolate."

Chase's eyes widened. "Do you, Nana?"

Leona looked at Lexie and Natalie. "I sure do." She took Chase's hand. "Come with me." She guided Chase into the kitchen.

Natalie glowered at Lexie. "Don't leave on my account."

Lexie walked over to get her things. "You ready, Connor?"

Connor reached for her laptop bag. "I am." He eyed Natalie. "I'm Connor, by the way."

"Nice to meet you." Natalie stayed focused on Lexie. "C'mon, Lex. Let's be adults about this."

Holding her overnight bag, Lexie flung her purse over her shoulder. "Careful, Connor. If my sister thinks you're with me, you'll be next on her list."

Natalie scoffed. "Don't be ridiculous. I'm married."

Lexie noted that her sister's main reason was marriage and not that they were sisters. "Since when do you care about that?"

Nat jutted out her chin. "You and Walker weren't married."

Lexie headed toward the front door. "You made sure of that, didn't you?"

Connor followed her.

Natalie put her hands on her hips. "I cannot believe we are having this same argument so many years later. Don't you think it's time to move on?"

Lexie put her hand on the doorknob. Connor came up behind her and stayed silent. "You've had ample opportunities to make this right, Nat, but you've failed every time."

Natalie grunted. "Oh, God. Really? You're going to bring up Dad again? You're like a broken record."

Lexie flung the door open. "It's called not excusing your behavior the way Mom does. She can look away, but I can't. Whenever you need something, you expect her and me to fall all over you. Mom concedes because of Chase. And when I don't, you get pissed despite all the crap you've pulled on me. But when it's the other way around, and we need help, you've got better things to do."

"I have a family, and I live in Arizona."

"You might as well live in Hong Kong."

"God, you love playing the martyr." She snorted. "You and Dad are so alike."

Lexie's anger swelled, and her heart pounded. She adjusted her purse on her shoulder. "As usual, you're the perfect daughter, and I'm the screw-up."

Natalie straightened. "I've never said I was perfect."

"You don't have to. You act like it all the time."

Natalie tightened her jaw. "You're just angry that I got what you wanted."

Getting nowhere with her sister, Lexie told herself to get out of there. "I hope you don't mean Walker, because that's a joke. You two deserve each other." She looked outside. "Where is he, by the way?" She was grateful not to see him. "Not here? Is he caught up with work? Again?" She couldn't stop herself. "Is that why you showed up? More trouble in paradise?"

Natalie's face tightened, and her body stiffened. "Why don't you and your friend go get yourselves a drink? It's what you do best, isn't it? I heard about your troubles from Mom. An overdose? Really, Lex? You expect us to believe that was an accident?"

Lexie went still. She itched to say something worse, but her throat was too tight to speak. Connor nudged her gently, and she glanced back at him.

"Let's go," he said calmly.

Her emotions whirling again, Lexie swallowed them back, and not answering Natalie, she walked out the door. Not looking behind her, she headed down the porch steps and toward the street. She kept walking until she got to the curb and stopped.

Connor came up behind her. "I'm over here."

Trying not to think, Lexie followed him to a car parked across the street. He opened the trunk and put her laptop bag inside. She handed him her overnight bag and kept her purse. He didn't say a word, put her bag in the trunk and shut it.

Moving on autopilot, she turned and got in the car when he opened the door for her. Before he could get around to the driver's side, Lexie did her best to collect herself. She was determined not to fall apart in front of him. She took several deep breaths and blinked her tears back. Her heart was still pounding, and she closed her eyes and focused her anger on her mother for not mentioning Natalie's arrival. Had Mom thought surprising Lexie would spur some sort of joyful reunion?

Connor opened the driver's door and slid in. He started the car and looked over at Lexie. "You okay?"

Lexie forced herself to act relaxed. "I'm okay."

"You don't seem okay."

She shut her eyes again. "These last twenty-four hours have sucked." He didn't respond, and she opened her eyes. "Sorry you had to see that."

"Don't worry about it. As you know, I've seen way worse."

She looked out the window at her mom's house. "You get another front-row seat to the misery that is my life. Lucky you."

"You want to talk about what happened in there?"

She scoffed. "God, no."

"Okay." He started the car and put his hand on the wheel. "Your mother seems nice."

Lexie looked over at him and couldn't help but smile. "She liked you."

He smiled back. "I guess it doesn't hurt that I look like Robert Redford."

"You heard that?" She groaned. "That's Leona Logan for you. Between you and my doctor at the hospital, she's already got me married off."

He chuckled. “Her heart’s in the right place. She’s your mom and wants you to be happy.”

Lexie dropped her smile. “If she wanted that, she would have told me about Natalie’s impending arrival and not sprung it on me.”

“Maybe she was surprised, too.”

“She came home from her trip early.” It hurt to think that her mother had come for Natalie. “I thought it was for me.” She dug her fingertips into her temples. “It’s days like this when I wish I could have a drink.” It surprised her when she said that out loud. Her insecurities flared again, and she braced herself when she expected him to say it was best if they went their separate ways.

He was quiet for a moment. “You hungry? When’s the last time you ate something?”

She rubbed her head. “Yesterday.”

He drove away from the curb. “Then we’ll eat.”

She set her purse beside her. “It’s okay if you just want to drop me off. I’m a big girl, and I understand if you don’t want to work with me anymore.” Her voice tightened, but she finished the sentence.

“Why wouldn’t I want to work with you?” He stopped at a stop sign and turned.

“I’ve given you plenty of reasons to run the other way, and I won’t blame you if you do.”

He glanced over at her. “You’re the most interesting client I have. And I like you. You’ve got problems, but who doesn’t? I’ve got plenty too, and the more we work together, the more you’ll learn about them. Nobody’s perfect, Lex. If they were, we’d both be out of jobs.”

Happy he was sticking with her, she relaxed, and her stomach growled. “Maybe, but this is a lot more than catching a cheating spouse or looking for a missing person.” She exhaled a deep breath. “Something tells me this is just the tip of the iceberg.” She paused. “You ready for that?”

He drove out of the gate and stopped at the corner. “Are you?”

They held a look, and that same heat rose into Lexie’s chest. A few hours ago, she would have said no. “I am now.”

“Then so am I.” He studied her for a moment and drove down the street.

Chapter Eleven

After Lexie ordered a turkey sandwich with chips and an iced tea, and Connor ordered the same, she pulled her temporary phone out of her purse. "Before I forget, let me give you this number so you can reach me."

He pulled out his cell, added her number, and she added his. Lexie didn't want to think of all the contact information she'd need in the coming days and debated whether to call Detective Carlson to inquire about when she might get her phone back.

Still holding his cell, Connor scrolled through it and held it out. "Not that I want to add to your crappy day, but I figure you should see this."

Lexie took his phone and read the headline. *Reporter suspected of alcoholism and murder.* Her heart sank, and she skimmed the article. It was as lurid and tasteless as the headline. She handed the phone back to him. "I repeat. I'm giving you an out if you want no part of this."

He put his phone on the table. "And I repeat. I'm not going anywhere." He gestured at his phone. "It's a stupid piece designed to sound as awful as possible. You can't let that stop you."

Lexie imagined who would see that. "People believe what they read."

"For maybe ten minutes, then they move on."

"Right now, the people I've worked with are questioning my reliability. My reputation may not recover. All the work I did to expose Rook and his organization? It could be down the tubes." She shook her head. "I hope this doesn't affect the investigation."

"You still think someone from Rook's society could be responsible for this?"

Lexie thought of Zephyr and had the unpleasant thought that her informant could be a member of the black birds. "I didn't think so. But now I'm not so sure."

"Anyone you can check with who might find out?"

She thought of Daniels and Rem and smacked her hand on the tabletop. "Damn. The detectives I worked with on the Rook case. I asked them to check out a few names and to find out more about the case against me. I bet they've tried to call." She picked up her phone again. "Maybe I can reach them." She did an internet search for the number of their division.

"You trust them?"

"Implicitly. Their names are Daniels and Remalla. You know them?"

"Oh, yeah." He smiled. "My team played against there's in the policemen's baseball league a year or so back. We won when I scored the winning home run."

Lexie found the number and dialed it. "I bet they loved that."

"There was plenty of cursing, but they were good sports. I've heard good things about those two."

Lexie held the phone to her ear. "All well deserved. I gave them a hard time when we first met. They were on a case I wanted the scoop on. They could have told me to take a hike plenty of times, but they didn't." A man answered, who identified himself as an officer, and she gave her name and asked to speak to either Detective Daniels or Remalla.

Several seconds passed, and Daniels answered. "You know you're a hard lady to reach?"

"I've been flying under the radar."

"I can imagine. You okay?"

She eyed Connor. "I'm doing better. You heard about the search at my place?"

"We read the article."

She groaned. "Crap."

"That's exactly what it was."

"Wherever this is coming from, they're doing a good job of making me look like a fool. And I know I told you already, but I swear I'm not drinking." She cringed when she recalled showing up at Daniels' place after she'd gotten drunk. Rem had been there, and Daniels had given her coffee to sober her up. "I know you may think otherwise, especially after..." she eyed Connor, "well, after I met with Miguel. But that was a weak moment I didn't repeat." She groaned. "Plus, I've made stupid comments about drinking, but that was me being an idiot." Anxious, she held her breath.

"You don't have to explain anything to me or Rem. We trust you. And without the info you got from Miguel, we might still be hunting the black birds."

"Still, I screwed up."

"But you got back on the horse. We've all been there, and that's all that matters."

She breathed a sigh of relief. "Thank you."

"No thanks required, but I've got some answers to your questions."

Shaking off the past, Lexie took the notebook out of her purse, found a pen, and opened it to a clean page. "What'd you learn?"

"Mel and Garcia found some additional member's names, but none that matched Mira Patel or Nolan Sorrento. I asked them to keep an eye out for anyone with a connection to Omnivista. They also found a couple of encrypted files they're working on opening. It's possible more members are listed there, so who knows?"

Lexie slumped. "Great. So there's no way to be sure."

"Not a hundred percent. They found one interesting name, though."

"Who's that?"

"Rook mentioned someone in his notes known only as Lynx."

"Lynx?" Lexie wrote the name in her notebook. "Who the heck is that?" She looked at Connor, who shrugged.

"Rook's notes suggest it's someone important. Mel and Garcia are working to figure out who it is."

"So basically, this mysterious Lynx could be behind this whole thing with me?"

"Could be."

She put a big question mark next to the name in her notebook. "So instead of getting some questions answered, we've only created more."

"Rem was thrilled, too."

"I bet. Any luck with Carlson and Justini?"

"I finally got in touch, but they're tight-lipped. Justini especially. If anyone thinks you're guilty, it's him. He wasn't very pleased when I told him we'd worked with you on the Rook case. He basically told me he and Carlson knew what they were doing and didn't need any help."

"Well, it was worth a shot." She sat back when the server brought the iced tea to the table. "Thanks for trying."

"I didn't give up that easy. I might have made another phone call or two. What I know so far is that there's a connection between the victim and your father."

Lexie tensed. "You know about my dad?" She glanced at Connor, who was listening.

"We do now."

She gripped the phone. "It's a long story."

"That you're not required to share, but Justini and Carlson are probably going to go talk to him."

She nearly dropped the phone. "What for?"

"Your dad and Patel obviously knew each other. They might talk to Patel's ex-husband, too. They'll be looking for any connection between you and Patel."

Lexie dropped her head back against the seat. "Hell. Why can't they believe that Omnivista may have something to do with this?"

"I think Carlson may lean that way, so she may be your best hope of getting Justini off your back, but that's not a guarantee."

"If they find something in my stuff from the search, I'm doomed."

"Well, you're still walking around, so that's a good sign. My advice? Start digging into Omnivista. Maybe you can prove their involvement before Carlson and Justini prove your guilt."

"Omnivista is a hard nut to crack. I'll start with Patel first and see where it leads."

"If you can find out what she planned to expose, that'll take a lot of heat off you."

Lexie needed to talk to Zephyr again. "Then that's what I'll do."

"You got some help? It's best not to go this one alone. Omnivista is no joke."

She looked up at Connor. "Yeah. I've got some help. Do you know Connor Diamond? He's a former detective."

"Connor Diamond?" There was a pause. "The name's familiar." His voice sounded distant. "Hey, Rem. You know a Detective Connor Diamond?"

"Connor Diamond?" Rem's voice traveled over the line. "That's the guy who beat us with that home run."

"Oh, yeah," said Daniels. "You're working with him, Lex?"

"I am."

Rem came on the line. "You tell that guy that we're ready for a rematch."

"He's no longer on the force," said Lexie.

"I don't care if he's working as a zookeeper, we want another shot at the title."

Lexie smiled. "I'll let him know."

Daniels spoke in the background. "Would you give me my phone back?"

"You tell him, okay, Lex?" said Rem. "And don't let this crap get you down. We know what kind of reporter you are. And if Diamond is better at baseball than investigating, let me and Daniels know. We'll do what we can to help. Just don't tell Lozano."

"I appreciate that."

Daniels came back on the line. "You know how to reach us. Call if you need anything. Is this your new number?"

"For the moment. Let me know if you learn anything about this Lynx."

"Will do. Stay in touch and tell Diamond that home run was a lucky break."

"I will."

They said their goodbyes and hung up.

Connor sipped his iced tea. "They're still pissed about losing that game, aren't they?"

Lexie set her phone down. "The grudge runs deep."

He chuckled. "Who's this Lynx?"

"They don't know. The name showed up in Rook's files. He or she must be a big player."

He raised his phone and started typing. "I'll make a note of it."

"And they didn't make much headway with Carlson and Justini." She told Connor about Patel's connection to her father and her father's current incarceration.

"I heard some about your dad from Frank. You think your father can tell Carlson and Justini anything that could hurt you?"

Lexie tried to think, but those days were too long ago. "Nothing comes to mind. Most of it is already out in the open."

Connor nodded. "Then let's focus on what we can. And that's Omnivista and Patel. She's the key."

Lexie wanted to tell him about Zephyr but had promised not to reveal her conversations with him. “Daniels said the same. We have to go on the offensive.”

“Agreed.” Connor studied his phone. “I did some digging on Omnivista. They’re a monster company. Since Sorrento took over, they’ve gone from being a large social media corporation to a full-on tech giant. They’ve got Vista, their popular social media app, but now their cell phone division, along with their smart devices, has taken over the market in a relatively short period. Sorrento’s been hailed as the Superman of CEOs.”

“He’s a powerful man.”

Connor scrolled with his finger on his phone. “Who’s got a legendary temper, from what I’ve read. His right-hand woman is Eliza Thorne. She’s running the AI division.”

“She is.”

Connor lowered his phone. “You know about her?”

“Only what you do. She and Sorrento would be the ones to watch if Patel got dirt on Omnivista.”

“You learn anything about Mira Patel?”

Lexie picked up her iced tea. “I know she was leading a large project for Omnivista in the AI division. She had concerns she took to her supervisor, who had to be Thorne, but Patel was ignored.”

“Who told you that?”

The server arrived with their food, and Lexie didn’t answer. She drank her iced tea until the server left.

Connor studied her. “Well?”

Lexie put her napkin on her lap. “I talked to someone who knew Patel.”

“Who?”

“I don’t know.” She picked up her sandwich and bit into it.

Not touching his food, he leaned up and rested his elbows on the table. "If we're going to do this, we have to trust each other."

She chewed, swallowed, and drank some tea. "I've been sworn to secrecy."

"By whom?"

She sighed and hoped she was doing the right thing. Since she didn't know Zephyr's real name, she could say she wasn't revealing a source. "He calls himself Zephyr." She told Connor about the secret phone and phone calls, including Zephyr's theory that Omnivista was collecting and selling customer's private information.

Connor sat back. "You realize this Zephyr could be playing you?" He ate a chip.

"I've considered that, but the more I learn, the less I think he is. He knows things, and he knew Mira Patel."

"So he says." Connor took a bite of his sandwich.

"I understand the risks, but for now, I have to take them. If he's aware of what's going on, he's my only shot at finding out what happened that night. To me and Dr. Patel."

Connor swallowed. "Just be careful."

"I will." She popped a chip into her mouth. "What are you gonna do next?"

Connor drank some of his tea. "I think it might be a good idea to talk to Nolan Sorrento."

Surprised, Lexie paused before taking another bite of her sandwich. "How do you propose to do that?"

"Call and make an appointment to meet him."

Lexie chuckled. "Yeah, right." She bit into her sandwich. "Good luck," she said through a mouthful.

"No luck required. I called earlier. I spoke to his assistant, Nila."

Lexie chewed and swallowed. "And?"

"I expected to be hung up on, or told that he was busy, but after I told her who I was, and why I wanted to speak to Sorrento, she put me on hold." He bit into his sandwich and chewed.

Lexie waited. "And?"

He took his time and finally swallowed. "I've got an appointment in Sorrento's office tomorrow at noon."

Lexie dropped her jaw. "You're kidding?"

"Nope. I'm not." He took another bite.

"Don't you think that's weird?" Lexie wiped her fingers on her napkin. "I mean, he's the CEO of an enormous company. Why would he make the time to talk to you?"

Connor shrugged. "His employee's been murdered. I'm sure Carlson and Justini have talked to him."

"They're the detectives on the case. No offense, but you're just an investigator. For all Sorrento knows, you're snooping to get dirt on Omnivista or even Patel."

"Maybe that's why he wants to talk. To find out what I'm after."

Lexie considered that, but it still seemed odd. "You think he knows you're connected to me?"

Connor paused before eating a chip. "It's possible. You're a reporter, so naturally you'd want to investigate. And since you're a suspect, it's logical to send me instead."

"Maybe Sorrento is a little worried himself. I doubt he likes this kind of attention."

"Guess we'll find out tomorrow."

"Just watch it, okay? Sorrento isn't stupid. He's talking to you for a reason."

"I've dealt with guys like Sorrento before. But I appreciate your concern."

"Guys like Sorrento? How many can there be?"

Connor drank some tea and set his glass down. "It's not about the money. It's about the attitude. Men like him are arrogant and entitled. They think they're bulletproof. I suspect Damien Rook was similar."

"He was exactly like that."

"Unfortunately, the type of person who can create a company like Omnivista, or Rook Enterprises, lets power get to their heads, and before they know it, they've crossed the line so many times and gotten away with it, they don't know where the line is anymore. Plus, they surround themselves with people who can't find the line either. At some point, though, that line gets longer and wider, and then they trip over it."

She picked up a chip. "Is that what you do? Remind them of the line?"

He pursed his lips. "I let them know I *am* the line, and stepping over me won't go so well."

She noted his eyes sparkled when he talked. "I bet you were an outstanding detective."

He chuckled. "Way better than I am at baseball."

They held a gaze, and Lexie's skin prickled. "You always get your man?"

His eyes lost their glimmer. "Not all the time. Detective work, while fulfilling, also sucks. Sometimes, the bad guys get away."

"Sounds like being a journalist." She nibbled a chip. "You know the apple's bad to the core, but you can't prove it."

He nodded. "Exactly."

The server returned and asked if they needed anything. They told her no and resumed eating their sandwiches. Lexie asked Connor about his daughter, and he lit up again. He told Lexie all about Brooke, how smart she was, how she liked to draw, and already liked a boy in her class because he'd picked up a crayon for her when she'd dropped it. When Lexie asked about custody, he told her he got Brooke most weekends and for longer periods during the holidays and summer. It wasn't perfect, but he and his ex were making it work. Thankfully, she was open to working with Connor and his schedule.

"What about you and your nephew, Chase?" Connor ate the last bite of his sandwich. "You two close?"

Finished, Lexie pushed her plate back. "I don't see him much." She didn't know what else to say without going into the reasons why. "He's a good kid, though."

"Your mom certainly loves him."

"He's the only grandchild, so she dotes on him."

"Too bad they don't live closer."

Lexie couldn't imagine living any closer to Natalie. She fiddled with the straw in her iced tea glass and didn't answer.

Connor wiped his mouth with his napkin. "You really don't want to talk about this, do you?"

She shook her head. "Not really, no. It upsets me."

"Then I won't pry. You can tell me when you're ready." He tossed his napkin onto the table. "Feel better after eating?"

Lexie recalled her previous day and morning. "After yesterday, I couldn't get any worse, so yes. The food helped."

Connor tossed his napkin onto his plate. "You mind if I ask a personal question?"

Lexie couldn't help but tense up. "I suppose you can."

"I heard what you said to Daniels. Who's Miguel?"

Lexie fiddled with her fork and debated how much to say, but was honest. "He was a receptionist at a law office where a prominent attorney, who was murdered, worked. Daniels and Rem were investigating and asked me to talk to Miguel. They thought he might open up to me, since he was reluctant to talk to the cops." She shifted in her seat. "I met him in a bar."

Connor didn't say a word.

Uncomfortable, Lexie took a second to gather herself. "I'd done that plenty of times before and never had a problem, but I wasn't in a good place mentally. The case was stressful. I'd been beaten up by two men who took evidence from me—"

"What?" Connor glared.

"Long story, and they were eventually caught. But the attack messed with my head, and then an ex contacted me. Someone I'd dated a year earlier for barely a month before I broke it off because it was an obvious mistake. I screwed up and talked to him, and he got the wrong impression. And the night I met Miguel, he was texting me all sorts of insults, and I lost it. The next thing I knew, Miguel and I were drinking a pitcher of martinis." She sighed. "I even brought a flask with me to the bar. That's how stupid I was." She stopped fiddling with her fork and put her hands in her lap. "I showed up at Daniels' place plastered, and he and Rem sobered me up." She looked up. "But despite my lapse in judgement, I got some good intel from Miguel." She clenched her interlaced fingers together. "The next day, I was mortified about what happened. I called my sponsor, Mickey, pulled myself together, and promised myself I'd never do it again. I've been sober since."

Connor picked up his tea, sipped from the straw, and set it down. "What did Daniels say about it when you spoke to him just now?"

She shrugged. "He and Rem have moved on. They aren't concerned."

"Good. I'm not concerned either, in case you're wondering."

Feeling a little shaky, she nodded. "It's okay if you are."

He pushed his plate back. "I can count on zero fingers the number of perfect people I've met. That includes me." He leaned closer. "Can I offer some advice?"

"Sure."

"Stop being so hard on yourself."

"Mickey tells me the same thing."

"Then start listening. Lighten up, Logan."

She couldn't help but chuckle at the absurdity of his statement. "Considering my current circumstances?"

"In spite of them. Think of the alternative. You could be at some desk job with a crappy boss, bored as hell, and wishing you were in the middle of an AI conspiracy and sitting with your Robert Redford-handsome investigator."

She couldn't help but laugh. "Good point."

"And thanks for being honest with me."

"You're welcome. Thanks for listening."

The server brought them their bill, and despite Lexie's objections, Connor paid it. A few minutes later, they walked out into the sunny parking lot.

"So, what's our next move?" asked Connor, walking toward his car.

Lexie hooked her thumb over her purse strap. "You talk to Sorrento. I'm going to go home, clean up the mess the cops left me with, and try to get hold of Zephyr. I need to know more about Mira Patel."

"Did he tell you it was okay to call him?"

"He never said it wasn't, but I guess I'll find out."

"Like I said, be careful. You don't know who this guy is."

"You be careful too, with Sorrento."

"I will. What do you say we meet up again tomorrow at my office and compare notes?"

Lexie went to search for her phone and recalled her temporary one. "Hell. This new phone is a pain." She dug into her purse. "Maybe it has a calendar I can use." She shoved things around until she found the phone. She swiped it open and started searching. "Let's see..."

"Lexie..."

"Hold on. I'm looking for a calendar."

"Never mind that. Get in the car."

She looked up. "What's wrong?"

Connor was staring across the parking lot.

She followed his gaze but didn't see anything other than the busy street.

He opened the passenger door. "Get in. Right now."

Lexie lowered her phone and hurried up to the door. "What is it?"

Still staring at the street, he waited for her. "I'll explain in a second. Buckle up." He shut the door after she got in and ran around to the driver's side. He slid into the seat and started the car. "Hold on."

Lexie secured her seatbelt. "Hold on?"

Connor punched the accelerator and raced toward the parking lot exit. Just as he neared it, another car—a brown two-door sedan parked along the street—pulled away from the curb and zipped away. Connor hit the gas and squealed onto the road.

Lexie grabbed the armrest. "What are you doing?"

"That car's been following us." He screeched to a halt at a stop sign and raced around the corner to follow the brown vehicle ahead. It had picked up speed and passed an SUV.

Lexie held on. "Are you sure?"

"I saw it when we left your mom's. I didn't think much of it until we left the restaurant, and it was parked across the street." He hit the gas and zoomed around the same SUV the brown car had just passed. The person driving the SUV honked at them.

The brown sedan approached a stoplight that flipped from yellow to red. The driver ignored it and flew through the intersection, drawing the ire of another driver, who also honked.

Connor sped toward the light.

"Connor. It's red." Lexie grabbed the handle above her window. A van drove across the intersection, and behind it was a delivery truck. "You're not going to make it." She braced and closed her eyes.

Connor didn't decrease his speed, and Lexie anticipated the collision when Connor cursed and slammed on the brakes. The car skidded and squealed to a stop, and Lexie opened her eyes to see them nearly miss the delivery truck, which also blared its horn.

The car rocked from the sudden drop in speed, and Lexie clutched her chest. Connor had stopped almost in the middle of the intersection. Other cars had slowed to prevent being hit and drove around him. The brown sedan was no longer in sight.

Conor cursed again.

"Are you crazy?" yelled Lexie. Another car honked and drove around them.

Connor eyed the traffic and carefully drove out of the way of the other drivers. He stayed on the road where the brown sedan had disappeared and looked around. "Do you see him?"

Lexie let go of the handle above her. "You almost got us killed."

"He was following us. Don't you want to know who he is?"

"Not enough to die."

Connor glanced at her and resumed his study of the street. After another minute of driving that did not result in finding the sedan, Connor turned a corner. "I'll take you home."

Lexie tried to assimilate what had just happened. Had someone really been following them? And if so, who? It didn't seem like a Carlson and Justini move, but clearly, whoever had been in the sedan did not want to be caught. Despite the end of the chase, Connor's knuckles were white from his grip on the steering wheel.

"Are you okay?" she asked.

His eyes stayed on the road, as if he expected the brown car to return at any second. "Sorry. I didn't mean to scare you."

"You didn't answer my question."

He finally looked at her. "Do you have an alarm system at your place?"

She stiffened at the change of subject. "Connor, what is the matter?"

He pulled up at a light and stopped.

"Connor?"

The light turned, and he drove down the street.

"Are you going to talk to me?" After a few seconds, it dawned on Lexie that maybe there was more going on with Connor. "Did that chase have to do with me? Or with you?"

That got his attention, and he shot her a look.

Surprised by his pale face, she widened her eyes. "Connor?"

He turned abruptly at the next corner. "We're going to my office instead."

"Why?"

He watched the road with wary eyes. "Remember when I told you that we all have problems?"

Nervous, she breathed easier when he stopped at another light and didn't race through it. "That was only two hours ago."

The light turned green, and he drove on. "Guess it's time to share."

Lexie sat back and stared through the windshield. "Am I going to have another reason to want a drink after hearing this?"

"I hope not, but I sure as hell will." He picked up some speed and drove down the street.

Chapter Twelve

Lexie followed Connor into his office. He walked to the mini-fridge and opened it. "You want some water?" he asked.

"Please." Lexie sat in the chair facing the desk.

He pulled two bottled waters out of the fridge. "Let's sit out front."

She stood. "If you want a beer, that's fine. It won't bother me."

"I'm good." He handed her one of the waters, and she followed him to the front room where he sat on the sofa.

She sat beside him and set her water bottle on the coffee table.

Connor cracked his open and tossed the cap onto the table. He stared at the bottle before sitting back. "Before we start, you didn't answer my question in the car. Do you have a security system?"

Lexie shifted to face him. "I do, but it hasn't worked since I moved in. Doris, my landlady, hasn't made much effort to fix it."

He set his water down and stood. "Wait here." He returned to his office.

Lexie reached for her bottle, opened it, and took a drink. He returned and held out a plastic-wrapped package. "Use this."

She put her water bottle on the table and took the package. "Is this one of those personal alarm systems?"

"It is. I bought it for someone else, but they never used it. I was going to return it, but now I don't have to." He sat again. "It will monitor your door and windows. It won't alert the police, but it will make plenty of noise if someone tries to get in." He reached for his water. "In the meantime, bug Doris to fix your system."

Lexie almost declined his gift but thought better of it. Unless she planned to move in with her mother, she would need something to monitor her home. "I can pay you for it."

"It's not necessary."

She set the package on the floor. "Yes, it is. My security is my issue. Not yours."

He paused. "That may not be entirely true."

Lexie rested her elbow on the back of the couch. "All right. Tell me what is going on. Who was following us?"

He scratched his jaw. "I can't be sure. I couldn't read the plate, but something tells me it wouldn't matter. They'd account for that."

"Who are they?"

He turned toward her and, like her, put his elbow on the back of the couch. "When I was a detective, my partner and I worked on a big case. It involved a crime family that ran a drug and human trafficking ring. Ax and I...Ax is, or was, my partner. His name's Jamie Axelrod, but everyone calls him Ax. We went undercover."

"Sounds dangerous."

"It was. I won't go into the gory details, but Ax and I got close enough to take down the leaders of the family, Leo Silva, and his son, Trey. They'd been running drugs and women all over the state for years, using their trucking company as cover. Ax and I were the first to get enough evidence to stop them."

Lexie recognized the names. "I heard about this. It was all over the news. That was you who broke it up?"

"Hardly. It required a lot of moving parts, but yeah. Ax and I were integral pieces."

Lexie thought back. "Didn't Leo and Trey Silva get life in prison?"

"They did." He took a drink of water and put the bottle back on the table. "But that didn't come easy. It required the testimony of Maria Silva, the daughter, who was just as complicit in the crimes. But she wouldn't testify without immunity, which the State gave her."

"Wasn't there another sibling?"

"Excellent memory. There is. Ricky Silva. He's a half-sibling. He suffered a traumatic brain injury at a young age and was living in an expensive long-term care facility. Ricky wasn't involved in the family business, but the family business supported him."

"What happened after the business went under?"

"Maria moved Ricky into her home. But I doubt Maria's suffering. She's as big a snake as her father and brother. She just got lucky. Ax and I were against offering her immunity, but the State needed an airtight case against Leo and Trey, and they wanted her testimony. Our case against her wasn't as strong, so she got the deal."

"I bet that was frustrating."

"That's one word for it. Ax and I believe to this day that we had enough to bring down the whole family, including Maria, but that's not the way it worked out."

"Still. Even if Maria is free, I can imagine she did herself no favors by turning on her family."

"I'm not too sure about that." He faced forward and leaned back against the couch. "I think we got played. Or at least the prosecutor did."

"What do you mean?"

"The Silva defense team did its job well. They knew we had their clients dead to rights. They also knew the amount of pressure on the State to bring the Silvas to justice. I think they grandstanded enough to sway the prosecution to offer the deal to Maria to ensure a conviction."

Lexie frowned. "You mean they wanted Maria to testify against her family?"

"Yes." He looked over at her. "Better to have two members behind bars instead of three. And with Maria free, she could take care of Ricky and ensure that what little remained of the business would continue."

"You mean she's still on the payroll?"

"So to speak. Certainly not in the same way, but Maria's not stupid. By staying out of prison, she can keep the family name alive and work to free her father and brother."

"Free them?"

He nodded. "She'll go through the usual legal channels...but who knows what happens when that's exhausted?"

"You're not suggesting she'd break her father and brother out of prison?"

"The Silvas aren't limited to Maria's immediate family. There are aunts, uncles, and cousins, too. Most of them scattered back to El Salvador when Leo and Trey were arrested, but they won't stay scattered. In fact, there's already been chatter that some have returned and might be mounting a comeback."

"That's ambitious of them, considering the scrutiny they'll be under."

"It won't happen overnight, and it won't look the same, but with Maria at the helm, it's likely to succeed. Ax is working hard to keep the Silvas on the department's radar, but attention spans are short, and there are always new bad guys to catch."

Lexie tucked her foot up underneath her. "It must have been hard for Ax when you left."

"It was hard for both of us, but he understood. All the hours we worked on that case? I barely saw Barbara, my wife, or Brooke. It was the main reason for my divorce. And even after the trial, the time commitment didn't improve. I had to make a change, and Ax gave me the green light. I wouldn't have done it without his okay."

After working with Daniels and Remalla, she understood the power and mystique of a strong detective partnership. "He sounds like a good guy."

"He's my best friend. Ax's been with me through some tough times."

"And I suspect you've done the same with him."

"You bet."

Lexie leaned against the cushions. "So, you ended up leaving the force after taking down the Silvas and bought this agency to spend more time with your daughter."

He shifted to face her again. "It wasn't just the time factor. It was the safety element, too. Taking down a family like the Silvas doesn't come without consequences. I'd hoped that by leaving the force, the danger level would decrease."

"Were you wrong?"

He hesitated. "Maria Silva doesn't just want to resume her business and restore the family name. She wants payback."

Lexie had considered that, but hoped she was wrong. "I'm guessing this isn't the usual threat level that most detectives expect?"

"Threats come with the territory, but Ax called me not long after I took over the agency. He's received some threatening calls, and he saw a strange car in front of his home. He told me to stay alert and pay attention."

Lexie tensed with concern. "You think whoever was following us was sent by Maria Silva?"

"I can't be sure of anything, but it has to be taken seriously." He pointed at the packaged alarm system. "That's why I want you to take that. Between what's happening with you and what could be happening with me, either of us could be targets."

Lexie made an uncomfortable deduction. "Are you saying I could be a target of the Silvas because of my connection to you?"

"It's unlikely, but it can't be ruled out. I've already talked to Barbara about taking precautions, and I'd be remiss if I didn't tell you the same."

Lexie tried to grasp what she was hearing. "So now I'm the potential target of the black birds, Carlson and Justini, Omnivista, and the Silvas?"

"Go big or go home." His face fell. "Sorry about adding more to your plate. I should have considered all of this before agreeing to take you on as a client. But now that you know the deal, I'll give you the same option you gave me. A way out. You can leave. No hard feelings. Just take the security system with you and use it."

She didn't think twice. "The way I see it, we need each other, don't you think?"

"I don't need you becoming a target because of me."

"And I could say the same. But if we don't do this, I'm on my own, and so are you."

"I don't like it either, but my problems aren't yours."

"And vice versa."

"But it's my job to help you. It's not your job to help me."

"Says who? I'm a journalist, aren't I? If these people are coming after you and Ax, maybe I can help maintain some of that scrutiny you're hoping for."

He sat up. "That's not what I'm asking. And I don't want you to be involved. You've got enough to deal with."

"I appreciate that, but that's up to me."

"Lexie—"

"Connor. Assuming my reputation survives this, I might be able to help. And I know what it's like to be targeted. Maybe the two of us working together is exactly what we need. And besides, aren't we getting a little ahead of ourselves? We don't know who was following us. So before we jump to conclusions and think the worst, maybe we ought to take some time before making a rash decision."

He scooted forward on the couch and put his elbows on his knees. "I've considered that our follower may have been watching you." He pulled on his shirt sleeve. "I don't like that either."

"Then what do *you* want to do?"

He groaned. "I wish there were an easy answer."

"If we were smart, we'd both pack up and leave town."

He raised the corner of his lip. "But we're not smart, are we?"

She scooted forward and, like him, put her elbows on her knees. "Unfortunately, we're incredibly stupid. But I want my life back, and I assume you'd like to live yours without fear of retribution. You and I going our separate ways won't accomplish either of those things."

"Working together may not either."

She shrugged. "There's only one way to find out."

He studied her. "You sure about this?"

"No. As you know, I've had some tough times, but I've learned the hard way how to move past them. I'm not going to stop now."

"You're a brave lady."

That familiar warmth fluttered through her, and the way he stared at her made her stomach churn. She thought back to the night she'd met him, when she'd been at her lowest. "Not always, but I'm working on it." She nudged his knee with her own. "You helped with that."

He smiled. "That was all you."

Her heart rate quickened. "I think we're good for each other. Don't you?"

"I do."

His eyes glittered as they looked into hers, and Lexie's perception of time slowed. Her cheeks warmed when her mind wandered, and she imagined kissing him. Without thinking, her gaze traveled to his full lips. Focused on him, she jumped when the office door opened. Connor did the same. A woman walked in. Tall and slim with olive skin and long, thick black hair, she stopped when she saw Lexie and Connor on the couch.

Connor's body language shifted, and he stood. "Sasha."

The woman, who wore tailored black slacks with a slim black turtleneck and silver jewelry, looked as if she'd stepped out of the pages of Vogue. She put her hand on her hip. "Connor." She eyed Lexie. "Hello."

Lexie stood. "Hi." She fought not to fidget with her clothes. Wearing her standard jeans, short-sleeved T-shirt, and Converse sneakers, she felt like a gangly teenager compared to the elegant Sasha.

Connor stepped around the coffee table. "Everything okay?"

"Yes." Sasha looked back at Connor. "Sorry to interrupt. I just thought I'd stop by to see about dinner." She glanced at Lexie again.

"Oh, sorry." Connor waved his hand toward Lexie. "We just ate."

Her brow furrowed. "We?"

"Yes. This is Lexie Logan. A new client."

"A new client?" Sasha arched an eyebrow at Lexie. "Lexie Logan?"

Connor gestured at Sasha. "Lexie, this is Sasha Ramos." He paused. "My...girlfriend."

Lexie fought to keep her expression neutral. The realization that Connor was seeing this gorgeous woman made her want to curl up on the sofa. Had Connor ever mentioned a girlfriend? She was certain he had not. She forced a smile. "Nice to meet you." She refused to look at Connor. Was he as uncomfortable as she was?

Sasha offered an unreadable expression. "I know you." She squinted, then widened her eyes and raised her finger. "That's it. You're all over Vista this morning. You're the reporter, right? The one accused of murder?"

"She's not accused of anything," said Connor.

"Not yet, anyway." Lexie didn't think her day could get much worse, but she was wrong. The articles about her were all over Vista, Omnivista's social media app? She found that curious. She finally glanced at Connor. “I should go.” The tension in the room swirled, and Sasha’s scrutiny made her uncomfortable.

“You don’t have to leave.” Connor spoke to Sasha. “I can catch up with you later. I’ll call you when we’re done.”

Sasha’s eyes narrowed to slits. She looked at Lexie and then focused on Connor. “Could we talk privately, honey?”

Lexie noted how she emphasized the word honey. “It’s fine, Connor.” She grabbed her purse, and the security system he’d given her. “I’ll call you.”

“You don’t have a ride. Just sit tight.” He eyed Sasha, who stood there with her hand on her hip. “Let’s talk in the office.”

“Great.” Sasha headed into the office, and Connor followed her. “I’ll be right back.”

Lexie could only nod. The minute the door closed, she dug through her purse, found her phone, and raced out of his office.

Chapter Thirteen

Lexie opened her eyes and looked at the clock. It was later than her usual time to wake up, but since she'd been awake until almost three am, she was glad she'd slept a few hours. Rolling onto her back, she stared at the ceiling, and her thoughts returned to the day before. After leaving Connor's office, she'd sent him a quick text telling him she'd called her mom, arranged a rideshare, and gone home. He'd sent a quick reply, apologizing and telling her he would get in touch after his meeting with Sorrento.

She'd kept herself busy the rest of the day cleaning up her home. It was a helpful distraction from the murder investigation, her mother and Natalie, and Connor and Sasha. But it wasn't foolproof, and she caught herself more than once thinking about Connor. She couldn't understand why it bothered her that he had a girlfriend. He hadn't mentioned Sasha, but Lexie hadn't asked either. She'd just assumed he was single.

And why should it matter? Lexie was in no position to start a relationship. Between her family issues, her history with lousy men and alcohol, and her current troubles, the last thing she needed was to get involved with someone. Until Mira Patel's murder was solved and Lexie's name was cleared, it would be wise to keep her distance from people, but did that mean Connor too? Between his issues and hers, she'd assumed they could be a productive team, but now she had to reevaluate.

After some thought while she cleaned, she'd convinced herself that Connor was only a business associate and who he dated was none of her business. They could continue to work together as friends only. That had kept her going until she'd gone through the items in her last box and found a picture of her and Walker together during better times, or at least what she'd considered better times.

That had thrown her. All the crap that had ensued after her breakup with him reared its head, and Lexie ended up stuffing the picture down the disposal and turning it on. It wasn't the most mature response, but it felt good. After that, she'd taken a shower and gone to bed, but her feelings about Connor had shifted. After what he'd done for her the night of her fight with Judd, did she have some sort of hero complex regarding Connor? Did she expect him to save her again?

Those thoughts, along with the fear of being accused of murder and wondering about Zephyr, had kept her awake. She'd tried to reach Zephyr when she'd returned home, but no one had picked up. That had bothered her more. Was Zephyr who he said he was, or was he playing games with her?

Lying in bed, she was finally honest with herself about Connor. It wasn't Sasha's or Lexie's history with him that was the problem; it was Connor himself. As much as she'd tried to deny it, she was attracted to him.

Groaning, she shut her eyes and covered them with her forearm. How could she be stupid enough to fall for a guy within twenty-four hours of meeting him? Granted, his role in saving her life had a lot to do with her feelings, but she suspected it was more than that. She genuinely liked him. It was hard not to. He was handsome, smart, independent, protective, and courageous. All appealing qualities rarely found in one man. And what made it worse was that she wasn't even looking for it. He'd just fallen into her life the same way he had all those years ago. And now she had to figure out what to do about it.

Tired of dwelling on her problems, she shoved the covers back and got up. She slipped on her robe, pushed her hair off her face, and went into the kitchen to make some coffee. Now that she'd finally confronted the genuine problem, she felt a smidge better. It made it easier to deal with. She just had to decide whether she could work with Connor while having a silly crush, or if it was better to move on? That question was hard to answer. Working with him meant risking a broken heart and enduring Sasha, but not working with him meant going this alone, and that would risk her freedom. Which did she value more?

Pondering the question, she stilled when she heard her phone ring. But it wasn't her temporary cell. It was Zephyr's burner.

She raced to the table and answered the phone. "Hello?"

The same filtered voice responded. "You try to call me again, I'll disappear."

Fed up with the cloak and dagger crap, Lexie raised her voice. "Listen, Zephyr. You came to me, remember? I never signed up for this. So if you expect me to help solve Mira's murder before I get accused of it, you need to work with me."

"If I get exposed, we both pay the price."

"Yeah, well, right now, I'm the one taking all the risks. You're going to have to take some too. And I'm still not sure I can trust you. Have you seen the articles written about me? How do I know whether you're the one who called the press?"

"Did you think this case wouldn't hit the news? You should know better."

"So you're not denying that you called them?"

"I didn't call anyone. Your most likely culprit is the cops."

Lexie walked back into the kitchen to start the coffee. "Cops hate the press."

"Not always. They can use them too. They want the press to accuse you of all the things they can't. Not yet, at least."

"Thanks for the vote of confidence." She added a filter to the coffee machine and put some grounds in it.

"If you want to prove your innocence, I'm your best bet. But if you don't trust me, I can't do anything about that. All I can tell you is not to let the past impede the present."

She stopped mid-scoop. "How much do you know about my past?"

"Enough to wonder whether I can trust *you*."

"If you can't, this won't work." She finished scooping, grabbed the coffeepot and brought it to the sink. She turned on the faucet and added water to the pot.

"How much have you told that investigator?"

That surprised her. "You know about him?" She thought of the brown sedan. "Were you the one following us yesterday?"

"You think you were being followed?"

"I don't *think*. We were."

"Then you've caught someone's attention. You need to be cautious."

"Thanks for the heads-up. But cautious of what?" She turned off the faucet and added the water to the machine.

"Mira had a USB drive she planned to give you. It had all the evidence against Omnivista and Sorrento. And since you don't have it, and you're being followed, I assume they don't have it either, and they're terrified you'll find it before they do."

Lexie tried again to remember anything from the night of Mira's call, but it was still a blank. "Why do you think the people following me were from Omnivista?" She slid the pot onto the burner and flipped on the machine.

"Who else would they be?"

"Someone from a past investigation. And Connor, the investigator, was with me. They could have been following him." She paused. "And how do you know Mira had a USB drive?" She returned to the table and sat.

"Because she told me on the day she took it from the facility. Her plan was to meet with you and give you the evidence. But Mira anticipated problems and acted accordingly. My guess is she realized her plans had gone awry and hid the USB. But where is the question you have to answer. And regardless of who it was who followed you, assume it was Omnivista. To assume otherwise could be fatal."

"You're telling me it's *probably* Omnivista?" She scoffed. "For all you know, whoever killed Patel took the USB, and Sorrento is letting the investigation play out, hoping I'll be arrested for the murder. He may have been the one to call the press just to make me squirm. Did you know the articles about me are all over their app, Vista?"

"No doubt they've configured the algorithm to show it to everyone. The more they can discredit you, the better."

"But that still doesn't mean that USB is out there."

"It doesn't mean it isn't, and I'd bet on Mira. My hunch is she hid it, and you need to find it before Omnivista does."

Lexie listened to the coffee percolate. "Any suggestions on where to start? I need something more solid than 'it's out there somewhere.'"

"You're further than you'd be without my help. Don't forget that. And if there's anyone to be wary of, it's the investigator."

Lexie sat up. "What are you saying?"

"Have you done your homework on him?"

Lexie dropped her jaw. "I know him. We have a history, and he's trustworthy."

"What you think means nothing. People change. Do your due diligence. If it's possible it was him being followed, find out why."

"He told me why."

"Get a second opinion. Trust no one. In my experience, anyone can lie."

Lexie sat in silence.

"And for now, be careful what you tell him. Especially about me."

Lexie poked at the edge of one of her notebooks. “You didn’t tell me how you knew about him.”

“Because I take my own advice. I did my research. You need to do the same.”

“You’re wrong about him.”

“Am I? Did you mention me to him?”

She hesitated. “I did.”

“You shouldn’t have done that.”

“If he’s going to help me, he should know.”

“Just be sure that’s what he’s doing.”

“He said the same about you.”

“I’m sure he did.”

More confused than before, Lexie squeezed her temples. “So I can’t trust you or Connor?” She snorted. “Why don’t I just hang up this phone and do this without either of you?”

“You can try, but without my help, you’ll fail. Whether or not you believe me, I’m in your corner.”

Weary with the back and forth, Lexie sighed. “You know about the search at my place? Justini and Carlson, the two detectives on the case, are itching to arrest me.”

“Then don’t sit around and feel sorry for yourself.”

She raised her head.

“Go see Edna Randall. She’s Mira’s best friend. If anyone knows anything, it’s her. But she’ll be protective of Mira, so be careful.”

Lexie sat back. “What does that mean, and where do I find her?”

“Lucky Louie’s. It’s an all-night dive bar. She’ll be there tonight after ten, sitting at the end of the counter near the bathroom. As for the rest, you’ll figure it out. I’ll be in touch.”

“But how do I—”

The line clicked, and he was gone.

Frustrated, Lexie cursed.

Chapter Fourteen

CARLSON WAITED WITH JUSTINI as the prison guard opened the cell door to an interview room and stood to the side. They walked in and sat at the metal table with three chairs.

The officer hooked his thumb over his belt. "Wait here." Leaving the door open, he walked away.

"Where else are we supposed to wait?" grumbled Justini.

Carlson looked around the grimy room with the barred window and concrete floor. She'd interviewed inmates in prison before, and it wasn't her favorite part of the job. She wrinkled her nose. "It smells in here."

"God knows when they last cleaned this place." He rested his elbows on the table. "You ready for this?"

Carlson adjusted her position on the chair. "Why wouldn't I be?"

Justini pursed his lips. "It's obvious you're on Logan's side."

"I'm on the side of keeping our options open. We investigate all possibilities. So far, nothing from Logan's search is pointing the finger at her as a murderer."

"Doesn't mean she didn't do it."

"You're going to have a hell of a time proving it without evidence. Which means we have to consider that Patel got killed by her employer and Logan got caught in the crossfire."

"We don't have evidence to support that theory either."

"It doesn't mean we discount it."

Justini tapped his finger on the tabletop. "Let's just see what Tobias Logan has to say."

Carlson opened her mouth to reply but stopped when she heard footsteps and the jangle of chains. She turned to see the same prison guard escorting a slender man in his late fifties with thinning hair, a wrinkled face and tired eyes toward them. He wore the standard orange prison garb; his wrists were cuffed in front of him, and his ankles were shackled.

He ambled toward them and entered the cell, where the guard sat him in the chair across from Carlson and Justini. "He's all yours." The guard left and closed the cell door behind him with a clang. "I'll be down the hall. Holler when you're done." He walked away.

Carlson eyed Tobias Logan, who sat slumped in his chair. She could imagine that at some point he had been a handsome man, and she could tell that Lexie had his eyes. "Mr. Logan?" she said. "I'm Detective Carlson and this is my partner, Detective Justini. We'd like to ask you some questions."

He studied them. "Can I see some identification?"

Carlson accessed her badge and held it out. Justini did the same.

Logan nodded and sat back. "What's this about? Haven't you guys done enough damage?"

Uncertain of what he meant, Carlson leaned in. "This isn't about you, sir. It's about your daughter, Lexie."

Logan's eyes flashed, and he straightened. "What happened? Is she okay?"

Justini interlaced his fingers. "She's in a bit of a scrape. And we're trying to sort things out."

"What kind of scrape?" Logan eyed them warily. "Is she hurt?"

"No," said Carlson, choosing not to mention the overdose. "She's well."

Justini, maintaining a relaxed demeanor, rubbed his nose. "What can you tell us about your daughter's character?"

Logan frowned. "What the hell does that mean?"

Justini shrugged. "You know. The way she acts. How does she conduct herself? What kind of person is she?"

"Why don't you talk to her and find out?"

"We have," said Carlson.

Justini tapped his finger on the table. "Now we'd like to talk to you."

Logan shifted in his seat as if deciding whether to answer. "My daughter's a good kid, but unfortunately she takes after her old man." He grunted. "And I wasn't the best role model."

"Can you elaborate?" asked Carlson.

Logan moved his legs, and his shackles rattled. "Meaning I was a drunk most of my life, and a hardheaded one at that. I thought I knew what was best, all the way until they closed my damn cell door." He snorted. "Natalie took after her mom; Jonah wanted nothing to do with me, and Lex, well, damn, she idolized me. The only thing I could do to save her was to get her out of my life." He looked away. "It's the only time she ever listened when I told her to do something."

Seeing Tobias almost shrink in front of her, Carlson guessed he was missing his daughter.

"Was your daughter a drunk as well?" asked Justini.

Logan straightened his shoulders. "What the hell kind of question is that?"

"A logical one." Justini scooted back in his chair. "You're the one who said she took after you."

Logan's face fell. "She drank, but she was one of those functional alcoholics. So was I until neither of us could hide it anymore."

"When did you two stop hiding it?" Carlson hoped he'd relax enough to open up and be less defensive.

Logan arched his brow at Carlson. "Hell. I guess I stopped hiding it after Leona learned about my affair." He raised his cuffed wrists. "And after these trumped-up charges. And Lex, well, after that damn loser boyfriend of hers ended up with Nat, it threw Lex over the edge." He paused. "Not that she wasn't already hanging over it."

Justini crossed his arms. "What do you mean by over the edge?"

Logan squinted at Justini. "She ended up with another loser boyfriend, only he was worse. He beat her up. Course, I was dealing with the trial, and her mom, well, Leona focuses on Leona. We tried to tell Lex to get rid of him, but she was too messed up to see the forest for the trees."

Carlson pulled out a small notebook and a pencil from her pocket. She flipped the notebook open and took some notes. "Have you got a name for the boyfriend?"

Logan scowled. "What for? He's history. Lex finally came to her senses."

"We'd like to talk to him," said Justini.

Logan scrunched his face. "Judd something. Ballard, I think."

Carlson scribbled. "Thank you."

"If you find him," said Logan, "do me a favor and punch him in the face. You can tell him it's from me." He smiled.

Carlson smiled back, wishing she could do as Tobias asked. "I'll see what I can do."

Justini glanced at her.

"I'd appreciate that," said Logan.

"Is your daughter violent, Mr. Logan?" asked Justini. "Does she have a temper?"

Logan snorted. "You don't beat around the bush, do you?"

Justini scratched his jaw. "It's direct, but I don't like to waste time."

Logan adjusted a cuff around his wrist and grunted. "When she was drunk, she could give you hell, that's for sure. But violent? I can't say that."

"Did she hit back when she was abused?" asked Justini.

"I hope to hell she did," said Logan. "I didn't raise my daughter to get punched without punching back."

"So if she were threatened," said Justini, "she could retaliate?"

Logan paused and raised his brow again. "What exactly are we talking about here?"

Justini softened his posture. "I'm just trying to get an idea of how your daughter carries herself. How does she handle stress?"

Logan sneered. "How does anyone handle stress? Not well. And if she's got you two breathing down her neck, I hope she does what I should have done."

"What's that, Mr. Logan?" asked Carlson.

"Keeps her mouth shut." Logan raised his cuffed wrists and pointed. "I learned the hard way that cops can't be trusted."

Carlson scribbled again on her paper. "Why's that?"

"Detectives are only interested in a guilty plea. The truth is not their game. Only their conviction rate." He shot a look at Justini. "And whoever is lining their pockets."

Justini fiddled with his watch. "What are you implying, Mr. Logan? That we're on the take?"

Logan's stare hardened. "I only know what I've experienced. And no one in the legal arena is trustworthy. Cops, prosecutors, judges. You're as dirty as this floor we're walking on." He scoffed. "I doubt you two are any different."

Carlson tapped her pencil on her notebook. "I'm sorry you feel that way. But I can assure you, all we want is the truth."

Logan narrowed an eye at Justini. "Is that what you want?"

Justini remained calm but smiled softly. "What I want is to find out why your daughter met with a woman who was one of *your* victims and why that woman ended up dead that same night. And why your daughter was later found lying in an alley near the crime scene, loaded with booze and cocaine."

Carlson put her hand on Justini's forearm. "Justini."

Logan's demeanor shifted, and he leaned forward. "Bullshit."

"You'd think we'd be in this stinkhole talking to you otherwise?" asked Justini.

"I don't care who the victim is. My daughter wouldn't kill anyone."

Justini raised his voice. "Her father stole people's life savings, slept around on his wife, drank his way to prison, and blames everyone else for his troubles. You said Lexie is just like you." He pointed. "That tells me she's just as unstable. I think she got drunk and went after the woman who threatened to expose her weaknesses and wanted the money you stole from her back. Isn't that what you would expect from your daughter?"

Carlson gripped Justini's arm. "*Justini.*"

Logan came out of his seat. "Yes. That's *exactly* what I would expect her to do. I hope my daughter defended herself."

"And if she was drunk, high, and angry about her own situation and her father's," said Justini, "would she kill?"

Logan yelled back. "I never asked her to do a damn thing for me."

"But she idolized you, right? Was she as angry at the system as you?" Justini got in Logan's face. "If you could get out right now, would you want to kill someone?"

Logan trembled. "You're damn right I would." He stopped and eyed Carlson, who didn't move. After a pause, he visibly calmed himself. "I'd *want* to, but I wouldn't actually kill."

Justini narrowed his eyes. "You'd get a drink first, right?"

Logan sneered again. "You know what you can do with that badge of yours? Go fu—"

Carlson closed her notebook. "I think we've said enough." She glared at Justini. "You ready?"

Justini didn't break his gaze with Lexie's father. "I think we're just getting started."

Carlson stood. "We're going. Now." She turned toward the door and yelled. "Guard."

Logan glared back at Justini. "I'm done talking to you. Go with your partner, *Detective*." He spoke to Carlson. "You want to speak to me again, leave him home. He's just like all the others. He'll put my daughter behind bars first and screw the truth."

The guard headed down the hall toward the cell.

Justini's stare at Logan hardened. "If she's guilty, she'll wind up just like her dad. I can promise you that."

The guard hit a button, and the door buzzed and slid open. "Let's go, Tobias."

"She's not guilty." Logan shuffled toward the door and eyed Carlson. "You do your job and prove her innocence."

Carlson slid her notebook into her pocket. "We'll find out what happened to your daughter, Mr. Logan. That's what *I'll* promise you." She didn't look at Justini.

Logan got to the door and turned back with a somber look. "Tell her..."

Carlson waited. "Tell her what?"

Logan paused and shook his head. Looking defeated again, he turned away. "Nothing." His leg shackles clinking, he left with the guard.

••••••••••

Connor sat on the leather couch outside Sorrento's office. Sorrento's assistant, Nila, who sat at her desk and typed at the keyboard, had told him to have a seat and wait.

After a few minutes, Nila's phone buzzed, and she picked it up. "Yes, sir?" She listened and regarded Connor. "Right away." She hung up and stood. "He's ready to see you, Mr. Diamond."

Connor stood and followed Nila to the door. She opened it, and he stepped into an enormous office. The far wall was all windows with a view of downtown. A couch and two chairs with an intricate oriental rug beneath them were in front of the windows, and a large conference table was in the opposite corner. In another corner was an immense desk with a leather chair and a bureau spanning the wall behind it. Two more high-backed upholstered chairs faced the desk. Expensive art hung on the walls, and along another wall was a bar with a granite counter and a mini-fridge. Various liquor bottles and crystal glasses were sitting on glass shelves above it.

Nolan Sorrento, wearing pressed pants with his trademark long-sleeved shirt and no tie, stood from his desk when he saw Connor. "Mr. Diamond. Come in." He looked past Connor. "Thank you, Nila."

"Yes, sir." Nila turned and left the office.

Connor, still trying to get used to not being addressed as Detective Diamond, admired the office. "Nice place."

Nolan smiled. "I think so." He waved at a chair. "Have a seat. Did Nila offer you a drink?"

Connor walked to one of the high-backed chairs. "She did. I'm fine."

Nolan stepped away from his desk and headed to the bar. "Something stronger?" He waved at the bar.

"It's a little early for me."

Nolan smiled and opened the fridge. "Me too." He pulled out an energy drink and opened the can. "Care to share?" He pulled down one glass and half-filled it. "I hate drinking alone."

Connor shrugged. "Sure. Why not?" It couldn't hurt to look friendly.

"Great." Nolan took down another glass and filled it with the rest of the drink. He tossed the can into the trash and brought both glasses over. He handed one to Connor and sat at his desk.

Holding the drink, Connor sat in one of the chairs. "Thank you for seeing me. I can imagine you're a busy man."

Nolan sipped his drink and set it on his desk. "I am, but this is a difficult time for all of us at Omnivista, and I'd like to help however I can." He crossed one leg over another. "Is it true you were a detective?"

Connor rested his glass on his knee. "You've done your homework."

"I like to know who I'm talking to. Normally, private investigators are wannabe cops whose greatest accomplishments are getting the perfect shot of a cheating spouse."

Connor chuckled. "That comes with the territory, but I'd like to think I'm more than that."

"Since you're investigating Mira's death, I'd say you're well on your way." He swiveled in his leather chair. "Do you mind if I ask who hired you?"

Connor tried to get a read on Nolan Sorrento, but it wasn't easy. The man was as slick as a wet tiled floor. "That's confidential."

"But easy to deduce. If Lexie Logan weren't a suspect in Mira's death, I suspect she'd be sitting in that seat, and not you."

"I can't say either way."

They held each other's gazes until Nolan sighed. "Okay, then, Mr. Diamond. What do you want to know?"

Connor debated which style to choose. Go fast and hard, or take it easy? "What can you tell me about Mira Patel?" Easy seemed a good place to start.

Nolan swiped at something on his pant leg. "I liked her. I didn't know her that well. She reported to Eliza Thorne, but her annual reviews were always excellent, and she was a hard and reliable worker."

"Did she have friends at Omnivista? Anyone she hung out with after work?"

"I wouldn't know. You'd have to ask Eliza."

"I'd love to talk to Miss Thorne if she's available."

Nolan kept a blank stare on his face. "Let's see how this goes first. We are all busy around here."

"But I'm sure she'd like to help too, wouldn't she?"

Nolan's lips tightened into a harsh smile. "That's why I'm here, Mr. Diamond, so if you don't mind, what's your next question?"

Connor tucked his glass between his leg and the chair and accessed his phone. He opened his note-taking app. "Was Mira unhappy at Omnivista?"

"No. Not that I'm aware of."

"Any problems with other employees? Or supervisors?"

"No. Again, we never had an issue with Mira, nor did anyone else."

Connor lowered his phone. "Then who do you think killed her?"

Nolan rested his elbows on the armrests of his chair. "I have no idea, but I'm aware the police have a suspect. Lexie Logan."

"What do you know about her?"

He shrugged. "Only what I read in the press."

"That's your sole source?"

"What other source would there be?"

Connor chuckled. "You're a powerful man, Mr. Sorrento. You could make one phone call and talk to the chief of police. I suspect you know more about this case than I, or Lexie Logan, do, or even the two detectives in charge of the case."

Nolan steepled his fingers and stared over them. "I spoke to Detectives Carlson and Justini. They seem to know what they're doing. I'm sure they'll get their man...or woman."

Connor decided it was time to press a little harder. "Are you aware that there are two theories regarding what happened to Mira?"

"Two?" asked Nolan. "You mean other than Miss Logan killing Mira because Mira threatened to expose Miss Logan's addiction? And wanted Lexie to pay back the money owed to her after Lexie's father stole it?"

That confirmed to Connor that Sorrento had inside knowledge of the case. "Yes. There is another theory. One I intend to explore. And it's that Mira had dirt on your company, Mr. Sorrento, and was going to share it with Miss Logan, but someone silenced Mira and discredited Lexie before that could happen."

Nolan tapped his index fingers together. "That's quite a story, but unfortunately, it's far-fetched. Mira was not a whistleblower."

"How can you be sure?"

Nolan smiled. "That's easy. Because there's nothing for her to expose. We run a tight ship around here, Mr. Diamond. I don't abide mischief or underhanded schemes. We are a scrupulous company with high expectations of our employees. And our customers are our highest priority. There's nothing untoward going on around here, and if Mira thought she was exposing something, we'd have no reason to stop her. We could easily disprove any accusations and use all litigation avenues necessary to protect our good name. Mira would have been risking quite a bit if she had planned to accuse Omnivista or any of its employees of something nefarious."

"If she had evidence, though, her risk would be minimal. Your risk, however, would be enormous, especially if that evidence got into the hands of the press. And Lexie Logan recently exposed another major conspiracy. She's a reporter with clout who could take damaging information like that national with a few phone calls."

Nolan retained his flat stare. "I suppose if you watch enough TV shows, I can see why you'd think that. It's a thrilling scenario. A huge global organization gets taken down by one rogue employee and an independent reporter. I'm sure Miss Logan is itching to write her first bestseller." He held out his hands. "She took down Damien Rook and got a popular podcast out of it." He chuckled. "I'm sure she's got six-figure dollar signs floating in her head." He sighed. "Too bad she had to go on a bender after killing Mira. Or she might have gotten away with it."

Seeing Sorrento's smug look, Connor imagined hauling the CEO out of his fancy office and cuffing his hands behind his back. "You're a confident man, Nolan."

"I didn't get into this chair by doubting myself."

"You understand, though, that I have to investigate this whistle-blowing theory."

"Of course."

"Great. Then you won't mind if I speak with Eliza Thorne or Mira's coworkers?"

He swiveled in his chair. "I think we'll leave that to the detectives."

"If you're so confident that Omnivista is as clean as a whistle, why not open the vaults and let people look?" He rubbed his jaw with the back of his fingers. "If it looks like you're hiding something, the rumor mill will only grow."

"We can't open the vaults, Connor. We have proprietary and confidential information that must remain that way."

"I'm not talking about giving away any state secrets, Nolan. I'm merely suggesting that we learn more about Mira and her role at Omnivista." He lifted his phone and read from his screen. "Didn't she work in the AI division, which Eliza Thorne runs? That's the sort of information I'm talking about. AI is so relevant today, but it's also misunderstood, which makes it ripe for sordid stories like Mira's murder to take on a life of its own. So before the whistleblowing theory hits the papers, and it will, why not get ahead of it? Let the public know about Mira's role and responsibilities." He studied his screen. "Mira was one of the original researchers on Vista, wasn't she? Who then got moved over into the smart devices and cell phone division? I can imagine she was privy to a lot." He lowered his phone. "It's a good thing Omnivista has such a stellar reputation and is one hundred percent legitimate. Can you imagine if it weren't?"

Nolan's composure slipped slightly, but it didn't last. He smiled, but Connor sensed his tension. "It's an excellent thing, but again. I'm going to have to deny your request to speak with anyone else. This tragedy has had a horrible effect on our employees, and I think it's best if we move on and let the detectives handle this case. I'm quite confident they'll disprove this whistle-blowing nonsense before the public weighs in on it." He stood. "And if that's the angle you came here to pursue, I'm afraid you've wasted your time." He checked his watch. "Is there anything else? I have another meeting to get to." He tugged at the edge of his sleeve.

Certain he'd gotten to Sorrento, Connor tucked his phone back into his pocket. He set his glass on the desk. "I didn't get to finish my drink."

"That's unfortunate. Nila will show you out."

Connor slid to the edge of his chair. "Before I go, there is one more question."

Nolan eyed his watch again. "Yes. What is it?"

"During my research, a name popped up that I wasn't familiar with."

Nolan sighed. "What name is that?"

"It's cryptic. All I have is Lynx. Does that ring a bell? Is there a Lynx connected to Omnivista?"

Nolan failed to hide the sudden stiffening of his torso and shoulders.

Gotcha, thought Connor.

"No. The name isn't familiar." He paused. "May I ask what you were researching? Maybe that will give me a clue."

"Unfortunately, that's also confidential."

"Then I'm afraid your time is up, Mr. Diamond."

Connor stood. “Maybe we could set up another appointment to meet? When you’re free? Or I could meet with Miss Thorne instead?”

“I think not.” He gestured toward the door. “Have a nice day.”

“You too, and thank you again for meeting with me. It’s been…enlightening.” He offered his most charming grin before exiting the office.

Chapter Fifteen

LEXIE STARED AT HER laptop screen, trying to focus. She'd spent the morning finishing her cleaning and clearing out her remaining boxes. That was one benefit of the police search; it had forced her to put away everything she'd never unpacked but the police had. She'd spent the afternoon drinking coffee and researching Mira Patel, Omnivista, AI, smart devices, Prometheus, and the required proof necessary to be arrested for murder. Eyeing the clock, she still had several hours before she had to meet Edna.

Rubbing her eyes, she closed her laptop and flipped through the many notes she had taken. Unfortunately, none of them could prove her innocence or belief that Mira was a whistleblower. She hoped that Mira's friend, Edna, would be more helpful.

Fidgeting with the belt on her robe, she recalled again what Zephyr had said. She'd researched everything on her list except for one person—Connor Diamond.

Staring at her closed laptop, she cursed, sat up, and opened it. She hated that Zephyr had made her question her trust in Connor. He was the one person she believed could help her, but she couldn't ignore that Zephyr had made a solid point. What did she know about Connor Diamond other than what he'd told her? She'd met the man once years earlier and hadn't seen him since. Any experienced journalist would do their due diligence. This wasn't just any case—her freedom was on the line.

She spent the next several minutes exploring Connor Diamond's name online and was relieved to find little to worry about. He had no social media presence, which, since he'd been an undercover officer, made sense. She found one mention of him in an article about the collapse of the Silva crime family and how he'd testified at the trial. There had even been a picture of Maria Silva talking at a press conference, and behind her was Connor, watching from a distance. His expression was impossible to read.

Lexie searched for his ex's name too and found that Barbara Diamond was active on social media. She posted frequently, mainly about her activities as a mom, her work as an event planner, and Brooke's various accomplishments as a first grader.

Taking a breath, Lexie drummed the tabletop with her fingers, and then reluctantly typed in Sasha Ramos' name. Several results popped up, and it dismayed Lexie to see that Sasha had once been a fashion model. And a well-paid one. As a teenager and into her early twenties, she'd walked the runways in New York and Paris and had been featured in several well-known fashion magazines.

Continuing to research, she saw that Sasha was now a style editor for *Flare* magazine. Apparently, modeling had never been challenging enough for her, and she'd gone back to school to pursue more mindful employment.

Tired of reading about how amazing Sasha was, she shut the laptop again and sat back in her chair, wondering what to do about Connor. She'd found nothing to suggest he was anything other than what he'd told her, but that incident of being followed stuck with her. Who had been following them? Were they following her or him? And if it was Connor, was his connection to the dismantling of the Silva family worth the risk? And could she work with a man she felt attracted to, who was dating a woman like Sasha?

That last question ticked her off. She was not the kind of woman to pine over a man with a girlfriend when she had a serious investigation to pursue, and one that could send her to jail. If she continued to work with Connor, she'd just have to put on her big-girl pants and get over him. How hard could it be?

Deciding she needed to eat something protein-related since she'd only had cereal for breakfast, she reached for her coffee cup and stood when her phone rang. Seeing Connor's name appear on the display, she hesitated. Her mind went in a million directions. Answer it? Let it go to voicemail? She recalled his meeting with Sorrento, grabbed the phone, and answered it. "Hey."

"Hey." His voice was relaxed. "How are you?"

"Great. How are you? How'd the meeting go with Sorrento?" She had no intention of bringing up their previous afternoon.

"Interesting. He's a cool customer."

She sat again and told herself to stay calm. "Did that surprise you?"

"No. But he's got something to hide. That cool exterior can be rattled."

"Really? What happened?"

He paused. "Before we get into that, I want to apologize for yesterday."

Her stomach tightening, Lexie put her hand on her head. "It's no big deal."

"I should have told you about Sasha—"

"Connor, it's fine. You're not required to inform me about your personal life."

"Still, it felt...awkward."

Lexie closed her eyes. "It's not a problem."

"And in her defense, I was supposed to call her about dinner, but after our little chase yesterday, I got distracted, I guess."

"I understand."

"I'm sorry if it looked like I blew you off, or if she was angry. She wasn't and didn't mean for it to—"

"Connor, really. It's old news. Let's just move on." She clenched her jaw when she thought she sounded too harsh. She softened her voice. "I'm a big girl, and Sasha seems nice." She had to fight not to groan.

"She's a good person. Maybe one day the three of us can have lunch."

Lexie almost choked, but cleared her throat instead. "Connor, let's worry about Sorrento and Omnivista first before we make any lunch plans. What happened with Sorrento?" She prayed he'd change the subject.

"Well, since we didn't get to finish our meeting yesterday. I thought we might get some dinner tonight, and I can fill you in, and you can let me know what you've discovered today."

"Discovered?"

"You're not the type to sit around, eat popcorn, and watch TV. Did you get your place cleaned up?"

She looked around. "I did. It's pretty respectable around here now. And I set up the do-it-yourself security system and used it last night." She had to admit she'd been relieved to have it.

"I'm glad you did. Any more press outside?"

"No, thank God, which is a good sign. My story must not be garnering too much attention. Not yet, at least."

"Good. Did you contact Zephyr?"

She had a moment of hesitation when Zephyr's warning flashed in her mind. But after a split-second, she discounted it. "I did. He told me about Mira's best friend, Edna Randall. Said she'd be a good source of information. I'm meeting her later tonight. Zephyr told me she's the best person to talk to about Mira and this missing evidence."

"Where are you meeting her?"

"Well, it's not exactly a meeting. He told me where to find her, and she may not be too thrilled to see me, so we'll have to see how it goes."

She eyed her notes. "She'll be at Lucky Louie's tonight at ten o'clock, sitting at the bar."

"Lucky Louie's? I know the place. It's open all night. Ax and I have been there a few times. It's not exactly the best place to meet a stranger, especially at that time."

"Well, I don't have a choice. I'm going."

"Then I'm going with you."

She tensed. "What for?"

"Lexie, you don't know this woman, and you still don't know anything about Zephyr, and it's possible you're being followed."

"I thought about that. I figured I'd drive to Mom's, leave the car out front, and then sneak out the back and get a rideshare. If anyone's watching, they'll think I'm at Mom's."

"How about I pick you up behind your mother's place? I'll drive you to Louie's."

"What if you're the one being followed?"

"Give me some credit. I have some experience with this. If I am, I'll lose them. Or find out who they are."

"Connor, is that necessary?"

"Lexie, you brought me into this to help, so let me help. And I don't want you to go to Louie's alone. How about this? I'll pick you up on the street behind your mother's at nine o'clock. Just tell the front gate I'm coming. We'll drive to Louie's, and while we wait for Edna, I'll catch you up on my conversation with Sorrento. Once she arrives, you can go talk to her, and I'll watch from afar."

"What if she sees you and gets spooked?"

"The way it sounds, she's more likely to get spooked seeing you, and she doesn't even know we'll be there. And if she turns tail and runs, I can see where she goes. Maybe I'll get a plate number."

"Let's hope it doesn't come to that. My hope is to get her to trust me. That may not be easy if she thinks I killed her friend."

"If anyone can get her to open up, it will be you. It's what you do best. Put people at ease. That's what makes you a great reporter."

Hearing his words made her heart rate pick up. But just as quickly, she turned off any gooey feelings and turned serious. "You barely know me, Connor. I could be a horrible journalist."

"You broke the Rook case, and Daniels and Remalla back you up. I'd say you know what you're doing. If those two trust you, then so do I. But you're also impulsive and a risk-taker, which means I'm going with you tonight."

"How do you know I'm either of those things?"

"You wouldn't be good at your job if you weren't. I've had some experience with the press. The best ones are like that."

"Connor, really. I'm capable of—"

"Text me when you're at your mom's. I'll be in the area and waiting to hear from you."

"Connor..." She wanted to tell him no, but couldn't deny she'd feel better having him there. She fiddled with her pencil. "...Okay...I give in."

"Good. See you tonight." He hung up before she could change her mind.

Cursing, she ended the call and dropped her head into her hands. Was this a good idea? To hang out with Connor at an all-night dive bar while she waited to talk with Edna? What would Sasha think?

Realizing that was not her concern, and all she was doing was her job, and she was simply meeting with a co-worker, she stood and brought her coffee cup to the sink. It made sense for her investigator to join her, and it would be safer. Besides, like her, he was only there to work.

Feeling better, she put her concerns aside and opened the fridge to make a sandwich.

•••••••••••

Lexie sat at the small, round wooden table on a rickety wooden chair. Both the chair and table had seen better days, but Louie's had seen better days too, so she couldn't complain. Around her were several other rickety tables and chairs, and it smelled of beer and cigarette smoke. The bar was on her left. It spanned the wall and had several worn leather barstools. Bright neon signs flashed on the walls. A small stage with a dance floor was at the back, but both were empty. A jukebox played a Garth Brooks song at a low volume. The wall on her right sported a few booths, and a pool table was in the corner. The floor was littered with peanut shells, the source of which came from the buckets of peanuts on the tables. A busboy near the stage swept them up with a broom, and she imagined he stayed busy, since the bar was open all night.

Connor was at the bar's counter, getting drinks. She'd asked for a club soda with lime, and he was getting a beer. A few other tables were occupied. Two men with big bellies wearing trucker hats sat near the stage, and behind Lexie was a four-top table with four women, all drinking cosmos and talking. The only other occupied table was in the corner, where a man in a motorcycle jacket, wearing a bandana, jeans and boots, sat alone, drinking a beer and eating peanuts.

Lexie eyed the bar. Connor was talking to the bartender, and there was one older gentleman sitting alone at the far end of the counter, but no one was sitting near the bathroom. It was still early, though, so Lexie hoped Edna would eventually show.

She and Connor had arrived at Louie's not long after he'd picked her up behind her mom's house. Lexie had been cautious on the drive to her mom's. Thankfully, the press had stopped harassing her, and she didn't catch anyone following her. Connor had seemed confident he hadn't been followed either. Lexie hoped that meant the Silvas weren't involved and would be one less problem to deal with.

After arriving at her mom's, she greeted her mother and nephew, but when Natalie came downstairs, Lexie had left out the back without saying one word to her sister. She explained to her mom that she'd be back late, would be dropped off at her car later, and not to wait up. Her mom wanted more details, but Lexie had told her she'd explain at another time and had headed into the alley.

Connor returned to the table carrying two glasses. He placed one in front of Lexie and sat beside her. "You sure you're okay if I have a beer?"

She nodded. "It's fine. Beer was never my liquor of choice, anyway."

Connor sipped his drink. "Does being here bother you?"

"No. I'm okay. In my early days of sobriety, I'd have avoided a place like this. The sights, sounds, and smells would have been tough, but I barely notice that stuff anymore. And what happened with Miguel was more about my mental state at the time." She glanced at the women drinking cosmos behind her. "In my glory days, I'd have joined those ladies and closed the place down if it weren't open all night."

Connor glanced at the women, too. "You were a martini girl?"

"Could drink them like water."

He wrinkled his lips. "Never been a fan."

She smiled.

"Have you had a moment or two in the last few days where you've wanted to drink?" He grabbed a peanut from the bucket. "And if I'm prying, tell me to shut up."

"It's fine. And yes. I had a moment after they searched my place and the press showed up."

"How did you handle it?" He cracked open the peanut shell and pried out a peanut.

She shrugged. "Powered through it. Normally, I'd go to an AA meeting or call Mickey."

"How often do you go to meetings?" He offered her a peanut.

She took it. "Thanks. And usually once a week." She popped the peanut into her mouth and chewed. "But sometimes once a month. I missed a few with the Rook investigation. I can't go too long though before Mickey gets on me."

"Did you make it this week?" He chewed on a peanut and tossed the shell onto the floor.

"No. I went to one right before this whole thing started." She caught his stare. "Don't worry. I'm managing."

"With everything going on, don't let it get away from you. Prioritize yourself."

She brushed an errant peanut shell onto the floor. "Won't matter much if I go to prison."

"You're not going to prison." He reached for another peanut. "What about your podcast? You keeping up with that?"

She sipped her drink. "I recorded the last one featuring Rook last week. Until the trials of certain prominent members start, there won't be much more to report, so I'm taking a short break."

"Good timing."

She didn't disagree. "So tell me. How'd it go with Sorrento?"

He wiped his fingers on his jeans. "Good. His office is the size of Louie's. And he's got a hell of a view of downtown. He wears expensive clothes and a pricey watch, but tries to act like he's one of us by not wearing a tie. He's smug too, with a colossal ego. He didn't like it when I suggested Mira might be a whistleblower. According to him, Omnivista is cleaner than his perfectly white teeth."

"No surprise there. Did you mention me?" Lexie stirred her drink with her straw.

"He did. He knows you're a suspect, and that Mira was one of your dad's victims. He suspects I'm working for you and believes Justini and Carlson will eventually prove your guilt."

She widened her eyes. "He said that?"

"Not in so many words, but the message was clear. Omnivista is not culpable in Mira's death, and you are."

"I'm sure that's what he told Carlson and Justini too." Lexie tucked a strand of hair behind her ear. "Any luck getting to talk to Eliza Thorne?"

"None. Sorrento circled the wagons on that one. Doesn't want anyone talking to Thorne or Mira's coworkers. Apparently, they're too busy and distraught over Mira's death."

"I figured. We may have to find a way around that."

"I was thinking the same. I can learn where Thorne lives and hangs out, and I might just have to bump into her."

Lexie eyed the bar but didn't see Edna. "Thorne won't say anything either. Like Sorrento, she'll protect Omnivista. If their dirty laundry is exposed, she'll go down with the ship along with Sorrento."

"She won't say anything, but I'd like to rattle her cage, too. Make them think they're not invincible."

Lexie sipped from the straw. "Unfortunately, they're holding all the cards. With no evidence, my ass is hanging out in the chilly wind, and let me tell you, it doesn't feel good."

"That's why it's time to follow Daniels' advice and go on the offensive." He drank some beer.

"I'm open to ideas."

He shifted toward her. "Right now, they think they're untouchable. But when I mentioned to Sorrento that Mira could be a whistleblower, that got under his skin. He didn't like the thought of his or his company's reputation being tarnished. Right now, the press has been focused on you, but what if we changed that?" He rested his elbow on the table. "It's time to put the focus on Omnivista."

"You mean do to them what was done to me?"

"Damn straight. Who do you know that would love a story about a potential whistleblower being murdered before she could get evidence to a seasoned reporter?"

Lexie sat back. "That would get more traction than me killing my blackmailer."

"Omnivista and Sorrento are far juicier subjects."

"We still don't have proof, though, that Mira had any USB drive with evidence that she planned to give me."

"Thus the word *alleged*. It works wonders. Reporters have written stories with far less."

Lexie started to make a list in her head of respectable reporters to call who'd want a story like that. Plenty of names came to mind. "It still doesn't solve our problems, though."

"But it'll make Sorrento and Thorne squirm. And the line they've been crossing that they think is invisible? It's suddenly going to feel pretty glaring. Exposure like that doesn't go away overnight."

Lexie rubbed her forehead. "Tell me about it." She considered her own negative press coverage and wondered if any reporters would even take her call.

"Hey," he said.

She looked over at him.

"You realize if the public has to decide between a monster corporation killing a whistleblower and framing a reporter, or a reporter killing her blackmailer who wanted her money back…they'll go with option one."

"You sure about that? Both theories are salacious. The public will devour them."

"But we have an advantage. If this Zephyr of yours is who he says he is, he can lead us to the proof we need."

"Now you believe him?"

Connor gestured toward the bar. "If Edna pans out, that will go a long way toward my trusting him." He paused. "Ultimately, though, it would be better to learn who Zephyr is."

"I'm sure Woodward and Bernstein said the same about Deepthroat, and it worked out okay for them."

"If Z leads us to the evidence, then sure. But if he doesn't, he's our only link to proving Mira's a whistleblower."

Lexie pulled a napkin from the holder on the table and set it under her glass. "We'll deal with that later." She eyed the bar again. "Let's handle tonight first and see if this Edna shows up."

Connor checked his watch. "We still have a few minutes, so she's not late."

Nervous, Lexie bounced her foot.

"I should tell you I talked to Frank. I called him with a question about the agency, and he asked about you. I told him you were fine, but I think he's worried."

"Hell. I meant to call him today." Lexie groaned. "Did you mention anything about us being followed yesterday?"

"No, I didn't."

"Thank you. That's the last thing I need. Both him *and* Mom on my case. I'll call him tomorrow."

"And you're my client, so what happens with your case is confidential. I won't discuss it with him."

Lexie appreciated that, but the word client was hard to hear, even though it was true. After a pause in the conversation, she needed to fill the silence. "So, you and Ax hang out here?"

"We have." He drank some beer. "It's a good place to come after a lousy day, or when you need to talk somewhere private during an undercover assignment."

She observed the surrounding patrons. "I can see that."

"I brought Sasha here once, but it wasn't her cup of tea."

Lexie gripped her glass at the mention of Sasha.

"She's more the piano bar with leather couches and fancy waiters kind of gal."

Lexie drank some club soda. “I can imagine.”

“Don’t get the wrong idea. She likes her dive bars too.”

Lexie tried not to think of Connor bringing Sasha to Louie’s. “They have a certain charm...and smell.”

He chuckled. “They do. It’s where I’m most comfortable.” He ran his finger down the side of his glass. “You can sit without being bothered and, no matter what you’re dealing with, feel pretty confident that the people around you are dealing with worse.”

Lexie wondered what problems he was referring to. “And that makes you feel better?”

He shrugged. “I guess that depends on how big the problem is.”

Lexie glanced at the two men wearing trucker hats, sitting together. “Something tells me their troubles aren’t as serious as mine.” She tipped her head at the biker with the bandana and glanced at the group of women sitting behind them. “Them too.”

“You don’t know that.”

“But I can assume.”

He rested both elbows on the table. “Listen, when I met Sasha, I thought she had the perfect life.”

Lexie kept her expression flat.

“And she does, but it didn’t come easy. Her parents immigrated from the Philippines when she was two years old, and she had a four-year-old brother. Both parents worked two jobs to pay the bills. She and her brother were basically raised by strangers and, when they got older, were home alone a lot. Sasha saw how hard her parents worked and, when she was old enough, started working at a drugstore to contribute. She was saving for college when a woman walked in and gave her a card for a modeling school. She told Sasha that she had potential. Sasha used some of her money she was saving for college and went to the school. A month later, they plucked her up and sent her to New York. She was sixteen and traveled on her own. For someone who'd never been to a big city, it was terrifying, but she did it. Within a year, she was walking the runways and doing photoshoots for major magazines, but her plan was still to go to college. She got her GED, sent most of her money home to her parents, and after saving enough, got her degree. Now she works for a major fashion magazine as an editor, and she bought her parents a house."

Lexie ran her hands through her hair and stared at the table. "She sounds amazing, but forgive me if I don't think that's a unique story. There are a lot of people who've worked their asses off to overcome a hard childhood, and most of them don't become models to do it."

Conor scratched his neck. "No. I know that. Her situation is unique. I guess my point is that no matter what you're facing, you never know what can happen that can change everything." He looked over at her. "So hang in there." He gestured toward the door. "Maybe Eillen Ford will walk in, take one look at you, and tell you that you have remarkable cheekbones."

Lexie smirked. "And she'll whisk me away to New York where I'll make a million bucks with my smile?"

"And Carlson and Justini will have no choice but to leave you alone or risk facing the wrath of millions of your fans."

"There's one problem."

"What's that?"

"Eileen Ford is dead."

He dropped his jaw and cursed. "Well, that sucks."

She couldn't help but chuckle. "It's a nice thought, though." She paused. "And thanks for the pep talk."

"You're welcome." He picked up his glass. "Sasha's given me a few when I've needed them." He drank more of his beer.

Sighing, Lexie had to admit it was silly to avoid the subject of Sasha. It was time to put on the big-girl pants. "How long have you two been dating?"

"Eight months."

Her heart thumped. "So, it's been a while."

"Yeah."

"That's good. I'm glad you've found someone special. And she's independent and knows what she wants."

He pursed his lips. "Barbara's like that, too." He set his beer down. "I guess I just like strong women." His gaze met hers. "They intrigue me."

She stared back, and it suddenly felt much warmer in the bar. Had they turned on the heater? "Sasha's a lucky lady."

He smiled softly and stared at his beer. "Thank you."

They were quiet for a moment, and Lexie asked the obvious question. "What does she think of your doing this tonight? You're out kind of late."

"It comes with the territory. Same with her, though. She's working late too. Some kind of photoshoot downtown."

"Then I guess it's working out." She didn't know what else to say. After another pause, she eyed the bar. "Still no Edna."

Connor seemed to shake off whatever he was thinking and sat up. "Don't give up yet. She'll show."

Settling in to wait, Lexie leaned back. "And if she doesn't?"

"You can tell Z to go fly a kite."

"What about Sorrento and Thorne?"

"I'll stick with them and try to talk to Thorne. By the way," he raised his hand, "I mentioned Lynx to Sorrento."

"You did? You think that was a good idea?"

"Why not? I wanted to see his reaction, and it didn't disappoint. I'd bet my next beer that Sorrento knows this Lynx."

Lexie's mind raced. "What do you think that means? Lynx was found in Rook's records. Which means Lynx is tied to some powerful people."

"So he's pretty powerful, too. And if Sorrento's worried that Mira exposed Lynx in whatever she was supposed to give you..."

Lexie held her stomach. "I bet he's not sleeping too well tonight."

"And he'll tear this city apart to get to whatever Mira had on Omnivista."

"Which means whoever was following us could have been sent by Sorrento."

"It's possible." Connor raised his finger. "I'll say it again. Be cautious. If there's any hint that Edna can lead you to Mira's evidence, tread carefully. We don't want to put Edna in danger too." He swirled his beer. "Assuming she shows."

Thinking the worst, but trying not to, Lexie held her breath when a woman entered Louie's and walked up to the bar. She stopped and talked to the bartender, then walked down to the last stool near the bathroom and took a seat. "Connor." She took a deep breath. "It's her."

Connor swiveled in his chair. "I'll be damned. Z came through."

The bartender made a drink and set it in front of the woman. Lexie took a swig of her club soda and set it down. "I'm going to talk to her."

Connor put his hand on her forearm before she could stand. "Remember what I said, okay? Anything can happen, so be careful."

Lexie felt the heat of his fingers through her sleeve. "Like you said to me earlier, this isn't my first rodeo." She stood.

"I'll be here if you need me."

"You just sit tight." She smoothed her shirt. "My fabulous cheekbones and I are going to talk to Edna Randall." She straightened her shoulders and headed toward the bar.

Chapter Sixteen

ELIZA THORNE KNOCKED ON the door of Nolan's estate. It was late, but the front lights were on, and she knew he was awake. She rubbed and stretched her tight neck. It had been a long day, and a stressful one, but it had ended on a positive note. She hoped Nolan would think the same.

The door opened, and Gerald, Nolan's valet, greeted her. "Good evening, Miss Thorne." He stepped back. "Come in."

She stepped inside. "Thank you, Gerald." She pulled off her scarf and jacket. "Is he out on the deck?" Nolan liked to spend his evenings enjoying his view of the city at night.

Gerald took her jacket and scarf. "No, ma'am. He's in his study. I'll show you back."

"Thank you."

Gerald hung her scarf and jacket in a closet and walked past the living area and down a long hall.

Since it was rare for Nolan to greet her in his home office, Eliza imagined he was still in a snit since his meeting with Diamond. They passed a den and kitchen, and Gerald stopped at a set of closed doors. He opened one and stepped inside. "Miss Thorne is here, sir."

Nolan sat on a large leather sofa, holding a drink and staring out at a lavish garden beyond a set of glass double doors. He stood. "Thank you, Gerald. Come on in, Eliza." He downed the rest of his drink and walked to the minibar in the room. "Go home, Gerald. It's late. And take tomorrow off. Spend some time with your family."

Gerald pursed his lips. "Are you sure, sir? I'm happy to stay."

"I'm sure." Nolan grabbed a bottle of liquor from a shelf. "Someone ought to have some fun around here."

Eliza stepped into the office. Nolan was clearly still angry. "Thank you, Gerald," she said. "Have a pleasant night."

"You too, ma'am." Gerald turned and closed the door behind him.

Eliza faced Nolan, who added an ice cube to his glass and took another swig. He pushed the liquor bottle away. "You want something to drink?"

Needing to keep a level head, she declined. "Where's Ramona?"

Nolan returned to the couch and sat. "Went to Chicago this morning for another fundraiser. She'll be back in a couple of days."

Eliza walked over to the sofa. "I see. Is that why you're back here in your office, getting drunk?"

He shot her a look and slammed his glass on the coffee table with a bang. "You know why I'm getting drunk." He sat back, unbuttoned his cuff, and rolled up his shirt sleeve. "Tell me what you're doing about it."

She noted his disheveled appearance and wondered if it was as clear to him as it was to her that despite his wonder-boy reputation, it was she who pulled him out of his messes. "I'm handling it."

He finished rolling up his sleeves and stood. "How the hell are you *handling* the fact that that low-life investigator, Diamond, got Lynx's name?"

She stayed cool. "I've spoken to my source. Lynx's name came up in Damien Rook's files. But all they have is the name. They don't know who Lynx is or his connection to Rook."

Nolan cursed loudly and called Rook several colorful names. "Rook should have known better. What the hell was he thinking?" He put his hands on his hips and started to pace. "They get a hold of Lynx, and we'll either be in prison or serving burgers at the local diner. Our friends will scatter, and everything we've achieved will be gone."

"I'm aware of your concerns, but you don't need to worry. Lynx's actual name is not mentioned in the files. If it were, we'd know it by now." She didn't tell him about Rook's encrypted records, which the police were currently trying to open. She didn't see the point.

Nolan stopped pacing. "But they know there is a Lynx. They'll want to figure out who he is."

She shrugged. "Let them."

He walked up to her. "What are you talking about?"

"They found the name in *Rook's* files. Not ours. Rook's mental state at the end wasn't stable. His friends and staff have all attested to that. Whatever they find is only the random notes of a doddering old fool in decline unless they have solid evidence. No one connected to Omnivista is mentioned. Besides, if something detrimental comes to light, it can be handled."

"There's that word again." He scowled. "Sorry, but that doesn't satisfy me."

"Don't forget who we are and what we can do."

He waved his hand at her. "We agreed certain things are off-limits. It's too risky."

"I understand, but the option is there if we need it."

He glared. "Nothing happens without my okay."

"Of course. My source will keep track of what's happening with the Rook investigation. If anything comes up, I'll know about it."

"And what about Diamond and Logan? They'll be all over this. Diamond is helping to prove Patel was a whistleblower. He wants to talk to you and Patel's coworkers. And just because I told him no won't stop him."

"We're monitoring him and Logan. And don't worry about Diamond. He's not squeaky-clean. My digging pulled up some interesting facts."

Nolan narrowed his eyes. “Do tell.”

“He was one of the detectives involved in the Silva investigation. He went undercover.”

“The Silvas took a fall. Their organization is in shambles.”

“For now. And the daughter, Maria, is free. There are some questions about how that happened. I don’t have all the details yet, but if needed, we might be able to use it.”

“Use it how? The issue is what Patel stole from us. And if Logan finds it before we do, Lynx is the least of our problems.”

“If we can discredit Logan *and* Diamond, that helps with the optics. And I know they’re looking for the USB drive. I’ve got someone on it.”

He frowned. “Please don’t tell me it’s the same clown who got caught following them.”

She shook her head. “He’s been handled too.”

“Good. Just make sure he keeps his mouth shut.”

“He will. He knows what’s at stake. We go down, he goes with us.”

Nolan paused. “How is the new guy?”

“Far more experienced. We’ve used him before.” She didn’t tell Nolan that the “new” guy had been the one to handle Mira. Nolan preferred to leave the details to her.

“Is he following them?”

“No, he feels it’s unnecessary. He has a better idea of how to stop them from digging into Patel.”

He turned, picked up his drink, and took a gulp. “Enlighten me.”

“I can’t.”

Nolan lowered his glass.

“He says it’s better if we have plausible deniability.”

“You trust him?”

“He came highly recommended.”

He tilted his head. “Don’t tell me. From your source?”

She smiled. "It's taken care of, Nolan. Relax." She took his glass from him. "Let me get you another." Eliza walked to the bar and put his glass on the counter.

Nolan came up behind her. "How come you never get ruffled? You're always so sure of yourself."

She picked up the bottle and added more liquor to his glass. "It's what you hired me for." She recapped the bottle and turned toward him. "You just need to trust me. Lexie Logan and Connor Diamond won't be a problem." She held out his drink.

He took it from her. "It's not just them. It's that damn drive."

"My friend assures me it will be located." She paused. "But it might get messy." She waited to see Nolan's reaction.

"As long as it doesn't come back to haunt us, Omnivista, or Lynx, I can live with messy."

She reached up and smoothed his collar. "Then enjoy your drink. And stop thinking the worst. This will all work out."

He took another swig and stepped closer. Eliza didn't move, but she could smell the booze on his breath. He leaned around her and set his glass on the bar. Studying her, he stroked her cheek with the back of his fingers. "Can you stay?"

Her skin tingled where he touched her. "Do you want me to?"

He took hold of a loose tendril of her hair and slid it between his fingers. "My wife is out of town and Gerald is gone. I've got the place to myself."

"It's late." She swallowed when he brought his lips closer to hers. "And it's been a long day."

"Are you tense?" he whispered. "Are your muscles tight?" He trailed kisses down her cheek to her throat, where he nibbled her skin. "I can give you a massage." His hands encircled her waist, and he ran them down her hips, cupped her backside, and pulled her against him.

The sensations racing through her made her gasp. "I have to be up early tomorrow." She tilted her head back as he kissed her neck. "I have a meeting with the boss."

His hot breath tickled her skin. "Good thing you'll be here." He reached up and pulled the clip from her hair, which came undone and spilled over her shoulders. "We'll make it a breakfast meeting."

Her breathing picked up, and she ran her hands up to his shoulders. "I can make that work."

"Good." He dragged his lips to her jaw. "Mmm, you smell good." He brought his lips close to hers again, but held off from kissing her. "You take care of Lexie Logan for me, and find that drive, and I'll give you a hell of a raise."

She rubbed her nose against his. "I want us to go on a vacation together. Just the two of us."

He ran his hands up her back. "Name the place, and it's done."

Grinning with satisfaction and eager for his touch, Eliza pressed her lips against his.

••••••••••••

Lexie walked up to Edna Randall and stopped behind her. Edna was holding her drink and looking at her phone. Her stringy blonde hair hung in her face, and she brushed it back. She wore jeans and an oversized sweatshirt, and her nails were painted black.

Lexie approached the stool next to Edna's. "Excuse me. You mind if I sit?" She gestured at the stool.

Edna looked up and down the row of empty stools. "You don't like personal space?"

"Actually, I'd like to talk to you. Are you Edna Randall?"

Edna lowered her phone. "Who's asking?"

Lexie sat on the stool beside Edna's. "My name is Lexie Logan."

Edna scrunched her face. "Do I know you?"

"No. You don't." She leaned against the bar. "But your friend Mira did."

Edna's face paled. "Oh my God. You're that reporter, aren't you?"

"I am a reporter, yes."

"You're the one they think killed Mira?" She grabbed her purse, which she'd put on the bar. "I have to go."

"Wait, Edna. Just give me two minutes. I didn't kill Mira." Lexie debated what to say to keep Edna from leaving. "But I want to find out who did."

"I can't help you." Edna slid off the stool and glared. "How did you find me?"

"I'm working with someone who knew Mira well. They were friends, and he knew Mira wanted to expose Omnivista's crimes. He told me to talk to you and that I could find you here."

She yanked her purse over her shoulder. "How can I possibly believe you? The police think you killed my friend." She jabbed a finger toward Lexie. "And it was your father who stole Mira's money."

"Whoever killed Mira wants everyone to believe I killed her because she was blackmailing me. But none of that is true."

Edna sucked in a breath and held her head. "They found you in an alley, didn't they? Almost dead from an overdose?"

"They did, but that wasn't my fault either. I believe I was supposed to die along with Mira. But I didn't. Now they need to make me look like a murderer and a drunk. But I'm neither. I swear I didn't kill Mira."

Gripping her purse strap, Edna studied Lexie with a sharp gaze.

"Please," said Lexie. "Just let me talk. If you listen to what I have to say, and still don't believe me, I'll leave. I promise."

Edna didn't move. "If you didn't kill her, then who did?"

"I don't know, but I suspect someone on Omnivista's payroll. I think Mira wanted to give me evidence that could destroy that company and the people who run it. Unfortunately, they got to her before I could. And now that evidence is lost. And I'm here to see if you can help me locate it."

Edna continued to stare with animosity.

"You'd think I'd be here otherwise? The last thing I want to do is upset you."

"How do I know I can trust you?"

"All I can tell you is that I'd like to prove my innocence. And accomplish what Mira couldn't. She lost her life to expose Omnivista's lies. Whatever she had on them, they were willing to kill to keep it hidden. And proving that will mean Mira's death meant something. She was determined and courageous, and not a blackmailer out for retribution."

Edna's gaze and the grip on her purse softened, along with her voice. "I told her for years to leave that company, but she wouldn't listen to me."

Lexie's tension eased. "Can you tell me why?"

Edna paused and pulled her purse off her shoulder. "Lexie Logan, huh?"

Lexie nodded. "Yes."

"Your father's Tobias Logan?"

"He is."

"You two close?"

Lexie glanced toward Connor, who was sitting at the table watching. "I haven't seen him since he went to prison. But before he was accused, yes. We were close."

After another long pause, Edna dropped her purse back onto the bar. "My dad was an asshole too." She slid back onto the stool. "Okay. I'll give you two minutes, and it better be good, or I'm out of here." She leaned up. "Hey, Len."

The bartender, who was at the other end of the bar, looked up. "Yeah?"

"Get me another." She spoke to Lexie. "You want something?"

Lexie shook her head. "No. Thanks."

"You sure about that? This seems like a conversation that requires alcohol."

"It does, but I don't drink."

"Not according to the papers."

Lexie swiveled back toward the bar. "Don't believe what you read. If what was printed were true, I wouldn't be here."

Edna picked up the drink in front of her. "Start talking, Miss Logan."

"Call me Lexie." She took a moment to collect herself. "First of all, thank you for listening. I know this must be a hard time for you."

Edna gripped her glass. "Get to the point."

"Okay. Just a few questions. You said you'd told Mira to leave Omnivista. Why? Was she unhappy there?"

Edna snorted. "Hell. Those people worked her to the bone. She was always at the office. They paid well, but what's the point if all you ever do is work?"

"What about her coworkers? Did she have friends?"

"She did, not that I ever met them. But she liked them. The one she didn't like was that supervisor of hers. Eliza somebody. That lady was a bitch."

"Thorne?"

"That's her. You'd think with all the work Mira did that Eliza would have been nicer, but she barely spoke to Mira and was always on her ass about something. Personally, I think it was jealousy."

"Jealousy? Over what?"

Edna finished her first drink as Len brought her another, and Lexie asked him for some water. "Mira was always the smartest person in the room. She could have run circles around Eliza, and I think Eliza worried about her job security."

Lexie thanked Len when he brought her a glass of water. "From what I've heard, Mira got excellent annual reviews and consistent raises."

"That's because Eliza's not stupid. She wasn't going to give Mira any ammunition to claim unfair treatment by a supervisor. So, no matter how hard Eliza was on Mira, Mira always got decent reviews."

"Decent? Not glowing?"

"Enough to say she was rewarded for her efforts, but not enough to move her up the ladder."

"That's not exactly the story Omnivista is telling."

"Doesn't surprise me." Edna took another healthy sip of her drink and then sighed. "God, I wish she'd listened to me."

Seeing Edna's grief, Lexie could sympathize. "How long did you two know each other?"

Edna grabbed a napkin from the bar. "Since high school. We hit it off in algebra and never looked back. I was never as smart as her, but my sense of humor was way raunchier." She smiled and dabbed her watery eyes with the edge of the napkin.

Lexie let Edna have a moment. "I'm very sorry for your loss." She thought of Lonny. "It's hard to lose a friend, especially like this."

"It's terrible." She sniffed, and her voice shook.

"You okay?"

She held the napkin to her eyes. "Every time I think I can't cry anymore, I surprise myself." She blew out a deep breath and composed herself. "But yes. I'm okay. Mira wouldn't want me weeping over her."

"What would she want?"

Edna dropped the crumpled napkin on the bar. "She'd tell me to move on and live my life. She was never very sentimental." She gave a sad chuckle. "After she lost her money and divorced her husband, she and I had one night of debauchery, and then she was over it. Oleg went one way, and she went another, and she didn't dwell on either him or the money again." She cleared her throat. "That's why I know she didn't blackmail you." She scoffed. "Hell, she made that money back within a few years. It's utter nonsense."

"I thought that's why she stayed at Omnivista. To recoup the money."

"It was at first, but there was another reason."

"Did she tell you what that was?"

Edna groaned and had more to drink. "She told me once that she was staying because she had to. There were things going on that had to be monitored. She had created them, and now she was responsible for them. But then, a few months ago, she seemed more stressed than usual. I knew something was on her mind, but she wouldn't confide in me. When I asked her why, she said it was to keep me safe."

"Was there anyone else she would have talked to?"

Edna grabbed an olive from the bowl on the bar.

"This ain't a buffet, Edna," said Len, who was wiping the bar down with a towel. He stopped in front of them and moved the bowl of olives.

"I'm a regular, Len. Get over it. And it's *one olive.*" She rolled her eyes as Len left the towel on the bar and walked away. "He's so cheap."

Lexie looked around Louie's establishment. "I can see that."

"Len took over after Louie died. Needless to say, the place has seen better days."

Lexie got back to Mira. "Did you say whether Mira had a friend she might confide in? Maybe a coworker?"

Edna rubbed her head. "There was one guy she met when she first started there. They were close. They worked together in the same department, but I think he ended up getting fired. That's the only person she ever mentioned to me."

Lexie held her breath. Was Edna referring to Zephyr? She put her hand on the bar. "Think, Edna. Can you remember his name?"

"Hell, no. That was years ago." She rubbed her jaw. "But he had a nickname."

"Can you remember what it was?"

Her eyes creased when she squinted. "Scratch? Or was it Match?" Her eyes widened. "Wait. No. It was Patch."

Lexie slumped. "Patch? You're sure?" It wasn't much to go on, but even minor details helped.

"I think so." She smiled. "He was good at fixing problems, if I recall, which Mira appreciated. Most people cause them."

"I hear that." Lexie drank some water. So far, Edna hadn't given her much to work with. "Anyone more recent she may have confided in? Was she dating anyone?"

Edna gasped. "Wait a minute. Yes. There was someone."

Lexie sat up. "Who?"

"A man." She grabbed her purse and dug through it.

"What man?"

"There was a person at work. They'd been talking for a while. I think he worked on the same team as her." She pulled out her phone. "Personally, I think Mira was smitten, but she refused to admit it. Said he was just a friend."

"Do you know his name?"

She opened her phone and tapped the screen. "Mira sent me a weird text a few weeks before she died. We were supposed to get together, but she canceled." She scrolled through her messages. "Here. She sent me this."

She held out her phone, and Lexie read the message.

Can't make it tonight. Rip and I have to stay to clear up some problems. If you don't hear from me tomorrow, I'm sorry.

Lexie read the message twice. "That's ominous."

"It scared me. I called her, and she told me to ignore it. That she was sleep-deprived. And she was fine the next day, so I forgot about it."

"Who is Rip?"

"That's the guy I think she liked."

"You never met him?"

"No, never."

"You know his full name?" Lexie had left her purse with her notebooks with Connor, so she pulled out her phone to use for notes. She hastily wrote what Edna had told her in an email to send to herself.

Edna held her head. "Let me think. I'm sure she told me." She looked up. "Maybe—"

A man walked up beside Edna. "Excuse me, ladies. Sorry to interrupt."

Lexie recognized the biker with the bandana who'd been sitting at the table by himself. He leaned over the counter.

Edna frowned at him. "No, thanks, pal. We don't want any drinks."

"I'm not here to get you a drink, Edna."

Edna's eyes widened, and alarm bells rang in Lexie's head.

"I'm here to warn you." He moved his arm beneath the counter, and Lexie heard a flick. "Keep your mouth shut about your friend." He jabbed his hand, and Edna grunted and gripped her stomach.

The man glared at Lexie. "Forget about Mira Patel, or you're next." He stepped back, and Lexie caught sight of the bloody switchblade in his hand. He closed it, slid it into his pocket, and walked toward the hall that led to the bathroom.

Moaning, Edna clutched her stomach with her hands. Blood seeped between her fingers.

"Edna!" Lexie grabbed Edna's arm as Edna slid off her barstool. Lexie tried to hold on to her so she wouldn't fall to the floor. "No!"

One woman from the table of ladies drinking cosmos was standing at the bar's counter. Seeing Edna, she screamed.

Edna went down on her side, and Lexie dropped to her knees and reached for her as Connor appeared beside her.

"Are you okay?"

All Lexie could do was nod as he kneeled beside Edna and looked at her stomach. After a glance, he stood, grabbed the bar towel and tossed it at Lexie. "Put pressure on it." He yelled at Len, who was standing frozen in place. "Call nine-one-one," he yelled as he raced down the hallway toward the bathroom.

Chapter Seventeen

LEXIE SAT IN THE waiting area outside the surgical ward. Lexie had gone with Edna to the hospital while Connor stayed behind to talk to the police. He'd arrived at the hospital just as Edna had gone into surgery.

While waiting, Lexie kept replaying the incident in her mind. The biker coming to the bar, Edna being stabbed, Connor running after him, and her putting pressure on Edna's stomach while blood pooled on the floor. For the millionth time, she chastised herself. How could she have been so stupid? She should have been more aware of who was in the bar. After having been followed the previous day, how could she have been so lax in her safety and Edna's?

Gripping her head, Lexie said another prayer that Edna would survive when footsteps approached. She looked up to see Connor holding out a cup of coffee. "Here," he said, sitting beside her. "Any news?"

Lexie took the cup. "Nothing." Her stomach turned at the thought of eating and drinking anything, and she set the coffee cup on the table beside the chair.

Connor sipped his coffee and grimaced. "That's terrible." He set the cup on the floor and eyed Lexie, who stared at the doors to surgery. "You know this isn't your fault."

Lexie dropped her head. "I should have been more careful."

"Lexie, he was in the bar before we got there. How were either of us supposed to know?"

Lexie sat up. "That's another thing. He was waiting for us. How did he know?"

"I'm pondering that. Edna is Mira's best friend. He must have expected we'd eventually seek her out."

"But at Louie's?"

"It's possible. If she goes there frequently, it's not that far-fetched."

"Why not just watch her house? Wouldn't that make more sense?"

"Maybe they were."

"They?"

He slid his jacket off and tossed it onto the chair beside him. "We have no idea how deep this goes. We're talking about a company with significant clout. If they want to hire multiple people to monitor anyone they fear could help us, they'll do it."

"That seems like an enormous risk. The more people you include in this thing, the more likely someone will talk."

"It depends on what you threaten them with. Look at the mob. They do a pretty good job of keeping members' mouths shut."

"You're comparing Omnivista to the mob?" She huffed in frustration. "God, Connor, who exactly are we dealing with here? I mean, they stabbed Edna right in front of me. In a public place. What the hell did Mira have on them that's got them this freaked out?"

"I don't know, but whatever it is, we're going to have to take more precautions." He paused. "Any chance you could stay at your mom's until we figure this out?"

"Now is not the time for jokes."

"I'm not joking. You shouldn't be alone."

"If they wanted me dead, I'd be dead. Besides, they need their scapegoat, and if I die now, that brings attention they don't want. It's way better if they have someone to take the fall for Mira's murder. And if they find the evidence before we do, all they have to do is sit back and let the chips fall where they may. Which means right on top of me." She eyed the doors again. "If we find that evidence, though, then you can worry."

"Lexie, there is nothing stopping them from breaking in and trying another overdose. It almost worked the first time, and if it happened again, it would play right into the addiction story."

"I've got the security system set up, remember? They try to get in, it's going to make a hell of a lot of noise. I already told my neighbor, Lynn, that if it goes off, to call me. If I don't answer and give her a code word, she calls the cops."

"It's a deterrent, but it's not foolproof."

Lexie leaned back against the chair. "I'll call Doris tomorrow and get on her ass about fixing the alarm, okay?"

"Still, is it that bad staying with your mother?"

"I stayed there plenty during the Rook case, and I've had my fill. And until Nat leaves, it's not an option."

"It's that bad between you and your sister?"

"It's that bad." Anxious, she ran her hands down her thighs. "Can we change the subject now?"

"Avoidance never solves problems."

She glared at him.

"Fine. I'll change the subject." He glanced at the doors leading to surgery. "Since we have some time, did you get a good look at the man who stabbed Edna?"

"I told you. It all happened so fast."

"I get it, but I need you to try. The police are going to ask. They may want you to meet with a sketch artist."

"I guess it's too much to expect that Louie's has cameras?"

"You really want me to answer that?"

"No." Lexie closed her eyes. The last thing she wanted to do was recall the man who'd attacked Edna, but she understood why it was important. The memory of Edna bleeding and falling to the floor made her stomach turn. “Okay. I’ll try.” She took a deep breath. “He had dark eyes and stubble on his jaw.” Her stomach rolled again, and she opened her eyes.

“You okay? Just take your time.”

Lexie blinked. “I’m all right. Just feel a little warm.” She waved her fingers at her face.

“You look a little pale. You sure you’re...” Looking behind her, his face fell, and he cursed.

“What is it?” She followed his gaze and saw Carlson and Justini enter the waiting area. She cursed too. “What are they doing here?”

“Something tells me this is their case. Just play it cool.” He stood as the detectives approached. “Detectives.”

Still feeling warm, Lexie didn’t get up. “Don’t tell me. You two think I stabbed Edna?”

“Your words,” said Justini, “not ours.”

Carlson narrowed her eyes at him and spoke to Lexie. “How is Edna Randall? Any news?”

Connor shook his head. “Nothing yet.”

Justini looked Connor over. “Detective Connor Diamond?”

Connor squared his shoulders. “Have we met?”

“Your reputation precedes you,” offered Justini. “You were on the Silva case.”

Connor relaxed, but his expression didn’t. “I had no idea I had a fan club.”

“I followed the investigation.” Justini raised the side of his lip. “Too bad about Maria Silva. I always thought she was dirtier than her father.” He held Connor’s gaze. “Didn’t you?”

Connor’s eyes blazed, and Lexie wondered about the silent communication between them. Carlson looked perplexed, too.

“As I’m sure you’re aware,” said Connor, “sometimes a case doesn’t always go the way you want.”

"Oh, I'm aware." Justini eyed Lexie. "I'm hoping to avoid that with Mira Patel." He slid his hands into his pockets. "We need to ask you two about what happened tonight. Why were you meeting with Patel's friend?"

Annoyed, Lexie sat up. "We thought we'd have a few drinks and talk. Any problem with that?"

Justini offered that same annoying look. "Were you drinking, Miss Logan?"

"What the hell kind of question is that?" asked Connor.

"A reasonable one," said Justini. "Detectives do that."

Connor didn't back down. "Assholes ask asshole questions."

The creases around Justini's eyes deepened.

Carlson raised her hands. "Okay. That's enough testosterone. Phil, Detective Diamond is not the enemy. It's been a long night for these two, and I'm sure the sooner we can get this over with, the better."

"I'm not a detective anymore," said Connor. "I'm an investigator. I'm working with Lexie to figure out who killed Mira Patel, since you two seem to be struggling with that angle."

"We're not struggling," replied Justini. "We just have different ideas about who the killer is."

"Maybe you should focus on the evidence then, and not your opinion," offered Connor.

"Is that what you did on the Silva case?" asked Justini. "Cause I heard otherwise."

Connor clenched his jaw.

Carlson stepped between them. "Focus, Phil. I need you to talk about what happened *tonight*. Nothing else. Can you do that?"

Justini stopped staring at Connor and gave an annoyed chuckle. "Sure."

"Good." She pointed at Connor. "That goes for you too."

Connor raised his hands. "No problem on my end."

Carlson sat next to Lexie. She leaned close and spoke in her ear. "Why the hell do we put up with men and their crap?"

Lexie didn't know what to think about Carlson. Was she genuinely nice, or only trying to make Lexie think she was a friend? "I think we're just used to it."

Carlson leaned back. "Tell me about it." She pulled out a small notebook and a pen. "Tell us what happened between you and Edna tonight."

After taking a slow breath to calm herself, Lexie went through how they'd gone to Louie's to talk to Edna about Mira and Omnivista.

"How'd you know Edna was Mira's friend?" asked Justini.

"It's called investigating," answered Connor. "I did some and learned that Edna went to Louie's regularly."

Lexie was relieved she didn't have to mention Zephyr.

"Did Edna have any information about this alleged evidence against Omnivista?" asked Carlson.

Lexie almost questioned the word alleged but didn't see the point. "She doesn't know anything about Mira taking evidence from Omnivista." She refrained from mentioning Mira's coworkers. "But she told me Mira sent her a strange text a few weeks before she died. Mira told her she was working late and that if Edna didn't hear from her, she was sorry."

Carlson scribbled in her notebook. "Did Edna ask Mira about it?"

"She did. Mira told her to ignore it. She was just tired."

Justini crossed his arms. "What about the man who stabbed Edna? Have you seen him before?"

"He was sitting at one of the tables, alone, when we arrived," said Connor. "He was on his phone with his back to us."

Justini regarded Lexie. "You were with Edna when she got stabbed?"

Lexie nodded. "I was."

"Did you get a look at him?"

Lexie clenched her eyes shut when the man's face appeared in her mind. "Not great, but I saw him." That same heat traveled over her skin. "He had dark eyes and a stubbled jaw. His jaw was square, and he had a switchblade." She pulled on her shirt when sweat popped out on her skin.

"He wore a biker jacket, jeans and boots, and had a blue bandana around his neck," said Connor. "I chased him down a hall to a back door. It exited to an alley. By the time I got there, he was jumping into a car with tinted windows. The car took off, but I got a plate number." Connor provided the make and model of the car and the license plate. "I'll bet my next meal, though, that it's stolen."

Carlson took more notes. "We'll check it."

"Any idea why Edna would be a target?" asked Justini.

Frustrated, Lexie scowled at him. "The man told Edna to keep her mouth shut about Mira, and told me to do the same, or I'd be next."

"Anyone else hear that?" asked Justini.

Lexie dropped her jaw. "You think I'm lying?"

Carlson closed her notebook. "No one thinks you're lying."

"Doesn't seem that way," said Connor with another withering look at Justini.

"Edna can certainly verify it," said Lexie. She almost added *if she lives*.

"Edna couldn't tell you anything about this *supposed* evidence Mira had against Omnivista," said Justini. "So why would she be a target?"

Lexie scoffed. "Maybe you can do a little investigating and find out. But I think the answer is obvious. At least to me."

"Me too," added Connor. "Whoever stabbed Edna, or whoever sent him, thinks Edna knows something, which suggests Mira had knowledge that could damage someone important."

"That's one theory," replied Justini, without elaborating further.

Frustrated, Lexie spoke to Carlson. "How do you work with this man?"

Carlson tucked her notebook into her pocket. "One day at a time." She stood and spoke to Justini. "You have any more questions?"

"Not until we talk to Edna." He glanced at the entrance to surgery. "Provided we can."

"She'll be okay," said Connor.

"Let's hope," added Justini. "For both your sakes."

"We were both there," said Connor. "I saw what happened."

"But you didn't *hear* anything, did you?" asked Justini.

Connor bunched his shoulders. "What are you implying?"

"Nothing." Carlson tugged on Justini's arm. "Let's go before the name-calling starts again." She spoke to Lexie. "We'll be in touch after we talk to Edna. And I'll arrange for you to speak with a sketch artist."

Tired, Lexie hugged her elbows. "Fine."

"And try to get some sleep." Carlson directed Justini out of the waiting area.

After they left, Connor cursed again and sat beside Lexie. "What an ass."

"He doesn't like me. That's obvious." She rubbed her fingers over her forehead. "Carlson seems almost human, but can I trust her?"

"Watch yourself with her. Pretending to be a friend is a common tactic."

"Should I have said something about Zephyr or the man named Rip?"

"Zephyr? No. He learns you mentioned him, he'll disappear, and we need him. And Rip? What's to say? If Carlson and Justini do their jobs, they'll learn about him."

"I don't want to look like I'm hiding anything."

"At this point, you have to rely on yourself. We need to find this Rip and talk to him first. Those two find him before we do, he's more likely to run instead of help."

"That's why I didn't mention him."

"We need to find biker man. That will prove Mira hid something significant, and that you're an innocent piece of this puzzle. Not the mastermind."

Lexie didn't like the sound of that. "Are you suggesting that Justini thinks *I* hired biker man?"

"That's exactly what he's thinking. I could almost hear his wheels turning."

Lexie slumped. "Hell."

Connor leaned toward her. "Is there anything about this guy that stood out? Any scars? Did he smell bad? Did he wear a watch? Any tattoos?"

Lexie opened her mouth to answer when an image flashed in her mind. A man's face. With dark eyes and a stubbled jaw. Only not in the bar, but outside. In an alley.

Her stomach lurched, and everything spun. Breaking out in a cold sweat, she grabbed the armrest to stay in the chair and felt Connor's hand on her arm.

"Lexie? Are you okay?"

She struggled to breathe. "It's him."

"Who's him?"

"That man. At Louie's." She sucked in air but couldn't get a deep breath.

"Lexie, you're hyperventilating. Take slow breaths."

She gripped his hand. "I...I know...I..."

"Know what?" Connor scooted closer. "I need you to slow your breathing."

"I...can't. It's...him."

"It's who? Do you know who the man from the bar is?"

Spots formed in her vision. She took another wheezy breath. "He...he's...the man...in the alley." She forced herself to take a deep breath to gain control, but her memories swirled and her heart raced.

"He's the one...who tried to kill me."

Chapter Eighteen

LEXIE PACED IN HER living room, the biker man's dark eyes still vivid in her mind. She'd barely slept. After her mini-meltdown in the hospital waiting area, Connor had successfully calmed her down long enough to get her to talk coherently. All she could recall, though, was the man's face. Connor understandably questioned whether Lexie had confused the biker with her attacker from the alley, but she hadn't. They were the same man. The problem was that she couldn't remember any details from the night of Mira's death. Had the man been alone? Had she met Mira? Who had drugged her?

Thankfully, Edna's doctor had emerged not long after Lexie's recall and told them that Edna had survived surgery. She'd been lucky, and barring any unforeseen complications, he expected her to make a full recovery. He told them it would be a while before she could be questioned, and to come back later that day.

Since it was well after midnight, Connor had taken Lexie straight home afterward. She'd texted her mom to tell her she'd pick up her car later and not to worry. Once home, Connor had insisted on checking her duplex, and Lexie, still trying to process her memories, let him. He'd found nothing and had left after getting her to promise to turn on the security system and call him after she got some sleep.

When he'd left, Lexie could see he was worried about her. She understood because she was worried too. The man who'd attacked her was out there, and now he'd come after Edna. The further they went down this road, the more dangerous it became.

Despite all that, she'd slept a few hours before getting up and making two phone calls. The first one had been to a reporter friend named Karen Grazer, who lived in LA and worked for the *California Gazette*. Lexie had met Karen three years earlier at a conference, and they had remained in touch. After getting hold of her, Lexie told Karen about her situation. Karen had questions and admitted she'd seen the articles and videos about Lexie. But after hearing Lexie's side, her interest had peaked. She'd agreed to pursue the whistle-blower angle but wanted to do her own checking and pass it by her editor. Lexie had no problem with that. Karen was a respectable reporter who wanted to cover her butt, which is what Lexie would do if the situation were reversed.

After talking to Karen, she made her second phone call. Now she paced in her apartment, waiting and hoping that something else would spark in her brain from that night in the alley, but so far, she'd had no luck.

The doorbell rang, and she walked over and looked out the peep-hole. Taking a deep breath, she opened the door. Detective Carlson stood on the front steps.

"Good morning, Detective," said Lexie. She pulled the door open. "Come in."

Carlson held two cups of coffee and held one out as she entered. "Black with sugar?"

Lexie took the cup. "Yes. Thank you." She shut the door. "Thanks for coming."

"You're welcome." Carlson looked around. "You've been busy."

"Yeah, well, when your officers emptied all my boxes, I figured it was time to put everything away." She stepped to the small break-fast table. "Have a seat."

Carlson pulled out a chair and sat at the table. "I'll admit. I didn't expect to be here this morning."

"I didn't expect it either." Lexie sat beside her. "And thank you for leaving Justini behind. Was he pissed?"

Carlson smiled. "He thinks I left something at home." She sipped some coffee. "I figured I'd wait and see what's on your mind before telling him anything."

Lexie nodded. "Probably a good idea."

"I heard Edna Randall made it through surgery."

"She did. The doctor thinks she'll be okay. I assume you and Justini will go talk to her today?"

"That's the plan. I suppose you and Connor will do the same?"

"Yes."

"If I asked you to leave this investigation to me and Justini, would you listen?"

"No."

Carlson unzipped her jacket. "Thought it couldn't hurt to ask."

"If you were in my position, you'd do the same. You don't strike me as a woman who'd leave the truth-finding to Justini."

"It's not just Justini. But you're right. If I were you, I'd do the same." Her gaze traveled around the room. "Where's Connor?"

Lexie poked at the lid of her coffee. "He's at home or at his office. Where else would he be?"

"I guess I just assumed you two were together."

That silly flutter shot through her. "We're not. He's just helping me out as an investigator."

"He's pretty protective of you."

"He's a former detective. And he helped me once, a long time ago. That's all it is."

Carlson pursed her lips. "If you say so."

Lexie didn't ask what she meant. "I guess I should get to the point of why I asked you here."

"I'm certainly curious." She drank some coffee.

Lexie settled back in her seat. "First of all, I want to trust you, but I'm not sure if I should. You act like you're a friend, but you could be playing the part."

Carlson hesitated. "I'm not trying to con you, Lexie. But I see things from Justini's point of view too. I just want to get to the truth."

"Justini thinks I'm a liar. Is that what you think?"

"Justini thinks you remember more than what you're saying."

"He thinks I'm lying about the biker man too, doesn't he? He believes I hired him to kill Edna before she said too much about Mira?"

"It's a theory."

"He'll find out soon enough that he's wrong. Edna will verify everything."

"Then you've got nothing to worry about."

"You sure about that? Even if Edna backs me up, Justini could still think I hired biker man. All Edna can do is confirm what was said. Justini could believe I was just playing a role to learn what Edna knew."

"He might. But I think the evidence that you and Edna were the targets that night is mounting."

"But you still don't have proof. Just like you don't have proof that I wasn't the mastermind."

Carlson sat up and rested her forearms on the table. "Why am I here? You want me to tell you where we are in the investigation?"

Lexie paused. "That would be a helpful starting point."

"I do that, and you tell me where you and Connor are with yours?"

Lexie shifted in her chair. "I can do that."

Carlson held Lexie's gaze as if gauging her honesty. "Deal." She eyed her watch. "But let's make it quick before Justini wonders where I am."

"I'm all ears."

"Fine." Carlson crossed one leg over another. "So far, we don't have much. The search of your home has produced nothing to suggest you knew Mira or Mira knew you, other than the connection between her and your dad. We've searched Mira's place and spoken to her coworkers but haven't found or learned anything useful. Omnivista can only tell us how wonderful Mira was, but not much else. And nothing from the crime scene implicates you either, other than where you were found and when. We have no murder weapon and no witnesses."

Hearing they'd questioned Mira's coworkers, Lexie debated whether to ask about the mysterious Rip, but decided against it. "Then why is Justini so hell-bent on accusing me?"

"He thinks you have an accomplice. Someone who helped you kill Mira."

Lexie widened her eyes. "He thinks someone helped me murder Mira? Who?" She sucked in a breath. "Biker man?"

"Maybe. Or Connor Diamond."

Lexie almost choked on her coffee. "You can't be serious."

"That's Justini for you. He thinks the worst first and works his way back from there."

"But why Connor? He's a former detective. I thought your kind stuck together."

"We do, but Justini's got something up his craw about Diamond. He won't say what, but it has to do with the Silva case."

"Connor was a crucial part of that case. If it weren't for him and his partner, the Silvas would still be in business."

Carlson sat back. "Is that what Connor says, or did you do your own research?"

"Why would I believe otherwise?"

"I'm not saying you should, but it's better not to assume anything." Carlson drank some coffee. "So before you attack Justini, maybe do some checking."

Lexie recalled Zephyr saying the same. "Connor is not my evil accomplice. No one is. I didn't attack Mira."

"How do you know if you can't remember?"

"Because I'm not a killer. If she'd done what you suspect—tried to blackmail me—I would have told her to get lost. Being an alcoholic isn't earth-shattering. It wouldn't have been easy being outed, but I'd have managed, like I'm doing now."

"Maybe she had evidence you were still using and had graduated to hardcore drugs. That stain is harder to remove."

"Other than finding me in that alley, is there any evidence of my being a user? Have you talked to anyone I've worked with? Anyone in my family? As you say, that stain penetrates. If I were using, it would be obvious. I just broke an enormous case that took months of research. You think I did that while high and drunk?"

"Your family would protect you. Your mother proved that. So would people who care about you."

"Oh, come on, Detective. It's not that hard to figure out. I'd have to be buying drugs from somewhere, wouldn't I? And do you honestly believe I could do what I do while dysfunctional? I worked with two detectives on the Rook case. And if I'd pulled any kind of loser crap like that, they'd have tossed me to the curb. If Justini isn't suspicious of everyone on the force, maybe he should talk to them."

"You got names?"

Lexie grabbed one of her notebooks, opened it, and pulled out a blank sheet of paper. She found a pen and wrote Daniels and Remalla's names, plus their captain's, Frank Lozano. She slid the paper toward Carlson. "Contact one or all of them. They'll tell you I'm not some hopped-up journalist on drugs hiding my habit."

Carlson took the sheet and studied it. "Daniels is the one who called, looking for updates on the case. Did you ask him to do that?"

Lexie shrugged. "I needed to know what I was dealing with. Not that it helped much. You and Justini told him to mind his own business."

"It is none of their business, but it can't hurt to follow up with them. Anyone else?"

"Frank Storm. He used to be a detective and an attorney. He defended my father. He knows me better than most." She took the paper back and added Frank's contact information. She slid the paper over. "He'll shoot straight with you."

Carlson took the paper. "Okay." She folded it. "Now it's your turn. What have you and Diamond turned up on your end?"

Lexie ran her hands through her hair and collected her thoughts.

"Before I forget, I brought this for you." Carlson pulled a cell phone out of her jacket pocket and held it out.

Lexie recognized her phone and groaned with relief. "Thank you." She took the cell from Carlson.

"Nothing regarding Omnivista or Mira was found, other than her original phone call, so I figured there was no point in holding onto it."

Surprised that it had some charge left, Lexie opened her phone and flipped through it. There were several missed calls and voicemails. "I appreciate it."

"Maybe don't mention it to Justini. He already thinks I'm taking your side."

Lexie put her phone on the table. "Are you?"

"Tell me what you know, and we'll see." She set her coffee cup on the table and waited.

Lexie debated where to start. "First off. That man in the bar who stabbed Edna? He was in the alley the night I was assaulted."

Carlson dropped her jaw. "When did this happen? And how come you're just now saying something?"

"Because I didn't remember until early this morning, while we were waiting to hear about Edna's surgery. You and Justini had just left."

"What do you remember?"

Lexie closed her eyes and saw the biker man's face again. "That's just it. I recall his face and being in the alley with him, but that's it." She opened her eyes to see Carlson raise her brow. "I'm not making this up."

"I'm not saying you are, but is there anything else? Did you see Mira?"

Lexie shook her head. "That's all I can remember. But it's a good sign. My memory is slowly coming back."

"*Slowly* being the operative word."

"What do you want me to do? Snap my fingers or wiggle my nose?"

"Have you considered hypnosis? That might jog a few brain cells."

Lexie hadn't considered that. "That's a good idea. You know someone?"

"If you think it will help and you're willing, I'll ask around."

Lexie slumped. "I can already hear Justini. If I remember something under hypnosis, he'll think I'm faking it."

"We'll deal with that later. Let's get back to what you know."

Lexie sipped some coffee and considered where to begin. "I think whatever evidence Mira was going to give me that night is still out there. Mira hid it, and now Omnivista has to find it before I do. That's why Edna was attacked and I was threatened."

"If you can't remember what happened, how do you know anything was lost? Maybe they're just trying to scare you away from pursuing whoever killed Mira."

Lexie hesitated. "Because I have a source."

Carlson paused. "This source have a name?"

"I can't give you a name. All I know is that they used to work at Omnivista and knew Mira. I got a phone call the day I got home from the hospital after my supposed overdose. I was told that Mira was going to hand over damning files about Omnivista."

"A phone call?" She picked up Lexie's cell. "On this?"

Lexie realized she'd have to come clean on the burner. "No. The source sent me a phone."

Carlson looked around. "How come we didn't find it in the search?"

"Because it wasn't in the apartment."

"Did you hide it?" Carlson put her palm on the table. "Lexie, if you're—"

"Do you want me to tell you what I know, or not? This is a source I have to protect."

Carlson took a second, but relaxed. "Fine. I'll shut up. For now."

"Thank you." Lexie searched for a notebook on the table and pulled it from a stack of them. She opened it and found her notes. "According to my source, Omnivista has been collecting its user data, which is immense, and misusing it."

Carlson offered a quiet snort. "You sure? If you're on Vista, you basically sign away all your privacy before you can access it. That's common with social media."

Lexie couldn't deny that. "That may be true, but it goes way deeper. Their user data is sold to whoever wants it, for a high price."

"Do you know how much money marketing companies pay for that sort of data? A lot. Hell. I recently searched for a new pillow, and now Vista serves me tons of ads for pillows. What's new about that?" She narrowed her eyes. "I hope your source gave you more than Vista misusing data."

"Think bigger, Detective. Marketing is one thing, but spying on you is another." She leaned forward. "Do you have Prometheus?"

"The smart device? Yes. I do. Doesn't everyone?"

"I don't, but you're right. It's everywhere. Which means it's privy to a lot. How would you feel if you knew it was listening, maybe recording everything you say?"

Carlson's hold on her coffee cup tightened. "That would be concerning."

"And it's not just smart devices and social media. It's cell phones, tablets, wearables, search engines, and I'm sure there's more. God knows where else Omnivista has access."

"They have gaming apps too."

"Exactly. My source called it—" She stopped cold.

"Called it what?"

Lexie looked at Carlson's cell phone, and a chill ran through her. "What kind of phone is that?"

Carlson eyed her phone and picked it up. "It's the V5, the latest..."

"...Vista phone?" Lexie stared at it like it like it was biker man. The ramifications of what Zephyr told her clicked into place. "Hell." She took the phone from Carlson.

"What are you doing?"

Lexie stood. "Thinking bigger." She paused and grabbed her phone too, even though it wasn't a Vista. She went into the kitchen, opened a drawer, put both phones inside, and closed it.

Carlson sat forward. "Are you saying they're listening to us?"

Lexie returned to her seat. "My source calls it Project Prometheus. He and Mira were recruited to work on it with the advent of AI. Only it got out of hand. Mira and my source went to their supervisor, Eliza Thorne, but were told their concerns were unnecessary, but they believed otherwise. My source was ultimately fired for his interference, but Mira stayed on. Partly because of the money my father stole from her and her husband, but mainly because she felt responsible for what she'd helped to create."

Carlson sat still for a second. "How does AI fit into this?"

"How does it not? AI is part of everything now. Think of all the data Omnivista collects. It's massive. AI aggregates, catalogues, and organizes it into usable piles that can be sold to the highest bidder, and I'm not talking about marketing companies. My source said that he and Mira created Prometheus." She recalled Zephyr's warning. "And my source says if it can be trained to zero in on certain individuals or groups, the ramifications are enormous. Classified information could be used to gain leverage over a competitor, reveal industry secrets or proprietary data, and use personal information against rivals." Her heart rate sped up. "And if you want to go really big, in the wrong hands, it could be used to sway elections, manipulate markets, or even destabilize governments."

Carlson sat still, but the look in her eyes reflected her doubt, but also her shock. "You think they can get all of that by listening to you on the phone?"

"It's not just listening. They can read your texts and emails, see your browsing history, track what you watch online, get your location and photos. Everyone does everything on their phones. If you've got a Vista phone or smart device, or use their social media, nothing is off-limits."

Carlson tapped her fingers on the table. "I don't know, Lexie. Personally, I think all these companies already have loads of personal data about us."

"Maybe they do, but it's what they do with it that matters. I mean, think about if you're talking to a witness or a perp, or your captain about a sensitive case, and your phone is on the table. Nothing you said would be private. That's the power of AI. Prometheus can determine the value of that data, and Omnivista sells it, but it doesn't end there. If someone is powerful enough, they could pay Omnivista to use Prometheus to manipulate the algorithms that control the data that reaches us. If done right, it could encourage certain behaviors among its users."

"That's not new. We've heard of this before, especially around election time."

"Maybe so, but it's usually tied to foreign governments. But this is in our own backyard."

Carlson paused. "And you think this AI is powerful enough to affect voter behavior?"

"I think that's just the tip of the iceberg." She recalled what Sasha had told her. "From what I've heard, unflattering articles about me are all over Vista. People believe what they read. It's the perfect way to discredit me, and all it takes is a change to the algorithm. It's easy to do. And with the way things are going with deepfake videos and voice and photo manipulation, the power of whoever holds this data is immense."

Carlson sat back and studied Lexie.

"If Mira got hold of evidence that proves Omnivista is spying on its users, selling their private information to God knows who, and manipulating their behavior, the scandal would reverberate across the globe and would have huge implications."

Carlson took a deep breath. "I've heard of stuff like this. There are all sorts of conspiracy theories out there. AI is changing everything."

"Exactly," said Lexie. "Most can't really absorb something this big or understand the enormity of what it means, and until now, it's only been theory or rumor. We've been told there are systems in place to prevent AI from going haywire. But personally, it's all bullshit. Sorrento took Omnivista and went all in, and now he's terrified he's gonna get caught."

"If this is true, then who has the money and clout to pay Omnivista for this kind of information, and then pay even more for them to ensure a certain outcome?"

Lexie took her own deep breath. She thought of Lynx. "Someone big. Really. really big."

They stared in silence until something buzzed, and they both jumped. Lexie realized it was coming from the kitchen. She stood and went to the drawer. She opened it and heard Carlson's phone ringing.

Justini's name was on the display. She picked it up and brought it over to Carlson.

Carlson took it as it rang again and answered. "Hey, Phil." She paused. "Sorry. I got delayed."

Lexie waited to see what else Carlson would say.

"I know. I'm on my way. See you in a few." She hung up, stood and slid the phone into her pocket. "None of this means anything without proof. Your source may just have a bug up his ass for Omnivista because he got fired."

"Mira didn't die, Edna didn't get stabbed, and I wasn't shot up with drugs because my source is pissed. Or because Mira was blackmailing me."

Carlson finished her coffee and set her cup down. "What's your next move?"

"If I knew, I'd tell you."

Carlson walked to the door. "Until we have more, I can't launch a full investigation into Omnivista on this."

"It's better you don't, because whatever you know, they know. Our best bet is to keep this quiet. Especially from Justini." She opened the door for Carlson.

Carlson stepped outside. "I'm still not sure what to believe. This is a lot."

Lexie leaned against the frame. "I can't tell you what to think, Detective. But my advice? Be careful with your phone and unplug Prometheus, because they're listening. And if you decide you believe me, that puts you in danger too." She paused. "Hold up." She walked back to the table, ripped off a piece of paper, and wrote on it. She returned to the door and handed Carlson the paper. "My other number. Use that to contact me if you've got delicate information."

Carlson took the paper and tucked it into her pocket, just as Lynn stepped out of her door with Foster.

"Hey, Lex." She eyed Carlson.

"Hi, Lynn." Lexie raised her hand. "Detective Carlson, this is my neighbor, Lynn. Lynn, this is Detective Carlson." Lexie had said little to Lynn about her issues but figured the search of her home had the rumor mill swirling. "She's investigating what happened to me."

Lynn looped Foster's leash around her wrist. "I've seen those awful articles on Vista. And I can't believe they searched your place." She offered a withering stare at Carlson. "I hope you know Lexie would never do what those awful people are implying. She wouldn't hurt anyone."

"I'm only trying to get to the truth," said Carlson.

"I hope so." Lynn locked her door. "And just so you know, I've never seen Lexie inebriated. She's helped me with Foster plenty of times, and I can always rely on her."

"Good to know," replied Carlson.

"Thanks, Lynn," said Lexie.

"I vouch for her a hundred percent." She spoke to Lexie. "Oh, and Doris came by about the alarm system. She said she's sending someone next week to fix yours and mine too."

"Good," said Lexie. "Better late than never."

"It should have been done months ago. I'm glad you complained."

"When I told her she would be liable if I got killed by the same person who killed Mira Patel, I think it swayed her."

"Let's hope it doesn't come to that," added Carlson.

"Let's hope," said Lexie. "How's it going with Mr. Cutie from the dog park?"

Lynn beamed with a smile. "I might be in love. He plays drums with his band on the weekends, works as a mechanic in his cousin's garage, drives an old Corvette with a cracked windshield, and barely has any money, but he writes poems, gives me flowers from his yard, and is writing a new song about me." She clasped her hands together. "I know it hasn't been long, but he may be the one."

Lexie fought not to react and sensed Carlson doing the same.

"I'm meeting him now. We're going for a walk in the park." She petted Foster's head.

"He sounds like a romantic," said Carlson.

"He is." She smiled again. "Take care of Lexie, Detective. Good neighbors are hard to find."

Lexie waved. "See you, Lynn."

"See you." Lynn headed down the steps with Foster.

"I'm glad you're getting your alarm fixed, and that she has a dog," said Carlson. "Until we figure this out, the more precautions you take, the better."

"What matters is what Mira stole from Omnivista. We find that, and my life gets better."

"Or a lot worse."

Lexie chose not to think about that. "Oh, and you may get a call from a reporter today or tomorrow about Mira."

Carlson stopped on the steps. "Care to elaborate?"

"Her name's Karen Grazer, and she's pursuing the whistleblower angle. I figured it was time to share my side of the story. Omnivista's not the only one who can use the press."

"You sure you want to poke the bear?"

"This is my life and reputation on the line. I have to defend both."

"You know I can't comment on the case."

"All you have to say is you're investigating all angles, including the whistleblower theory. That's all she needs."

"I hope you know what you're doing." She turned. "Just be careful and keep in touch."

"You too. Thanks, Carlson."

Zipping her jacket, Carlson headed down the porch steps.

Chapter Nineteen

Lexie had barely closed the door on Carlson when she heard Zephyr's phone ring. She ran to the table and dug through her purse to pull out the burner. "Hello?" she answered.

"I heard about what happened at Louie's. You should have been more careful."

Lexie bit back a curse. "I'm fine, by the way. And so is Edna. Thanks for asking."

"You're not taking this seriously."

"Excuse me?" Lexie squeezed the phone and imagined it was Zephyr's throat. "You could have told me that Edna was a potential target."

"Everyone connected to Mira is a target. How has that not penetrated yet? How the hell did you become a journalist?"

Lexie bit back an unpleasant reply. "We were careful. We weren't followed. What else were we supposed to do?"

"We? I told you to be wary of that investigator."

"You asked me to meet a stranger in a dive bar late at night. First you tell me I should be careful, and now you're telling me not to be?"

"It's obvious that neither of you is aware of the risks."

Lexie paced with frustration. "The man who attacked Edna was already at the bar. How were we supposed to know that?"

"He was at the bar because he expected you to show up."

"I didn't tell anyone about Louie's other than Connor."

"And who did he tell?"

"No one."

"One of you got sloppy."

"Zephyr, what do you think—?"

"You still don't get it, do you? This is about more than you or your boyfriend talking to the wrong person..."

"He's not my boyfriend."

"I don't care. This is about protecting your information. Your world got a lot smaller the minute Mira contacted you."

Lexie tried to keep up. "What are you saying?"

She heard him sigh impatiently. "How did you tell Diamond about Edna?"

"He called me. I—" She instantly realized her mistake.

"You spoke on the phone? What kind of phone does he have?"

She groaned. "It's older. I don't think it's a Vista phone. But *I* was on my temp phone."

"Doesn't matter. And if he's got a Vista app on his phone, it could be compromised. Did he talk to anyone else after he talked to you?"

"No, he—wait a minute." She shut her eyes. "He talked to Frank, who's basically my uncle. But Connor wouldn't have said anything about Edna or Louie's."

"You sure? What kind of phone does your friend Frank have?"

"That one I know. It's not a Vista phone." That made her feel better.

"Who's in Frank's household? Anyone there have a Vista phone?"

Lexie considered Frank's wife and held her head. "Maybe."

"That's what I'm talking about. You and your investigator are careless."

"Connor didn't tell Frank or anyone else about Edna or Louie's. I used a burner, and Connor's phone is not made by Vista. The man who attacked Edna must have somehow found out another way."

"You're naïve. And if you don't start taking this seriously, you'll be dead from another overdose by the end of the week."

Lexie sat at her breakfast table. "What the hell are we supposed to do? Use tin cans with strings to communicate?"

"Tell your investigator to get his own burner and use it with you. And warn him about what he says to others."

"What about my laptop?"

"It's fine for general research, but for anything specific regarding this case? No."

"How the hell am I supposed to investigate when I can't use the technology around me?"

"You'll have to work smarter. Get Faraday cases for both your phone and laptop. Airplane mode isn't foolproof. Did Edna tell you anything that might help find the drive?"

"She told me Mira worked with a man named Rip. Edna thinks Mira liked him. They were working late together a couple of weeks before Mira died." Lexie remembered Edna pulling out her cell just before the attack. "Edna showed me the text between her and Mira. Is it possible Prometheus already saw it?"

"If Prometheus has access, yes, but if it's a general text between friends, it wouldn't have been flagged. It's what Edna told you that matters."

"I planned to look for an employee list online to find this Rip, but obviously I can't do that."

"You can if you hide who you are. Buy a new laptop with cash. Refurbished is fine. Doesn't have to be expensive. Go to the airport, create a new generic email address, and use the third-party internet there to load the Vista app."

Lexie frowned. "Isn't that the last thing I should do?"

"The airport is busy, and plenty of travelers will be on Vista. Prometheus won't be able to distinguish you from anyone else. Once you load up Vista, go to Omnivista's page. They hold a lot of employee functions and post pictures online. Use their social media against them and search for this Rip."

"I have no idea what he looks like."

"Look for Mira's picture. If she liked him, he'll likely be in a picture with her. There's an annual company picnic every summer. Go there first. Or try the Christmas party. If Rip's employed there, he'll be in the pictures. Look for any corporate events. Names might be listed."

"It sounds like a long shot, but I've done worse with less."

"If Mira mentioned Rip to Edna, he meant something. But if you find him..."

Lexie sighed. "Yeah. I know. Mum's the word."

"If you get his full name, don't do an internet search on him. If Prometheus picks it up and connects it to you, Rip will be the next target."

"How the hell am I supposed to find him then?"

"Ever heard of the phone book?"

She scoffed. "Are you serious?"

"Get the name first, and we'll figure it out."

Trying to prevent a headache, Lexie rubbed her temples. "This is going to be next to impossible if I can't use the internet."

"You can use it if you do it right. Prometheus isn't everywhere...yet."

"Are you telling me I can't use any devices, even if a Vista app is not connected to them?"

"Theoretically, they should be safe. But there are no guarantees. The internet is interconnected, and just because you're on a device with no Vista presence doesn't mean Prometheus can't find you. It just might take longer."

"This is nuts. There has to be a way around him."

"Right now, there are some limits. Prometheus was built to handle large amounts of data in a short period. Spying on individuals is not its strong suit. But that might be about to change, which is why you can't dawdle."

"I'm not exactly twiddling my thumbs. But what do you mean?"

"Mira sent me a letter before she died. I received it yesterday."

"A letter? Like snail mail?"

"It's the safest way to protect critical information from the web. Remember that. Keep your notes off your devices, but don't let them fall into the wrong hands."

Lexie was glad she'd always written her notes in her notebooks. "I think I'm in the Twilight Zone."

"It's better than jail. The letter said that Omnivista is rolling out an update to Prometheus within the next three months. They're calling it Prometheus Two, and Mira believed Two would be built solely to spy on certain people. That allows Prometheus One to handle the big stuff and Two to handle the smaller stuff."

Lexie raised her head. "That sounds like a problem."

"A big one. Once Prometheus Two rolls out, Omnivista and Sorrento could be virtually untouchable. If you don't find that drive before then..."

"I might as well move to Antarctica?" She rubbed her neck.

"No place will be safe. So either Omnivista and Prometheus go down...or we do."

••••••••••

After hanging up with Zephyr, Lexie put the burner back in her purse and picked up her cell. She dialed Frank's number.

"Hey," he answered. "You're calling from your own phone."

"Yeah. I got it back."

"Where have you been? I was getting ready to call you."

"Sorry I haven't been in touch. It's been a crazy couple of days."

"I know you've got a lot on your plate, but just let me know you're alive, okay? And that's good news about your phone. They obviously found nothing incriminating."

"No, they didn't." Lexie finished the coffee Carlson had brought her and dropped the cup in the trash. "I need to talk to you about a few things."

"I need to talk to you, too." He paused. "You want to go first?"

"Not over the phone. Are you free right now? I need a ride to Mom's to get my car. We can talk on the way."

"Hold on." She heard his muffled voice and guessed he was speaking to his wife, Elaine. He came back on the line. "I can be there in thirty minutes."

"Great. Thanks. I'll see you then." She hung up and went into her bedroom to change.

Thirty minutes later, she sat in the passenger seat as Frank drove down the street. "Any more press?" he asked.

"Not so far."

"That's good. How's it going with you and Diamond? He working out?"

She nodded. "He is. He's helping me with the Mira Patel case."

"I figured. Any progress?"

"Some." She held out her hand. "I need your phone."

"What for? Is yours not working?" He pulled out his cell and handed it to her.

"It's working fine." She took her cell and his, put them in the glove compartment and shut it.

Frank glanced at her. "Something I should know?"

She debated how much to tell him. "I'm taking precautions." Seeing where they were on the drive, she pointed. "Turn here. Before we go to Mom's, I need to make a stop."

Frank pulled up at the corner. "You going to explain what's going on?"

"I will, but let's stop first."

Frank turned, and Lexie guided him down the road to an electronics shop farther down the street. He parked, and she jumped out and ran inside the store. It didn't take long to find what she wanted, and she was back in Frank's car within twenty minutes. Frank remained in the parking spot while she pulled out a newly purchased Faraday bag, opened the glove compartment, and put both his phone and hers inside it. She pulled out a second Faraday bag and put both her temp phone Frank had purchased for her and Zephyr's burner inside it. She didn't think they were as risky as the others, but after Zephyr's warning, she was taking nothing for granted.

"Why do you have two other phones in your purse?"

She put the Faraday bags at her feet. "One of them is the temp phone you bought me, and the other is backup."

Frank scrunched his face. "What is going on, Lex?"

Before she buckled her belt, she swiveled to face him. "I can't tell you much, but my investigation into Omnivista and Mira's death is revealing disturbing facts, and I don't trust that we aren't being listened to." She pointed at the bags.

Frank's expression changed to one of surprise. "Oh, come on, Lex. You've never struck me as a conspiracy theorist."

"We're talking about a global technological media company. They make phones, tablets, smart devices, and own a social media network with millions of users."

Frank rolled his eyes. "What do you think they're trying to do? Take over the world?" He chuckled.

Lexie didn't smile.

His face fell. "Oh, c'mon, Lex."

"I can't tell you everything, Frank. But let's just say that my world is different now, and I have to be careful."

"Is this what you wanted to talk to me about?"

"No. I wanted to ask about what Connor told you when you talked to him yesterday."

Frank narrowed his eyes. "What do you mean?"

"It's important, Frank. Think."

He hesitated and shook his head. "I don't know. He had a few questions about the agency. I answered them. I asked about you, and he said you were doing okay. He said he was going to see you later, and that he'd tell you to call me."

"Did he say where he'd see me?"

"No, but I assumed it had to do with the Patel case."

Lexie relaxed. "That's it? Did he say anything else?"

Frank shrugged. "I asked him if he was enjoying being an investigator more than being a detective. He said there were good parts and bad, but he missed being on the force and working with Ax. I mentioned it was hard for me, too, at first, but I adjusted."

Feeling silly, Lexie turned back to face the window.

"That's pretty much it. Oh, and he brought up an old hangout he said he'd be stopping by. A place called Louie's. Said it would be a blast from the past."

Lexie swiveled back. "He mentioned Louie's, the bar?"

"Yeah. So?"

"Did he say why he was going there or when?"

"No." Frank grumbled. "What the hell is going on, Lex?"

Lexie groaned. "Weird question, but just bear with me. Was Elaine around when you were talking to Connor?"

Frank stared back with a confused look. "She was at the dinner table on her phone. Are you worried she was eavesdropping?"

"No, but what kind of phone does she have?"

"Lexie..."

"Frank, please. What kind of phone?"

He scoffed and waved his hand. "She just got the latest Vista, I think. Why does it matter?"

Lexie deflated and fell back against the seat.

"What is going on? Why the twenty questions?"

"I'm just curious."

"Did something happen last night? Is that why all the worry about the phones?"

Conflicted, Lexie rested her head back. "Connor and I went to Louie's last night and met a woman who was friends with Mira, but someone beat us there. They tried to kill Edna while she was speaking with me."

Frank's eyes widened. "What? Are you okay?"

"I'm fine. And thankfully, Edna will be too. But someone knew we would be there, and I'm trying to figure out how."

"Maybe they were watching Edna."

"Maybe." A man talking on his cell walked down the sidewalk, and Lexie envied his ignorance.

"I think you're letting this whole Omnivista thing get to you, kiddo. I know they're big, but they're not omnipotent." He pulled away from the curb and drove down the street.

Lexie hoped he was right. "You said you wanted to talk to me about something?" She changed the subject because thinking about Omnivista gave her a headache.

"I do." Frank cleared his throat. "I saw your dad this morning."

Lexie considered bringing up Omnivista again. "And?"

"Those detectives, Carlson and Justini, spoke to him."

"Already? When?"

"Yesterday. He said he didn't give them anything, though."

"Give them? What could he possibly give them?"

"Nothing. They asked a lot of questions about you and your past. But none of that matters today."

"You make it sound like maybe it does."

"What happened eight years ago is history."

"What did he say, Frank?"

Frank stopped at a red light. "Judd came up. Justini and Carlson know you were in an abusive relationship. They asked for Judd's name, and I suspect they plan to talk to him next."

Lexie put her hand over her eyes and let out a low groan. "Carlson conveniently didn't mention that or her talk with Dad."

"When did you talk to Carlson?"

Lexie lowered her hand. "I invited her over. She stopped by this morning."

Frank dropped his jaw. "Are you out of your mind?"

"It's okay, Frank. I figured it was time to clear the air."

"She's a detective, Lex. You can't trust her to clear anything." The light turned, and he drove down the road.

"What do you think I'm going to do? Accidentally let it slip that I killed Mira? I've got nothing to hide."

"Just because she pretends to be your friend doesn't mean she is."

"Connor said the same."

"You should listen to him." He paused. "What did you two talk about?"

"She told me that nothing so far from the search of my place has produced anything incriminating, and she gave me my phone back. They also have no witnesses and no murder weapon. And I told her Justini's determination to prove me guilty is a waste of time. Omnivista killed Patel. Not me."

"She's Justini's partner, and when the you-know-what hits the fan, she'll side with him."

"Nothing will hit the fan if there's no evidence, and right now there isn't. She's on my side, Frank. She knows Omnivista is involved. She just has to guide Justini in the same direction."

"You're swimming in dangerous waters, kiddo."

"I have to do what I think is right, and I need her. You've always told me I have good instincts, and I'm trusting them. Like me, Carlson just wants the truth."

Frank shook his head. "Tobias said he got the impression they were gunning for you. He told them to take a hike." He tapped his finger on the steering wheel. "But something tells me Judd won't be so nice."

"I haven't seen Judd in years. And they're going to take the word of an abusive ex? Even Justini isn't that stupid."

"Still. Guys like Judd hold grudges." He turned at a corner.

"Maybe, but he's stupid, too. It won't take Justini and Carlson long to figure that out."

"Did you tell Connor that you spoke to Carlson?"

"No. Not yet. I'll see him later when we talk to Edna."

Frank glanced at her. "I know you can't tell me everything, and I get it. But I hope you'll trust Connor. I don't like you going alone on this."

She studied her hands. "I need to ask you something else." She looked over at him. "About Connor."

"Shoot."

Lexie hated the question. "How well do you know him?"

Frank shrugged. "Personally? Not too well, but I did my due diligence before I sold him the agency. He was a stand-up detective. He had several commendations, great recs, and no red flags."

That made Lexie feel better. "What about the Silva investigation? Did you hear anything about that?"

"Who hasn't? That was a hell of a case. Took months, and they brought down Leo and Trey Silva. That's no small task."

"What about Maria Silva?"

"What about her?"

"Connor told me they wanted to get her too, but she got immunity instead in exchange for her testimony."

"That's not uncommon."

"But for someone like her? Who's as dangerous as her brother and father?"

"I can't speak for the D.A. but I'm sure they had their reasons."

Lexie fiddled with the edge of her sleeve.

"What's this all about?"

"I've had more than one person suggest I look deeper into Connor. That everything may not be as it seems."

Frank scoffed. "Let me guess. Carlson and Justini?"

"Not Carlson, but definitely Justini. There was some unspoken communication between him and Connor when they met."

"Justini's an ass. He thinks he knows everything when he knows squat."

Lexie picked up on Frank's slight shift in his seat. "Are you saying there's something to Justini's ambivalence?"

"Rumors are just that, Lex. Rumors. If they were acceptable in a courtroom, I'd be history." He met her gaze. "So would you."

"What rumors, Frank?"

Frank stared off as if considering his answer. "It's been floated around that the reason Maria Silva got the deal is that she had a romantic relationship with a detective during the investigation. And her testimony could have hurt the case. The detective supposedly swayed the D.A. to go easy on her, which is nonsense."

Lexie straightened in shock. "Are you saying Connor had an affair with Maria Silva and advocated for her release?"

"That's not what I'm saying. You wanted to hear the rumors? That's the rumor."

"What do *you* believe?"

He stopped at a stop sign and turned again. "I believe it's all nonsense. Trey and Leo Silva are behind bars, and their trafficking scheme is over. Maria is left to pick up the pieces."

"Why is Connor getting all the bad press? His partner, Ax, went undercover too."

"He did, but his assignment was Trey. Connor got close to Maria. I guess she took a liking to him. What actually happened? I don't know, and neither does anyone else. But the D.A. offered her the deal, which tells me the case against her wasn't as solid."

"Even if she'd had an affair with a detective, he still would have testified against her at trial."

"Depends."

"On what?"

"Juries might not like the ethics of a cop sleeping with a suspect. It could go either way, especially if Maria were convincing on the stand. And what the detective said or did all comes into play. If Maria witnessed something that could have been used against the detective and hurt the prosecution, that could sway the D.A. to give her immunity to protect the case against Leo and Trey."

Lexie tried to keep up. "So the rumors are Connor got in too deep with Maria and jeopardized the case against the Silvas? And the D.A. had to clean up the mess?"

"I would take all of this with a grain of salt, Lex. Rumors like this get started and spread, and before you know it, Connor's suddenly the secret lovechild of Leo Silva. Connor and Ax did their jobs. They went undercover for months, which was physically, mentally, and emotionally exhausting. And what happened during that time is between Connor, Ax, and the D.A. Not us."

Lexie leaned back in her seat. She rubbed her head as she tried to think. Connor telling her *I like strong women* kept repeating in her mind, and her mind wouldn't stop chattering. If some part of the rumor were true, could Maria and Connor still be in a relationship?

"C'mon, Lex. You think I'd sell my agency and give my clients, and you, to someone who didn't know what the hell they were doing? Connor's a good guy. You can trust him."

For the first time since meeting Connor in his new office, she wondered if that was true.

Chapter Twenty

Frank pulled up at Leona's home and stopped at the curb. "You sure you're all right?"

Lexie eyed her car. "I'm okay, Frank. I just have a lot on my mind." She pulled Frank's phone out of the Faraday bag and handed it to him. "Thanks for the ride."

Frank took his phone. "I know you're overthinking this. No matter what happened with the Silvas, Connor is reliable, and he'll watch out for you."

Lexie put her regular phone and both burners in her purse and tucked both Faraday bags into the shopping bag. "He's not my protector, Frank."

"Lex, I know you think you're invincible, and usually you are, but somebody threatened you last night, so don't tell me you don't need a protector, because you do."

Lexie widened her eyes. "Is that what you told Connor?"

"I told him that if anything happens to you on his watch, his client list is going to get a lot smaller."

"You didn't."

"I did."

"That's not fair, Frank. He works for me. Not you."

"And as long as he does, I expect him to watch out for you."

"This is my problem. Not his."

"Bullshit. If you're his client, that's his job. You may see it differently, but I don't care."

"Frank—"

Frank put the car into park. "Lexie, you are too damn much like Tobias. You think you know better than anyone else, and you don't want to listen to anyone, but you're not infallible. You need help. On the Rook case, you had those two detectives, but they're not around for this one." He shifted and put his hand on the back of her seat. "So whether you like it or not, Connor's a part of this, and if you fire him, I'll find someone else, unless you drop the investigation and let Carlson and Justini take the reins."

Lexie scoffed. "That won't be happening."

"Then stop bitching and accept the help. Connor's in this a hundred percent. He doesn't want to see you hurt any more than I or your mother do. Or Tobias. Connor's experienced and not easily intimidated, which is exactly what you need. So stop worrying about the Silvas and focus on what's important. Your life."

Lexie slumped. "Am I that bad?"

"You're not bad at all. You're just a pain-in-the-ass, but I've been your dad's friend for so long, I know how to deal with that affliction. Tobias needs a few ass-kickings every once in a while, and so do you. Consider this one of them."

Lexie set her purse in her lap and looked up at her mom's house. She could see Chase sitting on the front porch steps, tossing a baseball up and catching it in a mitt. "Guess I was overdue."

Frank relaxed and glanced up at the house. "The good news is I only ass-kick the people I love."

Lexie smiled softly. "I love you too, Frank. And I hear you."

"Promise?"

"Promise."

"Good."

Lexie opened the door. "I'll keep you posted."

"You better. And before you go, maybe now's a good time to reconnect." He pointed toward the house. "He looks lonely."

Chase tossed the baseball again and caught it. Lexie could imagine how he was feeling staying with his mom and grandmother. "He does."

"No time like the present to connect with your nephew."

"Frank—"

Frank raised his hands. "I'm not saying you have to talk to Natalie. But none of what happened between you and your sister is Chase's fault." He leaned in to look closer. "And it looks like he could use a friend."

Watching Chase, Lexie nibbled her lip.

Frank sat back. "But you've already had one ass-kicking today, so I'll spare you another."

"I appreciate that." She stepped out of the car. "Thanks, Frank."

"You're welcome, kiddo. As usual, if you need anything, you know where to find me." He put the car back into drive.

"I do. I'll see you."

"I'll talk to Elaine. We'll do dinner soon."

"Sounds good. Bye, Frank." She shut the door, and after a wave, Frank drove off.

Glancing up at the house, she walked to her car. Chase saw her and smiled. "Hi, Aunt Lexie."

She smiled back, and telling herself to be a better aunt, she headed up the walkway. "Hey, Chase. You playing baseball?"

Chase caught the ball again. "You can't play baseball by yourself."

"No, I guess you can't." She sat beside him on the step and set her purse and bags down.

"You getting your car?" he asked.

"I am. Where's your mom and grandmom?"

"Nana's getting her nails done. And Mom's inside, talking to Dad." He set the baseball in the mitt.

Alarmed, Lexie straightened. "Is your father here?"

"No, he's on the phone. They're fighting." He picked up the ball and tossed it back into the mitt.

Lexie's heart fell. "I'm sorry to hear that. But parents sometimes fight."

"They fight a lot."

"They do?" She glanced back at the house. "That sucks."

"Mom tells me not to use that word."

Lexie looked back. "Why not? It's a good word."

"My friend Ricky uses it all the time. So does Dad."

"I bet your mom loves that."

"Not really."

Lexie reached for the baseball. "You like baseball?"

He nodded. "I like the Diamondbacks."

"You do?" She tossed the ball up, and he caught it.

"Dad and I watch the games if they're not on too late. And sometimes he'll play catch with me if he's not working."

"That's nice." Lexie guessed Chase and Walker didn't play catch often. "Is your dad coming to visit?"

Chase shrugged. "Nah. He has to work. That's what he and Mom are fighting about."

Lexie could hear the sadness in his voice. "I'm sorry about that."

He tossed the ball into his mitt. "We were supposed to go to a game before we left, but he got busy."

"Well, that's the good thing about baseball. There're always plenty of games."

"Yeah."

"Maybe we can go to one while you're here. Would you like that?" She couldn't believe she'd asked, but it had just spilled out of her.

His eyes lit up. “Really?”

“Sure. I can’t promise it will be the Diamondbacks, but it will still be fun.”

“I’d like that.”

“Chase?”

Lexie turned to see her sister standing at the door. Her eyes were red, and her cheeks were splotchy. “Come inside.” She wiped her cheek with the back of her fingers.

“I’m talking to Aunt Lexie.”

Natalie glanced at Lexie. “I can see that, but it’s time for lunch.”

Chase stood. “Okay.” He tossed the baseball to Lexie. “Bye, Aunt Lexie.”

She tossed the ball back, and he caught it. “Bye, Chase. I’ll let you know about the game, okay?”

“What game?” asked Natalie.

Chase headed up the front stairs. “Aunt Lexie is going to take me to a baseball game. Right, Aunt Lexie?”

“Sure am,” said Lexie, making eye contact with Natalie.

“You sure?” Natalie asked Lexie. “Aren’t you pretty busy right now? With your case?”

Lexie stood. “I can make time for a baseball game.”

“Maybe you could come too, Mom,” said Chase. “And Grandma.”

Lexie tensed.

“Maybe,” said Natalie. “We’ll see.” She ruffled his hair. “But don’t get your hopes up, fella. Your Aunt Lexie has a lot going on right now.”

Chase’s body language shifted.

Lexie hated his reaction. “Don’t worry, Chase. We’ll figure it out. Because not going to a baseball game sucks.”

Chase smiled again. “It sucks.”

Nat glowered. “Your aunt may use that word, but you don’t, young man. Got it?”

"Sorry, Mom."

"Go inside. There's a sandwich in the kitchen."

Chase waved. "See you, Aunt Lexie."

"See you, Chase."

Chase walked inside.

Natalie stepped out onto the porch. "I'd appreciate it if you wouldn't get his hopes up."

"I'm not. I'll take him to a baseball game."

"I heard what happened to you. The police think you killed that woman."

"I didn't."

"Mom said you can't remember."

"I can't, but it's still not true."

Natalie put her hand on her hip. "Well, until you do, maybe it's best if Chase stays close to home."

Lexie's anger bubbled up. "You worried I'm going to get drunk? Or arrested for murder? Or both?"

"He's just a kid."

"Who's sitting out on the porch while his mother and father argue on the phone. Which apparently happens a lot." Lexie told herself to shut up, but with Natalie, she usually overrode that instinct.

Natalie's gaze darkened. "That's none of your business."

"Walker's not coming, is he? Because he's too busy working? Or is it something else?"

Natalie's eyes filled. "Leave it alone, Lexie."

"Chase told me his father backed out of taking him to a game before you left, so I offered to do it. I won't take that back. So if he can't go, you get to tell him. Not me. But tell him the real reason. Not because you think I'm a drunk, but because it scares you he'll get close to me. And the last thing you want is for me to be the fun aunt."

Nat crossed her arms. "That doesn't scare me at all because we won't be here long enough, and God knows you never visit. Besides, he's already got Uncle Jonah. He's the fun one."

Lexie straightened in surprise. "Jonah? You've seen Jonah?"

"Of course. He visits when he can. He and Chase have gotten to know each other, and when Walker didn't take him to that game, Jonah did."

Lexie sputtered. "Where is he? What's he doing?"

"Why don't you ask Mom? He calls her too."

Lexie didn't know what to say. "Why hasn't he called me?"

"Because he talks to the people he cares about, that's why."

Lexie stood stunned on the porch step.

"I'll tell Mom you stopped by, but I doubt she'll believe me." Natalie turned, walked inside, and slammed the door shut behind her.

••••••••••

Lexie parked next to a Harley-Davidson motorcycle outside Connor's office but sat in the car and thought again about her conversation with Natalie. Jonah had been in touch with her and Mom, but not Lexie?

Lexie grabbed her phone, pulled up Jonah's number, but didn't call it. She considered whether Nat had lied to her, which was possible, but doubted it. And that led her back to questioning why Jonah had frozen Lexie out. She suspected she knew, though. Jonah and Dad had never been close, despite Tobias being the only father Jonah had known. His biological father had disappeared when Jonah was two, and Leona rarely spoke about him.

Growing up, Lexie had always sided with Dad, and Natalie had always sided with Mom. And after Dad's arrest and eventual trial, he and Jonah had barely spoken. Lexie had argued with her brother over the phone about how he'd treated Dad during that time, and Jonah would barely say a word, tell her she would never understand, and hang up on her.

They'd talked a few times since her father's conviction, but the conversation had always been distant and impersonal. Jonah didn't ask about her life, and Lexie didn't ask about his. She didn't even know where he lived anymore. Now that some time had passed, though, and Jonah was in touch with Natalie and Mom, Lexie had to consider whether now was a good time to thaw their icy relationship. But with Dad's parole hearing coming up, she wondered if that would only sidetrack any attempts to reconnect.

Deciding to deal with Mira Patel first and Jonah later, Lexie put her phone back in her purse and eyed Connor's office door. She'd called him before leaving her mom's, and he'd asked her to stop by.

Frank's ass-kicking echoed in her mind. Was she overthinking Connor's role in the Silva investigation? Was it any of her business whether Connor had slept with Maria and jeopardized the case against her? It wasn't, but if it were true, then Connor had not been upfront with her, which made her question what else he might be hiding. Was he still involved with Maria? Was he lying to Sasha, too?

Again, she told herself it didn't matter because it was all rumors. And Frank was right. All she needed was help with her current case. As long as Connor could prevent Lexie from being pulled into the Silva mess, and as long as she could keep working with him instead of swooning over him, it would work. At least that's what she told herself.

She got out of her car and headed up to the door. After going inside, she almost knocked on the inner door when she heard voices from inside the office.

"We need to talk about this," said an unknown male voice.

"What else is there to talk about?" responded Connor.

"You know what else."

Not wanting to interrupt, Lexie took a step back from the door.

"I'm not on the force anymore. It's out of my hands."

"Don't take that attitude. There's plenty you can do."

"What about you? I'm not the only one caught up in this."

Lexie frowned.

"You know where I stand. And I don't have the option to just up and leave like you did."

"C'mon, Ax. You know why I left."

"And you know why I stayed."

The door swung open, and Lexie jumped.

A tall man with short dark hair, muscled shoulders and arms, and a trim beard, wearing a motorcycle jacket and jeans, stood in front of her, but he was looking back at Connor. "I'm tired of talking in circles, CD."

"So am I," said Connor.

The man turned, saw Lexie, and froze.

Lexie stood frozen, too. "Sorry. I stopped by to see Connor." She didn't know what else to say.

The man, who was obviously Ax, looked her over. "You must be the famous Lexie Logan."

Connor walked up to the door. "Lexie?"

"Hi," said Lexie. "I hope I didn't interrupt."

"Thank God you did," said Ax.

"It's fine. Ax stopped by." Connor waved his hand at Lexie. "This is Lexie Logan, Ax. Lexie, this is my partner, Jamie Axelrod, otherwise known as Ax."

Ax held out his hand. "Pleasure."

Lexie shook his hand. "I've heard a lot about you."

"Same here." His warm fingers tightened over hers. "It never ceases to amaze me, CD." He let go of her hand.

"What's that?" asked Connor.

"How you always manage to surround yourself with incredible women."

Connor smirked. "It's my impeccable bedside manner. You should try it sometime."

Ax ticked up his brow. "It's not the bed*side* I'm interested in."

"And that's why you attract the women you do."

Ax pointed at Connor and spoke to Lexie. "Is he this annoying with you?"

Lexie eyed Connor. "He has his moments, but so do I."

"Then let me give you a warning. Get out while you're ahead."

Connor punched Ax in the arm, and Ax grunted. "Don't you have somewhere to be?" asked Connor.

"I do," said Ax, rubbing his arm. "Anywhere but here." He stepped past Lexie. "Nice meeting you."

"You too." Lexie pointed out the window. "Is that your motorcycle?"

"It is?" He grinned. "You ride?"

Connor made a snort.

"No. Never been a fan." A memory flared of Jonah driving a motorcycle. Her father had told him to get rid of it, but Jonah had refused and had taken Lexie for a ride, making her dad even madder. "My brother used to have one."

"You're missing out." He walked away and grabbed a helmet from the sofa. "You ever want to join me, let me know." He winked and put the helmet on.

Connor knitted his brow. "Get lost, Ax."

Ax smiled. "Love you too, brother. I'll be in touch."

"See you," said Connor. "And stay out of trouble."

"What for?" Ax chuckled, waved, and left.

"Sorry about that," said Connor. "He stopped by unexpectedly."

Lexie watched through the window as Ax got on his motorcycle, and it roared to life. "It's fine. I'm glad I got to meet him."

"He wanted to meet you too."

The motorcycle rumbled as Ax backed out, reversed gears, and shot away with another roar. Lexie again thought of Jonah. "He seems interesting."

Connor stepped back so she could enter his office. "That's one word for it. Come on in."

"Thanks." Lexie stepped inside, carrying her purse and shopping bag.

Connor closed the door. "You should have called earlier. I could have taken you to your car."

"It's fine." Lexie set her purse and bag on the chair in front of Connor's desk. "I needed to talk to Frank anyway."

He sat on the side of his desk. "How are you doing after last night? Did you remember anything else?"

"Unfortunately, no. Didn't sleep much either. How about you?"

"Same. Tossed and turned before I gave up and came into the office." He pointed at her shopping bag. "Did you do some shopping?"

"I did. For you and for me."

He raised his eyebrows. "Now I'm curious."

"Before we get to that, have you called the hospital to check on Edna? Is she strong enough for us to talk to her today?"

He crossed his arms. "I did, and she is, but bad news. She doesn't want to talk."

"You mean she wants to wait?"

"No. I mean she's staying silent. I called Edna's room and talked to a nurse, who conveyed that Edna doesn't want to speak to anyone about what happened to her or Mira."

"But Justini and Carlson will want to talk to her."

Connor shrugged. "According to the nurse, Edna is scared. She wouldn't even speak to me on the phone."

Lexie remembered what the biker man had said. "Her attacker warned her to keep her mouth shut."

"Which is exactly what she's doing. She may relax a little in a day or two, but for now, I say we give her some space."

"Is someone watching her?"

"I asked, and yes. There's an officer outside her door, so at least Carlson and Justini got that right."

"That makes me feel better."

He tipped his head toward the bag. "What'd you get me?"

"Before we get to that, where's your phone?"

He pulled it out of his back pocket. "Right here."

"Is it a Vista phone?"

"No."

"Do you have the Vista app on it?"

He shook his head. "No. Never been a fan of social media."

"Any Vista games?"

His eyes narrowed. "No. What are we talking about here?"

"We're taking precautions. Yours should be good, and so is mine, but it's better to be safe."

He eyed his phone. "Hold up. I lied about the games. I added a couple for my daughter, but it's kids' stuff."

"Are they Vista apps?"

He checked his phone. After a few swipes, he studied his screen. "One of them is." He lowered his phone. "Why?"

"Then it's not safe." She opened her shopping bag, pulled out a Faraday bag and handed it to him. "This will block cellular, Wi-Fi, Bluetooth, and GPS signals."

"A Faraday bag?" He took it. "Did something just radically change?" He put his phone in the bag, and Lexie put her cell in the other bag.

"I think I know how biker man knew we'd be at Louie's."

He set his bag on his desk. "How?"

"When you talked to Frank yesterday, you mentioned the bar."

His expression darkened. "Are you saying Frank is a mole?"

"No. That's not what I'm saying. But you have a phone with a Vista app, and Frank's wife Elaine has a Vista phone. And she was nearby when Frank spoke to you yesterday."

His jaw dropped. "You think someone was listening?"

"I talked to Zephyr this morning. He said we were careless. And he's right."

"I don't understand."

"We didn't realize the extent of Prometheus' reach. Zephyr assumed we understood the ramifications, but as many geniuses do, they assume logic where there is none. So he explained it to me in language I can understand, and, bottom line, we have to change the way we do things."

He walked around his desk, pulled his chair out and rolled it over to hers. "Explain." He sat.

Lexie moved her bags and sat too. She told Connor everything Zephyr had described to her about Prometheus and Prometheus Two. "That's why I got us Faraday bags. The burner Zephyr got me is safe, as is the one Frank bought for me, but we can't trust our cells." She dug into the shopping bag. "Which is why I got you this." She handed him a package. "Your own burner. It's the only way we can communicate with each other and be certain no one is listening."

He took the package. "I can't believe this is what we've come to."

"And any notes you take on the phone? They're compromised. So, print them and then delete them. And start taking handwritten notes."

He puffed out his cheeks. "Why do I feel like we've just jumped back in time fifty years?"

"Because we have. Nothing online is safe."

"How are we supposed to do research?"

"By being smart. There are ways to do it. Right now, this version of Prometheus is better with large amounts of data. Zeroing in on a few isolated individuals is not its strong suit. It will miss things or take longer to analyze the data. That will change with P2, but we still have to be careful."

"If that's how the biker knew we would be at Louie's, then that's impressive."

"True, but keep in mind, you spoke to Frank earlier in the day, so it had time to analyze and spit out what it thought was a trigger. If you'd had the conversation right before we left, Prometheus might not have found it in time."

"But that's not certain?"

"No, it's not."

He fell back into his chair. "Well, this adds a new wrinkle." He ran his hands into his hair. "How are we supposed to find this Rip without using the internet?"

"First, we need a laptop. Something cheap. Refurbished will work. You know where we can get one?"

He nodded. "I know a guy. Can't promise it didn't fall off the back of a truck, though."

"That may be even better." She stood.

"What then?"

She grabbed her bags. "I'll treat you to lunch. At the airport."

Holding the package, he stood. "Not my first choice, but okay."

Heading toward the door, she thought of Chase and turned back. "Hey. Do you like baseball?"

He grabbed his jacket. "Love it. My stepdad works in the front office for the Padres. I can get you free tickets if you ever want to go to a game."

She grinned. At least something was going right. "Perfect. Let's go."

"To a game?"

"No, the airport." She left his office. "It's time to find Mira's friend, Rip."

Chapter Twenty-One

Carlson knocked on the door of the small brick house with the shuttered windows and one lone leafless tree in the front yard. A car was parked in the driveway, and an RV sat beside it. Justini stood beside her with his thumbs hooked into his belt. Several seconds passed, and Carlson knocked again.

"Keep your shorts on," said a female voice from the other side of the door. "I'm coming." The door opened. A woman with graying hair pulled back into a messy bun, wearing a black skirt and a green blouse, stood there. "Yes?" she asked, buttoning the top button of her shirt.

"Ma'am?" asked Carlson, holding out her badge. "I'm Detective Sam Carlson and this is my partner, Phil Justini." Justini held out his badge. "Are you Suzanna Ballard?"

The woman adjusted an earring. "I am. What's this about?" She grabbed a jacket from a hook near the door. "And hurry it up because I've got to get to work."

"We're looking for your son, Judd," said Justini. "We'd like to talk to him."

Suzanna held her jacket. "He do something stupid?"

"No, Mrs. Ballard," said Carlson.

"This is about Lexie Logan," added Justini. "You know her?"

Her jaw dropped. "Do I know her?" She cursed. "That woman ruined my son's life."

Carlson bit her tongue and asked the obvious. "How so, ma'am?"

Suzanna put on her jacket. “That bitch sent him to jail. Accused him of all kinds of nonsense when she’s to blame as much as him. Since getting out, the only work he can find is maintenance jobs. He can’t even afford his own place.”

“Can we talk to him?” asked Carlson.

She straightened her jacket. “He stays in the RV. Good luck talking to him, though.”

“Why’s that?” asked Justini.

“Been working all night. He’s probably asleep.” She grabbed her purse from the table near the door. “Anything else?”

“When’s the last time you saw Lexie Logan?” asked Justini.

Suzanna glared. “The day they sentenced my boy to jail. And she better pray I never see her again.”

Justini slid his badge back into his pocket. “When’s the last time your son saw her?”

“Hopefully, the same damn day.” She stepped outside, closed the door, and locked it. “I’ve got to go. Just knock on the RV door.”

Carlson nodded. “Thank you, Mrs. Ballard.”

Suzanna slid her purse strap over her shoulder. “Does this have something to do with Lexie and that woman they found dead?”

“What do you know about that?” asked Carlson.

“Just what I seen on Vista.” She cursed again. “If that doesn’t prove Lexie is a troublemaker, I don’t know what does. She back on the sauce?”

“We can’t comment on the case, ma’am.” Carlson followed Suzanna down the steps to her car.

“That means yes.” Suzanna opened her car door. “I knew it.”

“Knew what?” asked Justini.

“That one day, her time would come, and the truth would come out.” She tossed her purse onto the front seat.

Justini stopped near her car door. “What truth is that?”

Suzanna's face tightened. "That she's a lying, conniving snake who will stab anyone in the back to protect herself." She pointed. "And if you're talking to her, don't believe a word she says."

"Good to know," replied Justini.

Suzanna jabbed her thumb toward the RV. "Knock loud, or he'll sleep right through it." She got into her car, started it up, left the driveway, and drove down the street.

Carlson shook her head. "Quite the woman."

"Indeed."

Carlson gawked at her partner. "Come on, Phil. You're not buying all that 'my son got a bad rap' crap, are you?"

Justini shrugged. "Depends. Let's talk to the son."

Carlson walked with him to the RV door, where Justini banged on it. "Judd Ballard? Police. We'd like to talk with you."

They waited several seconds with no response. Justini banged on the door again. "Judd Ballard? You awake? Police."

No response.

Carlson stepped up. "Let me try." She banged on the door with her fist. "Judd Ballard? This is Detective Carlson and Detective Phil Justini from the SDPD. We'd like to talk to you about your ex, Lexie Logan."

After a pause, she heard a thump, and a male voice responded. "One second."

"That got his attention," said Justini.

"I figured."

They waited as they heard more thumps, and then the RV door opened. A man in a dingy robe, with oily hair, a stubbled jaw, and puffy eyes, stood inside. He pushed the door open. "Come in."

"Thank you." Justini stepped into the RV, and Carlson followed.

Inside the small space was a narrow, unmade bed, a kitchenette with dirty dishes in the sink, an old TV across from a worn couch with clothes strewn over it, and a trash can overflowing with empty beer cans.

Judd picked up another beer can from the floor and tossed it into the sink. "How can I help you?" He brushed his hair back from his face.

Justini flashed his badge along with Carlson. "We'd like to ask you about Lexie Logan?" asked Justini.

"What about her?" Judd tightened the belt of his robe. "She in trouble?"

"We're investigating the murder of a woman who Miss Logan was supposed to have met." Justini stepped over a dirty sock on the floor.

"I heard about that." He eyed Carlson. "It's true the lady was shot?"

"It is," said Carlson. "When's the last time you saw Miss Logan?"

Judd slid his hands into the pockets of his robe. "After I got out of the joint. I went to see her."

Justini arched his eyebrow. "Really? What happened?"

Judd straightened. "She aimed a gun and threatened me." His eyes sparkled with apparent satisfaction.

Carlson decided she didn't like this guy. And judging by the amount of alcohol in his trash, she questioned whether he'd been drinking that night instead of working. "Could that have something to do with your abuse?"

He jutted out his jaw. "I never touched her."

"The court decided otherwise," said Carlson.

"That's all bullshit."

Justini moved closer to Judd. "The only bullshit around here is you. We know you beat her up. We saw the file. But we're not here about you. We're here about her."

Judd's smug demeanor evaporated.

"You say she waved a gun at you?" asked Justini.

"She did. Told me to leave her alone and not come back."

"Smart lady." Carlson wrinkled her nose when she caught a foul smell and wondered when Judd had last cleaned his dishes. "Did you do as she asked?"

"I did. I wasn't that interested anyway."

"What do you think would have happened if you'd stayed?" asked Justini.

Judd looked between them. "She'd have shot me in cold blood."

Carlson fought not to roll her eyes.

"Is she violent?" asked Justini.

Judd gave a snort. "Sure as hell is. People think I beat her up?" He put his hand on his chest. "You should have seen what she did to me."

Carlson glared at him. "Funny. I don't recall any pictures of you from the hospital. With your busted nose, black eyes and split lip."

Judd shifted on his feet. "That's because they didn't take me to the hospital. Just straight to jail."

"They put makeup on you for your mugshot?" asked Carlson. "Because you looked just fine."

He scowled. "I don't care what I looked like. I was protecting myself. She...she pulled a knife on me."

"Funny," said Carlson. "That wasn't in the report."

"That's because I left it out."

"Why would you do that?" asked Justini.

"Because she threatened me." Judd raised his voice. "She...she told me if I said anything, she'd send her buddy to take care of me."

Justini paused and eyed Carlson. "What buddy?" asked Justini.

"Hell if I know, and I didn't ask. But I know she meant business."

Carlson studied his eyes. "How do you know that?"

Judd hesitated and fiddled with the lapels of his robe. "She told me once that she'd met people on the force. And if she asked them to, they'd take care of me. I didn't believe her. But then her dad got into trouble. Lexie did some digging that no one knew about except me. She told me she'd found a source who could confirm everything her father was denying and who planned to testify against him. Lexie had a cop take care of the threat against her dad. And after our last fight, she told me she'd send that same cop after me if I fought the charges. I believed her."

Carlson set her jaw.

Justini pulled out his notepad and took notes. "You know who this cop is?"

Carlson directed her shock at Justini. Was he buying Judd's ridiculous story?

"Hell no," said Judd. "And I didn't want to know. Still don't."

Justini looked up from his scribbling. "Still?"

Judd looked around as if Lexie might be listening. "When I went to see her when I got out? She told me, if I didn't leave her alone, that same cop could pay me a visit."

Justini arched his eyebrow again. "That's interesting." He aimed an intense look at Carlson. "Don't you think, Carlson?"

Dismayed, Carlson didn't say a word.

•••••••••••

Connor sat in the airport, near baggage claim, watching the crowd. After leaving his office, he and Lexie had stopped by the home of a man who went by the name Rondo. Connor and Ax had busted him twice for stealing and selling stolen goods. Both times, he'd received a reduced sentence because he'd given them decent tips, which had led to the arrest of one drug dealer plus a serial home invader. He became a reliable informant, even though he continued to bend the law. Connor hadn't seen him in a year, but figured Ax still worked with him.

When Rondo saw him, his eyes widened in surprise. Connor had assured him he was only there to conduct business. He'd asked Lexie to stay in the car and talked to Rondo about what he was looking for. Rondo had come through; Connor had paid him a hundred bucks and walked out with a used laptop and charger that had belonged to Rondo's supposed aunt. The aunt had died and left the laptop to Rondo, who hadn't touched it. His aunt had only used it for emails and to search online for recipes, but little else.

To Connor, it was perfect. It was ready to use, had no connection to him or Lexie, and no association with Vista or any of its apps. Plus, they could use Rondo's aunt's email and password, which Rondo had provided, to create a login to Vista once Lexie installed it. It was a win-win. He'd even questioned whether it was necessary to go to the airport, but erring on the side of safety, Lexie chose to stick with the plan.

Sitting outside baggage claim while Lexie installed Vista on the laptop, Connor scanned the crowd. As a detective, people-watching was a good way to pass the time. Plus, he'd learned a lot about individuals by studying their body language. Just by looking at a person's eyes, he could often get a sense if they were lying. He wasn't perfect at it, but he'd honed his skills over the years.

"I'm in," said Lexie, typing on the laptop.

Connor leaned over and saw her open the Omnivista page. Colorful photos of staff popped up on the screen. She scrolled through them.

"You see any names?" he asked.

"Not yet." She sighed. "This is like looking for a needle in a—" She stopped. "Hold on. I think that's Mira." She pointed to a picture of a group of people in a park. "This must be the company picnic."

"Is she with a guy?"

Lexie scrolled through more photos. "Not yet."

Connor sat back and continued to watch the crowd again. When they'd arrived, they'd determined baggage claim was the most suitable spot. People came and went, and no one paid any attention, but Connor stayed aware. He hadn't caught anyone following them since the day they'd left the diner, but that didn't mean they were safe. He'd checked both their cars to ensure there were no trackers and had found none, but he remained vigilant.

A woman's voice came over a loudspeaker cautioning people about unclaimed bags and to report anything suspicious. Nearby, a group of people stood around a cordoned area where international passengers arrived. The doors would slide open, and people would emerge and peruse the crowd, then smile and greet those waiting for them. They came in groups, and the doors slid open again as several more people emerged after leaving customs.

Lexie groaned. "I see pictures of Mira, and there are men in the group, but no names. Hell. I'll look for the Christmas party."

Connor glanced at the computer and looked back at the arriving passengers. One older man emerging through the international gate caught his eye. He was probably in his sixties, with thinning hair and a paunchy belly. He wore a light blue cotton short-sleeved shirt and loose white cotton pants with sandals. He looked as if he'd just stepped off a cruise ship. He carried a white hat, and his gaze darted around as he looked for someone.

Studying the man, Connor sat up. He thought back to the Silva case. The more he watched, the more certain he was that he was looking at Eduardo Silva, Leo's brother. Connor's heart raced as the man approached the end of the cordoned area. He stopped, paused, put on his hat, and smiled. The crowd parted, and Connor caught his breath when he saw who was waiting for Eduardo. It was his niece, Maria Silva.

....

Lexie found the Omnivista Christmas party pictures and flipped through them. She got excited when she found a photo of Nolan Sorrento and his wife, Ramona, with their names added beneath the picture. Hopeful, she kept going and saw other pictures of staff with their significant others. There were several pictures, and she stopped at each one. Mira was in a couple with other people, but no names were mentioned. Lexie scrolled past the Christmas party and, almost ready to give up, she caught a post from Omnivista's annual Innovation Summit. She opened that folder and got lucky. One of the first pictures she saw was of Mira standing with a slender, handsome man. "Connor, look." Beneath it was the caption, "Mira Patel and Rip O'Dell."

"Holy...Connor. It's him." She clicked on the photo and copied it to the laptop. She glanced at Connor and realized he was studying the crowd. "Connor?" Lexie looked too, but saw only a mass of people. "What is it?"

Tense, he stood. "Stay here and don't move. I'll be right back." He walked away.

Frowning, she saw him head toward a section where international travelers arrived. Several people stood outside the doors, waiting for their loved ones. Connor passed a few and stopped. A man in a short-sleeved shirt, wearing a white hat, stood next to a slim woman with bright red lips and long black curly hair, wearing a white pantsuit. Lexie thought of Sasha, who was tall and elegant. This woman was petite, but just as beautiful.

The woman stopped talking to the man with the hat when she saw Connor. Connor said something to her. The man smiled and spoke in response. The woman looked Connor up and down with a penetrating gaze.

Something nagged at Lexie, and she studied the female more carefully. After a second, she cursed. "It can't be," she said under her breath. She went back to the laptop, opened another browser, and typed in *Maria Silva*. Pictures of Leo Silva's daughter instantly filled the screen, and Lexie couldn't believe it. Connor was talking to Maria.

"How is that possible?" whispered Lexie to herself. And who was the man? He bore enough resemblance to Maria that Lexie searched for *Maria Silva Family*. Several photos popped up, mostly of Leo and Trey, but she scrolled through and stopped on a man in a white hat and cursed again. It was the same man standing beside Maria. It was Eduardo Silva.

Lexie stared in shock. What were the odds that Maria and her uncle would be at the airport at the same time as she and Connor? Was it only a coincidence? Did Connor know they would be there? Or had he arranged this meeting when he realized he was going to the airport? But if he had, when did he have the chance?

Lexie thought of Connor's visit with Rondo. Had Connor arranged this meeting while Lexie had been sitting in the car? But why? What were the three of them talking about? Their body language indicated the intensity of their conversation. Both Maria and Eduardo appeared annoyed, and Connor looked angry. He said something, and Maria offered him a smug look. Eduardo smiled again. Connor pointed, and Maria spoke and put her hand on her hip. Then, out of nowhere, she looked over, and her gaze found Lexie's. Lexie froze. She couldn't look away. What else was she supposed to do? Hide behind the laptop?

Connor followed Maria's gaze and said something else, his face tight. Maria looked back, raised the side of her lip, leaned in, and kissed Connor's cheek, leaving lipstick on his skin. He stiffened but didn't pull back. She stepped away, but not before sliding her hand down his arm and brushing her fingers against his. Connor pulled his hand back.

Appearing confident, Eduardo took Maria's elbow, and they turned away from Connor as Maria offered Lexie one more look, and if Lexie were to interpret it, she could only define it with one word—satisfaction.

Chapter Twenty-Two

Connor returned and sat beside Lexie. He asked if she was ready to leave, and she told him she'd found Rip's last name, but with his attention still on the crowd, he barely nodded. She asked him who he'd been talking to, but he was evasive and diverted the subject back to Rip.

While Connor monitored their surroundings, Lexie typed Rip's name into a search engine but found too many Rip O'Dells to be useful. Then she searched his name along with Omnivista's and still had no luck. Wondering if even that was safe, she closed the browser window and debated her next move. Seeing Connor staring at the crowd as if a mama bear might rush out of it and attack them, she pulled the phone Frank had given her from her bag and searched on the laptop for the number of the station where Rem and Daniels worked. She could have called them from her cell, but it was better to contact them via a landline. After reaching the front desk, she waited while the officer redirected the call.

Rem answered on the third ring. "Detective Remalla. I hope your day is going better than mine."

Lexie glanced at Connor. "That's debatable."

"Lexie? That you?"

"It is."

"Don't have your cell?"

"Actually, I do but contacting you on a landline from a burner is safer."

There was a pause. “Now I’m curious. What’s up? How’s it going with Mira Patel?”

Lexie thought of biker man. “Making some progress. That’s why I’m calling. I’m wondering if you and Daniels can run a name for me? I need an address.”

“Sure.” He offered a grunt. “Shoot.”

“It’s Rip O’Dell. I think he was Mira’s boyfriend. He works at Omnivista. I need to talk to him, but have to find him first.”

“You got any other info? How old is he?”

“Based on his photo, I’d put him around forty.” She opened the email on the laptop. “I’m sending you a picture. What’s your email?” Rem gave her his email, and she sent him the picture of Mira and Rip. “It’s coming from a different email address, though.”

Rem was quiet for a second. “Who the heck is Mabel Toothacre?”

“Long story, but I may use that email again, so don’t spam it.”

“I’m not even going to ask. Okay. Let me do some digging, and I’ll get back to you.”

“Thanks, and this is just between you, me, and Daniels.” Connor glanced at her. “And Connor,” she said.

“He still helping you out?”

“He is.” If she’d been alone, she would have asked Rem about the Silvas. “We’ve had some interesting developments.”

“Should I ask over the phone?”

“Probably not. But if you can get me Rip’s info, maybe we can meet and I’ll fill you two in. I’ll buy you a coffee.”

The furrow between Connor’s brows deepened.

“You know I can’t refuse that. I’ll call when I have something.”

“When you do, call this number from a landline. Don’t use your cell.” She ensured he had the number of the cell she was using.

“I’m looking forward to that coffee. I sense there’s a lot to catch up on.”

"You could say that. And hey, Detective Carlson may give you, Daniels, or Lozano a call. I told her you'd vouch for me and my sobriety." She thought about her evening with Miguel. "You can tell her whatever you want."

He picked up on her meaning. "Don't worry about that. We'll tell her the truth. We worked with you through some tough times and had no issues, and we'd do it again."

"I appreciate that. And you might get a call from Karen Grazer from the *California Gazette* too, about the same issue."

"The California Gazette? I'm guessing you're taking the initiative?"

"You bet I am, before this gets any worse."

"I like it. And no problem. I'll let Daniels and Lozano know."

"Thanks, Rem."

"You bet. Just watch your backside."

"You do the same."

"Always. Good thing it's attractive." He chuckled. "Or so I've heard. See ya."

"See ya." Lexie hung up and dropped the phone into her purse. "You ready?" she asked Connor.

Connor scanned the crowd one more time and stood. "Let's go."

Lexie slid the laptop into its own Faraday bag, which she'd purchased when she bought the bags for the cell phones, and put it into her big purse. She stood.

Connor took her elbow. "Stay beside me."

His alertness made Lexie nervous, and she watched the surrounding people as if someone might charge them at any second.

Connor didn't say a word and guided her out of the airport and into the parking lot.

Once they were outside, Lexie couldn't help but breathe a sigh of relief. "Are you going to tell me what that was all about?"

Connor remained on alert. "Nothing for you to worry about."

Lexie stopped. "Don't patronize me. I know that was Maria Silva. And her uncle."

He finally looked at her. "How do you know that?"

"I'm not an idiot. I recognized her and looked her up online. It wasn't hard to find a picture of Eduardo either." She adjusted the strap of her purse on her shoulder. "Did you know they would be here?"

His face clouded. "How the hell would I know they would be in baggage claim outside international arrivals?"

"It's a hell of a coincidence."

He gaped at her. "What are you implying? That I contacted them sometime between leaving my office and arriving here? And asked to meet? What for?"

She threw up her hands. "I don't know. You're the one with a history with the Silvas."

"If I wanted to meet with the Silvas, I'd go to Maria's and knock on the door."

That got Lexie's attention. "You must know her pretty well."

"I spent months undercover with her, Leo, and Trey. So, yeah. I know her."

"You two didn't seem too pleased to see each other."

"We didn't exactly part on good terms."

Lexie wanted to ask what those terms were, but asked a different question. "What did you say to each other?"

"She was meeting her uncle, who had just arrived from El Salvador. I was curious why."

"Did she tell you?"

"He's here for a social visit, which is bullshit."

"You think he's here to help rebuild the family business?"

"Well, he's not here to work on his tan."

"How do you know that?"

He glowered. "Because I know the Silvas. They'll stay quiet publicly, but privately, they're up to no good."

Lexie took a moment to collect her thoughts. "Is it possible that maybe you're too caught up in this? You're pissed Maria Silva got away and now you suspect every move she makes? Maybe this really is a family visit. Maria's on her own now, and she's got to take care of her disabled brother."

His glower deepened. "I know what I'm talking about. I know Maria."

"Just how well do you know her?" Lexie said the words before she could stop herself.

He stared at her with an unreadable expression. "What are you suggesting?" He paused. "Have you heard something?"

She hesitated, but had to answer. "I asked Frank about the Silva case."

He made a derisive snort. "You're a journalist, Lexie. Since when do you listen to rumors and innuendo?"

She pointed toward the airport. "Since you just bumped into the woman you say you hate and she kissed you. You've got her lipstick on your cheek."

He rubbed his cheek with his fingers.

"And she gawked at me like she'd just won the crown at a beauty pageant, and I hadn't made the top ten."

"This has nothing to do with you."

"You sure about that?"

"Forget about Maria Silva, Lexie."

"I could say the same to you, Connor. You're not a cop anymore, remember? If she is up to no good, it's not your job to stop her. It's Ax's."

He stilled. "It's not that simple."

"Isn't it?" She waited, but he didn't answer. "Or is there more to this story?"

He looked away. "We need to go." He turned and headed to their car.

Frustrated, Lexie followed. "Connor."

He kept walking.

"Connor."

He got to the car and turned. "What?"

She walked up beside him. "If you need to handle the Silvas, tell me. Because you can't handle them and Omnivista at the same time."

Connor held her gaze. "I'm not leaving you alone on this."

"I repeat. You can't do both without jeopardizing one or both of us. So, decide now who you want. Maria Silva, or me?" She didn't mean to phrase it like that, but that's how it came out.

He clenched his jaw. "That is a stupid question."

"I don't hear you answering it."

He cursed under his breath and walked to the passenger side. "Get in the car, Lexie."

She unlocked the doors, and still not answering her, he slid into the passenger seat. She tossed her big purse onto the back and got behind the wheel.

He stared out of the windshield. "And I could have called Ax and had him check out Rip O'Dell."

She started the car. "You were preoccupied. Besides, the fewer people involved in this mess, the better. And something tells me Ax is about to get an earful about Eduardo Silva."

"Like you said. I'm not on the force anymore. He'll have to handle it."

Lexie blew out a sharp breath. "Connor, it's okay if you need to refocus your priorities." It was one way of saying *spend more time pursuing Maria Silva*, without actually saying it. Had Connor had feelings for Maria in the past?

"I am not refocusing anything. Let's get back to the case."

She thought about what Frank had told her. "If you're worried about what you promised Frank about helping me, I can talk to him."

He twisted in his seat to face her. "Screw Frank, his rumors and his clients. I committed to this case, and...I'm seeing it through. Okay?"

Lexie noted he'd said he was committed to the case and not her, and she hated how that bothered her. *Get over it, Lex,* she said to herself. *The man's in love with Sasha or Maria, or both. Better to stay clear of that mess.* Wondering how she always fell for the wrong guy, she put the car in reverse. "Okay." She hit the brakes when her phone rang from her purse in the back. She'd left both burners outside of the Faraday bags.

Connor reached behind her into the backseat. "I'll get it." He unbuckled his belt and leaned over.

"It's the cell Frank gave me." He handed it to her. "Thanks." She answered. "This is Lexie."

"Hey, it's Carlson. I'm calling you from my desk phone, just in case. Are you okay to talk?"

A plane flew overhead. "I should be."

"I thought I'd let you know I just saw your ex."

Lexie slid her car back into park. "You saw Judd?" She glanced at Connor.

"We did. You should know that he says you threatened him. He told us you were working with a cop who took care of a witness to your dad's crimes, and that cop would take care of him too, if Judd didn't leave you alone."

Lexie sat in stunned silence. "That's absurd. None of that is true. I didn't threaten him."

"You held a gun on him?"

Lexie muttered an expletive. "After he got out of prison, he came to see me. I scared him away with the gun you found at my place and told him to leave me alone. But that's it."

"You realize how this sounds. Did you know a cop on the force back then?"

Lexie dropped her head back onto the headrest. "No one who I could ask to threaten a witness to Dad's crimes or my abusive boyfriend." She looked at Connor again, who was frowning at her.

"What about Connor Diamond?"

Lexie shut her eyes briefly and reopened them. "He was the responding officer the night Judd was arrested. I didn't see him again until I lost my memory and became a murder suspect."

"Okay. I had to ask."

She lifted her head. "God. I bet Justini is all over this."

"Justini knows that anything your ex says has to be taken with a grain of salt. But it raises the question, why did Judd lie? How does he know enough to point the finger at your association with Diamond? It's like he knows we suspect you have an accomplice."

Lexie sat up. "You think someone got to him?"

"Your ex is living in an RV parked in his mother's driveway. He was sleeping in from a likely hangover when Justini and I arrived. And his mother holds a helluva grudge against you. My guess is Judd does too. He's ripe for the picking if someone offered him money to make you look guilty."

"Judd would take it in a second."

"That's my assessment."

"Great. Now what?"

"I'm going to dig into Judd's financials. See if I can find any extra money. You two going to see Edna?"

"Eventually."

"I'd advise against it. Justini and I went to the hospital, but she refused to talk. Doctor suggested we give her some time."

"Yeah. I heard. She's scared. And I don't blame her."

"Hopefully, she'll reconsider. By the way, I may have a hypnotist lined up, if you're still interested in jogging your memory."

"I am. You know when?"

"I'm hoping sooner rather than later. I'll let you know."

"That's great. Thanks."

"You have any other updates, keep me informed."

Lexie thought of Rip O'Dell. If she told Carlson about him, though, Carlson would tell her to back off and let her and Justini handle it. "I will. And thanks for the heads-up on Judd."

"You got it. I'll be in touch."

"Me too." Lexie said goodbye and hung up.

"What's that about?" asked Connor.

Lexie told him about what Carlson had said.

"Do you really think you should be talking to her? How do you know she's not feeding you whatever she thinks will get you to open up?"

"Because she came over earlier and we had a heart-to-heart. I told her about Zephyr's warnings and Omnivista. And she gave me my phone back."

Connor smirked. "That's the oldest trick in the book. She wants you to trust her."

"I realize that, but I need her too. I'm not the only one doing the talking. She told me what they have against me, which isn't much, and she just told me about Judd." Lexie set her phone on the center console. "She knows I didn't kill Mira. She even suggested a hypnotherapist to help jog my memories."

"How much you want to bet she'll be there during the session?"

"Who cares if she is? I didn't kill anyone. And if it helps to find biker man, and whoever helped him, I have to try."

"You didn't tell her about Rip."

She slumped. "I couldn't risk her and Justini getting to him before we do. They could freak him out. Besides, she already told me she and Justini spoke to Mira's coworkers and got nowhere. Now it's our turn. We'll talk to him first, and then I'll tell Carlson."

Connor sat back in his seat. "She won't be thrilled, and you might break this so-called circle of trust."

"If Rip O'Dell knows about whatever Mira took from Omnivista, it's a risk worth taking. He may not talk to the cops, but he might talk to us."

"We have to find him first." He buckled his seatbelt again. "Any ideas of what to do while we wait?"

Lexie stared out the windshield as another plane flew overhead. She thought again about what Carlson had told her, and an idea popped into her head. "Actually, I do." She put the car back into reverse and backed out of the parking space. "You said you could call Ax if we need something?"

"I can. What are you thinking?"

She headed toward the lot's exit. "Can he get Mira Patel's address?"

"What for?"

"Carlson's right about jogging my memory, but why wait for a hypnotherapist?" She glanced over at him. "Maybe it's time I retrieved it on my own."

He squinted. "You want to go to Patel's to remember what happened that night? What if you weren't even there?"

"There's one way to find out. And even if I wasn't, it can't hurt to learn more about Mira." She stopped to wait for another car to back out. "You think it's a bad idea?"

After a pause, he reached for his cell. "I'll call him."

Chapter Twenty-Three

LEXIE PARKED AT THE curb. "This is it."

Across the street was a small, one-story brick house surrounded by shrubs and big, leafy trees. A paved walkway cut through the overgrown grass, leading up to a porch and the front door.

Connor eyed the house. "The good news is, from what Ax learned, she lived alone. The cops searched it but found nothing linked to her murder."

Lexie surveyed the property. "It's quiet."

"It's not the crime scene, but it's still part of the investigation." He looked at her. "Does it ring any bells?"

Lexie shook her head. "No." She unbuckled her belt. "Let's get closer."

Connor took her arm. "Whoa. Hold up. What exactly is your plan?"

She shrugged. "I can walk up to the door, can't I? Ring the bell?"

"Sure, but what if someone answers?"

"I'll ask to look around."

He paused. "And if no one answers?"

She opened her door. "Let's just play it by ear."

"Lexie." He unbuckled his belt and got out of the car. "I don't have to tell you the implications if we get caught snooping around the murder victim's home."

"No, you don't." She opened the back door and dug through her purse. Finding the items she wanted, she pulled them out and tucked them into her jacket pocket.

"What's that?" asked Connor.

She closed the back door. "A precaution."

He shook his head and followed her up to the front door.

She knocked and waited. "Let's see what unfolds." He waited with her, and when no one answered, she knocked again.

"No one's home." Connor looked through a window.

"See anything?"

"It's dark inside."

Lexie stepped down the porch steps. "Let's go in the back." She took the stone walkway to the side of the house.

"Hold up."

Lexie got to the back fence and opened it.

"Wait a second." Connor took her arm again. "Are you sure about this? It's a hell of a risk."

"I'm fighting for my life, Connor. It's time I took a few risks."

He hesitated.

"I just want to look around. See if it jogs any memories. If not, we'll leave, okay?"

He cursed under his breath.

"What would Ax do in this situation?"

He snorted. "Hell. He told me to do this very thing. I told him to piss off."

Lexie opened the gate. "I'm liking Ax more and more." She walked through the gate and turned back. "Are you coming?"

He cursed again and walked through the gate.

Her heart rate picking up, Lexie walked down the side yard of the house. Glancing into the windows, she saw a dark interior with furniture. At the back was a garden that needed pruning and an outdoor seating area with a grill. She stepped up to the back porch and peered through a window. There was a tidy kitchen and breakfast table, and the back of the home was quiet. She tried the back door, but it was locked.

Connor peered through another window. "The good news is I don't see an alarm panel anywhere."

"Good." She tried to open a window.

"But that doesn't mean there isn't an alarm."

"Doesn't matter, because it's locked."

"Now I know why you're a superior journalist. You'll do anything for a story."

"I'll do anything for the truth."

Connor eyed another window and walked over to it. "Me too." He tried the window, and it creaked when it opened. He froze.

Lexie froze too, and waited to hear the blaring of an alarm, but nothing happened.

Still holding the window, Connor relaxed. "You sure about this? Once we go in, there's no turning back."

Lexie pulled the latex gloves she'd taken from her purse out of her pocket. She handed two to Connor. "Put these on."

"Guess I have my answer." He let go of the window, which remained in place, and put on the gloves.

Lexie put hers on too. "We'll go quick. I just want to look around."

Connor yanked on the window, which opened with reluctance. Once it was high enough, he lifted a leg and slipped inside the house. He turned and offered his hand to Lexie, who took it and stepped through the window and into Mira Patel's home.

They stood just outside the kitchen, and Lexie took a second to absorb the sounds and sights of the small home. It hit her that this was where Mira had spent her last hours before heading to the warehouse to meet Lexie and her death. After getting her bearings, Lexie walked around, hoping something familiar would spark in her mind, but nothing did. She sensed this was her first time in this home.

"Anything?" asked Connor.

"Nothing." She walked into the living room. Everything was neat and tidy, but dusty.

"Nothing's disturbed," said Connor. "No signs of breaking and entering."

Lexie stopped at a desk and opened the various drawers, noting the fingerprint dust on the wood. The cops had obviously been there. Not sure what she was looking for, she flipped through the various papers, folders, and notes, but nothing suspicious stood out.

Connor headed into the bedroom. "She was organized. Everything is in its place."

Lexie closed the desk drawers and joined him in Mira's bedroom. There were family photos on the walls and a colorful landscape painting behind the bed. She walked into the dark bathroom and saw two sinks and two mirrors, but only one sink had toiletries around it. Lexie looked under the cabinets but found little and closed them.

"Hey," said Connor from the bedroom. "Look at this."

Lexie went back into the bedroom and saw Connor standing in front of the closet. She walked over. "What is it?"

He pointed. "Look how organized she is."

Lexie noted the clothes were arranged by color, the shoes were all in clear shoeboxes perfectly stacked on shelves, and nothing was on the floor. "I wish my closet looked like this."

"Everything has its place, but look at that." He gestured toward the top shelf with shoeboxes.

"What about it?"

"There." He walked closer and pulled down a cardboard shoebox that had been tucked behind a clear one. "Why are all the other shoeboxes the same, but this one is different? That doesn't jibe with Mira's obvious need for continuity."

"Bring it in here." Lexie returned to the bedroom, and Connor set the shoebox on the bed and opened it. She sucked in a breath when she didn't see shoes, but newspaper articles instead. She reached for one. "What is this?"

Connor pulled one out and eyed it. "This is about the Rook case."

Lexie scanned hers. "This one too. I wrote this."

They pulled out more articles. They were all about Damien Rook and his secret society, many of them penned by Lexie. Lexie also found notes that listed her podcast dates.

"She was gathering information about you." Connor paused as he scanned another article. "I think she was vetting you."

Lexie scanned another article. "How did the cops miss this?"

"Someone must have thought it was another shoebox. Rookie mistake." Connor pulled out a photograph. "That's you."

Lexie took the photo from him and saw herself outside her duplex. "Was she following me?"

"Maybe." He pulled out another picture. "Is that Remalla and Daniels?"

Lexie studied it. It was from a diner where she'd met Rem and Daniels to discuss what they knew about the Rook case. "Hell. She'd been watching me this whole time?"

"She wanted to be sure she could trust you." He pulled out a piece of paper. "And not just you." He held it out to her.

She took it and dropped her jaw. Written in pencil was her name, along with the names Aaron Remalla and Gordon Daniels. Their addresses and phone numbers were listed too. Lexie's name was circled in marker, though.

"Looks like she was vetting all of you," said Connor with a measured gaze, "and she picked you."

Lexie's heart hammered against her ribs. Mira had been planning to blow the whistle on Omnivista, but she needed someone she could trust to help her, and after weeks of careful study and observation, and despite what Lexie's father had done to her, she'd picked Lexie. Knowing that made her chest tighten. Mira had trusted her, but Omnivista had gotten to her first.

Lexie lowered the paper. "We have to find out who did this to her."

Connor put the articles, photos, and papers back into the box. "We will."

"What should we do with this stuff? The cops should know about it."

"Put it back where we found it. Maybe you can put a bug in Carlson's ear about searching the house again."

"How am I supposed to do that without tipping her off that we were here?"

He picked up the box. "We'll think of something."

A car door slammed, and hearing faint talking from outside, Lexie ran over to the blinds and peered out. Facing the front of the house, she saw a woman with a phone to her ear stepping up the walkway. She stepped back from the window. "Someone's coming."

Connor brought the box back to the closet and put it on the shelf. "Come here."

Hearing footsteps on the porch and a key in the lock, Lexie ran over to the closet as Connor pulled her inside it. He closed the door, and they pushed themselves behind the clothes. Hearing the front door open and a woman's voice, Lexie moved deeper into the closet and found herself pressed into Connor's chest. He put his arms around her and pulled her close, and she buried her head in his neck. Her skin warmed at his closeness and the smell of his aftershave.

Lexie barely breathed as the woman's voice became louder as she came into the bedroom. It was obvious she was still on her phone.

"I know I shouldn't do this, Vicki," she said, "but I want my sweater back. If I wait, they may take all her clothes, and it will be gone."

Lexie heard a drawer open and close.

"No one will know. I have her key, so why not use it? I'll be in and out." Another drawer closed, and the woman laughed. "Don't be silly. I don't believe in ghosts. I'm her neighbor. Mira wouldn't care about this. Stop trying to scare me."

Lexie heard the woman walking through the bedroom. "Darn it. Where is it?" There was a pause. "Oh, wait. The closet."

Lexie instinctively pressed harder against Connor, and his arms tightened around her. The closet doors opened, and like a child pretending she was invisible, she closed her eyes and pressed her face into Connor's shirt.

She heard hangers sliding across the bar. "There it is."

Lexie peeked from the back corner and saw a hand reach in and pull a sweater from a hanger. "What a relief."

The woman stepped back and closed the closet door. Lexie let out a long-held breath and suspected Connor was doing the same.

"I'm so glad I found it. Thanks for staying on the phone with me, Vick. I needed your support." She paused. "Yes. It is a little spooky around here, knowing Mira is dead."

Lexie prayed the woman would leave, but she kept talking. "She has some nice things, though. I wonder who is going to get it all."

Standing in the dark closet, tucked behind Mira's clothes and pressed against Connor, Lexie started to sweat. She could feel the heat of his skin and his muscular chest and was certain he could feel her pounding heart.

"You know," said the woman, "Mira had this great blouse. I wonder..."

Connor reached up and scratched the wall. The sound was soft but audible. The woman stopped talking, and Lexie imagined her listening. Connor scratched the wall again.

"Wait. I hear something," said the woman.

Lexie calmly jostled some clothes.

"Um, I think I'd better go."

Lexie said a prayer of thanks.

"Maybe this ghost stuff isn't so far-fetched." The woman's voice became distant. "Don't start, Vick. I wasn't actually going to take the blouse." The front door opened and closed, the lock turned, and the house went quiet again.

Lexie didn't move, and neither did Connor. After several seconds, Connor pushed some clothes aside. "I think it's safe."

Lexie tried to step back, but the cramped space prevented it, and they moved together past the clothes. Connor pushed the closet door open, and Lexie stepped into the cool air of the bedroom. "Is she gone?" she whispered.

His cheeks red, and pulling on his shirt, Connor peered out the window blinds. "She's headed back to the street."

"Thank God. That was close."

"I'm amazed she didn't see us."

"She was too fixated on the sweater and stealing her neighbor's blouse."

"Talk about no respect for the dead." He eyed her. "You okay?"

Lexie did her best not to think about Connor's body pressed against hers. "Yeah. You?"

"That got my heart rate up."

"I'm sure you could tell mine was racing."

"I could." He stared at her, and she stared back. "It was getting hot in there," he said.

She swallowed and smoothed her hair. "It was."

They held a gaze until Lexie looked away. "We need to get out of here."

"I'm right behind you."

Lexie returned to the window, stepped through it to the back porch, and Connor joined her. He closed the window, and watching to ensure the neighbor was gone, they returned to Lexie's car. Lexie pulled off her gloves, opened the back door of her car, and heard Frank's burner phone ringing. Wondering who was calling, she pulled it out and answered. "This is Lexie." Connor handed her his gloves, and she tucked them into her purse.

"Lex, it's Rem. I've got that information you requested."

Lexie closed the back door. She noted how careful he was with what he said. "Are you calling from your cell?"

"I am, and since you're squirrely about that, I figured I shouldn't say much."

"Good idea." She got into the front seat and shut the door. "You want to meet? Get that coffee?"

"That's a great idea. Daniels is with me. How about we go to that diner around the corner?"

"Around the corner?" She glanced at Connor.

"Yeah, and you can tell me and Daniels why you and Diamond just left a certain someone's home, wearing gloves."

Lexie stiffened and looked up and down the street. A flash of headlights from a car parked down from hers on the opposite side of the road made her stomach tighten. "How the hell—?"

"You should know by now that our sixth sense is the seventh wonder of the world."

"Eighth," said Daniels through the phone. "There are already seven."

"Whatever," said Rem. "Head down the street and take a right at the stop sign. Go to the first light. There's a sandwich shop on the corner. We'll meet you there." He hung up.

Flummoxed, Lexie lowered the phone. “We’ve been made.”

Chapter Twenty-Four

Lexie sat in a booth in the sandwich shop's back corner, and Connor slid in next to her. It didn't take long for the bell to ring when the door opened again. Rem, with his familiar long dark hair, wearing a T-shirt under a jacket and blue jeans, and Daniels, with his short blond hair gelled back, in a long-sleeved shirt, a jacket and pants, sauntered over. They were an imposing pair, dedicated to their jobs and fiercely loyal to each other and their loved ones, and despite each of them having been through hell and back, they maintained their strong bond and good-natured humor. Lexie was glad they were on her side.

They approached the booth, and Lexie raised her hand. "Before you start, turn your cell phones off."

They looked at each other. Rem shrugged, and they pulled out their cells, turned them off and slid into the booth across from Lexie and Connor. A server approached, and they ordered drinks.

Daniels spoke to Connor. "I didn't expect to see you again until the next baseball game."

"Things change," said Connor.

"That they do," added Rem.

"How'd you know we'd be at Mira's?" asked Lexie.

Rem scratched his jaw. "After I talked to you, Lozano called us into his office. He was talking to Detective Carlson on the phone."

Daniels adjusted the sleeve of his jacket. "She asked a lot of questions about our experience working with you on the Rook case. We sang your praises."

"I appreciate that." Lexie hesitated. "Did you have to mention Miguel?"

"It didn't come up," said Rem. He glanced at Daniels. "Right?"

"Nope," said Daniels. "Didn't come up."

"Glad to hear it," added Connor.

Lexie didn't know how to interpret that and didn't ask. "Me too."

"And when she was done, we asked a few questions of our own," said Rem.

"Where was Justini in all of this?" asked Lexie.

Daniels glanced at the menu. "He wasn't on the call."

"That's interesting," said Connor.

Lexie nudged him. "I told you. Carlson is on my side."

"Maybe," offered Connor. He spoke to Daniels. "What'd you ask her?"

"We wanted to know what she had on Lexie, and based on what she told us, it isn't a lot." He eyed Lexie. "But your ex and your dad didn't help much."

Lexie went still. "Yeah. Carlson conveniently went silent on that."

"That's because she's not telling you everything." Connor leaned back as the server brought them water and poured coffee for Rem and Lexie.

Rem reached for the sugar. "Nothing your father or your ex said proves anything, but it's keeping Justini on your rear end."

Daniels set his menu down. "How come you didn't tell us about what happened at Louie's?"

Lexie added cream to her coffee. "Because you two are not on the case."

"You were almost killed," said Rem.

Connor drank some water and put his glass down. "The assailant went after Edna, Mira Patel's friend, who Lexie was there to meet. He didn't go after Lexie. I chased him into the alley, but someone was waiting, and they drove off."

"So there's two of them?" Rem added cream to his coffee.

"Yes." Lexie stirred her coffee. "And the one who came after Edna? I recognized him as one of my attackers from the night Mira died."

"Carlson mentioned that," added Rem, after sipping some coffee. "She said you hoped that meant your memory might start to come back."

"After the phone call," said Daniels, "Rem and I spoke to Lozano. It's obvious this case is way bigger than we thought. Carlson mentioned Omnivista and its potential reach but didn't go into detail. But we know how you work, Lexie."

"If anyone's got the scoop, it's you," said Rem. "You've got Carlson and Justini scrambling, and you, Connor, are giving Justini fits. Carlson subtly mentioned that he doesn't like you."

Connor rested his elbows on the table. "The feeling's mutual."

"He's thinking you're some sort of accomplice," said Daniels.

"That's nonsense," said Lexie.

"But you're right about the implications of this case," said Connor. "It goes way deeper than a murder investigation."

Rem nodded. "That's why, when we spoke with Lozano and figured you were trying to stir your memory banks, we thought you might go to the places that could trigger it."

"I suggested the warehouse where Mira died," said Daniels, "but Rem wanted to go to Mira's place first."

"After a rousing rock, paper, scissors battle, I won, and we went to Mira's." Rem sipped more coffee. "And as usual, I was right."

Daniels smirked at him and regarded Lexie and Connor. "So, what'd you find?"

Connor sat up. "Just so you know, it was my idea to go in. Not Lexie's."

Lexie gaped at him.

Rem chuckled, and Daniels smiled. "I hope you lied better than that when you were undercover," said Rem.

"We've worked with Lexie too long to believe that." Daniels grabbed a napkin from a dispenser on the table.

Lexie had to wonder if they knew about Connor's assignment with the Silva investigation.

"But we appreciate your loyalty, Diamond," added Rem. "It's good to know Lexie's in safe hands."

Connor lowered his voice. "Then I can assume this stays between us?"

"Just like this table. But we need to know the details." Rem studied the menu as the server reappeared to take their orders. He ordered a BLT with fries; Daniels and Lexie ordered a salad, and Connor ordered a chicken sandwich with chips.

Daniels handed his menu to the server. "After all we've heard, we have to assume that there is some connection between the Rook and Omnivista, especially with this mysterious Lynx."

"And when we pulled the file on Rip O'Dell, it made it more interesting." Rem put his napkin on his lap.

Lexie sucked in her breath. "Did you tell Carlson about O'Dell?"

Daniels shook his head. "No. I'm guessing you haven't either."

"No." She tilted her head toward Connor. "We want to talk to him first."

"What did you learn about him?" asked Connor.

Rem pulled a folded piece of paper from his pocket and slid it across the table. Lexie opened it and saw a photo of Rip's face. She scanned the report.

Connor did the same. "He was arrested for assault?"

"Two years ago," said Daniels, "but the charges were dropped."

"He's been working for Omnivista for four years," said Rem. He regarded Lexie. "Why do you think he was having a relationship with Mira?"

"Edna told me before she was attacked."

"How'd you find Edna?" asked Daniels.

Lexie paused.

"She has a source," said Connor. "Calls himself Zephyr."

Lexie leaned in. "He contacted me after I got home from the hospital. Told me he'd worked with Mira at Omnivista, and she was going to spill Omnivista's secrets."

Rem arched his eyebrow. "What secrets?"

Lexie rested her elbows on the table and intertwined her fingers. "If I tell you, there's no going back. You'll be down the rabbit hole with me and Connor."

"Did you tell Carlson?" asked Daniels.

"I did, but I'm not sure how much she believes me."

Connor kept his voice low. "Omnivista is a dangerous corporation, and Patel was going to expose its crimes. She planned to tell Lexie everything. That's what we found at her home. Lexie's articles about the Rook case and photos of you two, and Lexie. Mira had your names, addresses and phone numbers."

"She was vetting us," added Lexie, "trying to determine who to go to with what she had. She got killed first. But the information is still out there. She hid it, and Omnivista is looking for it, and that's why I think Edna was attacked. She must know something, or they're worried she does."

Daniels leaned up and rested his elbows on the table. "Now I know we need to be involved."

"Nolan Sorrento will kill to protect himself and his company, and has the clout, power, and ability to do it." Connor waved his hand.

"And who knows what this Lynx could do? If they get cornered, they'll attack."

Rem glanced at Daniels. "Sounds like another day on the job."

"I knew it had been quiet for too long," replied Daniels. "Tell us what you know."

Lexie took a deep breath and told them about Omnivista, Nolan Sorrento, Mira and Zephyr, and Project Prometheus One and Two. During her explanation, the server brought them their food, and they ate while she talked.

When she was done, Rem rubbed his shoulder and whistled. He'd barely touched his BLT. "And I thought Rook was bad."

Daniels stabbed some lettuce with his fork. "Rook was a powerful man, like Sorrento. You think he was involved with Sorrento and the development of Prometheus?"

"That group runs in the same circles." Connor ate a chip. "They knew each other, and this Lynx knows them both. I'd say Rook was aware of it, but Sorrento runs the show. He's the one pulling the strings. Eliza Thorne, who runs Prometheus and who was Patel's boss, is a close second."

Rem popped a fry into his mouth. "So we can't trust our phones or computers?"

Lexie poked at her salad with her fork. "Anything linked to Vista or any of its apps is a hard no. Connor and I use burners to communicate. And it's important to use a messaging app that's encrypted and deletes the messages after they're read. And don't keep your notes on the computer."

Connor pointed. "And be careful around others' devices too, and any home devices or wearables. They're listening."

"Hell," said Daniels, "Marjorie and I just bought a Prometheus device."

"Get rid of it," said Lexie. "Or at least unplug it. And be careful what you say to her. Her phone could be compromised too."

"She's got a Vista, so I know it is." Daniels shot a look at Rem. "What do you think, partner?"

Rem was chewing on a piece of bacon from his sandwich. "I'm thinking we should have kicked Lexie out of your car that day in the garage outside Pinnacle Properties."

Lexie recalled that day. She'd been hot on the story of missing protesters who opposed a recent development going up in a low-income part of town. Lexie wanted the scoop. She'd already met Daniels and Rem on a previous case when, on a separate story, she'd followed them to the small town of Elmwood and had almost gotten killed. Knowing they were on the protester case, she'd hounded them, which included surprising them in the garage outside Pinnacle's offices, until they agreed to share information with her. It was that case that had led them all to Damien Rook.

She snorted. "If you'd done that, you'd still be chasing Rook."

Rem narrowed his eyes, Daniels rolled his, and Connor smiled.

"So, now what?" asked Rem. "We start writing letters to each other to communicate?"

"It's not quite that bad," said Lexie.

"But close," added Connor. "You need burners. To talk to each other and to us."

"And be careful what you say around other people," said Lexie. "Lozano, too."

"What about our computers?" asked Daniels. "We still have work to do and reports to make."

"Just be careful what you say." Lexie put her fork down. "Like this Rip O'Dell. Don't mention him until we talk to him. If the biker man knows what's up, he'll target Rip too." She paused. "You have a slight advantage because you're not assigned to this case. Carlson and Justini will be the obvious ones to watch. But you'll still have to be cautious."

"About Rip O'Dell," said Connor. "You said something about his report got your attention. What was it?" He held up the report on Rip. "Assault is lousy, but not earth-shattering. And it was two years ago."

"It was that combined with where he worked before." Rem ate another fry.

Lexie wiped her fingers on her napkin. "Where?"

"For a tech company called BetaWerks." Daniels chewed a bite of salad and set his fork down. "Rip O'Dell was the COO."

"So?" asked Lexie.

Rem swallowed a bite of his sandwich. "BetaWerks was owned by Rook Enterprises."

Holding half his sandwich, Connor cursed.

Lexie dropped her head into her palm. "God. This is such a mess." She looked up. "What does that mean?"

"Speaking of messes, quick question." Rem licked ketchup off his finger. "Anyone in the market for a housekeeper?"

Daniels shot a look at his partner. "Seriously? You're bringing Greta up *now*?"

"Who's Greta?" asked Connor.

"My cousin," answered Rem. "She's working for a housekeeping service and is looking for clients. She does a great job, and I'm trying to help her out." He pointed at Daniels. "He refuses to use her."

Daniels huffed. "She's been arrested twice for shoplifting and got fired from her last job for stealing office supplies."

Rem scoffed. "I told you she returned all the stuff. She did community service for the shoplifting and paid her dues. I've never had a problem with her."

"Maybe that's because you're cousins." Daniels pushed his plate back.

"She's great at cleaning the house. She's got the arms and shoulders of an elite swimmer, and she's taller than me."

"What does that have to do with anything?" asked Daniels. "Other than it's best not to confront her if she pockets my watch. I'm not hiring a kleptomaniac to clean my home."

Rem's shoulders fell. "That's a little harsh."

Lexie was used to these verbal spars between the partners. "Can we focus, please? I think stopping Omnivista and finding who killed Mira and almost me is the priority over Greta."

Connor ate his last chip and dropped his crumpled napkin onto his plate. "Tell you what. We get through this alive, clear Lexie's name, and stop Sorrento and Prometheus, I'll give Greta a try. Cleaning isn't my strong suit."

"You're on," said Rem. "Thanks, Diamond." He eyed Daniels. "See? Was that so hard?"

"Can we get back to the subject, please?" asked Daniels.

"Is Rip a good guy or a bad guy?" asked Lexie.

"No way to know until you talk to him," said Rem. "But be careful when you do. If he's working with Sorrento, he could rat you out to your biker man."

"Or, he was Mira's friend," said Daniels, "and he may know where she hid her evidence."

"Looks like we're going to have to play this carefully," said Connor. "Any chance you'll let me talk to him and you hang back?" he asked Lexie.

Lexie scoffed. "Hell no. I need to speak with him. If he was on Mira's side, he'll know she was coming to me for help."

"And if he betrayed her?" asked Connor.

Lexie regarded the men at the table. Determined to learn the truth, she pulled her credit card from her purse pocket and set it on the edge of the table. "Let's go find out."

• • • • • • • • • •

Eliza Thorne sat at her desk, speaking on the phone. Her office door abruptly opened, and Nolan stomped inside, his face tense. Wendy, her assistant, stood behind him, her eyes wide.

"I'll have to call you back." Eliza hung up and stood. "Nolan."

His face taut, he stopped in front of her desk. "We need to talk."

Eliza waved at Wendy. "It's okay, Wendy. Hold my calls, please."

"Yes, ma'am." Wendy closed the door behind her.

Nolan spoke tersely. "I need to know what's happening."

"About what?"

His cheeks reddened. "That woman is in the hospital. Does she know something?"

"You mean Edna, Mira's friend? Don't worry about her. She's not talking."

"But what does she know?"

"I'm not sure she knows anything. Nothing indicates Mira told her what her plans were."

"So we're no closer to finding that drive?"

Eliza remained patient. It was important during Nolan's outbursts. "No. Not yet. But I'm hopeful."

"I'm so glad. But hope won't get you out of prison if that information falls into the wrong hands."

"I'm aware of the implications, but my contact assures me we're getting closer."

He raised his voice. "Care to elaborate?"

"We're monitoring the situation. We know Logan is looking for the drive. We believe she's attempting to recall her meeting with Mira. If she succeeds…"

Nolan shot out his hand. "We're screwed."

"Not if we can stop her first."

"How do you plan to do that? You already told me Logan's been successful in avoiding Prometheus."

"She has, but sometimes the old-school ways work better than the new ones."

"But how the hell is she doing it?"

"She and her investigator are using burners and avoiding anything Vista. It's effective, but not foolproof. P2, though, will help solve those issues."

He leaned over her desk. "Then we need to move the timetable up for P2."

Eliza shook her head. "We're already pushing our people to the—"

"Don't you understand what's at stake?" he yelled.

She held his gaze but didn't yell back. "Of course, but rolling out P2 before it's ready could be disastrous. We need to complete our testing."

He pointed. "If Lexie Logan gets to that drive before us, it's over. And if you think Lynx is going down without crucifying us, you're delusional."

"No one is going down, Nolan. I've got it under control."

"And what about that damn Rook investigation? Any word there?"

"They've made no progress regarding Lynx, and I doubt they will. And I'm monitoring Carlson and Justini's progress. Lexie Logan is still their primary suspect. My source is keeping me informed, and my man in the field is ready to go at a moment's notice. We're ready, Nolan. Edna is too scared to talk, and if Logan's memories return, we'll stop her. No matter what it takes."

"She's working with that damned investigator."

"We'll stop him too."

He jammed his hands into his pockets. "How do you plan to stop both of them without implicating us?"

Eliza smoothed her skirt. "We'll have to give the cops what they want. The person or persons who killed Mira."

He scowled again. "The more Logan digs, the closer she gets. Now Logan can say she was threatened, and Edna was attacked right in front of her. The longer this goes on, the more likely the police are to believe her."

"Logan's ex put it out there that Lexie has a friend on the force who is her accomplice. And her father didn't help his daughter's case either."

"That ex is about as reliable as my deadbeat stepbrother, and the father is a felon. Not exactly stalwart testimony."

"All we needed was to cast doubt on Logan's story, and it's working. So, when the time comes and they find her dead from an overdose because of her guilt over killing Mira, and find the murder weapon with her prints on it, it will all fall into place."

"That should have been done the night Mira died, then we wouldn't be dealing with any of this."

"And we'd have no idea where to find that drive. The only logical explanation is that Logan knows where it is. She just can't remember."

Nolan's cheeks turned redder. "And how are you going to stop her when she does? You don't even know where she is! And how did she find Edna?" He pulled his hands out of his pockets. "Or know to use burners and avoid Vista?"

Eliza took a deep breath. It was moments like these that she wondered how Nolan ran a billion-dollar corporation with such success. She closed the folder on her desk. This was the conversation she'd been hoping to avoid, and she braced for the reaction. "We believe she has a source."

He went still. "A what?"

"Someone who's familiar with Prometheus and who knew Mira. We're working on finding him or her."

His jaw clenched. "How long have you known this?"

"It became apparent once Logan started taking precautions to avoid Prometheus."

"And I'm just now hearing it?"

"That's because there's nothing you can do. I'm—"

"Handling it?" he yelled. "I keep hearing that instead of, 'it's handl ed.'"

"We'll find the source. The good news is that if this person had anything concrete or knew where the drive was, Logan would have already gone to the authorities. He's helping her only because she can be his eyes and ears. If he comes out into the open, he's doomed, and he knows it."

Nolan jammed his hands back into his pockets and paced. "I want P2's timetable pushed up. We need it to find this source."

"Nolan, I—"

He whirled on her. "You what? You disagree? There are too many ways this can all go wrong. I don't care what you have to do to get P2 ready, but get it done."

She scrambled to think. "We suspect we know where she's going next. Based on her movements and attempts to revive her memory, logically she'll return to the crime scene or talk to another friend of Mira's. It's what I'd do."

He stopped pacing. "What friend?"

"Possibly Rip O'Dell. Edna could have told her about Mira's connection to him."

He turned toward her. "Rip?"

"Yes, we're monitoring it. Based on what happens there, we'll determine what to do next, but if we wait it out, I think we'll get what we need, and this will be over sooner than you think."

He studied her with a piercing gaze. "You've got forty-eight hours. This doesn't get *handled* by then, I expect a full rollout of P2 as soon as possible. Do you understand?"

She held his gaze. "I do." She thought of the phone call she'd just received that Nolan had interrupted. "There's something else you should know."

His eyes glimmered, and the muscle in his jaw clenched again.

"Prometheus has picked up chatter about a newspaper article coming out in the *California Gazette*. Lexie spoke to a reporter, Karen Grazer, about Mira being a whistleblower. Grazer is following up and writing the article. It could be published as soon as tomorrow."

Nolan's stare darkened. "What are we doing about it?"

"Nothing. It's an article. It will get some attention, but Vista won't circulate it. Other papers may pick it up, but if we offer no comment—"

He erupted. "That's your solution?"

She leaned back. "Nolan, it's just an article..."

"Kill it."

"I'd advise against that."

He lowered his voice and spoke slowly. "Kill it, or you can explain to Lynx how we've become the bullseye, and not the dart."

"You kill it, and it only garners more interest. Things like this can get bigger if you fight them. We simply deny the story and continue to blame Logan. And when she ends up dead with the murder weapon beside her, the article will be forgotten."

Still glaring, Nolan never took his eyes off her.

Eliza didn't flinch. "I can manage this. It's what you pay me to do."

He pulled his hands from his pockets and jabbed his finger at her. "You better. Because if you fail, and this gets any bigger, *I'm* the one who will handle *you*." He stared at her without blinking before he turned and strode toward the door. "Keep me apprised." He walked out of her office and slammed the door shut behind him.

Chapter Twenty-Five

Lexie sat in her car across from Rip O'Dell's house. Connor sat in the passenger seat. "How long do you think we should wait?" she asked. They'd been watching for almost an hour.

Connor glanced at his watch. "You know the hours they keep at Omnivista. I doubt he's home." He looked back at the house. "There's been no movement."

"How can you tell? All the blinds are closed."

"True, but you'd still expect to see a light go on or off."

Lexie rested her elbow on the armrest. "I'm giving it fifteen minutes. Then I'm knocking on the door."

"Hold up." Connor pointed as a car stopped in front of the house.

Lexie instinctively scooted lower. "Is it him?"

Connor watched. "No."

Lexie sat up. The driver left his car, carrying a bag. He dropped it in front of O'Dell's door and jogged back to his car. "It's a food delivery."

"Look."

Lexie spotted the front door open. A hand grabbed the food and shut the door. "He's home." She shot a look at Connor. "He's been home this whole time."

"Assuming it's him."

Lexie opened her car door. "Let's find out."

"Lexie, wait." Connor got out of the car. "You sure you don't want me to talk to him?" He shut the door.

"I'm positive." Lexie crossed the street. "Let's go."

Connor followed. They got to the sidewalk and headed down the walkway toward O'Dell's front door. "What if O'Dell's working with Omnivista?" asked Connor.

"Then he won't help us, and we'll leave." She stopped on the walkway. "The worst he can do is call biker man, which I doubt he'll do while we're there."

"That's not the worst he can do."

Lexie widened her eyes. "He's not going to kill us in his home."

"He could delay us until biker man arrives."

"And then have biker man kill us instead? That's stupid. Omnivista isn't that sloppy. It brings way too much scrutiny."

"It's not a brilliant plan, but we have to consider every possibility."

"And if you sense that might happen, you can get us out of there. But we have to talk to him, regardless of the risk. What if he was Mira's friend or lover? What if he's devastated about what happened and wants to help? What if he knows where that drive is?"

Connor hesitated. "Okay. But stick close to me. I give the signal that we're done, you follow me out. No questions asked. You got it?"

"I got it." She turned and continued down the walkway. "Come on." She stepped up to the door. "Ready?"

"Ready."

She knocked.

They waited several seconds, and she knocked again. "Mr. O'Dell?"

They waited.

"Great," said Connor. "He's probably calling biker man as we speak."

Lexie knocked again. "Mr. O'Dell? Are you home? We need to speak to you about Mira Patel."

Connor eyed the street. "We should go."

The door opened, but a chain prevented it from opening wider. A man's face appeared, and Lexie recognized O'Dell. He was around

Mira's age, of average height, and clean-shaven with thinning black hair. "Who are you?"

"Mr. O'Dell? My name is Lexie Logan, and this is my associate, Connor Diamond. I'd like to talk to you about what happened to Mira Patel. We understand you were her coworker and friend."

His gaze traveled back and forth between them. "You were there, weren't you? When she died."

Lexie nodded. "I was. I almost died too."

"We'd like to talk about what happened that night," said Connor. "We don't need a lot of your time. Just a few minutes."

O'Dell shook his head. "I can't." He started to close the door.

Lexie stepped closer. "Please, Mr. O'Dell. It's important. I want to find out what happened to Mira. Don't you? I understand you were her friend."

His face, or at least the visible part, tightened. "I know what happened to her."

Lexie held still. "I didn't kill her, if that's what you're thinking."

"Lexie is as much a victim as Mira," added Connor. "We promise that whatever you tell us will stay between us, and when you want us to leave, we will."

"Mira came to me for help, and I plan to do just that." Lexie prayed he'd relent and open the door.

O'Dell kept staring. His skin was pale, and glimmers of sweat popped up on his forehead. After an agonizing wait, he closed the door. Lexie heard the jangle of the chain, and the door swung open. Rip stood there in a bathrobe. His hair was disheveled, and he tightened the sash on his robe. "I'll give you ten minutes."

Relieved, Lexie stepped inside the house. "Thank you."

"We appreciate it." Connor walked in with her.

O'Dell closed the door behind them. "Sorry about the mess."

Lexie entered the living room to find clothes strewn over the furniture and food bags littering the coffee table. The TV was on, but the volume was low. To her left was the kitchen. More food bags were on the counter, and dirty dishes filled the sink.

O'Dell walked over to the couch and grabbed some of the clothes. "I haven't been right since Mira died. I've taken the last two days off." He tossed the clothes onto a nearby chair. "Have a seat."

Lexie walked over with Connor, and she sat on the sofa. "We're sorry for your loss."

Connor remained standing. "And we're sorry to bother you at a difficult time, but is it true you worked closely with Mira?"

O'Dell ran his hand through his hair. "Yes. She was a good friend."

Lexie took a deep breath. "I'm sorry to get personal, but were you more than friends?"

He looked over at her with haunted eyes. "Who told you that?"

"Edna, Mira's friend, told me." She raised her hand at Connor. "That's why we're here."

"Mira was murdered, but not by Lexie," said Connor. "Mira contacted Lexie and told her she had information about Omnivista. But she died before she could give it to her."

Lexie shifted to the edge of the couch. "Someone got to her before me and then tried to kill me too. They failed, but now I'm a suspect. The killer is still out there, but so is the information Mira was trying to give me."

His eyes widened. "What?"

"Omnivista is looking for it," said Connor, "and we have to find it before they do."

O'Dell held his stomach. "You have no idea what you're up against." He shook his head. "And you shouldn't be here." His gaze traveled across the room and settled on something.

Lexie followed his gaze and mumbled a curse when she saw a Prometheus device sitting on a desk against the wall. Blue light glowed from its edges.

Connor saw it too.

O'Dell put his fingers to his lips. "Yes. Mira and I were more than friends, but she never told me a thing about her plans. I woke up to the news of her death like everyone else, and I know nothing about any information Mira planned to give you." He eyed the device. "Mira kept her intentions to herself, and I can't help you." He waved at the door. "I think you should go. I want no part of whatever Mira was involved in. I've worked with Omnivista for years, and all her fears and worries amounted to nothing. AI can be scary, but it's not the boogeyman. I tried to tell Mira that, but she wouldn't listen. And now she's dead, and I'll never forgive myself."

Lexie's heart raced, and she stood. "None of this is your fault."

Connor caught her attention and pointed his finger at the door.

"I'm sorry we bothered you." Lexie stepped away from the couch.

O'Dell walked with them to the door. "I wish I could help you, but I can't. And if you know what's good for you, leave Omnivista alone." He opened the door, and she and Connor stepped out onto the porch.

"Sorry to bother you, Mr. O'Dell," said Connor.

O'Dell stepped out with them and closed the door. He spoke low. "Do you have cell phones on you?"

"We left them in the car," said Lexie.

"Good." He looked around. "I knew exactly what Mira was up to. She told me what she was planning. I said it was too risky and not to do it. That Omnivista would know, but she did it anyway." He held his head. "I was so stupid. I should have stopped her."

Lexie understood his regret. "She had a USB drive with all the evidence she'd collected. Did she tell you anything about it? Do you know where she hid it?"

"No. She said she planned to give it to you. You didn't see her that night?"

"No," said Lexie. "Or at least I don't recall if I did. I don't remember a thing."

"Then how do you know you don't have it?" he asked.

"Because I woke up in a hospital bed with nothing but a hospital gown and my mother standing over me. My clothes were gone, and there was no drive in my purse."

"Would Mira have given it to someone else?" asked Connor.

"She didn't give it to me," said Rip. "I'm as baffled as you are. Are you sure Omnivista didn't recover it?"

"Pretty certain," said Lexie. "Otherwise, they wouldn't have come after Edna."

"They went after Edna?" asked O'Dell. "Hell. I shouldn't be talking to you."

"We'll keep it quiet," said Connor, "but if you can think of anything that might help...anything that Mira may have mentioned about the meeting with Lexie."

O'Dell shook his head. "I wish I—" He stared off. "Wait a minute."

Lexie straightened. "Do you remember something?"

O'Dell rubbed his neck. "The warehouse where they found her...she'd mentioned it before."

"What did she say?" asked Connor.

"She'd been there years ago. It belongs to Omnivista, but hadn't been used in a long time. But now they've moved shipping in-house and are using the warehouse for overflow. It's still a work in progress and there's more to do, but there's a team that works there now."

"Why would she meet in a warehouse that's in use?" asked Lexie.

"Because currently, it's only for overflow. All the staff leave by five. It's one of the few teams that do. If she had planned to meet you late, the place would have been empty. Plus, she'd have access."

"What about security?" asked Connor.

"My guess is it's low. Not fully updated yet. Knowing Mira, she checked all of that and figured she could get in and out undetected."

Lexie still couldn't recall being inside a warehouse. "Maybe she was wrong about that security."

"You said Mira was familiar with the warehouse?" asked Connor.

Rip nodded. "When Mira first started working at Omnivista, she told me she had a good friend who was on the Prometheus team with her. On long days, they'd disappear and smoke pot somewhere quiet. The warehouse was one of those places."

Lexie thought of Zephyr. "So, there was something about that warehouse that made it ideal for her to meet with me? Any idea what?"

O'Dell tucked his hands into the pockets of his robe. "All I know is she'd meet her friend there, and they'd smoke in one of the backrooms. Back then, they almost lived at work, and as long as they met their deadlines, the supervisor looked the other way."

Lexie eyed Connor.

"I'm not saying she hid anything there," added O'Dell, "but that's what she told me."

Connor studied O'Dell as if gauging his honesty. "There's something we need to ask you about, Mr. O'Dell. Did you once work for Damien Rook?"

O'Dell furrowed his brow. "For a time. Why?"

"We're curious. Why did you leave?" asked Connor.

O'Dell put his hand on the doorframe. "Because Rook was showing signs of instability, and I could read the writing on the wall."

"We've also learned there was an assault charge against you two years ago," added Lexie.

His face dropped. "Wait. Do you think I had something to do with what happened to Mira?"

"We have to be sure," said Connor.

O'Dell glared for a few seconds, but answered. "I got into a stupid bar fight two years ago. Thankfully, after tempers calmed, the charges were dropped." He crossed his arms. "Does that satisfy your curiosity?"

Lexie paused. "We had to ask."

After a pause, O'Dell's shoulders dropped. "I suppose I understand, considering what you're up against. But I can assure you, I played no part in what happened to Mira, other than letting her down." He looked away.

Lexie could imagine how he must feel. "We're going to find who did this."

He looked back. "I admire your courage, but you're facing a formidable opponent."

"What do you think?" Connor asked Lexie.

O'Dell stepped closer. "If you're considering going to the warehouse, I'd highly advise against it. If they catch you..."

"We understand the implications, Mr. O'Dell," said Lexie, "but if that drive is in there, we have to find it before Omnivista does."

"Call me Rip. If you're going to get yourselves killed, we should be on a first-name basis." He paused. "You understand that if Mira got what I think she got from Omnivista, it will take the entire company down."

"We understand," said Connor.

"And like any predator fighting for its life, it will kill to protect itself?" asked Rip.

Lexie knew they had no choice. They had to go to the warehouse to look for the drive, or at least stir up her memories.

Connor spoke to Rip. "I suggest you take tomorrow off too, Rip."

Rip's expression softened. "I appreciate what you're doing for Mira. I wish I were as brave, but please be careful. If you follow through with this...and get caught," he expelled a long breath, "...God help you both."

••••••••••

Daniels signed the paperwork and closed the folder. He handed it back to Officer Shelby. "Thanks, Shelby. Make sure that gets to Records."

"You got it, Detective." Holding the folder, Shelby headed back out the squad doors as Rem walked through them, sucking on what Daniels suspected was a chocolate shake.

"I guess the BLT with fries wasn't enough?" he asked Rem.

Rem sat at his desk. "That sandwich was heavy on the L and T. It's a crime how little bacon there was."

Daniels straightened his desk. "God forbid you don't get enough bacon."

"We agree on that much." Rem took another sip from his shake. "Hear anything from Lexie or Diamond?"

"Not a word."

Rem set his shake down. "Do you think we did the right thing? Letting them go off on their own?"

"What choice did we have? We're not on the case. And we can't call Carlson and Justini and tell them. They don't grasp what's at stake here, even if Carlson is on Lexie's side."

"But if something happens..."

Daniels rubbed his face. "Yeah. I know. But Diamond is a seasoned investigator. He can handle himself and watch out for Lexie."

"Waiting isn't my strong suit."

"It's not mine either, but until we know more..."

"Yeah." Rem sat up. "Where's your phone?"

"In my desk drawer."

"Good. So's mine." He leaned in and kept his voice down. "Do you have any doubts about what Lexie told us?"

Daniels moved a folder on his desk. "You don't believe her?"

"It's not that. But consider that her only source for all this is this mysterious Zephyr, who can't be identified. What if he's not who he says he is?"

“I sense Diamond is worried about that too, but what would be the point? Trying to take down a massive organization and its AI project is not something you do in your free time.”

“Exactly. The scale of this is hard to comprehend. How is it possible that one company could spy on people all over the world? We’re talking colossal amounts of data. What if Zephyr is just some pissed-off employee with a grudge trying to stick it to his former employer?”

Daniels rested his elbows on his desk. “What happened to Mira is real, and so is what’s happening to Lexie. Edna too. Someone’s hiding something.”

“Hiding a secret or two is one thing, but hiding billions is another.” He paused. “I mean, think of the ramifications if Prometheus is the real deal.”

“I can’t stop thinking about that. When you came over for dinner the other night, we talked about the Odwalla case and our testimony in the Phillips trial. Plus, what we’d learned about that carjacking ring, all while Prometheus sat on my table. It heard everything.” He snorted. “Think about the conversations between lawyers and clients, doctors and patients, husbands and wives, and teachers and students. Or the scientist discussing his latest breakthrough, or the CEO talking about sensitive information. And don’t get me started on politicians. Nothing is safe anymore.”

“But how is all that data handled? And who has access to it all?”

“That’s Zephyr’s point. Wherever it goes, it’s sorted and grouped and distributed. I don’t get all the tech behind it, but there must be triggers that pique Prometheus’ interest. Based on that, it’s determined who gets listened to even more. That must be why it takes a little longer for Prometheus One to zero in.” He rubbed his forehead. “And who has access depends on Omnivista. There are plenty of high-powered players out there who would pay top dollar for that kind of information.”

He shrugged. “Hell, for all we know, someone with enough clout pays Omnivista to get Prometheus to listen in on certain people.”

“But not everyone has Vista. They can’t listen to everyone.”

“Not yet, but something tells me this rollout of Prometheus Two could change that. Don’t ask me how, but it scares me.”

“It scares the hell out of me too.” He shook his head. “Maybe that’s why I’m trying to find the cracks in Zephyr’s story. I’m hoping it isn’t true.”

“Your gut is as solid as an oak tree. What’s it telling you?”

Rem hesitated and sat back. “That maybe Damien Rook’s case was just a walk in the park compared to this.”

Daniels grunted. “My gut says the same.” He eyed his watch. “Let’s just pray Lexie and Diamond get some help from O’Dell.”

“Or Lexie remembers something of value that will lead to that drive.” Rem scratched his jaw and sat up again. “After we leave today, we should stop and buy burners.”

“I was thinking the same.”

Rem lowered his voice. “Just out of curiosity, how hard has it been for you not to dig into Nolan Sorrento and his Omnivista gang?”

Daniels looked up when another detective entered the squad room and waited until he walked away. “It’s killing me. But we can’t risk triggering Prometheus.”

“Our computers aren’t linked to him and have no connection to Vista.”

“Maybe not, but our system is linked to a bigger one, and who says Prometheus is the only one doing the spying? Let’s not forget the human factor.”

Rem clutched his shake. “You think there’s more than one spy?”

“You saw the Rook organization and how widespread it was, and Omnivista is twice as big. I don’t trust anyone except you and Lozano.”

“That’s not a lot of people.”

"Tell me about it."

Rem picked up his shake and sucked on the straw. He rocked back in his chair. "There is another option."

Daniels understood exactly who Rem was talking about. "It's a last resort."

Rem raised the corner of his lip. "Great minds think alike."

"Why does that concern me?"

"It's not a bad idea."

"No, it's a terrible one."

"Snoop could do exactly what we need without any worries about getting caught."

Daniels held up his hand. "Don't even say his name."

"Hey, what happened before was a mistake. It won't happen again."

Daniels scoffed. "A mistake? He hacked into the SDPD computer system and changed all his priors. Then he tripled my commissary bill, and I couldn't buy an apple until I paid it, and he gave you three unpaid parking tickets. We looked like idiots."

Rem shrugged. "We eventually got it sorted out."

"He's a menace, and he should have done more time."

"But he's a genius with computers. This whole Prometheus thing? I bet he'd do loops around it. We could do some research, and Prom Boy wouldn't know a thing."

"Prom Boy?"

"Prometheus needs a nickname so we can keep it quiet."

"And that's what you came up with?" He shook his head. "This is where the great minds think alike concerns me."

"It's something to consider."

"Prom Boy?"

Rem smirked. "No, bonehead. Snoop. He owes us for all the crap he's put us through. Maybe it's time to call in our favor." He raised an eyebrow.

Daniels reluctantly considered it. Before he could respond, though, the squad doors banged open, and Lozano walked in with Detectives Mel and Garcia.

Lozano passed Daniels' desk. "You two. My office." He strode past them.

Rem stood. "What's up?" he asked Mel and Garcia.

"You're gonna love this," said Mel, who followed his partner behind Lozano.

Daniels stood and pushed his chair in. "This ought to be good."

Sucking on his straw, Rem walked with Daniels into Lozano's office. Daniels shut the door behind them. "What's up, Cap?"

Lozano slid his jacket off and put it on the back of his chair. "Tell them, Garcia."

Garcia, who had a folder tucked under his arm, pulled it out. "We've made some progress on Rook's encrypted files."

"What'd you find?" asked Rem.

Mel put his hands on his hips. "You remember how we found the name Lynx in the files, but we couldn't link the name to anyone?"

"That's a little hard to forget." Daniels eyed the folder, and his heart skipped. "Are you saying you found Lynx?"

"Not saying that at all," said Garcia, "but we found something else." He opened the folder. "Research accessed a photo. They sent it to me and Mel. We asked them to print it, and we just showed it to Lozano."

Lozano sat at his desk. "You're going to want to see this."

"Does this relate to Omnivista?" asked Rem, with a glance at Daniels.

Daniels understood his partner's concerns. "If you've got phones on you, put them in Lozano's drawer, or turn them off."

Lozano grunted, and Mel and Garcia stared with confusion.

"Trust us," said Rem. "We'll explain later."

After a pause, Lozano took out his phone and put it in his drawer. Mel and Garcia added theirs, and Lozano closed it. “I can’t wait to find out what’s going on,” said Lozano.

“Be careful what you wish for,” said Daniels. “What you got, Garcia?”

Garcia lifted a photo from the folder and held it out. Rem and Daniels got closer, and Daniels immediately recognized a tan Damien Rook, who was wearing a Hawaiian shirt and Bermuda shorts. He stood with another man with silver hair, wearing a hat, shorts, and a button-down, short-sleeved shirt. On the other side of him was Nolan Sorrento, wearing similar clothing and smiling.

“Who’s the guy in the middle?” asked Rem.

Daniels’ heart skipped again. “Is that...?”

Lozano rolled up one of his shirt sleeves. “It is.”

“Who?” asked Rem.

Daniels’ mind whirled with the implications.

“Senator Richard Blackwell from the great state of Texas,” said Mel. “Attorney and heir to the Blackwell Oil fortune. He’s chair of the Armed Services Committee plus a prominent member of the Intelligence Committee.”

“We believe this was taken in Cancún." Garcia chuckled. "Texas senators seem to like it there."

Lozano grunted.

"Can’t be sure of the year, though,” added Garcia. “Needless to say, he’s a powerful man."

Lozano wiped a handkerchief across his face. “Who apparently knows Damien Rook and Nolan Sorrento well enough to go on vacation with them.”

Rem dropped his jaw, and Daniels stood frozen in place. Daniels didn’t like where this was going. “Are you saying...?”

"Based on what you told me," said Lozano, "this Lynx was part of Rook's world and now Sorrento's." He aimed a pen at the photograph. "There aren't many at that level who can instill fear in men like them."

Rem, who'd lowered his shake, eyed Daniels. "Something tells me Senator Richard Blackwell could."

Daniels deflated. "If Blackwell has access to Prom Boy's intel, there's no telling the damage he could do with it."

Rem uttered a groan. "He'd be damn near unstoppable."

Lozano scowled. "Who the hell is Prom Boy?"

Chapter Twenty-Six

Lexie sat in the passenger seat with Connor behind the wheel. After leaving O'Dell's, Connor insisted on returning to his office and switching cars. He'd grabbed a few things, and they'd driven to the warehouse, which they now watched from across the street. It was well after five o'clock. The sun was almost down, and there'd been no activity for over an hour. "It's definitely quiet around here," said Lexie. "I can see why Mira chose this spot."

"It's almost too quiet, but I see your point." Connor had walked the perimeter of the warehouse not long after five to check for security cameras, but had found none. "You'd think they'd have more security, especially after Mira died here."

"It certainly makes Omnivista seem overconfident. It's like they know no one would dare try to do what Mira did. But I suspect this area will get a security facelift soon. You know how red tape works. Heck, I can't even get my security fixed, and it's been weeks."

"That's because of your landlady."

"And a company like Omnivista probably requires ten signatures from ten different people just to get approval."

"Maybe." He checked his watch.

"Do you have flashlights?" she asked.

"They're in the trunk." He leaned over and pulled up his pant leg.

Lexie stared. "Is that a gun?"

He pulled out a small pistol and checked the chamber. “Of course it is. What kind of investigator do you think I am?” He returned the gun to its holster.

“I didn’t realize you were armed.”

“Old habits die hard.” He swiveled toward her. “Listen. When we go in, you stick beside me, okay? No heroics. And if something happens, you get the hell out. Don’t wait for me.”

“What exactly do you think is going to happen? We’re just looking around.”

“And you should know that any plan can fall apart at a moment's notice, so stay alert.”

Lexie eyed the warehouse with uncertainty. “I’m familiar with plans falling apart.” Since they’d arrived, she’d been waiting to remember something about this place, but so far, nothing. “But you be careful too. No heroics, as you say. We get in and we get out.”

“Deal.” He took hold of the door handle. “Are you ready?”

She slid the burner cell from Frank into her pocket and took a deep breath. “I’m ready.”

They opened their doors and stepped out of the car. Connor went to the trunk and pulled out gloves for each of them, took a flashlight, and handed one to Lexie. “This has a little extra firepower.”

Lexie looked at it. “Is the light extra bright?”

He took it and switched it on. “This works the light, but if you move the switch up another notch, it becomes a stun gun.” He flicked the switch and pressed a button. The flashlight crackled, and blue light arced from the top.

Lexie jumped. “Where’d you get that?”

“It’s good for unexpected situations, and this is classified as one.” He shut the trunk. “Let’s go.”

Putting on their gloves and watching their surroundings, they jogged across the street to a side door of the warehouse. Connor tried it, but it was locked. "Let's try around back. Less chance of a car driving by."

Lexie followed him down the side and around the back. They jogged up an alley and stopped beside another door. Connor tried it, but it was also locked. "What do we do?" asked Lexie.

"Keep an eye out." Connor pulled a small leather pouch from his pocket. He opened it and pulled out a long tool, which he slid into the lock.

Lexie told herself to stay calm. "Great. Now we're breaking and entering."

"How'd you expect to get in here?" He used a second tool and maneuvered it into the lock.

Lexie looked around, and her uncertainty grew. Seeing a nearby trash bin, her stomach rolled, and perspiration broke out on her skin. Feeling sick, she put her hand on the wall. "Connor..."

"One sec. Almost there." He wiggled the tools.

Lexie had to take a long, slow breath. This place was familiar.

There was a click. "Got it." Connor turned the knob and opened the door. He paused, poked his head through the doorway, and listened. "No alarm. So far, so good." He put his tools back in his pocket.

Lexie's throat turned dry. "I was here."

Connor put his hand on her arm. "I know."

She shot him a look. "What?"

He pointed toward the trash bin. "That's where they found you that night. I read the report."

"You what? How come you didn't tell me?"

"Because you needed to remember on your own. And you did. That's a good sign. Do you recall how you got there?"

She tried to think and had a vague recollection of being half-carried by someone but didn't know who. "Someone brought me out here."

"Once we go in, your memories may all come back. Are you ready for that?"

She faced the open door. "I have to be." She braced and pushed back her fear. "Let's go."

He studied her for a second and nodded. He stepped inside. She followed, and he closed the door behind them. It was dark, so they switched on their flashlights. They were in a small reception area with a desk, a chair, and wood-paneled walls. Beyond that was another door with a clear, square plastic panel in the center. Feeling as though she'd been in this room before, Lexie walked over, peered through the panel, and saw a spacious warehouse. She pushed the door and entered the space. Instant recognition hit her. The smell of paper and ink, the shelves with various-sized boxes, and the long conveyor belts that guided the packages to their proper destination brought it all back. She'd walked into this room just as she had now—at night and with apprehension. "I've been here," she whispered.

"What do you remember?" Connor flicked his light around the room.

Lexie blinked as if that would help her recall. "I didn't know where to go. And I was nervous."

"I can imagine."

Lexie spotted double doors on the opposite side of the conveyor belts. Her heart rate picked up. "I went through those doors."

Connor aimed his light. "Come on." He headed toward the doors.

Lexie stuck close behind him. Her skin was clammy, and she tried to slow her breathing.

"You okay?"

Lexie nodded. "Hanging in there."

Connor pushed one door open and pointed the light. "It's a hallway." He stepped through, and Lexie did too. Using her flashlight, she saw a short hall with offices on either side. A mailroom was on her left, and across from that was a door marked *Break Room*. At the far end of the hall was an illuminated *Exit* sign.

Lexie poked her head into the mailroom. It had a desk with a monitor and a phone on it. Various folders and piles of paper were on the desk, and a mail chute was in the wall. "I wasn't in here."

"What about here?"

Lexie turned to see Connor standing in the break room. She joined him and saw the small refrigerator, sink and tables and chairs for staff to sit. Something about it stirred in her mind. It wouldn't form, but her stomach flipped again. "I'm not sure."

They left the break room and closed the door. Continuing down the hall, Lexie passed the restrooms. Across from them was a door marked *Supervisor*. She wondered if these were the back rooms where Mira would come to smoke pot with Zephyr. The *Supervisor* room felt familiar. "This is it." Lexie's flashlight shook. "This is where I met Mira."

Connor hesitated. "Center yourself. Take a second and relax."

Lexie was nowhere near relaxed, but she closed her eyes for a second and reopened them. "I'm ready."

Connor opened the door. He flashed the light around the space, which didn't look like a supervisor's office. A long conference table was pushed against the wall, and there was a whiteboard above it.

Lexie walked inside and noticed the fingerprint dust covering various spots around the room. She stopped short when she almost stepped on a large stain on the floor. She gasped when a flash of memory hit her. "This is it. This is where I met Mira." She stepped back from the stain. "Is that…? Oh, God. Is this where she died?"

His flashlight illuminating the stain, Connor crouched beside it. "Looks like blood."

Lexie clutched her stomach. "Why isn't this a crime scene?"

"It was." Connor stood. "This whole warehouse was likely locked down. But it's since been reopened, especially if Omnivista bitched enough about it." He eyed the stain. "Looks like they cleaned the blood as best they could, but they're going to have to rip up the floorboards."

Lexie's vision swirled, and she balanced herself on the wall. "She was murdered here."

Connor walked closer. "Do you need to leave?"

Composing herself, she shook her head. "I'll be okay."

"What do you remember?"

Lexie fought to slow her swirling thoughts. It was all coming at her at once. "She was sitting at the conference table when I walked in. It was quiet, and no one was around, but the light was on in the room."

"Did she have anything with her?"

Lexie scrunched her eyes shut. "She had a crossbody knapsack slung across her chest." She ran her fingers from one shoulder to the opposite side of her waist. "We talked, and she told me who she was and why she'd contacted me. She talked about Omnivista, how I had to be careful, and said we had to hurry." Lexie gripped her flashlight. "Mira pulled a small envelope out of her knapsack and handed it to me. She told me to get out and tell no one about what I had. There were instructions inside telling me what to do to protect the information and to follow them to the letter, or we'd both be killed. I took it, put it in my purse, and walked out. I was cautious and walked fast. I didn't see anyone but...but..." Her vision swirled again and swayed on her feet. "Oh, God." She grabbed onto Connor when her knees buckled.

Holding onto her, he got his arm under her knees and lifted her into his arms. "Hang on. I got you." He carried her out of the room and into the breakroom, where he sat her in a chair. "You still with me?"

Lexie leaned over and held her head until the room stopped spinning.

Connor found a roll of paper towels on the counter and wet a few at the sink. He brought them over. "Here."

Lexie took them and covered her face with them. She couldn't stop shaking. "It happened in the hall."

"What did?"

"I...I...passed the mailroom and...and...someone was there. Before I could do anything, I felt a sting in my neck." She rubbed her neck where she recalled being jabbed with something. She lowered the towels and found it hard to speak. "They...he...someone...brought me in here and shut the door." She dropped her head again. "Oh, no."

"Take your time." Connor rubbed her shoulder. "Did you see any faces?"

"No. I couldn't stand. Everything was moving." She froze. "Someone asked me questions." Her heart pounded harder against her chest. "About why I was there."

"Was it more than one person?"

She tried to recall, but it was too fuzzy. "I can't be sure. But I...I think it was biker man." Another memory made her moan. "He wanted me to drink." Gasping, she clutched her stomach. "But I didn't want to." She grimaced. "He hit me in the head." Tears clouded her vision and ran down her cheeks. "He forced me to drink." More tears surfaced. "I tried to fight, but I was too scared. And...and the more I drank, the easier it got." Overwhelmed by the onslaught of emotion, she sobbed. Connor pulled her closer, and she buried her face in his neck. "I couldn't do anything."

"It's okay," he said softly. "You did what you had to do to survive."

"I wanted to stop, but then I couldn't fight anymore. He asked me about Mira and went through my purse. He found the envelope and took it. I asked him to let me go, and he laughed." Her tears slowing, she pulled back. "He made me drink more and told me he'd take care of me. I was barely thinking by then. He stood me up and half-carried me outside into the alley." She clenched her eyes shut again. "And he jabbed me in the arm with something else, and I went limp and fell. He...he left me there and went back inside."

Connor spoke softly. "Is that all you remember? What about Mira?"

"I don't know. I was too out of it." Lexie groaned and wrapped her fingers in his shirt. "But after he went back inside, I think I heard a shot. That must have been when I passed out." Fresh tears emerged. "That had to be when Mira was killed." Barely able to hold it together, she dropped her head back onto his shoulder.

He stroked the back of her head until she slowly calmed again. "You back with me?" he asked when she looked at him and sniffed.

Lexie wasn't sure how to answer. Her body trembled, and she was shivering but sweating. "I don't know." She wiped her face with the damp paper towels.

"Deep breaths. You'll feel better." He rubbed her arms. "But we broke into a dark warehouse by ourselves where Mira was murdered, so don't take too long."

Reality pierced her emotions, and she straightened and collected herself. "And we still haven't answered the bigger question. Where's that drive?"

Connor picked up his flashlight from the floor where he'd put it and flashed it around the room. "You said he brought you in here and questioned you. And took the envelope?"

Lexie held her elbows after another shiver. "Yes."

"That makes no sense. If he had the drive, why are they still looking for it?"

The question pulled Lexie out of the past. "I don't know." She wiped her face and neck again. "He went back into the warehouse after leaving me. You think he somehow lost the envelope?"

"No. I don't think so."

Lexie sucked in a sharp breath. "You mean Mira gave me a fake drive?"

"She must have. She must have suspected you two weren't alone."

"Then where's the actual drive? She must have had it with her."

He waved the light. "You okay to walk?" He stood and held out his hand.

She took it and stood on shaky legs. Connor supported her until she got her bearings. "Do you think it's still in the other room?" she asked.

"Let's find out. Hold on to me if you get dizzy again."

Feeling better, Lexie walked with him into the adjacent room. She aimed the light around the conference table and walls. "I don't see any hiding places."

Connor shone his light in her direction. "Think about it. If she came here to smoke pot, that's not something she'd carry around." He redirected the light at the floor.

"You think there's a hiding place?"

"It's a long shot. Where'd you hide your pot when you were younger?"

"Who says I smoked pot?"

"Most teenagers do. I hid my stash at the bottom of my underwear drawer."

Lexie thought back. "My brother kept his in the garage in an old toolkit. I'd sneak back there and steal a joint. I think he knew but never told on me."

"That's what good brothers are for."

"My parents would disagree, especially my dad."

Connor used his foot to press on the floor. "Look for any loose floorboards. You start at this end. I'll start over here."

Lexie got down on her hands and knees and studied the wood with her light. She pressed and tugged at any place that looked loose. "Nothing. You?"

Connor had done the same as her and was on his knees. "Nothing."

"Don't you think biker man would have already done this?"

"I'm sure he did, but obviously he didn't find anything."

"That doesn't bode well for us." Frustrated, Lexie moved under the conference table, still poking at the wood floor, when another flash of recall hit her. She rose and almost hit her head on the underside of the table. "Connor." She flashed her light at him.

"Yeah." He dug at a floorboard with no success.

She scooted out from under the table. "When I entered this room to meet Mira. She was standing in that corner. Over here." She crawled over to the far corner. "She was kicking the baseboard."

"Kicking?" Connor crawled over to the same corner.

"Not hard. More like nudging." She illuminated the place where she remembered Mira standing and saw a minor crease in the paint. "Look." She poked at it with her nail, and a section of the baseboard moved.

"I'll be damned." Connor pulled out his lock-picking tools again and used one tool to wiggle the baseboard loose. He pulled it free, and Lexie saw a narrow compartment behind the wall. Inside was a small, opaque plastic bag.

Lexie's heart thumped as she reached for it.

A man's voice spoke from behind them. "Thank you."

Lexie whirled to look behind her. Connor did the same just as the man swung something long and narrow and hit Connor hard on the head.

Chapter Twenty-Seven

Lexie shrieked as Connor dropped his light and fell limp to the floor. Blood trickled from his head. "Connor!" Holding her flashlight, she went to his side, but he didn't move. She shook his shoulder, but he was out cold.

"Get up."

Shaking, Lexie turned toward the man. She shone her light on him as he walked to the wall and hit the light switch. Light brightened the room, and she squinted, but she recognized Connor's assailant immediately. It was biker man.

Still wearing his motorcycle jacket and a blue bandana, he held a heavy metal pipe and grinned at her. "I knew you'd come back here eventually."

She eyed Connor, who now had a substantial amount of blood pooling beneath his head. "He needs a hospital."

"I think you need to worry more about you." He stepped closer. "I said get up." He pulled a gun from his waistband and aimed it at her.

Trying to stay calm, she slowly stood. She thought of the stun gun in her light, and using her thumb, she flicked the switch the way Connor had shown her.

He pointed at the baseboard with the pipe. "I figured she'd hid it somewhere. I looked but missed the baseboard. You did a much better job. I appreciate the help."

Lexie raised her hands. “Just take it. Leave me and Connor alone. I can’t touch you. Not with the power of Omnivista protecting you.”

“Sorry. It doesn’t work like that. I know you won’t leave this alone.” He set the pipe down and leaned it against the wall. “You and I have unfinished business.”

Feeling the panic rise, she talked to him. “What happened that night? How did you know Mira was meeting me?”

He chuckled. “Mira should have known she’d get caught. She believed she’d covered her bases, but she wasn’t as smart as she thought.”

“That envelope you took from me. It wasn’t what you’d hoped, was it?”

“It was a blank drive. Worthless. Too bad we didn’t know that before she died.”

“You knew she was going to meet with me?”

“We knew everything.”

“And I was supposed to die?”

“Hell, yes. But we’ll remedy that tonight.” He stepped back and used his gun to gesture toward the pipe. “Pick it up.”

She didn’t understand.

“I said, pick it up,” he yelled.

Lexie jumped, moved toward the pipe, and picked it up. Her heart skipped when she saw the blood at the other end of it.

“Wipe my prints off with your shirt.”

His plan became obvious. “You want it to look like I hit Connor?”

“Do it.”

She tucked the flashlight under her arm and hastily used her shirt to wipe down the pipe.

“Now hold it like you’re going to swing it.”

Her hands shaking, she did as he asked.

“Now put it back where it was.”

She set it back against the wall. "Now what?" Her voice shook, and she took hold of the flashlight.

He patted his jacket pocket. "Now, we'll finish what we started." He waved the gun. "Move. Go to the breakroom."

Lexie eyed the door to the hall. If she went through it, she'd be a dead woman. She suspected he had drugs in his pocket, and they were meant for her. "You're not stupid enough to try the same thing as before. Knock me out and leave me to die?"

"When the cops find him unconscious, and you dead from an overdose, that will confirm that you were working with him and you came here to kill Mira, who they suspect was blackmailing you." He smiled. "After you're dead, I'll take the drive and shove ten grand in that hiding spot. They'll think that's the money you planned to give Mira, but when things went awry, one of you hid it with plans to come back for it. And when you did, you got greedy and killed him for it."

She couldn't believe that was his plan. "That is ludicrous. Why, after all that, would I kill myself?"

"Guilt. You killed your lover for what? Ten grand? You couldn't help but take a hit to deal with it, only you took too much."

"The cops will never buy that."

"It doesn't really matter what they believe. All I want is the drive. There will be an investigation, but without more to go on, they'll either blame you, or your case will go cold. And him?" He eyed Connor. "He never saw me coming. If he lives, I doubt he'll remember much anyway. And if they believe he was your accomplice, they won't care what he says to defend you." He shrugged. "And you'll be dead, so his word is all he'll have, and that won't be enough. Omnivista will make sure of that."

She cringed at the thought, gripped her flashlight, and eyed the hallway.

"Stop wasting time and move." He stepped closer.

Lexie turned and walked through the door, but slowly, allowing him to get closer. Sensing he was eager to get this over with, she stopped. He came up behind her. "I said move."

She held still. "I'm not going to walk myself to my death." She steeled herself and prayed he couldn't read her mind. If he took her flashlight, she wouldn't survive.

He cursed, came up behind her, and shoved her. "I said move!"

She swiveled, jabbed the flashlight into his stomach, and pressed the button. The weapon crackled, and biker man screamed and jerked. His body stiffened, and he fell forward at her feet, his gun beneath him.

She had a split second to make a decision. Hit him again or go for Connor's gun. She'd heard too many stories of tasers only temporarily taking down suspects, and biker man was a big guy, and she couldn't run and leave Connor behind.

She raced into the room where Connor was still lying motionless. Blood ran from his head and collected in a large puddle on the floor. She dropped beside his feet and pulled on his pant leg. Hearing a groan from the hall, she yanked harder and saw the gun in its holster. Pulling Connor's pant leg higher, she grabbed the handle, but it snagged on Connor's hem.

Biker man cursed loudly, and she saw his feet, which were sticking out into the room, move and then disappear. He grunted and cursed again.

Panic set in, and she tugged harder without realizing she wasn't getting anywhere. She had to calm down. She stopped staring at the doorway and focused on the gun. She put the flashlight down and used both hands to pull the pant leg farther up. Finally getting it high enough, she freed the gun just as biker man staggered into the room. He appeared slightly dazed, and his skin was pale, but he was coherent enough to realize what she was doing.

"You bitch." He raised his gun.

Lexie aimed and fired three times. Biker man jerked again. Blood spurted from his chest. He fired wildly into the wall, his knees buckled, and he crumpled to the floor.

Chapter Twenty-Eight

Lexie sat in the back of Detective Carlson's vehicle outside the warehouse. Despite the blanket draped over her shoulders, she shivered. Police lights swirled, and the warehouse that had been so quiet only an hour earlier was now lit up with light and bustling with law enforcement. To her dismay, the press had arrived. She could see their camera lights beyond the police tape on the other side of the street. Thankfully, since she was in the car, they didn't know she was there. Lexie doubted that would last long. She expected that this would be the lead story on that night's news. She cringed at the thought.

Her phone was still in her pocket, but other than nine-one-one, she'd called no one. All she could do was relive that moment when she'd shot biker man. After he'd collapsed, she'd been shaking so hard she'd almost dropped the gun, but she was aware enough to pull out her phone to call for help. Connor remained unconscious, and while she waited, she'd pulled herself together long enough to realize she couldn't let the drive be discovered. The risk was too great it would fall into the wrong hands. Hearing the approaching sirens, she'd crawled back over to the baseboard and closed it. She'd made it back to Connor's side just as the police and EMTs arrived. The EMTs immediately began treating biker man. They'd checked Connor too, but had taken biker man first. A second ambulance had shown up, and Connor had been loaded onto a stretcher. She'd wanted to go with him to the hospital, but Carlson and Justini had arrived by then and told her they'd needed her to stay and answer questions.

Reluctantly, she'd watched Connor get driven off in the ambulance. Carlson had directed her away from all the activity while Justini remained inside the warehouse. Carlson had asked her about what had happened, and Lexie did her best to answer her questions without mentioning finding Mira's hiding place. She told her about meeting Rip O'Dell earlier and how they'd decided to visit the warehouse to help jog her memory, but they hadn't expected the biker to show.

Carlson had listened, and to her credit, kept her opinions to herself, but Lexie imagined how it must have sounded. It was stupid to break into the warehouse where Mira had been murdered to remember the night of her death, but Lexie had emphasized it was her only option. After hearing Lexie's story, Carlson had asked if Lexie wanted her to call anyone, but Lexie told her no. She'd call her people once she got to the hospital, assuming she didn't go to jail. She'd asked Carlson to contact Ax, though, to tell him about Connor. Carlson had done so, guided Lexie to the back of Carlson's car, told her to wait, and then disappeared. Lexie had been sitting there ever since.

After a long wait, Carlson finally returned, slid into the driver's seat and shut her door. "How you doing?"

Lexie sniffed and wiped her eyes. "I've been better."

"Me too."

"Are you going to arrest me?"

"Justini's been on the phone with Eliza Thorne. At the moment, they're not pressing charges against you for breaking into the warehouse."

Relief flooded through Lexie.

"And I called the hospital. The person you call biker man, whose ID says is George Constable, is in emergency surgery."

"He's still alive?"

"Last I heard, but it's touch and go."

"And Connor?"

"Don't know. He made it to the ER, though. Ax should be there by now."

"Good."

"And I called Daniels and Remalla. I figured they'd want to know. They're heading to the hospital, too."

Lexie could imagine what they were thinking. "Thanks."

Carlson shifted to face Lexie. "You want me to call anyone else?"

Lexie couldn't imagine dealing with her mother right now. And if she called Frank, he'd feel obligated to call her mom. "Not right now." She pulled the blanket closer around her shoulders. "I'd like to go to the hospital, too. I want to check on Connor."

Carlson studied her closely. "Are you telling me everything?"

Lexie didn't flinch. "You don't believe what I told you?"

"You broke into this warehouse to retrieve your memories?"

"And it worked."

"What do you recall about the drive?"

"That night when I met Mira, it was taken from me by biker...I mean George Constable. But it turned out the drive was fake."

"How did Mira know to give you a fake drive?"

"She must have realized we weren't alone."

"If she gave you the fake one, she must have had the real one too. What happened to her after you left the room?"

"That's the one thing I can't answer. I don't know."

"Did you see anyone else?"

Lexie shook her head. "No."

"Mira could not have been alone the whole time you were in the breakroom with Constable. Since she didn't escape, someone must have been with her. And since the drive wasn't found on her, it was either taken or she hid it."

"If Omnivista has it, I doubt George would have been waiting for us."

"Which suggests it was hidden."

Lexie looked out the window.

"Is that why you were really here? To find it?"

Lexie thought fast. "Partly. We searched for the drive, but George interrupted us."

Carlson continued to stare. "Why didn't you tell me about Rip O'Dell?"

Lexie sighed. "Connor and I wanted to talk to him first."

"Dammit, Lexie. We had an agreement."

"I don't recall you telling me you went to see my father. And you didn't tell me about Judd until after you questioned him."

"None of that mattered until after we spoke with them."

"I could say the same thing about O'Dell."

Carlson muttered something under her breath and turned to face the wheel. "Why do I get the feeling you're hiding something?"

Lexie changed the subject. "Can I go to the hospital now? I grabbed Connor's key fob before he was put in the ambulance. If you can drop me off at his car so I can avoid the press..."

"No need. I'll drive you."

"You don't have to do that."

She started the car. "No, I don't. But I will." She eyed Lexie through the rearview mirror. "You shouldn't be alone right now."

Lexie suspected that was true. "Can we at least swing by Connor's car so I can get my purse?"

Carlson pulled away. "Sure."

• • • • • • • • • • •

After Carlson dropped her outside the emergency room and drove off to park, Lexie walked into the hospital. Anxious, she approached the nurse behind the counter when she heard her name called. She turned to see Daniels and Rem.

"Glad to see you're not arrested," said Daniels.

"Are you all right?" asked Rem.

Lexie nodded. "I'm okay. How's Connor?"

Daniels pointed toward the ER doors. "He's back there. Ax is with him. They're doing tests. That's all we know."

"Did you come on your own?" asked Rem.

"No, Carlson drove me. She's parking." Staring at the doors that led to the ER, she wrung her hands. "God, I hope Connor's okay."

"Come here," said Rem. "Sit down. You're as pale as the monochrome paint on the walls."

Feeling a little faint, she followed them to the waiting area and sat.

"Do you want some water or coffee?" asked Daniels.

"Water, please. Thanks." Lexie set her purse on the ground. On the way over, she'd checked Zephyr's phone and had seen one missed call. Lexie guessed he'd heard about the night's events and tried to reach her.

"Be right back." Daniels walked away.

Lexie held her elbows. "You two don't have to stay."

"You've had a hell of a day," said Rem. "I've had a few myself, and it's better not to be alone."

She rubbed her head. "I'm managing."

"Lexie, you shot a man who may not survive. That can do a number on you."

"I shot a man who was going to kill me."

"It's still traumatizing."

She replayed the shooting in her mind and shivered again.

"You're lucky to be alive."

The ER doors opened, and Carlson walked in. She saw Lexie with Rem and headed over. "Any news?"

“No,” said Lexie. She introduced Remalla and Daniels, who returned holding a bottle of water. He gave it to Lexie and shook Carlson’s hand.

“Nice to finally meet face-to-face,” said Rem.

Carlson paused. “I assume you’re both up to speed with Omnivista and the Prometheus problem?”

“We’re aware,” said Daniels.

“If that drive exists,” said Carlson, “it needs to be found.”

“We’re aware of that too,” said Rem.

“They know what you know, along with Connor,” Lexie said to Carlson. “But you’re the only people who do.”

“What about this Zephyr?” asked Carlson. “Any word from him?”

“No, but I haven’t exactly been available.” Lexie kept his phone call to herself.

“You think he might know about this hiding place in the warehouse?” asked Carlson.

“Hiding place?” asked Daniels.

Carlson’s phone rang. She pulled it from her pocket, answered, and, holding up a finger, walked away.

Rem arched an eyebrow at Lexie. “What hiding place?”

Lexie opened her water bottle. “She thinks Mira hid the drive in the warehouse.”

“Wasn’t the warehouse already searched?” asked Rem.

“I assume so,” answered Lexie.

“So, what’s the issue?” Daniels sat beside Rem.

Lexie took a long drink of water.

“Lexie?” asked Daniels.

Lexie capped her water bottle. “Where are your phones? The personal ones, not the burners.”

Rem pulled his cell out. Daniels patted his pocket. “I need to leave mine on.”

"Give them to me." Lexie took both, put them in her interior purse pocket, and zipped it shut.

Rem shook his head. "I will never get used to this."

Lexie glanced back at Carlson, who was still talking to someone. "She thinks Connor and I know where the hiding place is."

"Do you?" asked Rem.

Lexie hesitated. "Maybe."

"You found it, didn't you?" asked Daniels.

Lexie took a second when she recalled finding the spot just before Connor was hit on the head. "We found it behind the baseboard, but before we could get the drive, biker man showed. And before the police arrived, I closed the spot up again." The water bottle crackled as she gripped it. "I can't risk it falling into the wrong hands."

Rem whistled. "Well, this is a turn of events. No one else knows?"

Lexie shook her head.

"We've got to get to it before someone else does," said Daniels. "If Omnivista is looking for it, they could go back to the warehouse."

"Biker man, whose name is George Constable, by the way," said Lexie, "knows where it is, but he won't be saying anything anytime soon."

"Still, it's not safe." Daniels eyed Rem. "Maybe we can get to it."

Lexie straightened. "Absolutely not. You two don't need to get any deeper into this. Nobody does. I figure I'll wait for the uproar to die down and go back for it."

Rem dropped his jaw. "You want to break into the warehouse again?"

"What choice do I have?"

"No way." Daniels sat back. "Rem and I are cops. We can—"

"You two are not on this case. You walk in there, and Omnivista and Prometheus will know it. Plus, there's press everywhere. That puts you on Sorrento's radar. No, we have to wait. Besides, you don't know where to look."

Rem paused. "You sure about this, Lex?"

"I'm not sure about anything." Lexie ran her hand through her hair. "Right now, I just want to be sure Connor is okay and then figure out what to do."

"We can't take too long." Daniels leaned up and spoke softly. "Rem and I came across some new information, which makes it obvious why that drive is so valuable."

Lexie perked up. "What's that?"

Rem watched Carlson, who remained on the phone. "We found a vacation picture in Rook's files. It's of Rook and Sorrento with Senator Richard Blackwater. They looked pretty chummy."

Lexie's mind flipped back to an article she wrote a few years ago about the senator from Texas. "He's one of the most powerful men in the Senate. He was friends with Rook?"

"Seems that way." Rem turned back to face Lexie. "Sorrento, too."

Lexie sucked in her breath. "You don't think he's Lynx, do you?"

"No way to know," said Daniels. "But if he's caught up with Rook and Sorrento, it's not good." A phone rang from Lexie's purse. "And if he's on that drive...we're in bigger trouble than we realize."

Lexie pulled the ringing phone out of her purse and handed it to Daniels.

He took it. "It's Marjorie. Be right back." He stepped away and answered.

Lexie tried to imagine the what-ifs if Blackwater was Lynx. "My God."

"I said the same," said Rem, "only with a few more colorful words."

"I wrote about him once. More than a few sources mentioned he was corrupt, but none agreed to go on record. They were too scared."

Rem blew out his cheeks. "That makes me feel so much better." He nodded at Carlson. "Heads up. She's coming over. Better to keep this between ourselves."

"You think?" Lexie offered Carlson an uncomfortable smile as Carlson hung up her phone.

"That was Justini. Guess what? George Constable is not George Constable. The ID is fake, and the address matches up to a George Constable who died twelve years ago at the age of ninety-two."

"Then who is he?" asked Lexie.

"That's the big question." Carlson hooked her thumb into her belt. "Justini's been talking to Thorne and Sorrento. Neither admits to knowing this George nor why he was at the warehouse."

Lexie scoffed. "They're lying. They sent him."

"What's Justini think?" asked Rem.

The crease between Carlson's brows deepened. "He's questioning whether Lexie and Diamond went to the warehouse to retrieve something damning regarding Mira's death. They met with the fake George, whom they hired to take out Edna, and George wanted more of the pie, and Lexie killed him after he laid out Diamond."

Lexie gaped at her. It was exactly the scenario biker man had expected the police to buy. "And what would Justini think if biker man had succeeded and left me to die from another overdose? That I killed myself when everything went awry and I couldn't handle the guilt?"

"Tell me he's not buying that," said Rem.

Carlson scratched her neck. "All of that feels more realistic to him than some out-of-control corporation and its evil CEO in collusion with hired guns who kill people to protect the corporation's secrets."

Rem grunted. "That feels way more realistic to me."

"Me too," said Lexie.

"They also found drugs in his pocket and a syringe." Carlson eyed Daniels as he returned to the conversation.

"That was Marjorie," said Daniels. "J.P.'s running a fever. She wants me to pick up some medicine on the way home."

"We can do that." Rem gestured toward Carlson. "Wait until you hear the latest." He filled Daniels in on Carlson's updates.

"Those drugs were meant for me," said Lexie. "That confirms my story."

"Not if he was your dealer," said Carlson. "Or at least that's what Justini's thinking."

Daniels smirked. "Carlson, you may need to consider another partner sometime soon."

Carlson returned her cell to her pocket. "He's just doing his job."

The doors to the ER opened, and Ax walked through them. Lexie stood and hurried over. "Ax. How is he?"

"He's okay. Stitches in his head and a severe concussion, but so far, no brain swelling, which would mean surgery. They're keeping him to make sure that doesn't change. He's damned lucky he didn't have a fractured skull."

"Is he awake?" she asked.

"In and out, but loopy. I stepped out to let you know he's doing okay."

Lexie held her stomach. "Thank you." She introduced him to Daniels, Rem and Carlson, who'd joined them.

"We'll need to talk to him," said Carlson.

"Not today, you won't," said Ax. "He can barely tell you his name right now." He pointed. "I'm going to go back in. I don't want to miss the doctor. They'll move CD upstairs when they find him a room."

Some of the stress drained from Lexie. "Thanks, Ax. Once he's awake enough, I'd like to see him."

"He's not there yet, but once he comes around, I'll come and get you."

"I'd appreciate that." She spoke to Daniels and Rem. "You guys don't need to stay. Go get that medicine for J.P., Daniels."

"You sure?" said Daniels. "We can make sure you get home safe."

"I can make sure she gets home," said Ax. "Once CD gets situated." He spoke to Lexie. "If you don't mind waiting."

"I'd prefer to wait," said Lexie.

"Okay," Ax said. "Give me your number. I'll text you with updates."

Lexie gave him her cell number, and he excused himself and returned to the ER.

"You sure about this?" asked Rem.

She understood his concerns and knew he was thinking about the drive. "There's not much we can do until morning."

"I'm not sure you should go home alone until we have this sorted out," said Carlson.

"You can't stay with your mother?" asked Rem.

Lexie grimaced. "Between her and my sister, who's in town, I'd rather face George again." She paused. "I'll be okay. I'll be with Ax, and when I get home, I'll text you, Carlson. Okay?"

"And text us first thing in the morning," said Rem. "We'll talk." He held her gaze.

Lexie nodded. "We'll talk."

Carlson looked between them. "Anything I should know?"

"Let's see if Justini plans to arrest me first." Lexie found her purse and gave Rem his cell phone back.

Daniels rubbed his jaw. "Makes you wonder why Omnivista didn't press charges."

"It's not good optics," added Carlson. "Arresting the woman who shot the man who may have killed Mira Patel. There's a lot of dust that needs to settle before any decisions are made."

"Which is why I think I'm safe. For now." Lexie spoke to Daniels and Rem. "Thanks for coming. I appreciate your help."

"You stay in touch, okay?" asked Rem.

"I will."

"See you tomorrow." Daniels patted Rem on the shoulder and followed him out of the ER.

Lexie took a long, deep breath. “You don’t have to stay, Carlson, unless Justini expects you to get me to spill all my secrets.” She sat again in the chair.

Carlson sat beside her. “Forget Justini.” She took out her cell phone, turned it off and put it in her pocket. “Be honest with me, Logan. You know where that drive is, don’t you?”

Chapter Twenty-Nine

LEXIE INTERLACED HER FINGERS and rested her elbows on her knees. She didn't answer Carlson. She'd been lucky enough to avoid a direct question like that until now, and straight-out lying to a detective made her squirm.

Carlson huffed. "Damn it, Lexie. I spent most of that phone call talking Justini out of hauling you off to the station for questioning. Eventually, he'll insist, and so will my captain. I can only put them off for so long. If you know something, now is the time to say it before you have to answer these questions in an interview room in front of a two-way mirror."

Lexie bounced her foot. "It's not that simple, Carlson. We're not talking about stolen money or lost jewelry. If that drive ends up with the wrong people, Prometheus will never be stopped."

"At some point, you're going to have to trust me."

Lexie met her gaze. "And you're going to have to trust me."

"You can't do this alone."

"I'm not alone."

"Connor is injured, Zephyr is anonymous, Daniels and Remalla are not on this case, and you're keeping me at arm's length."

Lexie couldn't deny any of that. "Mira came to *me*. She trusted me."

"She trusted you to do what's right. Not handle everything by yourself."

"Carlson, I—"

The ER doors banged open, and Sasha raced in. Wearing leather boots with snug jeans and a white long-sleeved blouse, and with her smooth glossy hair brushing her shoulders, she banged on the counter of the front desk with her palm. "I'm here to see Connor Diamond." Breathing fast, she smacked the counter again when the nurse didn't immediately answer. "Where is he?"

Lexie stood. "Sasha?"

Carlson stood too.

Sasha looked over. "Lexie Logan?" She stomped over. "Were you with him?"

"I was." Lexie gestured toward Carlson. "This is Detective Carlson."

Sasha barely acknowledged the detective and pulled out her phone. She texted someone and put her phone away. "What the hell happened?"

"Connor and I were attacked, and he was hit on the head." Lexie figured Sasha had little interest in hearing the whole story.

Sasha looked Lexie over. "You seem okay."

"I am. I shot the man who hurt Connor. He's in surgery."

Sasha flapped her arms. "How did Connor get hurt?"

"He was helping me. The assailant surprised us."

Carlson spoke. "Lexie's quick thinking saved his life."

Sasha didn't look convinced. "If she were that quick," she pointed at the ER doors, "Connor wouldn't be in here, would he?" She cursed and eyed the ceiling. "God. When will he learn? He's always trying to *save* someone."

The ER doors opened, and Ax walked through them.

Sasha turned. "There you are."

"I got your text. He's with the doctor. Once they find him a room, they'll move him upstairs."

"I want to see him."

"He's still pretty out of it."

Sasha glowered. “Now, Ax.” She glanced back at Lexie. “Unless he’d rather see the person who put him in here.”

Lexie didn’t say a word. Neither did Carlson.

Ax hesitated, but stepped aside. “Right this way.”

“Thank you.” Sasha stomped away and through the ER doors with Ax.

“Pleasant woman,” said Carlson. “Who is she?”

“Connor’s girlfriend.” Dejected, Lexie sat again.

“Girlfriend?” Carlson sat beside her. “But I thought...”

Lexie dropped her head back into her hand. “That we were together? No, I told you we weren’t.”

“Huh. She doesn’t strike me as his type.”

“Apparently, she is.” Lexie’s stomach twisted. Sasha was right. This mess was all Lexie’s fault.

Carlson nudged Lexie’s arm. “Take what she says with a grain of salt. Situations like these can bring out the worst in people, and they end up apologizing later.”

“I understand that.”

Carlson paused. “You like Diamond?”

Lexie closed her eyes. “It doesn’t matter what I like.”

“Yes, it does.” She paused. “If we were sitting in a bar...scratch that, sitting in a coffee shop, I’d dive right into the girl talk, but right now, we have more pressing matters.” She turned her phone back on. “Please think about what I said. Don’t go this alone.”

Lexie thought about sitting at a bar. Every cell in her body wanted a drink. “I will.”

Carlson turned on and checked her phone. “My captain called.” She stood. “I’ll be right back.” Holding the phone to her ear, she turned and walked out of the waiting area.

Her emotions swirling, Lexie gripped her temples. She heard the ER doors open again and looked up to see Ax returning. He came over and sat beside her. "How you doing?"

She groaned. "Not great."

"Sorry about Sasha. I hope she didn't make too big a scene."

Lexie fell back in her seat. "I don't think she likes me."

"You've spent more time with CD in the last forty-eight hours than she has in the past week. She's just jealous."

Lexie snorted. "Jealous? Her? Of me?"

"Why the hell not? Connor likes you. That's obvious. He's just too damned caught up in being Mr. Nice Guy. That's plagued him since I've known him, and as much as I've tried to teach him some of my bad boy ways, it's failed every time." He rested his booted foot on his knee. "Hell. The whole reason he's with Sasha is because of me. I introduced them after he and Barbara split. I thought I was helping him get out of his rut. He just needed a fling to get back on the horse. And she was perfect for that. She's married to her work and wasn't looking for anything permanent."

Lexie sat up. "What happened?"

"It was just a fling at first. They dated for a few weeks, but between the Silva trial and CD going back and forth with Barb, it didn't last. Until Sasha called him months later when her brother got into trouble for throwing a brick through someone's window. They reconnected and have been dating ever since."

"It seems pretty serious. He told me she's his type. And she's gorgeous."

"Don't get me wrong. Sasha is a formidable woman. There aren't many like her. She's ambitious, smart, passionate, and beautiful. But she's not the one for Connor."

"Why wouldn't he want all of that?"

Ax crossed his arms. "Because he wants something more. It took me a while to figure it out, but one night, I finally did."

Curious, Lexie shifted in her seat to face him. "Not that I care, but now you have to tell me."

He smiled at her. "This secret is just between you and me. I was right in the middle of something embarrassing when it hit me. CD knows what I'm talking about, but only because he walked in and caught me."

Lexie knitted her brow. "Is this going to be TMI?"

He leaned over and lowered his voice. "I was watching Christmas movies. The super sappy ones that make you want to barf candy canes and chocolate, but you can't turn them off. I love them."

She didn't understand. "What does that have to do with what Connor wants?"

"He loves strong, beautiful women who challenge him, but what he really wants is the HEA."

"The happily ever after?" She straightened in her seat. "Everyone wants that. Don't you want that?"

"Sure I do. But I don't dwell on it. And I don't fit the traditional mold of the HEA hero."

Lexie eyed his motorcycle jacket, worn jeans, and stubbled jaw. "I think you fit it better than you think."

He chuckled. "Maybe, but I'm more the spicy romance novel. I can play that all day. Connor's the Christmas movie. You may not see the spice on screen, but you know he smolders." He grinned.

Imagining Connor smoldering, Lexie fidgeted in her seat. "Why can't he have that with Sasha?"

"Because Sasha is like me. Spicy romance novel. She's not looking for a HEA. Not right now, at least. Connor is the hero at heart, but she's not looking to be rescued."

"And I am?"

"He rescued you once before, didn't he?"

Lexie slumped. "Yes, he did." She sighed. "Is this what this is? He's just trying to save me?"

"Don't take it the wrong way. You obviously can take care of yourself. So can Sasha and Barbara. But everyone needs help at some point, and when you do, Connor wants to be the guy. He thrives on it." He shrugged. "Some women like that, and some don't. Sasha tells him she likes it, but deep down, I doubt she does." His voice turned gruff. "She's not honest with him, and that pisses me off."

"She doesn't strike me as a woman who often needs help."

"There's nothing wrong with asking for help. Sasha sees that as a weakness, but I see it as a sign of strength. It's difficult, and too many people are lousy at it." He poked at the armrest. "I should know."

Lexie thought about her conversation with Carlson. "Asking for help means trusting someone. That's hard to do."

"Discernment is key. You talk to the wrong person, you're screwed." He stared off and bobbed his foot up and down. "But Connor is the most trustworthy man I know." He looked back at her. "I think you'd say the same."

Lexie didn't know what to think. How had she ended up in this personal conversation with a man she barely knew in the waiting area of the ER? Perplexed, she leaned over and eyed the floor. "I don't know what I know anymore. I just want Connor to be okay."

"He will be." He leaned over too. "Has anyone asked you how you're doing?"

"Sure."

"I don't mean in a casual way. I mean in the *how are you doing* way?"

She sensed the meaning behind his words. "You sound like a man who's been asked that himself."

"More times than I care to admit." He smoothed his jeans. "My old man drank for years, and we were estranged until he got sober four years ago. He works hard at it. It's easier now, but he still goes to meetings and speaks to his sponsor on a weekly basis." He looked at Lexie. "When's the last time you spoke to yours?"

Lexie's throat tightened. "I'm overdue."

"Been to a meeting recently?"

"Last month."

"I've heard you've been through a lot lately, not counting tonight."

She pushed the hair off her face. "You could say that."

"Sorry if this is too personal, but how badly do you want a drink right now?"

Lexie groaned. "If there were a bar in this waiting room, I'd be making a martini."

He nodded. "May I suggest that you not neglect yourself? Call your sponsor tonight and go to a meeting tomorrow."

Knowing he was right, she expelled a shaky breath.

"Connor would tell you the same, but he's incapacitated, so I have to be the HEA guy. Just for tonight, though. I'll revert to my spicy self tomorrow."

"You're pretty good at being the HEA guy."

"Connor's an excellent teacher, but I've helped him with his spicy side, so we're even."

"You two remind me of Daniels and Remalla. You're good partners."

"Doesn't happen often, but when you find it, you hold on to it. Through thick and thin."

She thought of the Silva case. "I hear you've both been through plenty of that."

"More than I care to share."

"It must have been hard when he left the force."

"Devastating, but we're navigating our way through it." He patted her arm. "Just like you'll navigate your way through this."

Thinking about how close it came for her and Connor, she leaned back again. "He almost died tonight."

"So did you, but you're both still standing, which means there's more to be done."

Lexie wondered whether Carlson had left or was still on the phone. "I might get arrested tomorrow."

"*Might* doesn't matter. Deal with what you know."

She nibbled her lip. "What I know is that I want to talk to Connor. I need his advice."

"I can't promise he'll give it, but we can try."

"Sasha's with him."

He checked his watch. "Give it five minutes. Tops."

Lexie eyed the doors to the ER. "You know something I don't?"

"Sasha is not the type of lady to sit and watch her concussed man sleep in the ER. And there's a patient in the adjacent room moaning and asking for more meds. Her phone rings constantly. Work will call, and she'll find a reason to leave. Just sit tight."

Surprised, Lexie reached for her water bottle just as the ER doors opened and Sasha walked out, holding her cell phone.

"What'd I tell you?" Ax stood and approached Sasha. "How's he doing?"

"He's barely conscious."

"He's got a concussion. He'll be better tomorrow."

She raised her phone. "I've got a work thing. I'll be back in the morning. Can you tell him?"

"Sure."

Lexie wondered what Sasha had to do at nine o'clock at night, especially after her boyfriend had almost died. They shared a look, but neither said anything.

"Make sure he gets plenty of rest," said Sasha, still staring at Lexie.

"I will. Glad you could stop by."

Sasha glared at him. "Of course. Have a good night."

"You too."

With a last look at Lexie, Sasha walked out of the ER.

Connor stood by the ER doors. "You ready?"

"You think now's a good time?"

He pushed the door open. "Better late than never. Just don't get your hopes up. He may not be very conversational."

Lexie grabbed her water bottle and purse and headed toward the doors. "Let's go."

Chapter Thirty

Lexie walked past the nurse's station, and Ax pointed her toward a hall to her right. "He's in room three."

"Where will you be?"

He smiled. "Just saw Connor's nurse go into the coffee room. Thought I might join her."

Lexie smiled back. "Just so you know, spicy romance novels have HEAs too."

"Maybe, but people read them for the spice."

"Not everyone."

He nodded. "Maybe." He waved his hand. "Go talk to him."

Ax walked away, and Lexie approached room three. The door was partially open, so she knocked softly and poked her head in. Connor was lying in bed with a sheet pulled up to his chest and a bandage around his head. A machine beside his bed softly beeped his heart rate, and his eyes were closed.

Lexie whispered. "Connor?"

Hearing a loud moan from a nearby room, she pushed the door open and walked in. She closed the door, tucked her water bottle into her purse, and ensured her phone was tucked into the Faraday bag. She placed her purse by the wall and sat in the chair beside his bed. He didn't stir. "Connor?"

His arm was resting on top of the sheet, and she put her hand on his wrist. She watched his chest move up and down as he breathed. "It's me. Lexie."

His eyelids twitched, and he opened them. His gaze found hers, and for a horrifying moment, she wondered if he recognized her. He blinked and whispered. "Lex?"

Relief coursed through her. "It's me."

He looked around the room.

"Sasha was here, but she had to go. She'll be back tomorrow."

He looked back at her. "You okay?"

"I'm okay. Do you remember what happened?"

He stared at the ceiling with dull eyes.

"We were at the warehouse where Mira died. We were looking for the—"

"—drive." His face paled. "Did we find it?"

Clearly, his memories were affected. "That's when you were hit on the head."

He frowned at her.

"I'll tell you what happened. Just close your eyes and listen." She looked around the room. "Where's your phone?"

"Ax has it." He swallowed and closed his eyes. "Tell me."

Lexie told him about confronting biker man after his attack on Connor, and how she escaped after tasering him and shooting him with Connor's gun. He kept his eyes closed, but Lexie could tell from his expression that he was listening. She told him how she'd closed the hiding spot, waited for the police, and how he and the biker man were taken to the hospital.

She slid her hand down his wrist until he grasped her fingers. "I should have been there," he whispered. "You almost died."

"He surprised both of us and almost killed you."

"I'm sorry."

She squeezed his hand. "Connor, if we're going to blame someone, blame me. But we can discuss that later. That drive is still in the warehouse, and I can't let it stay there."

His eyes abruptly opened. They were still glassy but more alert. "You stay away from there."

"If someone finds it..."

"You can't go back."

She scooted closer. "It has to be found. I can't risk Omnivista finding it. Biker man knows where it is. If he survives, he'll tell someone, but if he doesn't, they'll..."

"It doesn't matter. They may already know."

Lexie narrowed her eyes. "What do you mean?"

"Prometheus."

For a second, she didn't understand until his reasoning popped into her head. "You think Prometheus was listening to our conversation in the warehouse?"

Connor closed his eyes again. "If George had a phone..."

Lexie dropped her jaw. Connor was right. If fake George had brought a Vista phone with him, which he likely had, or at least a phone with the Vista app, Prometheus could have heard everything they'd said. According to Zephyr, Prometheus would need time to sort through the data, but it wouldn't take long for the AI to be triggered. Hours at most, which meant they were almost out of time.

Connor shifted and winced. "You can't go back."

She looked to see him staring at her. "Carlson asked me about the drive. She suspects we found it."

"Tell her."

Lexie clutched his fingers. "It's not safe."

"It's not safe for anyone. She's a cop. You said you trusted her."

Lexie hesitated.

"Lexie."

She leaned closer. "I don't know what to do."

"Ask for help. It's not worth your life." His thumb traced over the back of her hand. "Please."

She saw the worry in his eyes and relented. "Okay."

"Thank you." He closed his eyes again. "Promise me."

"I promise." She could hear the fatigue in his voice. "Carlson and Justini will want to question you tomorrow, but don't be surprised if they try tonight."

He nodded slightly and winced again. "Head hurts."

She resisted the urge to brush back a lock of hair that had fallen onto his forehead. "You rest."

His body relaxed, and his breathing softened.

Lexie heard another muffled groan from the room next door. A man shouted. "Where's my pill, you lousy doctors?"

The door opened, and Ax walked in with the nurse. "Sorry to interrupt," said Ax, "but good news. They found you a room, partner."

Connor kept his eyes closed. "Good."

The nurse moved closer to Connor's bed and checked his machines. "We'll get you upstairs soon, Mr. Diamond."

Connor cracked an eye open. "Ax."

Ax leaned over the bed. "What do you need, buddy?"

Connor glanced at Lexie. "Make sure she gets home safe."

"Already taken care of. Now that you're situated, I'll take care of her."

"Thank you."

"You got it."

There was another knock, and an orderly with a wheelchair stood at the door.

"Looks like your chariot has arrived," said the nurse.

"We'll go," said Ax. "You get some rest, partner, or at least as much as you can with these nurses poking and prodding at you."

"I'll try," said Connor. "Be careful."

"Always, and I'll see you tomorrow," said Ax. "You ready?" he asked Lexie.

Lexie picked up her purse. "I need to talk to Detective Carlson before we leave."

Connor opened his eyes, and Lexie leaned over him. "I'll be back in the morning."

"You better." Connor paused. "Go home...and trust Carlson."

She squeezed his hand and left with Ax.

• • • • • • • • • • •

Lexie walked out of the ER and saw Carlson in the waiting area. Carlson walked over. "There you are."

"I saw Connor. They're moving him upstairs."

"That's great," said Carlson. "Any chance you thought about what I said?"

"I'll go get the car," said Ax. "I'll pick you up outside."

"Thanks, Ax." Ax left, and Lexie eyed Carlson. "Connor agrees with you."

"I'm glad to hear it, but do you agree with me?"

Despite what she'd told Connor, Lexie still hesitated.

"Your time's running out," said Carlson. "My captain is leaning toward Justini's side. Justini is on his way here."

"What for?"

"To get updates on the fake George, maybe talk to Connor, and if that doesn't work, maybe talk to Edna." She pointed. "And they'll want to speak to you first thing tomorrow. They want you to come to the station."

"Justini can't know about the drive."

"Then tell me before he gets here."

Lexie took a deep breath and prayed she was doing the right thing. "If I tell you, this stays between us. You bring Justini in or your captain, or you mention it to a friend on the phone or write it up in a report, you endanger lives. And if you go get the drive, you risk yours as well. Omnivista can't know."

"I understand the implications. But if we're going to do this, it has to be now. Before Justini shows, I can find a reason to go back to the warehouse, and he can wait for me until I get back."

"We also have to consider that Prometheus overheard the conversation between me, Connor, and George, and if he did..."

"Then we have even less time."

Lexie's heart rate picked up. "You'll call me? When you find it? Make sure it's my burner, and your phone is off."

"I will. But once I have it, I'll have to hide it until we can figure out what to do with it."

"Where?"

Carlson paused. "I'll stop at home and put it in my gun safe."

Lexie didn't know if she liked that or not, but had little choice. "Just be extremely careful. If anyone sees you..."

"I understand. Now where is it?"

Lexie almost changed her mind, but remembering her promise to Connor, she leaned close and told Carlson where to find the drive.

• • • • • • • • • • •

Lexie opened her door, and Ax walked in first. She stood in the entryway while he checked her duplex.

"All clear." He walked out of the bedroom. "You sure you're okay to be alone?"

Lexie resisted the urge to check her watch. The entire drive home, all she could do was think about where Carlson was and what she was doing. "I'm okay. After everything that's happened, I doubt anyone will stir up any more trouble tonight."

"If you need anything, call me. Now that you're important to Connor, you're important to me."

"I appreciate that." She set her purse on the table. "I just want to take a hot shower and get some sleep."

"And call that sponsor?"

She smiled. "That too. And go to a meeting."

"Sorry if I'm prying."

"You're not. Connor would tell me the same."

"He would." He walked to the door. "Lock it."

"I will. And thanks, Ax." She held the door open as he walked out. "Connor's a lucky guy," she said.

"He's got you and me in his corner. The man hit the jackpot." He waved. "I'll see you tomorrow at the hospital."

"Provided I'm not arrested."

He glanced back. "Deal with what you know, remember?"

"I'll do my best."

"Night."

"Night."

After she closed and locked the door, she headed straight for her purse. She pulled out her burner from Frank, but Carlson hadn't called. She cursed and sat at her breakfast table, wondering what to do besides wait.

Eyeing the time, she realized she'd better contact her mother and Frank before the events at the warehouse hit the news. Using her regular phone, she called each of them, answered their questions as best she could without telling them too much, and did her best to convince them she was okay and didn't need to spend the night anywhere else but at home. With everything going on, she needed to be on her own.

After talking to them, she returned her cell to the Faraday bag and considered calling her sponsor, Mickey, but couldn't stop worrying about Carlson. Her mind raced with potential problems. What if Carlson were caught? What if Prometheus informed Omnivista, and they got to the drive first? What if Carlson interrupted someone else searching for the drive? Lexie couldn't sit still, and when Zephyr's phone rang, she jumped. She grabbed it from her purse and answered. "I'm here."

Zephyr responded. "Where the hell have you been?"

She bit back an unpleasant response. "In case you haven't heard, I've been through hell and back tonight looking for that drive. Connor's in the hospital, and I was almost in the morgue."

"I heard about the excitement at the warehouse.

"Excitement? That's one word for it."

"Fill me in. Did you find O'Dell?"

Feeling as though her visit with O'Dell was ages ago, she told Zephyr about the events of the day and evening.

"You told Detective Carlson?" asked Zephyr with dismay.

"I had no choice. I couldn't go back to the warehouse, but I couldn't leave the drive. What did you expect me to do?"

"The more people involved in this, the more likely Mira's plans will fail."

"Don't you think I know that?" She sat at her table. "But I can't go this alone."

"I hope to hell you know what you're doing."

"If you think you can do better, I'll happily let you."

"Prepare yourself for the worst, but if Carlson finds the drive, you'll have to open it."

Lexie squinted. "Thank you for that wise advice. Please tell me you didn't say such illuminating things like that to Mira."

"It's not as simple as you think. Mira likely encrypted it, or it may have a password. And you can't open it on any computer. Prometheus will be hunting for it. If it picks up the scent, you'll be no safer than you are now."

Lexie slumped over the table. "How am I supposed to read it then?"

"If there's a password, we'll deal with it. And you'll need an air-gapped laptop to open it. One that doesn't connect to the internet."

Lexie couldn't believe this. Finding the drive was only half the problem.

"What's important now is to keep the drive hidden and pray Omnivista doesn't know you've found it."

Her head pounding, Lexie squeezed her temples. "So finding the drive is just the beginning."

"You better believe it."

Lexie's other burner phone rang, and she straightened. She hoped this mess would end soon because she was tired of managing three cell phones. "I have to go. That's Carlson."

"Be careful. And toss this phone after tonight. I'll get in touch with a new one."

"But—" She couldn't finish her sentence because Zephyr had hung up. She answered the other burner. "Carlson? It's me."

"Lexie." Carlson's breathless voice traveled over the line. "I just left the warehouse."

Lexie could barely breathe. "Did you find it?"

"I went to the room and found the loose baseboard, but there's nothing there."

Lexie froze. "What? Did you find the bag?"

"No. There was no bag. There was nothing. If the drive was there, it's gone now."

Lexie's head throbbed, and her heart fell. Defeat shot through her belly, and she fought the urge to be ill. At the same time, she thought of Zephyr's warning. Had Carlson betrayed her?

"Lexie? You there?"

Discouraged, Lexie dropped her head into her palm. Whether Carlson was lying, or someone else had found the drive, the game was over. Omnivista had won, and there was nothing Lexie could do. "They got there first." Lexie wished she had a drink. Realizing she'd failed, she fought back tears. "Go back to the hospital, Carlson. It's over." She took a long, shaky breath. "Prometheus won."

Chapter Thirty-One

CARLSON SAT IN HER car outside the warehouse and stared out the windshield. The crime scene unit was finishing and loading up their van, reporters were preparing to broadcast their live news reports from across the street, and officers remained at the scene, ensuring no one without authority accessed the warehouse.

While talking with Lexie, Carlson heard the dejection in her voice and understood it. After all she'd risked, someone else had beaten her to the drive. Thinking, Carlson replayed the events of the last two hours in her mind, wondering if she'd missed something. She'd spent most of that time at the hospital, while Justini... She sat up. "Justini was here," she said to herself. She tried to grasp the possibility that her partner had found the drive, and if he had, what had he done with it? Was he working with Omnivista? Or was he so determined to prove Lexie guilty that he'd hide evidence? She found either scenario hard to believe. Determined to learn the truth, she picked up the phone and called him.

He answered on the first ring. "Carlson? Where the hell are you?"

"I told you. I went back to the warehouse."

"And I told you to stay at the hospital. That I was on my way. What the hell is going on?"

Carlson didn't mince words. "Did you take it, Phil?"

"Take what?"

"You know what. The USB drive. That Mira hid in the warehouse. Did you find it? Did you give it to Omnivista?"

Justini went silent, and Mira's heart thumped. After a long pause, Justini finally responded. "Are you out of your ever lovin' mind? Did you get hit on the head like Diamond?"

Carlson fell back in her seat. Could she believe him? "Where are you?"

"I'm at the damn hospital, where you should be. Is that why you went back? Did Logan send you on some wild goose chase? Trying to convince you that this evidence exists? She's playing you, Carlson, and you should know that. There was never any USB." He uttered a snort. "How the hell did you become a detective at such a young age?"

Carlson shut her eyes. Was he right? Had Lexie been lying the entire time? Had Carlson been so easily fooled? Too tired to think, she dropped her head and rubbed her shoulders. "Persistence, lots of coffee, and putting up with old farts like you, Phil."

"Old farts like me are way smarter. Remember that."

She pinched the bridge of her nose. "Sorry Phil. I'm not thinking too straight. Have you talked to anyone yet?"

"Diamond's getting moved to his room, and I've been told I'll have to wait until tomorrow to question him. Edna, though, is a different story. She's awake. You care to join me, or would you rather run all over town doing Logan's bidding?"

Figuring she deserved that, she sighed. "I'll head that way."

"I'll wait with bated breath."

A rap on the window startled Carlson. She looked to see Officer Henley, who was in charge of the scene, standing outside. "See you soon, Phil." She hung up with Justini and opened her door. "Hey, Henley. Everything okay?"

He nodded. "Fine, but you were asking about anyone who accessed the crime scene this evening?"

Carlson got out of the car. "I was. You learn something?"

Henley looked to his left. "Byers. Get your butt over here."

A young officer who didn't look more than eighteen jogged over. "Yes, sir."

"Tell her what you saw," said Henley.

Byers looked at Carlson. "What I saw?"

Henley rolled his eyes. "The other detective, Byers. Who visited the scene?"

Carlson tensed. "What other detective?"

"Oh, yeah," said Byers. "Detective Sykes."

Carlson put her hand on her car door. "Tell me about him."

Byers shrugged. "He said he was from another division. He thought this crime lined up with another in his area. Wanted to look around."

"He show you an ID?"

"Sure did."

"What did he look like?"

Byers' eyes widened. "Did I do something wrong?"

"No. But what did he look like?"

"Taller than me. With a mustache and glasses. He wore a knitted cap over his head and one of those long coats."

"Like a trench coat?"

"I guess."

The night was cool but not cold enough for a trench coat and cap. "When did he get here?"

He shrugged. "Maybe thirty minutes ago. He left about ten minutes before you came back."

Carlson cursed inwardly. "Thank you." She got back into her car.

••••••••••

Emotionally exhausted, Lexie stood and went into the kitchen. She'd had no dinner but also had no appetite. She poured herself some juice, ate a few bites of a banana, and took some aspirin. Her mind wouldn't stop, and all she could do was question what she'd done wrong. Had Carlson found the drive and kept it? Was she working for Omnivista? Had she taken Justini's side?

In her heart, she couldn't believe that was true. She suspected they'd run out of time. Prometheus had overheard everything, and Omnivista had sent someone to get the drive before Carlson had made it back. She cursed herself for leaving the drive behind, although that would have involved plenty more risks, but that didn't matter right now.

Angry and upset that she'd failed Mira and herself, she left the rest of the banana on the counter, left the kitchen, and went into her bedroom. Trying not to think about going to the liquor store to grab a bottle of vodka, which would be easy because there was a store five minutes away, she flipped on her do-it-yourself security system, grabbed her robe, went into the bathroom and started the shower. She wanted to forget about everything - the drive, Omnivista, Prometheus, Mira, Connor, Sasha, Natalie, Jonah, her father, and her mother, who would no doubt tell her she should have stuck with reporting on lifestyles or entertainment.

Doing her best not to dwell on her failures, she stripped off her clothes, stepped into the bath and let the hot spray soothe her mind and body.

••••••••••

Driving away from the warehouse, Carlson called Justini again.

"Now what?" he asked.

"Hey, do you know a Detective Sykes?" Justini had been around long enough that Carlson felt confident that if there were a Detective Sykes, Justini would have heard of him.

"Sykes?" He paused. "There was an Allen Sykes, but he retired probably ten years ago. Why?"

"Because I was just told that a Detective Sykes visited the crime scene. He left before I arrived. He told an officer that he thought it resembled another incident in his division, but I think that's bullshit." She gave Justini the description of Sykes.

"I don't know who the hell that is." Justini went quiet. "What are you thinking with that wacky brain of yours, Carlson?"

"I think he came here looking for whatever Mira planned to give Logan."

Justini muttered something. "Can I offer an alternative theory? Maybe he was there to collect the money Logan and Diamond left behind?"

"That makes no sense. We didn't find any money."

"We haven't found any secret drive either."

"There's no proof that fake George was working with Logan and Diamond. This whole blackmail idea is not panning out. Even if George survives, we can't trust him to tell us the truth."

"About that...I just checked. George died in the operating room."

Carlson stopped at a light. "Damn it."

"Agreed. Which leaves us only Connor Diamond and Edna. I'm outside her room, and I can hear the TV. The officer outside her door says she's better today."

Carlson considered her next move. Should she try to find Detective Sykes? Something told her that the fake detective had the drive and was long gone.

Disappointed, she drove when the light changed. "Go easy on her, will you? Try to be a little patient."

"Let me see if my pleasant bedside manner will sway her. You're not the only one who has one."

"I'll be there soon."

"I'll put you on speaker. You can join in if my bedside manner gives way."

Carlson wondered whether Prometheus would be listening, but imagined Justini's response if she mentioned her concerns. And as a detective, she couldn't go around using burner phones. She figured she'd hear what Edna had to say and deal with any repercussions later. "Okay."

Carlson heard a knock and Justini's voice. "Here goes." There was a pause, and Justini said hello to Edna. He told her he was in the area and, when he heard her TV, he thought he'd stop by. He mentioned his partner, Detective Carlson, was on her way but was on the phone to join the conversation.

Over the phone, Carlson said hello to Edna and told her to take her time and not feel rushed.

Edna was quiet at first, but not resistant, and Justini, to his credit, didn't push. He asked her how she was feeling and would she feel comfortable answering some questions about her attacker? "If you're scared," said Justini, "you don't need to be. What you say will be between us, and there's an officer outside your door."

Her voice a little shaky, Edna said she'd been thinking about what happened to her and to Mira, and despite her attack, had reconsidered, but didn't think she knew much that could help. Justini encouraged her and started with her attacker. She described fake George and reiterated what Lexie had said George had told them at the bar. That gave Carlson hope Justini would believe Lexie.

"Had you seen this man before?" asked Justini.

Edna went quiet.

"Edna, it's okay if you have," said Justini. "We need to know."

After a pause, Carlson felt a flare of hope when Edna said she'd seen him. "Where, Edna?" she asked over the phone.

Edna spoke softly, so Carlson turned the volume up to listen. "Outside Mira's house," said Edna, "about a week before she died. He was in a car with another man. I had a weird feeling they were watching Mira, but I told myself I was overreacting." Carlson heard a sob. "I wish I'd paid more attention."

"You're sure one of the men in the car was the man who attacked you?" asked Justini.

"Yes. He had on the same blue bandana."

"And the other man?

"He was harder to see. But he wore glasses and a knit cap."

Carlson gripped the steering wheel. Was the mystery Detective Sykes the same man in the car with George? "Did you notice anything else, Edna?" asked Carlson. "The smallest detail could help."

"Yes," she said. "The reason I noticed them was because they looked cramped in that small car."

"Small car?" asked Justini. "What kind of car?"

"It was an old Corvette. I used to have one, and it's not big."

Carlson's skin prickled. She recalled Lexie's neighbor, Lynn, telling her that her new boyfriend drove an old Corvette. Was that just a coincidence? Her stomach clenched. "Did that car have a cracked windshield, Edna?"

"Yes, actually. It did."

Carlson braked and pulled over to the side of the road. "Justini, take me off speaker."

There was a click, and Justini's voice returned. "Yeah?"

"Hold on the line," she said. "I'll be right back."

"Carlson, what is—?"

Carlson clicked over to call Lexie, but after dialing her number, Lexie's phone went straight to voicemail. "Shit," said Carlson. She clicked back over to Justini. "Justini, that same car belongs to the new boyfriend of Lexie Logan's neighbor. That's no coincidence. If he's the mystery Detective Sykes, and if he didn't find what he wanted at the warehouse, or he did and wants to tie up loose ends, Lexie's in trouble. Logan's not answering her phone. Get over there. Right now. I'm already on my way."

Before Justini could utter a response, Carlson hung up and, her tires screeching, made a rapid U-turn.

Chapter Thirty-Two

Lexie came out of her steamy bathroom wearing her robe. She removed the towel wrapped around her hair, blotted it, and hung the towel back up in the bathroom. After returning to the bedroom, she took off her robe and put on a pair of sweatpants and a sweatshirt, and combed out her hair.

Numb with fatigue and disappointment, she left the bedroom. While in the shower, she'd decided that her next phone call would be to Mickey. She needed to talk to someone before she took a bad turn and reached for a drink. Her phone was not on the table, though, where she thought she'd left it. Digging through her purse, she stopped, and a chill ran through her when she didn't see any of her three phones.

"Looking for these?" asked a male voice from behind her.

She whirled and saw a man standing near the sink. He was tall with a mustache and wore a knit cap and gloves. Her three phones were on the counter, next to a brown paper bag and a bottle of tequila. Fear rippled through her, and frozen in place, she realized she recognized him. She held onto the back of a chair to steady herself. "Rip O'Dell?"

He smiled at her. "I turned off your phones. It's better if we're not interrupted."

She fought to remain calm. "What are you doing here? How did you get in?"

"Your friend, Lynn. She has a copy of your key. And now, so do I."

She didn't understand. "Lynn?" Her heart raced when she remembered Lynn's latest boyfriend. "You're the man she met in the park?"

"She told me about you. She made it easy for me to find a way in."

Lexie eyed her door, which was still locked.

He chuckled. "I came over here after we met this afternoon. Once I knew you and your investigator were going to the warehouse, I had to be ready in case you found that drive. I unlocked your bedroom window and removed its alarm sensor. You really should invest in a more reliable security system."

She couldn't believe what she was hearing.

"I entered through the window while you were in the shower." He chuckled again. "Your door is still locked, and your alarm is still on. It's perfect, really. When I leave, no one will know I was ever here."

Horror raced through her, and her skin broke out in goosebumps. She shook her head. "But why?"

His smile vanished. "You know why."

She fought back panic. "I don't understand."

"Where is it?" he yelled.

She stepped back.

He grabbed the paper bag and liquor and advanced toward her. "Where is the drive?"

She backed into her table. "I don't have it. You got to it first."

"Liar!" He dropped the bag on the table and opened it. He pulled out the small, opaque plastic bag she recognized from the spot behind the baseboard.

"That's it," she said.

He dug into the bag and dumped the contents on her table. "Four old joints and a lighter."

She gaped at the items. Mira had indeed hidden her pot inside the room in the warehouse. Lexie didn't know what to say.

"You took it, didn't you? Where is it?"

"I...I don't know. I didn't have time to take anything before George showed up."

"But you had time after you shot him." He sneered at her.

She shook her head again. "But...I didn't. I just closed the baseboard. I assumed the drive was still in there."

"How stupid do you think I am?"

"I...I..."

He reached out and grabbed her hair. She screeched, and he pulled her forward, grabbed a chair and shoved her into it. "I'm not leaving here without it."

She desperately tried to think. She had to buy some time. "You betrayed Mira, didn't you? You befriended her, and she told you her plans?"

He brought his face close to hers. "Mira was a brilliant and beautiful woman, but she had her flaws."

"She trusted you."

He stared into her eyes with a hard gaze and pulled off his mustache. "I'm pretty good at deception. I knew she was up to something. She didn't tell me everything, but I knew enough to suggest she should be followed. And then, the day before she decided to betray Omnivista, she told me she was going to contact you. That sealed her fate."

She hated hearing that Mira's plan was doomed from the start. "Why did you have to kill her?"

"She gave me no choice."

"Why didn't you take the drive then?"

He loomed over her. "Because we thought we already had it. She gave you an envelope with a blank drive. She fooled us."

Her fingers shook, and her voice trembled. "What happened that night?"

"You know what happened."

"I don't. George took me into the other room. He drugged me. If you had confronted Mira, she wouldn't have had time to hide the drive." She was grasping at anything to keep him talking.

He glared, and his eyes shimmered. "I didn't want to kill her. I liked her, and if she'd listened, she might have survived."

"I was supposed to die, wasn't I?"

"George was responsible for you. I was in charge of Mira. After George took you into the other room, I watched the hall from the restroom. I waited for Mira. I planned to confront her and see what she would say. When I saw her leave, I came out of the bathroom. She took one look at me and knew. She ran into the mailroom and slammed the door. I was disappointed when I realized she would not be cooperative. I went to the door and knocked; she had nowhere to go."

Shaking, Lexie tried not to cry. "But she was shot in the other room."

"I opened the door and saw her. She cursed at me and called me a coward. I grabbed her and took her back to the other room. I figured it would be better to finish things in the same place you two met. Makes it cleaner when the cops investigate."

"And you shot her."

He straightened, reached back into the paper bag, and pulled out a gun. "With this." He set the gun on her table.

Lexie sucked in a hard-fought breath.

"They'll find it here after they discover your body." He reached into the bag. "Along with this." He pulled out a bag of drugs and a syringe. "You'll finally kill yourself tonight."

Lexie didn't think it was possible for her fear levels to rise. "No."

"Yes." He leaned close again and pulled her head back by her hair. She winced. "If you tell me where the drive is, I'll make it quick and easy. No pain." His gaze darkened. "But if you make it hard..."

Desperate, Lexie prayed for a way out of this. "I'm telling you. All I saw was the bag. Nothing else. I assumed the drive was inside, but I never looked. She obviously didn't hide it there."

He yanked her hair and shoved her to the ground. She hit the floor with a grunt. "Is it here?" he asked.

Staying on the ground, she turned and scooted away from him. "It's not, but feel free to look. That's not going to help with your *I killed myself* story. Why would I toss my own place?"

He glared again and reached for her. She screamed when he grabbed her, pulled her up, and shoved her against the wall. Her head hit hard, and she lost her breath. "We'll do it the ugly way then." He dragged her back to the chair and roughly sat her back in it. He gripped her by the throat and leered at her. "Don't move." He let her go and grabbed the tequila bottle. "Time for a drink."

The panic she had tried to keep at bay rocketed through her. She couldn't let him do this. The memory of George forcing her to drink made her want to gag. But back then, she'd already been drugged. Now, she had her full faculties.

Before he could open the bottle, she jumped out of the chair. If he were going to do this, she wouldn't make it easy. She got to the door and unlocked it, but he grabbed her before she could escape. He tossed her back to the ground and kicked her in the stomach. The oxygen whooshed out of her, and she curled inward, holding her stomach. Fighting to breathe, she braced for another kick when he stepped over her.

"I'll bring the bottle to you unless you want to tell me where the drive is. You do, and I'll start with the drugs instead."

Lexie sensed he was rapidly losing it. The more she fought, the harder it would be for him to sell the story that she had done this to herself. But he didn't seem to care. When he stepped away, she fought to get up. Getting onto her hands and knees, she sucked in some air, crawled to the door again, and saw the front table. She'd placed a small statue of a frog on it that her dad had given her years ago. She'd never been able to get rid of it. It was a reminder of happier times. Thinking fast, she crawled toward it.

"Where are you going?"

She reached up and grabbed the statue just before he dragged her backward. He saw it and laughed at her. "You going to hit me with that? Give it your best shot." He held the tequila bottle, gripped her hair, and hauled her into a sitting position. "Time for a drink."

She started to cry and stopped fighting him. "Please don't do this."

"Last chance. Where is the drive?"

Tears slid down her face. "In the bedroom. In my closet. I found it, just like you said. I hid it after I got home."

He narrowed his eyes but lowered the bottle. "Get up. Show me."

O'Dell yanked her to a standing position, and Lexie gripped the frog. "Move," he said. He shoved her forward into her bedroom.

Barely holding it together, she continued to beg him to let her go. As she walked past her bedroom door with him behind her, she grabbed the edge of it and slammed it into him. He barely moved with the contact, but he cursed, grabbed her arm and yanked her close. "You shouldn't have done that."

Her nearness to him gave her leverage, and she hauled her knee back and directed it into his groin. At the last second, he moved and avoided a direct hit, but the impact was hard enough for him to cry out and buckle to his knees. She dodged around him, but he caught her ankle and she toppled to the floor. Enraged, he threw the tequila bottle at her. It glanced off the side of her head, hit the floor, but didn't break. It rolled toward the table.

Seeing stars, Lexie forced herself back onto her knees. Breathing fast and terrified, she got up and headed for the door when he was suddenly there again. He grabbed her by the back of her head and, still holding the frog, she threw it at the window in her living area. It hit and cracked the glass; the frog shattered, and her high-pitched alarm began to shriek. Keeping the system active had worked against him. Hearing Foster bark, Lexie prayed Lynn was home and would contact the police.

Cursing, he tossed her roughly back to the floor and stomped back to the table, where he picked up the gun. "Last chance. Where is it?" Sweat rolled down the sides of his face.

Lexie touched her head where the bottle had hit her, and her fingers came back bloody. Seeing the gun aimed at her, she could see O'Dell had fully lost it. She held out her hand. "Rip. Don't."

He took a step closer. "George should have done this at the start. You're a miserable bitch."

Lexie scooted away to put some distance between them, but if he fired, that was it. "If you shoot me, they'll know it was you. Omnivista will turn on you."

"Fuck Omnivista. They're not as omnipotent as they think." He took a step closer and straightened his aim.

Seeing the wild look in his eye, she braced and said a silent *I'm sorry* to her mother when she heard a loud bang on the door. Someone shouted, "Police!" and the door flew open with a loud crack.

Rip swiveled the gun and fired. Lexie turned away, rolled into a ball, and kept her eyes shut. There was another gunshot, and Lexie heard two more rapid-fire shots before it all went quiet.

• • • • • • • • • • •

In a shooting stance, Carlson didn't move. She'd come in behind Justini, who'd been hit but had fired back. Carlson shot the gunman twice. He collapsed and dropped the gun. Her hands shaking, Carlson immediately called for backup, declared an officer was down, and requested an ambulance. She kicked the assailant's gun away and checked his pulse. He was still alive, but unconscious. She raced to Justini, who was conscious but lying on the floor against the wall. Examining his wound, she saw he'd been hit in the shoulder.

Grimacing, he pushed her back. "I'm okay. Check on Logan."

Relieved his wound didn't appear life-threatening, she ran to Lexie's side. She was curled up in a ball and not moving. "Lexie. Are you okay?" She touched her shoulder. "Lexie, it's Carlson."

Lexie moved, and Carlson heard her whimper.

"It's okay," said Carlson. "It's over." She jostled her shoulder. "Lexie?"

"Carlson?" Lexie slowly unfolded, and Carlson saw blood running down her face and neck.

"Take it easy. Ambulance is coming."

Lexie moaned and clutched her stomach. "It's Rip. Rip O'Dell." Tears ran down her face, and she tried to sit up. "He thought I had the drive."

The alarm continued to wail, and Carlson winced at the sound. "How do I turn the alarm off?"

Lexie told her where the remote was. Carlson found it and switched it off. The apartment went quiet, although Foster continued to bark, and Carlson helped Lexie get into a sitting position on the floor. "Stay here." She straightened and walked over to the man she'd shot. Taking a good look at him, she recognized O'Dell from when she and Justini had questioned Mira's coworkers after her death. She guessed O'Dell was also Detective Sykes.

She spied a tequila bottle on the floor and drugs on the breakfast table. Getting an idea of what O'Dell had planned, she went into the kitchen, found two dishtowels and brought them over to Justini. She pressed one of the towels against his wound. He grimaced and cursed, and she told him to keep pressure on it. He nodded, and she returned to Lexie with the second towel and put it against her head. "You better?"

Lexie looked at her with frightened eyes, and more tears escaped and slid down her cheeks. “Is Justini okay?”

“He’ll live. He’s hit in the shoulder.”

More tears surfaced. “You two saved my life.” She took the towel from Carlson and held it against her head.

Distant sirens wailed in the distance. “No. Edna did.” She told Lexie what Edna had said about the men in the Corvette. She regarded O’Dell. “He pretended to be a detective to gain access to the crime scene at the warehouse. He must have taken the drive and come here to shut you up.”

Lexie shook her head. “He didn’t have it.”

Carlson tensed. “He thought you did?”

Lexie nodded.

“So where the hell is it?”

Lexie looked at O’Dell with dismay. “I don’t know.”

The sirens grew louder, and Carlson could hear them pull up outside. “Stay put. The cavalry is here.” She stood and ran outside to meet them.

Chapter Thirty-Three

Two days later, Lexie sat in the hospital breakroom on Connor's floor. He was due to be released later that day, but because she hadn't seen him since his arrival in the ER, she'd stopped by. The day before, she'd spent most of the day in bed. After she, O'Dell, and Justini arrived at the hospital after O'Dell's break-in, O'Dell and Justini had gone into surgery. Lexie had remained in the ER while they did tests and stitched her head. Her mother and Frank had arrived and argued over who she would stay with after she was released. Lexie had chosen Frank until her mother had told her that Natalie had flown out earlier that evening to see Walker and had left Chase with her. Hearing that, Lexie agreed to stay with her mom. Thankfully, her tests had shown no serious damage, and the doctors had let her leave at three o'clock in the morning.

Exhausted and thankful to be alive, she'd fallen into bed and slept until noon. Chase had woken her, saying a detective was there to talk to her and asking if she wanted breakfast.

After rousing herself, she'd gone downstairs to see Carlson, who'd told her Justini was doing fine after having a bullet removed from his shoulder. O'Dell had made it through surgery but was in a coma in the ICU.

Her mother had insisted Lexie eat, and while she cooked, Lexie gave her statement to Carlson, telling her everything that had happened between her and O'Dell. She was happy to hear from Carlson that Justini was ready to admit that Lexie was telling the truth about Mira and Omnivista, especially after what Edna had told them, the murder weapon being found, and O'Dell's impersonation of a detective and assault on Lexie.

After Carlson had left, Lexie ate and went back to bed. She didn't get up until a nightmare of O'Dell forcing her to drink tequila woke her. That had shaken her, and she'd called Mickey. They'd talked for an hour, and she'd agreed to meet him for a coffee and an AA meeting that night. Despite her weariness, she went and was glad she had. They'd agreed to meet again the following week.

That morning, she'd called Connor, and he'd told her he was due to be released that day but couldn't be sure when, so encouraged her to stop by. Ax had told him what had happened with O'Dell, and he wanted to see her.

Eager to see him too, Lexie agreed, but when she arrived at the hospital, Barbara and Brooke were with him. Not wanting to interrupt, she'd gone to get some coffee in the breakroom. That gave her some time to call Daniels and Remalla and get them up to speed with all that had happened.

After hanging up with them, she pulled out her phone and reread the article in the *California Gazette* that had been published that morning. A few local news stations had picked up the story and tried to contact her, but Lexie had given the scoop to Karen. After what happened to Lexie, Grazer had delayed and rewritten her article to include updates about George Constable and Rip O'Dell's involvement in Mira's death. Lexie had spoken to Karen the previous day and told her about her recalled memories, and the assaults on her and Connor. Karen had planned to follow up with Carlson and attempt to get comments from Nolan Sorrento and Eliza Thorne. The latter had been unsuccessful, but Carlson had confirmed Lexie's account of how Constable and O'Dell had targeted Mira as a potential whistleblower and were being investigated for her murder. Without Mira's data from Omnivista, though, more evidence was required to confirm her intentions.

The article did not frame Omnivista in a positive light, and Grazer had called Lexie earlier to tell her other major news outlets had picked up her story and it was going national. That made Lexie smile. She understood it was temporary, though. Unless fresh evidence emerged, the story would lose its pull after a few days, and the spotlight on Omnivista would dim, but for now, Sorrento and Thorne would have to stay out of the public eye. That accomplishment gave her plenty of satisfaction, and she reveled in it because she suspected Thorne was scrambling to do damage control. If the rumors about Sorrento's temper were true, Lexie could imagine his reaction to the negative press.

"Lexie Logan?"

She looked up to see Dr. William McCabe, the doctor who'd treated her after she'd been found in the alley. Surprised, she put the magazine down and stood. "Dr. McCabe?" He stood in the doorway wearing his doctor's coat with his embroidered name on the pocket and a stethoscope around his neck. He looked as handsome as she remembered. Lexie was glad her mother wasn't there.

"I was on my way to see a patient," he said, "and saw you." He pointed at her head. "Are you all right?"

She touched her bandage. "I am. Just a few stitches. Nothing serious." She stepped closer. "I'm here to see a friend."

"How's the memory loss? Anything come back?"

She nodded. "All of it, actually."

"Good. Did it help sort things out?"

"You could say that. I'm still working on it."

"Glad to hear it." He studied her with his dark brown eyes. "I should tell you that during your stay, your mother gave me your phone number."

Lexie dropped her jaw. “You’re kidding? She shouldn’t have done that.”

“No, she shouldn’t have, which is why I didn’t use it.” He crossed his arms. “She’s quite the lady. She didn’t think I had a brain in my head until you were about to be discharged.”

“She can drive people a little crazy. Me especially.”

“But she loves you. That’s obvious.”

“I know she does.”

He studied her again with a hard-to-read look. “I’m glad you’re doing better.”

She imagined what he was thinking. “If you’re worried that I’m drinking or doing drugs, I’m not.”

“I saw all that crap about you on Vista. I figured it was all nonsense.”

“It was. I’m sober and despite everything, feeling pretty good.”

He smiled. “I’m happy to hear that.” He paused. “Since you’re here, I might as well ask, do you mind if I use your number? Maybe we can get a coffee sometime?”

Lexie didn’t expect that. “Coffee?”

“Is that okay? It’s fine if you say no.”

Lexie considered her life now. “I’m still working through some things related to my supposed overdose. It’s hard to explain.”

He pursed his lips. “I understand. Timing is important.”

Lexie thought of Connor. Why was she pining for him when he loved someone else? “But maybe in a couple of weeks? That might work better for me.”

His posture relaxed. “I don’t mind waiting.” He gestured down the hall. “I’ve got to go, but I’ll call you in two weeks. We’ll get that coffee.”

Suddenly nervous, she rubbed her arms. “I’d like that. I’ll see you later, Doctor McCabe.”

“Call me Bill. Take care, and I’ll see you, Lexie.” He stepped away and walked down the hall.

Unsure of what had just happened, Lexie stood still, thinking, when a nurse stopped by to ask if she was Lexie Logan. She said yes and was told that Mr. Diamond was looking for her.

Still reeling from her talk with Bill, she went to Connor's room and knocked on the door.

"Come in."

She entered to see him lying on the bed, but wearing his street clothes. He had a bandage on his head but was significantly more alert than when she'd last seen him.

"Hey," she said.

"Barbara and Brooke just left, but the nurse told me you were here." He eyed the bandage at her hairline. "Looks like we're twins."

She eyed the larger bandage on the back of his head. "Not quite. I didn't get knocked senseless." She sat in the chair next to his bed. "How do you feel?"

"Still have a dull headache, but I'm much better. How are you?"

"Considering everything, I'm doing pretty well." She gestured at his clothes. "You ready to go?"

"As soon as they give the okay. Ax is picking me up."

"Good."

"He feels terrible about what happened to you. Keeps telling me he should have stuck with you longer."

"Wouldn't have mattered. O'Dell would have waited until he left."

"I'm not feeling great about it either. You hired me to help, and I end up in here, and left you to fend for yourself."

"I survived, and so did you. That's all that matters."

"I'm not sure I agree." He sighed. "Still didn't find that drive, though."

"No. We didn't." Seeing his phone on the side table, she picked it up, put it in the drawer, and closed it. She'd put her own phone in the Faraday bag after talking to Daniels and Rem. "But I'm not giving up."

"I didn't suspect you would, but where else is there to look? We've run out of options."

"I realize that, but Carlson and I were talking, and we have some ideas."

He sat up. "What ideas?"

Lexie recalled O'Dell's words with a shiver. "O'Dell told me what happened the night Mira died. He said that after George took me, he was watching when Mira left the room where I met her. He stepped out and confronted her. When she saw him, she ran into the mailroom."

"She must have been trying to hide."

"I don't think so. Why run into the mailroom when she could have headed into the warehouse and the front exit? That gave her a better chance of escaping. It doesn't make sense."

"Maybe she thought she could lock herself inside."

"That room doesn't have a lock. Going in there was a death sentence."

"What are you saying? That she meant to go in there? Why?"

"Why does anyone go into the mailroom?" She waited for him to figure it out.

His eyes widened. "You think she *mailed* the USB drive?"

"Why not?"

"But to who?"

Lexie shook her head. "I don't know."

"That makes no sense. Mira didn't have time to grab an envelope, scribble an address and find a stamp."

"She would if the envelope were already prepared. All she'd have to do is drop the drive into it, seal it, and drop it into the chute." She leaned in. "I think that was her backup plan. Something spooked her when we were talking. She gave me a fake drive, and after I left, she left too, but O'Dell stopped her."

"But you saw her poke that baseboard with her foot, like she was closing it."

"I did, but I never saw her hide anything. Maybe she was checking to see if her pot was still there after all these years. Who knows?"

Connor hesitated. "That sounds pretty thin."

"But not impossible."

"And if she mailed it, who would she trust enough to send the drive?"

That was harder for Lexie to answer. "I don't know. She wouldn't have sent it to me since I'd already been compromised. She had Daniels and Remalla's addresses, but they haven't received anything. So I don't know where it went."

"Maybe she hid it in the mailroom?"

"Carlson thought of that and searched it, but no luck."

Connor leaned back against the pillow. "I don't know, Lexie. Whoever she sent it to would have received it by now, and since we've heard nothing, maybe Omnivista got hold of it."

"I doubt it, or why send O'Dell after me?"

"Or maybe whoever has it doesn't know what they have?"

"Or, they haven't opened the letter yet. Not everyone's great with their mail. God knows I can build up a stack before I go through it."

"Mira had to have thought about this."

"I agree. She would have picked carefully. All we can do is wait." She fell back into her chair. "The question is, what do we do in the meantime?"

He turned toward her and paused. "You and I need a break. Especially you."

Meeting his gaze, she felt the same silly warmth spread through her. Connor was definitely a HEA guy. She wondered if Dr. McCabe, or Bill, was. "Now's not the time for a vacation."

"Not a vacation." He swung his legs over the edge of the bed. "I think it's time for a baseball game." He aimed a charming grin at her. "You in?"

She thought of Chase and couldn't help but smile back. "I'm in."

••••••••••

Three days later, Lexie sat beside Chase in decent seats at Petco Park, the Padres' stadium. Connor had gotten them all tickets, which included him and Sasha, Ax and his date - a buxom blonde accountant named Noelle, Lexie and Chase, and Leona and Natalie. Natalie had returned a day earlier. According to Leona, Natalie had said little about her time with Walker, which told Leona that the trouble in paradise continued. When Nat had learned they were all going to the baseball game, she, to Lexie's surprise, asked to join. Connor had gotten her a ticket, and they were all in attendance. Leona sat with Natalie at one end of the aisle, and Connor and Sasha sat at the other end. Ax and Noelle, and Lexie and Chase took up the middle seats.

During the seventh inning stretch, Connor and Ax had gone to get some beer, and Sasha, Noelle, Leona, and Nat had gone to the restroom. Lexie stayed back with Chase and tried to relax, although her mind wandered. The game had been a good one; the Padres were in the lead, and Chase was loving it. Natalie had even maintained a civil attitude. Lexie guessed she was either preoccupied with her marital problems or it was because her sister had almost died twice in one day. Regardless, she'd said little to Lexie, and Lexie had said little to her. She'd spoken little to Connor too, which wasn't hard since he sat at the end with Sasha, who'd come to the game wearing strappy heels, an oversized Padres jersey with leggings, big silver earrings and sporting a bold red lipstick. Even her hair looked perfect. Lexie had pulled her hair into a ponytail, thrown on some old jeans and a Padres T-shirt, and didn't even consider jewelry. She wore almost no makeup.

She and Ax had talked, and she'd engaged with Noelle too, who was a pretty lady, up on current events, and funny. She and Ax had met recently when he'd been talking to witnesses after a robbery. She couldn't tell him much about the robbery, but she'd given him her phone number, and this was their second date. Judging by the way they were touching each other, Lexie guessed the first date had gone well, confirming that Ax was definitely the spicy romance guy.

For the umpteenth time that day, she thought of Zephyr and wondered if he'd given up on finding the drive and stopping Omnivista, since she still hadn't received a new burner phone from him.

"Aunt Lexie?"

Stirred out of her thoughts, she reached for some of Chase's popcorn, which was almost gone. "Yeah, Chase?"

"You think we could do this again sometime?"

She smiled at him. "Sure, if you're in town. Why not?"

He ate some popcorn. "Mom says we might stay a little longer."

Lexie chewed her popcorn and frowned. "Really? Did something happen?"

Chase shrugged. "She's mad at Dad."

Lexie guessed that much. "I'm sure it will work out. Sometimes parents just need some time apart."

"Yeah." He held up his bag. "Can I have some more?"

Lexie started to answer when Natalie returned. "That's your second bag, Mr. Hungry Pants." She scooted down the aisle past Lexie. "Aren't you full?"

Leona followed. "I can get him some." She sat next to Nat.

"He's fine, Mom," said Nat.

"Can I get a hot dog too?" asked Chase.

"A hot dog?" asked Nat. "You already had one."

"I'm still hungry." Chase pouted. "Please."

Sasha returned to the aisle, but instead of sitting in her seat, she walked toward Lexie and stopped beside her. "You mind if I talk to you for a second?" she asked.

Surprised, Lexie tried not to act that way. "I don't mind."

She sat next to Lexie. "I wanted to apologize to you about the way I acted in the ER when Connor was hurt. I was upset and overreacted. But it was nothing personal. Connor explained what happened, and I know none of it was your fault."

Lexie grabbed her cup of lemonade but didn't drink it. "It's fine. I didn't take it personally. It's hard when you have a loved one in the hospital. It can mess with your head."

"It definitely messed with mine, and I took it out on you."

"Don't worry about it. I'm just glad he's okay."

She put her hand on her chest. "Me too. It's such a relief. It really makes you appreciate what you have every day and not take the people you love for granted."

Lexie sucked on her lemonade and lowered her cup. "Yeah, it does."

"Which is why, when my lease is up next month, Connor and I are moving in together." She smiled.

Lexie forced herself to smile back. "Really? That's great."

"We've been talking about it, and the timing wasn't right. But now it is."

Lexie looked up as Connor and Ax returned, carrying beers. Noelle was draped over Ax. "You're in my seat, Sash," said Ax. He eyed Lexie.

"Sorry, Ax." Sasha stood and spoke to Lexie. "Thanks for listening. And sorry again." She tilted her head. "I hope we're good?"

Feeling numb, Lexie nodded. "Yeah, we're good."

"Great." Sasha went back to her seat, and Connor sat beside her. He offered Lexie a glance, but she looked away. Ax sat next to her. "Everything okay?" he asked Lexie.

Lexie tried to focus on the game. "Couldn't be better."

He raised an eyebrow at her, but Noelle returned to Ax's side and took a beer from him. "Thanks, hon," she said.

Ax put his arm around her. "You got it, babe."

Lexie sucked her lemonade until it was gone. The game resumed, but she needed to move around. She hated that Sasha's revelation was bothering her more than she cared to admit. "You still want some popcorn, Chase?"

"Can I, Mom?"

Nat narrowed her eyes. "Just popcorn. No hot dog."

"I'll get it." Lexie stood. "I'm going to get some more lemonade."

"Are you sure?" asked Nat.

"I'm sure." She eyed Chase. "What size?"

Chase grinned at her.

"Extra-large," said Lexie. "Got it." She scooted past Ax, Noelle, Connor, and Sasha. "Be right back." She stepped down to the main ramp, which led to the concessions area. Spotting the popcorn stand, she stopped and bought a super-sized popcorn and headed to the next-door vendor that sold lemonade. She had a few people in front of her and munched some popcorn while she waited.

A woman came up beside her, turned and smiled. "Hello, Miss Logan. I was hoping to get you alone. Do you mind if we talk?" She gestured toward a section of tables and chairs.

Recognizing Maria Silva, Lexie choked on a piece of popcorn and coughed. She blinked to be sure she wasn't delusional.

Maria didn't seem fazed. "I realize this is unexpected, but I saw you in the stands from my box. And when an opportunity shows itself, I take it."

Lexie was tongue-tied. If Maria had seen her, she'd certainly have seen Connor and Ax. Lexie eyed the line she was in. "I'm waiting to get some lemonade." She didn't know what else to say.

Maria looked behind her. "Delano."

A tall man with broad shoulders and an intense gaze stepped out of the crowd.

"Take Miss Logan's place in the line. Get her a lemonade and one for me as well."

"Yes, Miss Silva." Delano stood in front of Lexie as if the decision were made.

Lexie shook her head. "That's not necessary. I really don't think—"

"Just a few minutes of your time. That's all I ask." She waved her hand at the tables. "Please."

Lexie glanced at Delano and noticed another man of similar stature and intensity standing in the other direction from Maria. She deduced they were bodyguards. Still unsure, but also curious, she stepped out of line. "Okay."

"Thank you." Maria walked to a free table and sat.

Lexie joined her. She set her popcorn down next to the napkin dispenser and was honest. "I must admit, I find it highly coincidental that you saw me from your box. You don't strike me as a baseball fan."

"My brother loves baseball, and he needed to get out of the house. And it's not my box. It belongs to a friend. For obvious reasons, a box is preferred over the general seats."

Lexie could imagine. Her brief time in the press paled compared to Maria's. "If you saw me, then you saw who I was sitting with."

"I did. But that doesn't concern me."

"I doubt Connor and Ax would be thrilled that I'm talking to you."

"I'm aware of that. Does that bother you?"

Lexie couldn't be sure if it did.

"Because if it does, then perhaps I misjudged you."

Lexie squirmed in her seat. "How do you even know who I am?"

"I saw you at the airport with Connor, and I read those vile articles about you on Vista."

"Did you believe them?"

"Did you believe the ones about me?"

Now that they were talking, Lexie's nerves settled. "I'm not on Vista, but I've heard things. I know about you and your illegal family business, and I know you received immunity for testifying against your father and brother."

"All of that is true, but you don't know everything. I'm not the villain everyone makes me out to be."

"Connor and Ax would disagree." Lexie rested her elbow on the table. "And I trust them way more than I trust you."

"With good reason. Because you've only heard *their* side of the story."

Lexie narrowed her eyes. "What are you trying to tell me?"

"Everything if you're up for it."

"I don't understand."

Delano walked up with two lemonades and placed them in front of Lexie and Maria.

"Thank you, Delano."

"Ma'am." He stepped back into the crowd.

It was clear to Lexie that Maria commanded a great deal of respect from her staff, but whether it was out of fear or love, Lexie didn't know.

Maria sipped some lemonade. "I did my homework on you. You're a competent journalist."

"I'd like to think so."

Maria pulled a napkin from the dispenser and wrapped it around her drink. "I've had numerous writers approach me, wanting to tell my story. None has interested me until I became aware of you."

Lexie sat in shock. "Wait a minute. Are you saying you want *me* to write your story?"

"I do."

Lexie chuckled sarcastically. "I'm not stupid, Miss Silva..."

"Call me Maria."

Lexie had no intention of doing so. "You picked me because of Connor, didn't you? This is your way of throwing his inability to put you in jail in his face."

"Far from it. I picked you because you're independent, which I admire. You don't have a boss telling you what to write or investigate...unless Connor has more sway over you than I expect." She set her cup down. "But judging by his coziness with the woman he's with, I'm guessing not."

Lexie tucked a loose tendril of hair behind her ear. "Connor has no sway over what I do, regardless of who he's with."

"Good. I'm glad to hear that."

"But I still don't think this is a good idea. I'm sure there are plenty of qualified independent journalists you could talk to."

"You broke the Rook case."

"I *helped* break the Rook case."

"And you've successfully cleared your name from a murder charge, not that Vista will print any articles about it."

Lexie thought about the missing drive. "Nor do I expect them to."

"Your name and reputation have taken a hit." She paused. "A story like mine could change all that."

Lexie crossed one leg over another. "That may be true, but even so, it's better if we—"

"You'll have full access to my life. Ask any questions you want. About the past, present, or future. You can feature me in a podcast. Nothing's off-limits. And if you want to write a book, I'll give you my blessing. I have no doubt it would be a bestseller."

Lexie contemplated the idea. Full access to Maria Silva would be a fundamental change in her career. Now that the Rook story was running its course, she'd have a slew of new material. But she couldn't shake the thought that Maria was using her to get to Connor, and she didn't like playing games. "As tempting as it sounds—"

"Before you say anything else, I haven't gotten to the best part yet."

Lexie waited to hear what Maria would surprise her with next.

"This isn't just about me. It's also about my family. Their business and...police corruption."

Lexie went still. "Excuse me?"

"You think the police didn't know about my father's activities? You think they didn't benefit from them? You think there weren't officers who looked the other way after taking bribes? You think I got immunity just for my testimony?" Her gaze turned as intense as Delano's. "I know things, Miss Logan. Things that could take down some powerful people. It's not for the faint of heart. You've handled investigations like this, and survived, and now I want you to take on one more."

Lexie tried to grasp what Maria was offering. "If that's true, then talking to me could be a death sentence. For you...and your family. Never mind me."

"I can take care of my family, but I understand your concern. We'd have to be discreet. No one can know we're talking until the last moment."

"You expect me not to tell anyone?"

"It would be impossible to do this otherwise. Unless...you're worried about what others may think...or what they may have done wrong..."

She realized Maria was referring to Connor.

"But if who you're thinking of is innocent," said Maria, "that should not be a concern."

Lexie couldn't believe that Connor or Ax could look the other way with the Silvas, but she couldn't deny that there was a lot she didn't know. "How can I trust you? From what I've heard, you're as guilty as your father and brother. Maybe this is some elaborate plot to smear the very people who put your loved ones away and took down your family's empire?"

"That will be for you to judge. If that's what you suspect, then write it. But if you suspect otherwise, you'll have to write that too." She leaned closer. "Believe me, Miss Logan. I know what the police and public say about me, and I don't approach this subject lightly. I know you'll require proof, and I'll provide it."

Lexie's mind raced with questions. She had expected none of this, but now that it was here, she couldn't ignore it.

"The choice is yours." Maria stood. "I'll give you some time to consider it." She tossed her lemonade cup into a nearby trash can. "I'll be in touch." She glanced back at Delano, who was still standing nearby. Seeing her look, he approached.

"Enjoy the rest of the game," she said as she, Delano, and the third man who'd been watching disappeared into the crowd.

Chapter Thirty Four

RUNNING LATE, REMALLA RACED down his stairs. Greta was in his front room running the vacuum. He headed into his kitchen, grabbed the pot of coffee from the machine, and filled his thermos. His phone rang, and seeing who it was, he cursed and answered. "I know. I know. I'm late. I lost track of time."

"Lozano's wondering where you are," said Daniels. "I told him you were moving slowly after that chase yesterday. You couldn't keep up with me."

Rem lowered his thermos. "*I* outran *you*."

"That's what happens when you leave the storytelling to your partner."

Rem screwed the lid onto his thermos. "I'm on my way, and Lozano is going to get the truth when he reads my report, slowpoke."

"That would require you to write it first."

Rem smirked. "I'll be there in twenty minutes." He spotted Greta and shook his head. "Make it twenty-three. I've got to pay Greta."

"Make sure she didn't take anything for her upcoming garage sale, or for her father's birthday."

Rem sat his thermos on the counter and ran into his room. "Be nice, or the discount she was going to offer you for her services will be long gone."

"I'm willing to take that chance. See you soon."

"See you." Rem hung up and slid his phone into his pocket. He dug into his sock drawer and pulled out the cash for Greta. Thinking of what Daniels had said, he recounted his stash and was glad to see none was missing. Chastising himself for questioning his cousin, he jogged back into the other room.

Greta had finished and was returning the vacuum to the front closet. "Here you go, Greta. Thanks for the great job. I gotta go." He handed her the money and jogged back into the kitchen.

"Hold up, Aaron." She walked into the kitchen. "Don't forget about the cleaning supplies I told you about. You're out of a few things. I gave you that list."

He patted his pocket. "I got it. I'll pick it up on the way home." He grabbed his thermos.

"And don't forget your mail."

He tried not to groan. "I got it already." He headed out of the kitchen.

"No, you didn't. It's in your drawer."

He stopped. "What drawer? Since when has it been in a drawer?"

"Since I put it in this one." She walked into the front room.

Rem followed, and she opened a drawer in the front table and pulled out a stack of mail. "Here."

He took it. "What's this? Why is it there?"

"Because I put it in there when I clean. It's a mess otherwise." She closed the drawer. "You're welcome." She tucked his money into her bra. "I'll finish upstairs and lock up when I leave."

Holding his mail, he stared at it as she went upstairs. "Great. Thanks." He sighed, put his thermos down and quickly flipped through it, looking for anything important. Most of it was trash, and he tossed it on the table to throw away. He found his electric bill and set it aside, along with a letter from his mother, who still preferred snail mail over email. At the bottom of the pile, he stopped at a plain manila envelope, which had his name and address but no return address.

He pulled it out and put the rest of the mail down. Staring at the envelope, a tingle of uneasiness crept up his spine. *No,* he thought to himself. *It couldn't be.* Suddenly nervous, he ripped the envelope open. Inside was a piece of paper, and at the bottom was a USB drive.

He tipped the envelope, and the small USB fell into his hand. He gaped at it, trying to absorb what he was holding. Breaking out in a cold sweat, he whispered the first words that came to mind. "Holy Prom Boy."

What Happens Next?

The USB drive wasn't lost. It was delivered. But not to Lexie. And the note inside the envelope changes everything:

"If Lexie Logan is dead, destroy this."

But Lexie is very much alive...and someone wishes she wasn't.

To save her herself and her kidnapped sister, Lexie must confront an enemy who sees everything... and secrets that could destroy her world.

Dive into *The Silent Sister,* where the lies get darker and the dangers get closer.

Enjoy an excerpt of *The Silent Sister* below.

And while you wait for book two, discover Detectives Daniels and Remalla.

Lexie first appears in the *Detectives Daniels and Remalla* series in book seven, *Dominion.* She gave Daniels and Rem such a hard time, I kept bringing her back, and now she's got her own series. But Daniels and Remalla go way back before Lexie appeared.

These two detectives face unexplained evil, unsolved cases, and their own demons. If you like a little paranormal mixed in with your mystery, plus a couple of bantering detectives whose trust in each other sees them through the worst of times, then this series is for you.

Start with *Haunted River*, or go big with the omnibus, ***Shadows and Secrets***, which includes the first three books in the series – *Haunted River*, *Of Breath and Blood,* and *Of Body and Bone.*

How did it all begin with the detectives?

Daniels and Remalla were first introduced in the prequel series, *The Family or Foe Saga.* A murderer with a mysterious background and powerful abilities is out for revenge against the family he believes wronged him, and Daniels and Rem won't escape his vengeance.

This series can be read before or after the detective series.

Want more from J.T. Bishop?

Subscribe at jtbishopauthor.com to get two Daniels and Remalla prequel novellas, *The Girl and the Gunshot*, and *The Magic of Murder*, plus future books, for free, in addition to extra content.

A Note from J.T.

When Lexie Logan first showed up in *Dominion*, I immediately liked her. She was driven, ambitious, and determined to get to the truth. And I loved her dynamic with Remalla and Daniels. She gave them a hard time, didn't cater to them, and steadfastly stood up for herself. Then came Illusions, and the fun continued as Lexie inserted herself into that investigation too. The idea that she might make a great protagonist began to form, and I entertained the idea of giving Lexie her own series.

Then came *Vendetta* and *Black Bird,* and her role developed and her back story popped into my head. Lexie is complicated and confident, but carries a lot of baggage. I showed a hint of that in *Illusions* and *Vendetta* and decided to flesh that side of her out more. I like her flaws and how she's working to overcome them, and her family drama adds to the mix. It gave me plenty to write about when I started *The Forgotten Night.*

But starting a new series is always a risk. You don't really know until about three books in (or longer) if it's going to be successful. But I always listen to my gut, and my gut was saying *write Lexie*, so I did. I'd planned to start her first book after I finished *Vendetta*, but so much was happening in Daniels and Remalla's world, that I felt it would be better to wrap that story line up with *Black Bird*, get Daniels and Rem at a good stopping point, and then focus on Lexie.

It took longer to write than I expected; Lexie was caught up in a murder investigation and suspected of the crime, while trying to bring down a corrupt corporation and their AI technology. It's been a challenge, but a positive one. I'm comfortable with murder mysteries with a little paranormal thrown in, but this book is different. It's got a murder mystery, but it's a technothriller with zero supernatural suspense. (The suspense is there, but no ghosts or bad guys who shoot fire from their fingers.) My other recent books focus on male partnerships and Lexie, although she works with Connor, is more of a lone wolf. I wanted to try something new, though, and offer readers another glimpse of what I can offer. Plus, they'll discover Daniels and Rem and hopefully love them as much as my avid fans do, and that's a big plus.

So, what's next? Book two, *The Silent Sister*, is already underway, and I know there will be a book three. What happens after that is up to fate. But don't worry. I haven't forgotten *The Redstone Chronicles* or *Daniels and Remalla*. They'll each have a new book coming out with all the mystery and paranormal you've come to expect from me.

Right now, though, I'm going to enjoy my time with Lexie. I can't wait to see where she's headed and what happens between her and Connor, her father, and the rest of her family, plus learning Prometheus' fate. There are plenty of secrets to reveal as we head down her multi-lane highway of a journey. I promise it's going to be a fun road trip full of big reveals, and I hope you'll join me along the way.

I'm thrilled to share *The Forgotten Night* with you. And now that it's here, I'd love to know what you, the reader, thought. Reviews are crucial to the success of a book, and I'm eager to hear your opinion of the first book in Lexie Logan's series. I welcome your comments too.

Now, on to the next book!

Books in Chronological Order

Although recommended but not required, in case you prefer to read in order...

Red-Line: Prelude to The Shift, a short story (subscribers only)
Red-Line: The Shift
Red-Line: Mirrors
Red-Line: Trust Destiny
Curse Breaker
High Child
Spark
Forged Lines
**
The Girl and the Gunshot, a novella (subscribers only)
A Hamburger Christmas, a novella
The Magic of Murder, a novella (subscribers only)
First Cut
Second Slice
Third Blow
Fourth Strike
Murder Unveiled
Haunted River
Of Breath and Blood

Lost Souls

Of Body and Bone

Lost Dreams

Of Mind and Madness

Lost Chances

Of Power and Pain

Lost Hope

Of Love and Loss

Lost Lives

Dominion

Lost Time

Illusions

Lost Love

Vendetta

Black Bird

The Forgotten Night

About the Author

AWARD-WINNING AUTHOR J.T. BISHOP is a writer of mystery thrillers with a paranormal edge. Growing up, she read Stephen King, Mary Higgins Clark, and Dean Koontz, devoured every episode of The X-Files, and watched plenty of TV shows with great partnerships that leave you wanting more. She loves tangled relationships, unexpected twists and turns, heart-stopping love stories, and the complications that come with all the above. Throw in a little supernatural fun and she's hooked. Her evil plan is to hook you, too.

She's the author of *The Red-Line Trilogy* and its sister series, *The Fletcher Family Saga*, which features touches of urban fantasy, light sci-fi, and paranormal romance. She's also happily writing mystery thrillers featuring two charismatic detectives who may occasionally encounter a supernatural villain or two, and a crossover series which follows the exploits of a gifted, but troubled, paranormal P.I. and his spunky sister.

She's also thrilled to introduce a new series featuring independent journalist Lexie Logan, a spin-off character from her detective books.

All the above keeps her busy, but in her spare time, she loves good movies, tasty food, an unfortunate sugar addiction, and traveling.

Acknowledgements

Another book is complete, and again, I have many to thank. This doesn't happen alone, and I am indebted to family and friends for their help, support and encouragement. It is truly appreciated.

I also want to thank my Beta and ARC teams. You guys keep me on my toes, ensure I write a great story, and help with early reviews. Thank you for being honest and offering your guidance.

I love writing about the bonds between loving family, deep friendships and the ties that hold them together. Plus, my fascination with the unknown thrown into the mix makes for a satisfying story and hopefully, adds a little more thrill for my readers.

I especially want to thank my fans. Hearing from you and knowing that you're enjoying my books makes all the hard work worthwhile. None of this would matter without your tremendous support. If I can help you escape from this crazy world for a short period each day, then I've done my job.

Here's to more stories, more fun, and more time for yourself. If you can have a little of that each day, you're on the right track.

Enjoy an excerpt from Book Two of Lexie Logan, The Silent Sister

"WHAT DO YOU MEAN Natalie's staying in town?" Lexie gripped the steering wheel as she drove down the street toward Remalla's. "Since when?"

Her mother, her voice strained, responded. "Since this morning. She thinks it's better if she and Chase don't go home."

Lexie bit back a curse. "That is ridiculous. Chase goes to school in Arizona. Walker is there. So is there home."

"She's enrolling Chase in school here and plans to look for a job."

Lexie scoffed. "Natalie hasn't worked since the day she said, 'I do.' And I don't see her waiting tables or making coffee. And what about you?"

"She's hoping I'll help with Chase."

Lexie's anger bloomed. "I bet she does. Did she even bother to ask? Or did she just assume? You're supposed to go to the Grand Canyon next week with Gary."

"That's been postponed."

Lexie stopped abruptly at a stop sign. "You've been looking forward to that. You need to tell Natalie to find her own childcare. That's not your job, Mom." She hit the gas and drove down the street, trying not to speed.

"He's my grandson."

"Chase is her responsibility. Not yours." Lexie clenched her jaw. "Where is she? Is she there?" Lexie had every intention of telling her sister what she thought of her plan.

"She went to the grocery store. And I didn't tell you this to make you mad. I just thought you should know."

"Well, I am mad. This is just like Natalie. She's got a lousy marriage and instead of dealing with it, she's using Chase to get Walker to do what she wants, which is likely to end some fling he's having on the side. And once he does that, she'll uproot Chase again and go home."

"Lexie, you don't know that."

"Once a philanderer, always a philanderer. I should know. He cheated on me with her. What did she think would happen?"

"She says she needs to get back on her own two feet. She wants to support herself. That's why she needs to get a job."

Lexie turned a corner into Remalla's neighborhood. "She's giving you all the woe is me crap, isn't she? Well, don't buy it. Walker makes a very good living, and Natalie is not poor or stupid. She's got money; she's just pulling the sympathy card. She'll tell Walker she's going back to work, and Chase will go to school here. Walker isn't going to go for that. He loves his son, and she'll manipulate Walker to get what she wants. It's how Natalie works."

"I think you're being too hard on her."

"And I think you're not being hard enough. Tell her to go home and figure out her life. If she and Walker decide to separate or divorce, then a court gets to decide who has custody and whether Chase can be moved to another state. Not Natalie." Lexie pulled into Remalla's driveway.

"She just needs time. That's all."

"Yeah. Time to mess with her husband and get what she wants, without actually fixing anything in their relationship. Meanwhile, Chase gets taken away from his dad and friends while Natalie plays her games."

"Lexie, please. You two need to find a way to be sisters."

Lexie snorted. "Sorry, Mom. I wish we could be, but this is not the way to do it." She spotted Remalla's silhouette in the window. He had the curtains drawn back and was watching. "I have to go, Mom. I'll call you tomorrow."

"Just be nice when you talk to your sister."

Lexie undid her seatbelt and opened the car door. "That's like asking me to smile because it makes me look prettier."

"Well, it does."

Lexie rolled her eyes. "Don't say that to any woman, Mom. Trust me on this." She grabbed her big purse and shut her car door. "I've got to go." She said goodbye and hung up, still angry that Natalie had the gall to expect so much from their mother without even discussing it with her.

Seeing the porch light come on and Rem open his door, she redirected her thoughts to why she was there. Rem had called her thirty minutes ago, asking her to come over, and he'd explain when she got there. When she tried to ask questions, he refused to answer. On the way out the door, she'd been wondering about the urgency when her mom had called to tell her about Natalie's decision.

Now that she was at Rem's, though, her questions returned. What had Rem all ruffled? It made her think about the USB drive Mira Patel had hidden before her death that had yet to resurface. Did Rem know something? Zephyr, her source after Mira had died, had still not resumed contact. The burner he'd told Lexie he'd send to her had never arrived. Had he given up on finding the drive and taking down Mira's employer, the tech giant Omnivista?

She stepped up the stairs. "Hey."

"Come inside." His voice was clipped, as if he were impatient. His usual casual demeanor was absent.

Lexie noted his pale features. “What’s wrong?” She went inside. “Where’s Daniels?” Remalla’s partner, Detective Gordon Daniels, was not there, which surprised her. Where there was a Remalla, there was usually a Daniels.

Rem closed the door. “He’ll be here any second.” He pointed at the front table. “Put your purse down.” He returned to the window and looked outside.

“Are you okay?” Lexie set her purse on the table.

“He’s here.” Rem returned to the door and opened it.

Lexie looked out the window to see Daniels pull up and park behind her car. He got out and jogged up to the porch. “Sorry. I had to wait for Marjorie’s mom to show up to watch J.P. Marjorie’s working late tonight.”

He walked inside and Rem shut the door behind him. “It’s fine. Lexie just got here. Have a seat in the living room.” He locked the door and adjusted the curtains to ensure they were closed.

Daniels frowned at him. “What is going on? Why the weird phone call and the urgent meeting?” He paused. “Does this have something to do with why you were so distracted today?”

“You could say that. And I wasn’t distracted.”

Daniels smirked. “You only ate half of your cheeseburger and fries, you didn’t argue when Lozano asked you to redo that report, and when Overton offered you a candy bar, you turned it down. I half-considered whether I should call a doctor.”

Rem took Daniels’ arm. “Just come in here.” He paused. “Oh, and leave your phones on the front table.”

A tingle raced up Lexie’s spine. Something was definitely up if Rem was worried the AI called Prometheus was listening. They’d eased up on the phone surveillance since their search for the USB drive had stalled, but now Rem was clearly worried. Her phone was in her purse, and she left her purse on the table. “You know something, don’t you?”

"Shhh," said Rem. "In here." He pointed toward his living room.

Daniels put his phone next to Lexie's purse and joined her on the sofa. "What's going on, partner?"

Rem paced. Once he saw Daniels and Lexie were waiting, he pulled up a cushion on an adjacent chair and slid out an envelope. "I got this earlier today, before I came into work. I didn't want to say anything because I was too paranoid."

Lexie's skin broke out into goosebumps. "Is that what I think it is?"

Rem turned the opened envelope upside down, and a USB drive slid out and fell into his palm. "Greta put some mail in the drawer, and I didn't know it. I found it today."

Lexie recalled Greta was Rem's cousin and housekeeper. Staring at the dive, Lexie couldn't speak.

"Holy..." Daniels slid forward on the couch. "Is that...?"

Lexie stood and took the drive from Rem. "It can't be."

"Oh, it be," said Rem. "There's a piece of paper in the envelope, but I haven't read it yet."

Lexie eyed the envelope. "Why not?" She took the envelope from Rem.

"I was too freaked out, and it felt like it should be a shared experience." Rem, still pale, sat in the chair. "And if it says something crazy, I didn't want to keep that to myself all day."

Daniels eyed Lexie. "What does it say?"

Lexie removed the paper and read from it.

If Lexie Logan is dead, destroy this before it destroys you. If she's alive, give this to her and tell her to find Sister Helena. And that the wind will set her free.

Lexie lowered the paper. "The wind will set me free? What does that mean?"

"And who is Sister Helena?" asked Daniels.

Rem leaned forward. "Whoever she is, we need to find her because the drive is password-protected."

Lexie sucked in her breath. "You tried to open it? Are you crazy?"

Daniels gaped at his partner. "You wouldn't read Mira's note, but you were willing to read the drive?"

Rem huffed. "All I did was plug the USB into my laptop. Prom Boy can't be watching for every USB that's read all over this city, state, and beyond. It would blow his circuit board."

Lexie narrowed her eyes. "Prom Boy?"

"You know." Rem offered her a knowing look and whispered. "The AI eavesdropper we're all trying to avoid?"

Lexie got the gist. He was referring to Prometheus and didn't blame him for not wanting to say the name aloud. "You took an enormous risk. If Prom Boy picked up the scent..."

"There's no scent to pick up," said Rem. "Not yet, anyway. I got a password request, which I expected. Mira Patel wouldn't leave the information on that drive vulnerable to whoever had it. What if the mailman had delivered it to the wrong address? I just wanted to know what I was dealing with."

"And if it had opened?" asked Daniels.

"Then you'd be wondering where I was right now, because Prom Boy would have tattled on me and I'd have disappeared along with the drive."

Daniels rolled his eyes. "Considering where you hid it, I wouldn't be surprised."

"Where else should I put it? The first place anyone would look would be the safe."

"I can think of a few places." Daniels raised his eyebrow.

Rem grimaced and shifted in his chair. “I wasn’t quite ready to go that far.” He eyed the drive in Lexie’s hand. “The question is what do we do now?”

“Where the hell is Connor?” asked Daniels. “Shouldn’t he be here?”

Lexie couldn’t stop staring at the USB drive. “He’s out of town with Sasha. He’ll be back tomorrow.”

“Who’s Sasha?” asked Rem.

Lexie lowered the drive. “His girlfriend.”

“His girlfriend?” asked Daniels. “Since when?”

“Since almost nine months ago.” Lexie sat on the sofa. “Didn’t I mention her?”

“No, you didn’t,” said Rem. He spoke to Daniels. “I doubt that will last long.”

“Assuming he figures it out,” added Daniels.

Lexie looked up. “What are you two talking about?”

Rem shrugged. “Nothing.”

Lexie didn’t bother to ask and reread the letter. “I’ll tell Connor tomorrow. But obviously, our next move is to find Sister Helena. Mira must have told her the password.”

“Any ideas where to start?” asked Rem. “And how to do it without alerting Prom Boy?”

Lexie thought of Zephyr again. He’d be the one to ask. “Zephyr’s gone dark. And if that doesn’t change, I’ll have to dig into Mira’s past. Helena must be someone important to her.”

“We can help, but it could get tricky,” said Daniels. “We can’t risk anyone knowing we found the drive.”

Lexie imagined the implications if Nolan Sorrento, the CEO of Omnivista, or Eliza Thorne, the head of the Prometheus project, learned of the USB’s discovery. All of their lives would be at risk. “I don’t think you two should do anything.”

Rem straightened. “What do you mean?”

"Mira said to give this to me, and you did. I'm the one who should assume the risk. Not you two."

Rem pointed at himself. "She sent that thing to me. She vetted all three of us. That puts all of us in the crosshairs."

"Agreed," said Daniels. "And you need help."

"Connor will help me if he wants to."

"He wants to," added Rem. "He won't leave you alone on this."

"And neither will we," said Daniels.

Lexie clutched the drive. "That's silly. There's no reason for—" The familiar sound of her ringtone from the other room interrupted her. "That's me." Wondering if it was her mother again, she stood. "Be right back." She went to her purse and grabbed her phone. Natalie's name appeared on the display. Her anger reigniting, Lexie couldn't help but answer. "I can't talk right now."

"Then you shouldn't have picked up," said Natalie. "And what business do you have telling Mom that she's not responsible for taking care of Chase?"

"Because that's your job. Not hers. If you're having marital troubles, go deal with them. Don't make Chase the victim of your petulance."

Natalie's voice rose. "Who the hell are you to tell me about my life, when yours is a mess?"

"My life has nothing to do with this."

"Doesn't it? You've been carrying a torch for Walker for years, and you're still angry that I've got what you want."

Lexie told herself this conversation was pointless, but couldn't shut up. "Yeah, I'm so jealous of you leaving your husband, who I suspect is cheating on you, and probably not for the first time, and you moving in with Mom. What a magnificent life I'm missing out on."

"I'm doing what is best for me and Chase. You wouldn't know anything about that."

"No. You're doing what's best for you. Chase is just a convenient bargaining tool."

Natalie gasped. "Go to hell, Lexie. At least I can handle my problems without drowning them in a bottle of booze."

Lexie stiffened. "Yeah, you prefer the more mature way of manipulation and deceit. You should be proud. It's a good thing Dad's not around to see this. He'd tell you exactly what he'd think."

"All Dad would care about is where to get his next drink, and I doubt he'd have much good to say about you either, considering how you abandoned him when he needed you the most."

Heat bloomed on Lexie's cheeks. "Maybe you ought to look in the mirror, sis. I didn't see you doing Dad any favors. Probably because if you'd left Walker alone for over twenty-four hours, he'd have found somebody prettier to spend his time with."

Natalie sucked in a breath. "You are such a—"

Lexie waited for the slur, but heard nothing except a loud clatter, as if Natalie had dropped the phone. "Natalie? Don't stop now. What am I?"

There was a distant shriek and another clatter. "Natalie? You there?" She turned to see Daniels and Rem watching her from the other room. "Natalie?"

A man's voice came on the line. "You want to see your sister alive again? Find that drive."

Lexie went cold. "Who is this? Where's Natalie?"

"We'll be in touch." There was a click, and the line went dead.

Lexie clutched the phone. "Natalie? Are you there? Natalie?"

Daniels and Rem came over. Their expressions reflected their concern. "What's wrong?" asked Daniels.

Stunned, Lexie lowered her phone. "I...I think...they took her." Her heart hammered, and she could barely utter the words. She put the phone to her ear again. “Natalie?” Her fingers shook. “Please answer me.” There was only silence.

Rem furrowed his brow. “Who? Your sister?”

Her heart racing faster, Lexie nodded, and her breath caught. “Natalie was there, and then she was gone. And someone came on the line and told me to find the drive if I want to see my sister alive again.”

Rem and Daniels shared an intense look. After a second, Daniels grabbed his phone. “I’ll call Lozano.”

www.ingramcontent.com/pod-product-compliance
Lightning Source LLC
LaVergne TN
LVHW010630110826
845149LV00014B/2817

9781971350028